Late and Soon

by D. R. Mozes

Copyright © 2023 D. R. Mozes
All rights reserved.
ISBN: 979838621262

For my father and mother.

Acknowledgments

The process of writing this book was unusual. I wrote it over ten summers while I was teaching at high school English ten months per year. I had a year to write during a sabbatical. Both of those parts of the process took patience from my wife. She also had to listen to me talk about the book, a lot. She read it more than once. She offered criticism balanced with love.

David Van Biema was an early-draft reader and was more encouraging than the book deserved then. Ben Cosgrove read a better draft and was also very encouraging. John Loonam's suggestion led me to re-order the whole story. If it's better, that credit goes to him. If not, my fault. Dana Isaacson worked on the book in a 2019 version and was extremely helpful. I recommend his text-doctor services without reservation.

I listened to a bunch of people about the East Village scene of the 80s, including Randy Rattray, who turned me on to his friends, Ande Whyland and Dany Johnson, authentic downtown pioneers and artists.

Zoe Pettijohn Schade and Colin Hunt are two amazing artists who attended Cooper Union and let me ask them a thousand questions about their times there. All deviations from the letter and spirit of Cooper's art school are my errors or choices, not theirs.

Hunter College of the City University of New York gets thanks for that sabbatical. A sabbatical is a way to have better teachers. It's not a waste, even if the teacher does not publish their work afterwards. It's not a vacation. It's not a gift, even though it deserves thanks. It's an investment in professional development. For me, the chance to spend a year writing has most certainly informed my teaching, particularly of novels, in more ways than I can list here.

Table of Contents

Acknowledgments 5

1. On Beauty 7

2. Metropolitans 28

3. No Listings 51

4. Crit 68

5. Out to Lunch 83

6. A Party 90

7. A Time to Break Down and a Time to Build Up 109

8. Becoming An Artist 126

9. Summer of Discontent 157

10. Anger 182

11. Department of Returns 202

12. The Child is the Father of the Man 218

13. A Friend 233

14. Hand in Hand with Wandering Steps 240

15. Life Three 263

1. On Beauty

Wednesday, October 25, 2006, 7:32PM, New York City.
In the kitchen of his apartment, David Bar Mizrachi, five-foot-eight, dark walnut skin, tight curly black hair, brown eyes, picked up a small picture frame from atop the fridge.

It contained a drawing of himself as a child in 1971, his mother Judit (born 1931, immigrant from Hungary to New York, 1956), and his father Saul (born 1938, immigrant from Yemen, 1950 to Israel, 1956 to New York). It was a sketch Bar made with pencils on lined loose-leaf paper from a black and white polaroid. Bar retained a memory of struggling to draw his father's face. It was much darker than his mother's, closer to mahogany, his mother closer to eggshell, her favorite paint hue. The exposure on the camera had been set for her. He had lightened his dad's face to make him visible. Still, they were more beautiful, more vibrant in their youth than in his later memory of them. There was a willow tree's luxuriant hangings in the background and tall, insistent grass rising above their ankles in the foreground. His drawing had a fair approximation of one-point perspective. The light, correctly, all came from the same place. Probably he got the light from the photo, not knowledge of how to draw light. Even so, not bad, he thought to himself; the picture had some beauty. The figure of Bar at five is off to one side, playing some game time has lost, crouched over, half covered by the grass, wholly involved with an unseen object, the space between him and the other figures graphically showing the mental distance between them.

He looked up at his kitchen again: the four-burner Hotpoint stove, the cheap fridge, a card table he made from plywood, two-by-fours, and sheetrock screws, two mismatched chairs he had found on the street at different times and had repaired, the vinyl tile floor he had promised himself to cover in hardwood but never did. At one point he had been proud to have scavenged and cheapskated his way to living adequately enough, but now he looked at the cheapness with shame, though his girlfriend's eyes. It wasn't charming, cozy. The table wasn't DIY-personal. It was shoddy, roughly done. The chairs were less than second-hand, and make-do. It made him feel sick.

He could renovate the kitchen himself. He knew from his father how to do the work. But he couldn't even afford the materials. A new stove, new appliances... He'd have to renovate his life before he could do the kitchen. Stop being an artist. Was he truly an artist anyway? If an artist makes art and no one sees it, is he an artist? If an artist draws a forest of drawings and every picture in it falls flat, will it make a sound?

It was all nauseating.

No – that wasn't what was making him feel sick. It was – suddenly, he felt dizzy in a familiar way. He was seeing the kitchen from two slightly different angles. It wasn't true dizziness, but visual confusion. The nausea was there because of the doubling of his angles of view. The two images of the kitchen diverged, then collapsed together, then separated again, as if his head were in two places, moving into the same space and then out again. This double vision had happened to him before. He called it a "palimpsest"; that was his name for the phenomenon that had occurred from time to time – sometimes one happened and then another quickly followed, and sometimes none occurred for years. They were always memorable: two images superimposed, but it wasn't just because of what he saw. It was also two feelings about what he was seeing.

"Bar? What's going on?" Eva, his girlfriend, with whom he had been living for two years, the woman he loved, called to him from the living room. He could not answer while the palimpsest was happening. When he tried to speak, it was as if he had also to speak from the other voice, too, but couldn't, as if that voice were controlled by someone else, but that someone else was also, somehow, "him."

Palimpsest: a parchment or other surface on which the original writing was erased to make room for later writing. A trace of the original is still there. Or, it's anything that's re-used but still shows the original underneath. Two moments, at once. Two feelings of what's going on.

He didn't know why they happened. It was as if he were experiencing whatever was happening again, sometimes feeling the difference between the two contexts, sometimes only having the visuals doubled, or not quite doubled. Sistered, as when a carpenter sisters a joist or a stud, the new one's not quite in the same place. It was always disconcerting, like a super-charged déja vu, except these things, the events happening "now," had not happened before.

In this palimpsest, he turned and saw Eva from his present angle and also from a foot to the left. She was standing in the doorway of the kitchen. He was not standing a foot to the left, where he also saw her from, he was certain of that. Closing one eye made no difference. Also, the feeling from the other angle, and he thought it was coming from that angle and not the one he was actually seeing through, was of gratitude and love, as if he were returning to her after being somewhere far away, as if he hadn't seen her in a long time. Yet, they were living together now for a while. He saw her every day.

He didn't feel the same way in the present self. He felt constriction. She would bring up their ongoing conversation again. It was just a matter of time. But in the "other" angle, he desired this conversation. How could that be?

Then it ended. He saw her from one point of view: the right one.

They happened before. There was nothing he could do about them, and they went away quickly enough. He felt his throat closing and coughed a few times, loudly.

The palimpsests always made him think of the person he called The Chanel Lady and the thought of her made him wonder if he should tell Eva about meeting with her this past week. It was a momentous occurrence, a huge, bewildering chance dangled before him, but he doubted that Eva would listen to this. Not now. He put The Chanel Lady in the back of his mind.

"Bar? What're we doing for dinner?" It's reasonable to ask about what we are doing for dinner, he told himself. Yet his feeling was one of being intruded upon. He wanted to retreat into his thoughts. "Bar? You said you didn't want to do anything, so I didn't do anything. Should I have?"

"No, no, I'm going to. I'm just ... I just need some water." Eva had not heard the other voice. Only he could see or hear the palimpsests. He did not bring up the palimpsests with her; it was better not to. He did once and she reasonably recommended a shrink and he told her it didn't work out, she wrinkled her nose in a way that he understood to mean she didn't like his answer. To him, it wasn't shrink material so much as a physics problem. It did not seem possible that it wasn't actually happening. In any case, the shrink he had seen said if they weren't happening often and they weren't ruining his life, he could ignore them, but should come in for at least ten more sessions to discuss them.

Bar went to the sink to pour himself a glass of water that he didn't need, passing that picture again, triggering his memory of Springs thirty-five years earlier, circa 1971. It had been a fishing village before all the fishing village shacks became summer cottages. They stayed in a small house a friend of mom had lent to them for a week in July (a raised ranch, 1100 square feet, about the size of his present apartment in the City). The friend, name and face now unremembered except for a fat white double chin, must have taken the polaroid. Bar's mother had said something like, "How wonderful. We have so few pictures of us as a family." Bar did not remember her handing the picture to him; perhaps Bar had procured it without permission. He remembered seeing her standing in the yard, wearing white jeans and a white sleeveless shirt, holding a tall drink and laughing as he sat inside the small cedar shingle house whose yard ran down to the Peconic Bay, seeing her tip her head back while smiling. He didn't like that, the tipping. He remembered thinking, that's fake. Also, his father laughing at the man's jokes. His father being open and friendly.

"Are you going to make supper?," Eva asked. (Eva The Beauty: ETB.) The constriction released. "Yeah, sure." He wanted to a moment to look at this picture before assembling the meal. Just a moment, please. But he did not say this; he merely stood, looking.

In 1971, he had gone into the house to draw or perhaps he had been sent so that the grownups could speak more freely. He remembered feeling the rarity of his mother appearing to be happy, or at least momentarily without care and he remembered his parents and the friend coming into the house through the screen door that squeaked and glowing over the picture, and his father, holding a can of Israeli beer, saying something about being present at Bar's birth, a subject he brought up from time to time as if to claim credit for the child's existence, as if having been present at his conception were not enough. His memory of his mother, when she still lived at home, was of her face screwed up to fight with his dad, mostly, but not entirely, because of his intermittent employment, his increased drinking, the fat beer belly that resulted from the drinking, and her general expression of being trapped, but all of that came later. Here, she was smiling, his dad was working for Schlomo on renovations, and wasn't drowning sorrows that had not yet arrived. It was hard to sort out one past from the layers of the others.

"We can order in," ETB called, having gone back into the living room and sat on a couch. Bar had made the couch himself. His father had taught him how, a long time ago. "Or I can go down to Mofungo and get some chicken," she offered.

"Don't go down," Bar said, implying a whole conversation about how the neighborhood was too dangerous, which implied another about finances, future plans, children, schools, and the end of art in which he would suddenly become accountable for every decision he had ever made that led to this moment/situation/predicament/conflict. The feeling of constriction returned.

"What? I can't hear you."
"Don't go."
"Are you sure, it's your..."
"No, yes. I'm sure."

He no longer had the original photograph. He noted the perspective in the drawing, the space. Impressive. He knew how to make them all appear to be set within a grassy, wooded landscape, even then, when he was what? Five?

Yes. Had he invented her smile? Did he remember her laughing because of the drawing, or had he made the drawing accurately to reflect the event? No: she was not smiling at his father. Since Bar had drawn the truth of the smile, directed at the host, the picture struck him as real. It held up after these decades despite not being an archival piece of paper, resisting the ravage of time, yellow only on the edges, probably because of the glass frame, he thought. He should spray it, make it archival.

"I'll toss a salad," he said, loud enough for her to hear. "There's hummus and chicken and good olives and we still have tahini left."

Bar put the drawing back up on the refrigerator and looked out his window onto the Hudson River and the memory of Springs faded into other moments when his father had said things about Bar's birth. Saul (dad) would periodically start to talk about Bar about it with a creepy half-smile on his invariably stubbled face. "There was a red-head nurse, and screaming from the other room," he would begin, smiling. Then the focus would go out of his eyes and the strength of his hand would begin to crush the invariably present can of beer. Bar remembered the feeling of wanting to escape from whatever room this story was being told in. He had wanted to be allowed to go color and draw and read and be himself.

"Okay. You mean the paprika chicken? I like that."
"Yeah, some of that." Paprika chicken: mom. Israeli/Middle Eastern salad: dad.
"I got two cupcakes. Shouldn't've?"
"Yeah, that's fine."
"What?"
"Good!"

Bar had heard of this nurse so many times that he imagined he could see the day of his birth itself as if, impossibly, he were remembering it. It is October 25, 1966. His father is wearing a double-knit thin green sweater, V-neck over no shirt, a thin gold chain with a Star of David on the sternum, black, close-fitting wool and polyester pants, and a yellow/tan leather jacket that his thick shoulders stretches when he wears it. The jacket is off. The sweater sleeves push up to his elbow reveal powerful carpenter's forearms and strong hands used to using claw hammers, furniture clamps, and table saws. Saul isn't reading anything; he's looking around furtively. Into the waiting room comes the red-haired nurse in a white uniform and white semi-circular hat, her arms covered in freckles and light-colored hairs. "Very pretty," Saul reported to his son, "of course she notices that I am staring at her. She try not to smile. She doesn't know I'm the husband of you mother who screams in the next room. Is one of those things; she knows that I know that she's staring at me." He winks. "Don't tell you mother this story." Another wink. "A delicious cherry, this girl. She's blushing; you know the white ones, how their face show how they feelings, but she's not shy, no, not this girl. It would be fun. But," and Saul would throw up his hands at the inscrutability of fate, "it wasn't the time." Bar liked to listen to his father pronounce words. He said "hhhwite," with an initial push of air, instead of "wite." "It" being unnecessary to define.

To make sure Bar understood the lesson of the story, Saul explained, "You hev to push, push, push. Then, you get. They like it, the push." "Dad," "No, they do. But that time, no, I let her go." Bar retained a memory of his father's face saying, "push." It was one of the ugliest things he could think of.

"Okay but are you starting? I'm kinda hungry," Eva said, now standing in the kitchen doorway.

"Yeah." He looked at her. She was beautiful. She was wearing a NYU Law t-shirt and gym shorts, her hair tied back. She caught him staring at her face and smiled, knowing what he was thinking, multiplying the beauty factor by 1.8. Maybe 2.3.

"I'm sorry, I didn't eat anything for lunch. I was in court all day."

"Yeah. Don't be sorry."

Bar opened the fridge and took out olives, lettuce, tomatoes, a cucumber, peppers, some not-new parsley, and parmesan. There was another drawing on the fridge, a portrait he had done of his father in 1976, a decade before Saul died. (There was no corresponding photo.) He had drawn that picture "from the model" thirty years ago, as a boy sitting on the floor in the living room, looking up at his dad watching television, or rather sitting in front of the television, his chin stubble tucked into his chest, not asleep but not quite awake. Nodding. The television had almost certainly been tuned to a ballgame, the rules of which his father did not understand, the sound off or very low, Yemenite folk songs playing on a record player that sat on top of the set. By then, Bar had learned to turn the record over, or to stop it, himself, when it reached its end. (He had been quite self-sufficient as a boy. An only child. A latch-key kid. He had to use his latch key even when his father was home sometimes.) He had chosen not to show his dad's left hand holding the beer, but had acquiesced to realism enough to have drawn the hand incongruously holding a phantom of the beer. The picture showed extraordinary detail in the hand that was oddly clutching nothing. Bar remembered that he felt calm and easy when he focused this way, shutting out all else. He felt, even though his father was not exactly awake, that they were together because Bar was drawing him. Bar remembered feeling calm when his father was not exactly awake.

"Salad's almost done."

"Good. Don't put in too much parsley."

"We don't have any parsley. This stuff's gone."

"Oh, okay."

Constriction. "It was bad so I threw it out."

"Okay," she said, meaning, why didn't you get more? Given that her hours saving poor people from eviction were longer than his hours saving them from flat tires on their bicycles, and that instead of buying parsley he had probably whiled away an hour drawing something; that is to say in her view: in his, it was not "whiling." The question of how chores ought to be split was a fraught one, unspoken only at the moment. What's your time worth? Are you taking something from someone you love by not cleaning that mug?

He remembered his father waking up. Bar showed this picture to him. Bar remembered not understanding why looking at the picture turned his father's face angry or why there had been a quick move to take it by his mother, just before his father could snatch it from Bar's hands. She spirited it away, into her room, into a folder that Bar discovered after she moved out years later. He remembered crying in surprise, his parents yelling at one another, both claiming to act on his behalf, and Bar wishing he had drawn nothing instead of just exactly what he had seen, mostly.

"I mean, it would be okay if we could order in," she said. Here it comes. "Like if we lived somewhere else, like where people can order in, as opposed to living in a restaurant desert, or where people can walk to the corner chicken place and feel like they're not risking their life."

"Uh-huh." Now that it was coming out into the open, he exhaled, realizing that he had been holding his breath.

"Just saying."

"Uh-huh."

Bar remembered his and Eva's first date, in 2004. He had picked her up at the bike store. It had taken some balls but it was his birthday then, too, and when she came in with a flat, the air taken from both the tire and his lungs (she took his breath away, he was breathless) yet he felt, put some air in your voice now, or forever shut the fuck up. On the date, he told Eva about his parents. It was kind of a rant. "My childhood was chaotic," Bar had begun. "Toleration of chaos varies."

"What?" The restaurant was loud with people in their twenties and thirties in groups of two to six. Lots of dark wood, atmosphere, and low prices.

He repeated himself, louder. "Domestically, I mean. Who does the dishes first, who picks up the socks. Also in art. Some people can only tolerate Kandinsky, for example, until mid-1908. Before that, he's still painting stuff.

Things in the world. After, it's the drive toward abstraction, you know? Which in his case produced a series of splotch-fests that reached a height in *Composition VII*, his so-called 'first abstraction,' though if you look at a random detail from earlier works, it's much the same thing. (Side-issue: was his trajectory inevitable?) Some folks can't stand splotchy. They need order, and expect art to give it to them. Art, for them, IS order, the way we order the chaos that we perceive, like maps and charts, or like building a house against the storm. Did you know that the first Puritans who came to America didn't think the natives were people, or not really people, not people like them, because they didn't have houses? The natives, I mean. They were savages who 'ranged up and down.' That was the term. You're not a person if you 'range.' Gotta have a house in this land of milk and honey. Anyway, art that seeks out the opposite is a like, uh,…"

"Like leaving home?" she had said.

Wasn't that brilliant, when she said that? Wasn't it wonderful when she smiled at his funny phrases and the rolling brilliance that he was using to avoid any chance of silence, of just staring at one another? She was really listening, he thought. But had he said anything to compliment her? No, he just went on, "Yeah, yeah, or like a map that leads you off a cliff. Others, however, seek out the anti-art in art, the chaos inherent in the drive to order things. Their favorite singer is Lou Reed and their goddess is Eris, which means 'disorder,' or 'strife.' Eris was the one who threw the Apple of Discord …" yeah, yeah, blah, blah, "…over-emphasis on aesthetic concerns. On beauty. That's what I do."

"You do beauty?" she asked, smiling and amused. Or was she smiling out of politeness? She didn't do that, he discovered later, as he was discovering things about her, or not as much as other women he knew. She didn't do polite laughs. A tough broad, Eva. That, too, attracted him.

"Yeah. No, I mean, 'do,' well." He laughed. He was nervous. "My artistic focus."

"That's interesting," she had said, thoughtful. She had worn a little make-up; all she ever wore was a little but then she herself was so fantastically beautiful, her cheekbones so high and her mouth so perfectly shaped that her choice to eschew external artifice was an expression of the casual privilege of the stunning. He did tell her that, recently. She took it as a half-compliment, half-accusation. He remembered thinking that starting to talk about beauty with a woman as beautiful as this might be delicate. "Why do you do it?"

A three-piece rhythm section started a shuffle and he hadn't heard her. "I'm closer to the wild-siders," he said.

"Trying to recapture the chaos of youth?" Looking at her smile was like gazing at a light bulb.

He shrugged, trying to appear nonchalant, though he felt quite chalant. "Not *lost*." He started talking again, this time about tachyons and Black holes and the idea of light. She pushed her food on her plate. She interrupted him. "You don't have to do that."

"Huh, sorry. Do what?"

"Talk to impress me. I'm impressed. You're very cute, and I'm flattered," she said, and leaned across the small table and kissed him, the bold girl. "It seems so uncertain," she said.

"Yeah," he said, not having an answer to so obvious an observation. He remembered his manners. "Tell me about why you're trying to save the world."

"Ha, hardly. I save very few people," she said, thoughtful. "The story I tell, and it's just a story, it doesn't explain everything, is that one day in synagogue. Shul attendance meant getting dressed up, going with dad, and playing in the back with other girls, until I was twelve and my dad said I had to get a Bat Mitzvah and I was complaining a lot because my friends didn't need to get one, just the boys. Dad read the torah stories with me and talked about them with me and that was basically the most attention I ever got from him. I was loving that part. I stopped complaining. I went to study with the rabbi, in his office, me and one boy, and the rabbi said the torah teaches us to help other people, not just ourselves and not just our families."

Bar waited. "That's it? A revelation from the rabbi? Instructions from two thousand years ago?"

"Well, my dad is a lawyer with the Justice committee in the House of Representatives. Mom's a shrink for Medicaid patients. There's that," she said and smiled.

"You have to live up to them. I meant that as a question."

"No. I'm a spoiled middle-class girl from Fairfax. Sometimes I think I could easily fall into a life of luxurious ease and sit around doing nothing. I think I have to fight that. I went to a rich suburban public school and then Georgetown and now N.Y.U. Law. My parents are able to pay. I never had to struggle."

"Listening to that makes me feel narcissistic."

She smiled again. "No, no. We need art, too, Bar."

"Why?"

She looked thoughtful again while Bar stared at her and reminded himself he wasn't there to draw her. "Because we can't see as well without it."

"That's good. Still."

"I'm working on it. I never had a date with an artist before. Everyone I know's a lawyer or some professional. I never had a date with someone like you."

Bar felt a nice big fat rush of feeling at that comment such that he couldn't speak. She reached across the table and took his hand and they smiled together. The waiter came to interrupt the love fest.

 The date had been in a restaurant. Which one? Of course, she would remember, and he felt a pang for forgetting, as finished with the lettuce and moved on to the tomatoes. It was somewhere downtown. Was it the bar in Soho or the Italian place over near First Avenue? The one that closed recently, replaced by something nouvelle and expensive, gentrified out of existence. Must've been near the law school. She hadn't graduated yet. Or was it near the bike shop, his employer? He remembered that they talked a lot, until the restaurant that had been full at dinner time was half empty. She said, wasn't it lucky that he, Bar, had asked her out when he did. After dinner, he walked her to her place. He kissed her again, a low-tension act of moving in for the kiss since she'd broken that ice at the dinner table, and as he walked away he wondered if her searching glance post-kiss had meant he should've tried to invite himself up.

He couldn't have; the first dates of that era were a series leading from a resigned acknowledgement that no female person would ever wish to spend time with him again, to a slow astonishment that the decade-long drought might be ending. He had wanted her not to see his excitement lest she smell it as desperation. He had been way too wound up to take her home and slip cooly and mildly into sex. He had to ease back into it. He had gotten overly used to being along.

Of the many beautiful women in the big city, this one's beauty, was something to which Bar was specifically attuned: she was olive-skinned with large brown eyes and heavy eyebrows. She was fit, meaning strong. About his height, maybe a little taller in shoes with any heel. What mattered more was the quickness of her face, the vibrancy in her expressions, like a cinema of her feelings, a projection of humanity that, he felt, was not something he was just making up. He was receptive to her codes. Her beauty lay between her self and his eye, a transmission of living energy.

Also, she had kissed him.

Yeah, yeah, said his friend Jon when he tried that out on him. But the cheesiness did not reduce how much Bar felt all this to be true.

The last two years with Eva had been a series of spiritual and physical revelations, each subsequent consummation devoutly to be wished.

Oh, yeah: it was Arturo's.

Bar chopped the cucumber, pausing to look across Riverside Drive at the rising construction site, the neighborhood travesty, the only building between the Drive and the Hudson River, which when finished will block the view of the water now publicly available to anyone strolling along the Drive's otherwise magisterial, Versailles/Champs Elysées-tree-lined street. The partially completed building faced Bar with two large uninstalled picture windows above a straight line of differently colored brick such as passed for ornament in this cheapskate's "modern" piece of architectural trash. The empty eyes of the building and its taciturn mouth stared back at Bar as if a minor god of commerce, projecting contempt for his artistic notions, for art apart from pragmatic concerns.

Now it was ending with Eva? Because of money? Could that be true?

Time passing means Eva's older means let's have a baby means make real money means stop being an artist means realize you're not an artist anyway. Give up.

Bar thought about the first time he asked for a raise at work. It was a year ago, 2005, Bar's, what? Near his twentieth year working there? when Adolfo, the senior bike mechanic, former star of Team Mexico, had let slip how much he was being paid. Adolfo had been re-telling the story of quitting Team Mexico when the other star got to fuck more girls than him. Then Adolfo went into his oft-repeated discourse about how climbers were superior, in some register of purity, over mere all-round team leaders such as the one who got to fuck more girls. Adolfo said, "Not prettier girls, just more girls. Like I am a better mechanic, so I get more." Adolfo fixed Bar in a stare expressing his lingering rage at someone long ago while Bar wondered what he was doing repairing a front derailleur next to this person. He thought about his conversation with Sally, the poet with blond, almost white hair pulled into a side pony tail, sometimes on the right, sometimes on the left. Sally's general refrain was about the difficulty she had writing after work.

"Keep up the good fight, Bar. After a few years, though, believe me, it can get to you. I hardly write more than a page a day if I'm lucky, coming home..."

Bar had heard it before, over the years. Her sacrifices for her art, the T.V. dinners, the dates she forewent, the disdain of her peers and family, the tragic squandering of her education, and so on. Not that he didn't feel for her. The real difference, for Bar, between fixing a bicycle and capturing what he had just seen of Sally's earnest self-pity was that when doing repairs he had to think. It wasn't mindless enough. But when he went home tonight and sketched Sally from memory he would be able to stop thinking and become an assemblage of hand muscles, tendons, bone, an eye or two, connective tissue between these, and a pencil. "I should go work on Wall Street," Sally said, as she did from time to time, though Bar saw no chance she would last a day in a frat-boy finance job.

If he, Bar, went to work on Wall Street, though, he thought he could do it. The sell-out aspect of it would bother him. The element of figuring things out would be fun, not making money as an end, but figuring out how. It would just tilt the balance of thinking and feeling almost wholly over to thinking all the time, and about something unimportant that everyone else thinks is the only important thing. That was the way to stop being a person.

"Bar? Is everything okay?" Eva had risen from the couch and was approaching the kitchen. "You're doing that thing. I see you, like you said. Really see. I see your eyes look through me. You're here, but you're not here.

Where are you?"

"Yeah, what? It's all ready. Do you want wine? It's chicken so...red?"

Eva laughed and said, "Sure."

He had lived inside this tight calculus of work, art, and life, for two decades now, and Adolfo was gone, some say back to Mexico City to live with his aunt, who had money from the Mexican movies, and Bar was now Chief Mechanic, which meant making a few dollars more per hour in 2006 than he did in 1987. Yeah, it had been eighteen, no nineteen? Years. His fortieth loomed before him like a waterfall he was about to go over. Sixteen or seventeen years before Eva. The day job, as opposed to making art. Not good enough any more.

They ate in the kitchen, as per what had become usual, on two railroad ties that Bar had turned into incredibly heavy bar stools, at the hand-crafted butcher-block counter that he had made from eight real butcher blocks (retrieved from a three-quarter yard dumpster on the Upper West Side). They'd been used by real butchers with divots and carved spots where the honest laborers had put in their years. The table's symbolic authenticity pleased Bar every time he sat at it. When Eva first saw it, she asked whether he had found it, "in the garbage."

"Mm. Thank you."

"I love feeding you," he said, taking a sip of wine.

"I was starving."

"Yeah."

"Maybe I'm pregnant."

"Yeah. Huh?"

"I'm not. But what if I was?"

"Then you shouldn't have that merlot. Wait, what about the condoms..."

"I want to have a child, Bar. I'm almost thirty."

"I want to have children too, but..."

"But what?"

"Why are we talking about this?"

"No, no, no. You can't do that. Why *aren't* we talking about this. That's the better question, your honor. I bring it up and you always somehow squirrel off into some...*discourse*..."

"Eva,"

"Bar?"

He looked at her without speaking. Still, so utterly beautiful. The lines around the mouth. Had he ever really captured...

"You can't keep working for ten dollars an hour."

"I make more than ten. I thought we were talking about children. You're changing the subject."

"No, this is the subject. You're worth more than…you're an artist, Bar. Your work is beautiful."

"Beautiful? Not like your face."

"Bar,"

"Not like New York City is beautiful. In spite of its ugliness. No, because of that. That power." He wanted to say, please, *please*, like James Brown, and begin by kissing her belly. He wanted to take her into the bedroom but the subject that he was trying to distract from felt like a wall, so instead he said, "Every visual aesthetic experience, including anti-aesthetics, involve beauty. Of course, an idea of beauty has to include sex and desire, not just love."

"Bar, don't show off just to avoid…"

"You met me because I was making ten dollars an hour. It was a Sunday. I fixed your gears." He leaned over to kiss her on the mouth. She turned her head. The market for sex recently had experienced a downturn in those parts. He mentally noted the ironic distance between her "pregnancy" and the lack of proximate cause.

"Thank you for fixing my gears. I wouldn't have you fixing anyone else's gears ever again," she said, but he saw her strain to make the joke. "It was a Saturday."

"Beauty is the ultimate concept," he said, going back.

"As in conceptual art," she said, trying.

"Something we always will return to. Even in seeing dirty as beautiful. The beauty of that derelict building down there, for example."

"Bar, this isn't an intellectual …"

"Your beauty, for example," he said.

"For example what? I'm ugly, dirty beauty, like the city?"

"No. Beauty as energy, as power. But I love you so how would I know?" She smiled.

"I don't trust my subjectivity. I organize reality according to my predilections."

"So I'm not really beautiful?"

"Yes, you are. Objectively. Your face is in the Encyclopedia Britannica."

That might've gotten a smile in days past, but now it received a furrow in her brow.

"I think you're beautiful, too, Bar," she said, looking at the inert remote. "It's not as important to me, I suppose."

"Maybe it is. Maybe that's why you're…"

"It's more of a big deal for guys. It matters to you, more. What if I got into a face-scarring accident? What if one of my 'hoodlums' as you not-so-gently refer to my clients…"

"Only the hoodlum-ish ones."

"…decides I got him a bad deal and throws acid in my face. Or cuts me with a razor like they do at Rikers every day..."

"I would think you're beautiful. I would incorporate your scars into a new concept of perfection. Enough with the eye-roll. That's the inner-outer thing. I half-create that which I perceive."

"I thought you said you were getting past that. The whole looking at girls thing." She looked out the window. The light on the building across Riverside was lurid now, a red streak whose backlighting made it seem even more dour and forbidding. "Look, the building is staring at us like we're some kind of fools."

"I've been past it for years. Your beauty matters to me. You're not 'girls.' That general category. When I'm staring, I'm thinking about you and also looking at you. That's what drawing is for me. I'll never be completely past it. I draw..."

"Because I'm worried that it seems like you're stuck."

"We talked about..."

"Yes, but sometimes I still think you are."

He said nothing. This was not right.

"Did you talk to Gary Mitchell about the bike store?"

"At first, when you told me what your art was about, when you showed me all those pictures of women, I didn't understand. I thought it was … it seemed wrong. Like, voyeuristic."

"It is voyeuristic. I look at people."

"Women, mostly."

"Mostly. The more recent work is hardly flattering. Except the ones I do of you. Those are still voyeuristic."

"But when I got to know you, when we talked. You have so much integrity. Bar? You're so … I'm trying to find the words. You're strict with yourself, even harsh. Your art … I don't think I understand yet. I'm not sure I will. It doesn't make me think you're creepy. You're not one of those guys who go after twenty-year-olds and ask them to take off their bras."

"Thanks. I appreciate the unlimited support. At least I'm not one of those. I've cleared that moral hurdle."

"I'm sorry I'm not … I think we should talk openly. I think we should always have talked openly."

"And Uri?"

She looked away from him. "Yeah."

"What does 'yeah' mean?"

"Uri's why I'm saying this. Bar?" She tried to look at him.

"What?"

"Did you talk to Nicholas Gatianne about his idea?" she countered. "I mean, I know you said you're not Black-black, but you are dark."

"I'm not Black. I'm not a descendant of slaves. I have no African genes."

"So what? And how do you know? Haven't you been mistaken for Black a hundred times? Did you tell me that? Why can't you let him sell your art? This is what I mean by harsh. You're cutting off a means of getting what you want because you won't tell a story that's … "

"That's not true."

"You must have been affected by your coloring. You can't not. What do the genes matter? You must've had, I don't know, some kind of heightened empathy because of that. Why do you…?"

"Because I don't think there's any integrity in taking advantage political leverage that comes from the suffering of people that I am not, I don't know, one of. I could go ahead and draw Black people but not say I'm Black. I don't even believe in the abstract idea of identity politics in art to begin with. Picasso wasn't a Spanish painter. He was a Cubist. Besides, I did talk to Nick. He said, and I quote, that my art is 'unreconstructed humanism with no conceptual punch and no identity issues that could be fodder for discussion. You make yourself less than relevant, not the next thing.' That's such a load of crap…"

"No, no it's not. Art's supposed to tell us what the next thing is. It feels like you live so deep in your own head, that …" She stopped.

"Yeah, but …" Bar stopped. They both looked at their food long enough for Bar to begin thinking about what Nick said again, assembling counter-arguments as if they were arrows, and watching them hit an impregnable shield and fall to the ground.

"You're staring at me," she said. "Sometimes, I mean, I know you do that. I know when you're staring. I mean like you're drawing me. It feels…it's a lot."

"I'm sorry."

"No, no. No one ever looked at me that way. I love your staring and I love your integrity." She dropped her eyes again. He walked back to his drawing and mirror setup. "Only when,… Sometimes I want to hide it. Hide from it."

"Your soul is beautiful."

"You see? That means you don't really see my soul, because if you did…" She seemed more upset at this idea than made sense to him. "I don't want to spend my entire life working as a lawyer, and having nothing else. I mean, of course I have you but I mean also, I want some thing else. No that's not it. I want children, not just some 'thing.' I've always wanted children. I told you that when we met."

"Not when we met."

"The second date, then."

"Yeah. Maybe."

"I don't want to become my dad. His whole life at the office. Typical. He hung out with us kids on strained Saturdays, sometimes taking us to synagogue, sometimes doing things that had nothing to do with us because he didn't know us. And then he retired and pretty soon after he had a heart attack and died before he had a chance to get to know us. I don't want that."

"He had kids."

"He did, and he didn't."

There was a long pause during which he could not look at her and she seemed similarly unable to find his eyes.

"You don't know some of the things I want. I think...I've been lying. Not lying. Not telling everything. I'm far from perfect." She got up from the couch and put the remote on the low table and sat on it, facing him. "I'm worried about things, Bar. I want things. When I think about having to take care of a child…"

"I know."

"You're not doing anything about it."

"Yes, I'm going to figure out what I said. About buying the bike shop."

"The bike shop where you've been an employee for umpteen years!" she yelled. "Where you've just earned measly paycheck after measly paycheck, letting your boss exploit you while you pretended not to care or actually didn't care because you were fostering your incredible faith in your art, and I want to have that faith, too, and I do, I do, Bar. I see your work and I think it's mind-blowingly good, no great, but I don't have faith in other people seeing that."

"Or in me selling it. What did Gary…?"

"I don't."

They sat quietly, both looking down. She let him take her hand. She pulled her hand away to wipe a tear.

Quietly, she said, "It's art. Come on. You could get discovered when you're dead."

"Yeah, like Art."

She smiled, getting the joke. "He died of AIDS."

"So? Actually, it was suicide."

"He died young, and he had AIDS." She looked down again. "I'm thirty-one and three-quarters."

"I know."

"I see you, too, Bar. I see the anger, caked over resentment and bitterness. Like your father, like you described him."

"Leave him out of it."

"Okay, I'm sorry."

"I think about my father every day."

"You said leave him out of it."

"What happened with Gary Mitchell?"

"I think of what you said about your dad when I see you either clinging to your signature style, so-called…"

"Clinging?"

"Okay, so I'm a lawyer and I can't tell shit about art except that I can, a little; you've explained it to me, and I read what you told me to read and so know about the excitement of becoming an artist in the 80s and something else I know is about people clinging to things and I know other people change sometimes..."

"Okay."

"Okay what?"

"I'll change. I am changing. Look, I'm doing this stupid self-portrait idea of Gary Mitchell's."

"Would you stop calling him that? He's Uri. Not a *Star Trek* character. You called him that when you were nerdy teenagers."

"Fine, Uri. Yeah. I'm doing Uri's idea. I'm rich …"

"...in what I afforded not to buy,'" she said, finishing the quote from Thoreau that she had heard from him too many times. "No, that can't work. It's not true anymore. We live on what I make,"

"In my apartment, that I own,"

"In this crappy neighborhood. This apartment is worth, what? Ten thousand dollars?"

"With Hudson River views."

"...and crappy schools that, if we had a kid, we'd have to figure out how to send away from here..."

"It's a nice pre-war with high ceilings. It's got to be worth a few hundred thou."

"...and what I make is shit. It's not fair to do that with a child,"

"The people around here send their kids to those schools. If it's good enough…"

"It's *not* good enough for them. They have no choice but you do have a choice. I just spoke to that waitress again, on the corner? She's sending her kid an hour on the train. In 6th grade, Bar. She's twelve. And Thoreau didn't have any kids. If somehow Thoreau had a child he'd have given the kid up for adoption so he could 'simplify' his life. That's selfish."

"So let's send our kid an hour on the train. So, wait, it's okay for you to make shit, but I..."

"I stop tenants from becoming homeless!"

"Which is more important than making art," he said evenly. "Right? That's what you mean?" As her voice rose, he felt his own dwindle into a kind of squeak.

"Yes, it is! If it's art no one sees! You can't really be an artist if no one ever, EVER, sees your art! Making art isn't enough. And yes, you are so stuck! It's narcissism. You're whole big focus on Bringing Back Aesthetics. It's masturbation!"

He looked away this time. Kayaker dude had followed his dream out of view.

"I'm sorry," she said.

"Yeah," he said in a barely perceptible tone. "The thing is, artists, it's hard to say what makes one successful in the market and another unsuccessful.

People hated Picasso until the late 30s, for instance. He was born in 1881, so that means he was in his 50s..."

She said nothing: that was what she said, nothing, so he stopped talking, as if she had interrupted him. She picked up her fork, idiotically, and stared at it. She put it down. She said, to the fork, "I don't think Uri's going to give you the capital to buy the bike store."

"Why not?"

She looked at him with an intense pain that he did not understand.

"What happened?"

The only response was her pained look. It was like a parody of how she looked when he came, a look of concern and almost pity for him.

"Did he say he doesn't have it, because that's shit. He just sold the rights to some I.T. work, I don't know, he was telling me about it." She said nothing.

After a minute during which he let the silence happen, she said, "I kissed Uri." She turned her head to look at him. "I'm sorry."

He felt the bed sinking under him as if it were a whirlpool and he sat up quickly to make the feeling go away but it made the vertigo worse and he felt a tear, though abstractly, clinically, in a way that that was unusual for him but also that it must be because he felt as if the building were falling down, he was falling down, and she was falling away. The world was being shot on a Dutch angle and the dolly shot was starting to spin. He thought about the concept of jealousy and how arbitrary it was while also being wholly jumbled by jealousy. And fear. He thought this was purely because of what he just heard her say, and it was, but it was also a second palimpsest, an after-shock of the first one, except that in this one he mostly had a feeling, less a visual doubling. The second feeling was the diametrically opposite feeling to the one he was having now: he felt secret satisfaction at what Eva was saying, happiness that she was kissing Uri because ...

"I'm sorry," she said again, and touched him.

... the palimpsest stopped. He felt that there was a reason for this inexplicably positive feeling at hearing that the love of his life kissed his one of his two oldest friends, but he didn't get it. It's as if the radio cut out when she touched him.

"I'm so sorry," she repeated. She explained it. The Soho lunch she went to with Uri, to talk about Bar, to see if he could help, very dry white wine, going up to Uri's giant, airy, well-lit photographer's loft with sexy pictures of models everywhere, and Uri's attention, his strong looks, his persistence, the apparent coherence of his life and confidence of his manner, his put-togetherness,

"You told me about his looks already. You kissed him because he has a square jaw and he wears fashionable, well-fitting jeans and gives off an air of arrogant self-assurance?"

"It was a mistake. I'm so sorry. I kissed him only for a minute and then when he...when I took a breath and thought about it I left right away. Don't blame him, he's been your friend forever, it's my fault, I wanted..."

"You wanted a rich guy," he said. He spoke in despair. He hadn't realized it was such an emergency. Or that time was already up. He thought he could eventually agree to her terms. But selling out of any kind, it would take time. He would have to unlearn Die Yuppie Scum and Reagan Equals Death and all the punk shows he ever attended and his whole childhood and his firmly ensconced belief that artist were ascetics and that the trick was to find low rent, to live low, keep your head down and make your art and let the world spin until it decided it was ready for your particular consciousness. He was now realizing just how much Eva did not sign on the dotted line of that contract. The furious debate about Eva, whether she wanted wealth after all, was settled. She had always wanted it. Every time he allowed himself to believe otherwise was narcissistic cherry-picking of evidence. Her own purity, the choice to practice tenant advocacy instead of something that paid, that was predicated on money to be brought home by the guy and it was always something to be rationalized as her partnership with Evil. She wanted a justice-infused transfer of wealth, perhaps from a stock-broking partner, some uber-capitalist. Or, she doesn't care; she just wants enough to ensure that her genetic material receives a quality education. The debate was moot. What's "enough"?

"No, no, I was confused, it was all a kind of whirl,"

"You went to my friend to help me because he's rich." This was the second sea swell of the evening. He sank into it. "You thought he could help me because Uri's loaded. You went to his rich-person's apartment, his bachelor pad full of poster-sized pictures of barely post-adolescent girls some half of whom he's screwed, a hobby of his – actually two hobbies, one being the photography and the other being the preying on girls who've recently turned eighteen – in fact, I have to wonder why I am, was, still his friend – and *that* turned you on..."

"Bar..."

He still felt as if he were floating, as if this coming-to-terms were not happening. He felt as if he were looking at himself from above, like some of the palimpsests, another angle, but this is something else.

"I've always known I would be an artist, no matter what. I've always been an artist. Maybe not always. Since I was a kid."

She took his hand again. "Maybe you're an artist, but you're stuck, Bar. Do you do something different from when you were a kid? You draw the same way you drew when you were eighteen and still in Cooper. It's not 1986. You draw pictures of me and at first I was flattered and I thought you did that because you loved me,"

"That is why,"

"No, no it isn't. I mean, yes, you do but you only draw women and their bodies. It's not enough."

"I am not stuck. I'm getting better. I'm focusing."

"Ugh, Bar!" She cries. "I'm crying because maybe you're right. Maybe you just can't change and I was wrong to start hoping that you could."

"Do you want to be with Uri? Huh? Is that what you want? Because..."

"No, Bar," she took back her hand and shuddered. "I *so* do not want to be with him. He's...Uri's cheesy and him kissing me was gross, even if it was my fault. I want to be with you. And I want to have a car so I can take our baby to the country once in a while, like my parents did."

"I ride a bike."

"Ok, fuck this." She jumped off the bar stool, quickly went to the coat rack, and violently pulled on her short black leather jacket.

"Where are you going?"

"For a walk."

"You want me to..."

"Nope. I'm not asking you for a thing." She fussed with the jacket.

"Are you coming back?"

"I'm coming back."

"When?"

"I don't know," she said, and shut the door hard. He heard her steps on the hallway stairs; she didn't wait for the elevator. "Tonight," he heard her say in the hallway, the building's old tile floor and marble walls reverberating the word.

"Why'd you even go see him? This is my deal with Uri. Did you have any idea before you went...any feeling...? You're beautiful when you're angry," he said to the doorway, and laughed because it was true. He closed the door gently.

Bar went into the extra bedroom that currently was his drawing studio but that, he knew, would have to go to the child. The hypothetical one. He had been calling it "Hypo" until Eva had objected. When was that? Two nights ago? That would be before The Disaster that he just heard had happened. The ontological question about that, he thought, was similar to the one about the French Revolution: did it all start at once, or was it slowly building up until it became inevitable?

He finished his glass of wine, refilled it. Perhaps it would mollify the pit he felt in his stomach, the depths of which he hadn't felt since...when? Since his father died. He finished his salad by forcing himself to eat.

At the end of the counter sat a small sketchbook and a set of HB, 2B, 6B, and 9B Faber pencils in a rubber band. He disassembled the pencils, flipped open the book to a blank page, and started drawing Eva in the moment as she reached for her jacket, just before she left now. The curve of her waist. Rhyme that with the curve of her hair. One toe pointed. Her ass in those jeans. Yes, he was doing what she said. How had he gotten stuck? I'm not an artist any more, he thought. I'm a pornographer, no different from Uri. Correction: an artistic pornographer. Correction, I don't screw women recently graduated from high school. What's the difference between an artistic pornographer and an artist?

What am I, if I'm not joking? When did I start thinking I was an artist, and when did all of that go wrong? In high school, drawing Stacey, my first girlfriend. And my teacher, Kincaid, she told me I could become an artist. But it was before that. I always drew.

He put down the pencil, which he had kept hovering over the page for a full minute, and wiped his eyes.

It's true that drawing Stacey was something he accomplished as much with his dick as with his right hand.

Hadn't Picasso painted his desire?

Isn't defensive self-pity a bad strategy for making powerful art?

He thought, I don't know anymore, and Eva is unhappy, and it's true that I can't keep doing this.

He wandered over to the large, comfortable easy chair facing the Hudson River (a chair reclaimed from the street, repaired, reupholstered more or less badly). He started thinking about the very odd meeting with The Chanel Lady. Yes, he was right not to dare tell Eva about this. He had once started to describe his years-long relationship with this mysterious personage, and Eva had cried and thought he, Bar, was most certainly delusional and perhaps worse. He had tried to say that The Chanel Lady was a middle-aged woman in a pink wool Chanel suit whom he had seen at various key moments in his life, a woman who seemed not to age, and who seemed able to appear and disappear. Not only did she not age from when he first had seen her, that time on the dock in Springs when he was a boy, for instance, but she never changed her outfit, either. So that when he saw her, late in his teens, on the Queensborough Bridge, and she was walking along the pedestrian/bike lane in the same heels and pink wool suit, she was instantly recognizable but also oddly transplanted from that time a decade earlier on the dock.

Perhaps she was a delusion. The problem with this theory was that she satisfied no clear psychological need in him. There was no pattern to how he felt when she appeared. Such as when she appeared last week (same age as when he was eighteen, same suit) offering him an "opportunity," he could not connect that event to the others in any simple way.

If there's anything to this Chanel Lady at all, he thought, I'm going to find out. I'm going to discover what she is, that she's a whole lotta nuthin', and then I'm going to become a conventional person. If Uri won't lend to me I'll find someone else. I'm not above capitalism. I'm not above anything anymore.

Maybe I am stuck, he thought. When did that happen? I'd have to go back far. If I do that, it's going to take a long, long time. Years. Decades.

I could save dad. I could go back, take the "opportunity," and do it.

Yes, but that really is decades.

Do it.

Bar walked over to the phone hanging on the wall next to the fridge and dialed a number, thinking, this would be the ultimate finagle. He waited. He heard the now-familiar yet so odd Eastern-European-ish voice say "Hello?" through the wires.

"It's me, Bar Mizrachi. Beam me up, Scotty."

"I do not understand."

"I'm saying yes. Do you get that?"

"Please come immediately. There is a window. It closes. Closed. It is closing. Unless you come."

2. Metropolitans

Saturday, October 25, 1986, around 11pm.

A picture in Bar's sketchpad: a pencil drawing, eleven-by-fourteen on sketchpad paper, the scale of the stadium behind them is made clear by contrast with the human figures in front and by the cars on the street below. The night lighting came from several directions: the nearby overhead incandescent bulbs about twelve feet above the subway platform, the stadium's own lights, and two sets of tiny car headlights (rendered by careful erasures). Most of the stadium was done with cross-hatching, while the human figures celebrating nearby were a combo of stippling and circling, smudged carefully (on the clothing, for example). The figures were composed to suggest a contained chaos, an exuberance that was limited to the lower-right quadrant, which felt nearest to the viewer via the use of perspective (while the stadium floated mostly in the upper-left). None of the celebrating figures were looking at the viewer. Looking at the picture, viewers expressed feeling a range from vicarious pleasure to jealous exclusion from their joy.

Though Sharpey had given him cab fare, Bar couldn't very well throw that away on a cab, as it otherwise represented four meals at the Kiev or Dojo's that he wouldn't have to cook for himself. He hadn't visited dad since the beginning of September. It would be good to go home, he thought. He would get up in the morning and make breakfast for…all three of them, because now there was the question of Claudia. There would always be the question of beer with dad. It might leave him in a state in which the visit, in a subjective sense, did not take place, having not been perceived or remembered by its central figure. Claudia's presence, though, meant reinforcing images of Claudia's body that Bar never intended to print on his optic nerve in the first place.

Bar did not bike this time. Normally, he would have as he almost always biked everywhere in the city, the bicycle an extension of his body, two wheels instead of, part of, his two legs, a multiplication of his life force in the form of speed and the feeling of power. Even when it sucked, as when it was below the freezing point, or in the rain, or against a bitter wind, still it felt better to bike than to be moved by a machine full of other people or to walk like a fool at three miles per hour. To ride a bike was to bring together the best of self-reliance and the unalienated simplicity that Thoreau talked about in his rant about walking from Concord to Boston. Bar had biked to high school, seven miles over the Queensborough Bridge every morning from Queens to Manhattan where he learned algebra from his teachers and sophistication from his peers, and seven miles back to learn about bitterness and conflict from his parents. While biking, his teacher was himself, his thoughts his own, his direction a matter of which way he leaned.

But Bar's bike betrayed him that evening with a slow leak that had not announced itself until he started wheeling it toward his door. No time to change it. Better just go.

Bar got off the uptown Lexington line and ran down to the platform of the Flushing line. The train ground into Grand Central Station, a decrepit, once-grand arched hall made in a once-grand city. Bar waited near the "No Spitting" sign, a reminder that the former glory of the architecture had been accompanied by tuberculosis. It smelled of piss, objectively, but Bar floated above it as he considered his lessons, and as he considered girls physically visible and in his mind's eye. Claudia. He dispelled this forbidden image with images of Stacey, which were crisp and sharp. These led forward to the girl whose name he forgot in his art history class at Cooper Union, and the girl whose name he never knew whose studio space was next to his own, and then a girl waiting for the Seven.

He got on. So did the girl. An admonishing lurch zoomed Bar zoomed back into the train car as it entered the tunnel under the East River.

Bar looked. Three unrelated Latina women sat in corners of the car; one was reading a Sagrada Biblia. A Russian lady, jolie laide, about fifty, a red leather miniskirt, long-sleeve purple blouse, gold earrings, black heels. Two Black men in tan canvas construction work clothes, maybe around forty, chatted on the two-seat bench at the far end to Bar's right.

A tall Latino man, about twenty, purple jeans, a big soft fro, was in the middle of the train, trying vainly to get a signal on his radio though they were still underground. He cursed at the radio in Spanish, puta's and maricon's, until the old lady with the Bible spoke sharply to him in Spanish from across the car. She was a quarter his size, but he said "Sorry mami" nevertheless.

Bar took out a small sketch pad and drew her, her finger raised in rebuke (but not at him), the wrinkles on her face, the mole near the left side of her chin, her trench coat and sweater, her lumpy body, her wooden cane, her shaved and re-painted eyebrows, the arthritic hand holding the Sagrada Biblia. He turned the page and drew the young man, his fro framing his thin face, his focused look down at the radio, his long brown arms bent at the elbows that hit the back of the grey resin bench, his long legs forcing his knees up. He focused on the fro's interesting texture. His Mets t-shirt under the denim jacket. He was happy making these drawings. He was alone among others, not answering to them, not bothering them, taking nothing from them but the way they showed themselves to the world.

When the train emerged as the line elevated into the Queens evening at Vernon-Jackson Avenues, the radio snapped from fuzz into the crowd at Shea. Its owner yelled out to no one, everyone, "Oye, hombre, ¡es la Serie Mundial!"

Vin Scully, the radio announcer, said, "McDowell just isn't very lucky tonight."

"What's going on, man? What's the score?" said one of the Black men in the far corner. His Mets hat jarred with his patchwork brown and tan leather jacket and brown work coveralls.

Bar did smudge work on the Latina woman.

"I don't know yet. I just turned it on. Listen, he's..."

"Who?"

"I don't know. Come over here and listen if you want to hear the...shhh."

Scully: "Spike Owen. Three for three, turning around to hit left-handed." Scully's voice added drama to the most mundane athletic choices. "Turning around" was said as if momentus.

The two men from the corner had moved over. "What's that? A little TV? Let's see." Bar looked again.

"Mierda, Would you shush? It's three-two Sox."

"Shee-it."

The train lurched around two "S" turns, its wheels, like all subway train wheels, lacking a differential, screeching through the curves. The Latina woman across from them rolled her eyes and frowned. Bar wished he could photograph her. Her and the older Russian. He stared at the Latina, memorizing. She reminded him of a figure in a Goya; he tried to remember which.

At Queens Plaza three modern-orthodox Jewish boys got onto the train.

Scully, his voice like opera, singing the words, "Owen makes a bunt."

"Shee-it."

"Would you stop saying that?"

"What's it, three-two, Sox?"

"Listen, PEOPLE?" The Puerto Rican man stood, making use of his height. "Solo habla...HEY! SOLO durante comerciales, ONLY talk during commercials only. Si? Can we agree?"

The Black men and the orthodox boys murmured yes and attempted library quiet in the rumbling, screeching car as it went by the rail yards of Long Island City, the still, graffiti-bombed trains visible in the yard's klieg lights, whorish color on all cars.

"Look at how long ago it was, since the Red Sox won the Series," Vin said, building tension needlessly.

"Holy shit, a Model T cost Eight-hundred thirty-five dollars."

"A quart of milk cost fourteen cents."

"Thirteen point nine."

"I can't see the T.V. It's too small."

"Shut up!"

"Sorry," said a few talkers at once.

Vin: "They're letting Schiraldi close." Emphasis on "letting," as if that decision were the most astonishing since the choice to invade Normandy.

"Is that bad?" Bar asked. He surprised himself, saying anything aloud to strangers.

"No, no, man, that's good. Clemens is fucking scary. Schiraldi's a douche," said one of the Black men, this one wearing a heavy, sheep-lined denim jacket with a construction company logo on the back. Bar noted the deep lines on his face. The man's eyes caught Bar looking. Bar looked down at the man's hands and their lines. The man and his friend looked nothing alike, in their faces, except they were both "Black." One pinched-nose, thin lips, the other wide nose, bigger mouth, large eyes. Bar wondered, again, if they thought he was "Black," as so many had done before.

"Schiraldi's what?" said his friend. "One of the best closers in the league," said thin lips.

"He's a douche. They savin' Clemens." Yet, if I close my eyes, Bar thought, I can hear Blackness in both of their voices. A thing I do not have.

"Schiraldi ain't got nothing on my man McDowell," said the other man in the multi-colored leather. That's a cool coat, Bar thought.

"Looks like your man McDowell just walked the bases loaded."

One of the orthodox boys said, "They going with Orosco." Bar saw the zits on his face, the dweeby buttoned shirt, and the thick glasses, the pasty skin. Is it possible that this boy will ever reproduce?

Or that I will? He thought of his short history of interactions with female humans with shame.

Bar felt stupid not knowing who Orosco was. He hadn't even watched the playoffs.

The religious Latina woman said, "He is Puerto Rican, much better than the white boy." She said "white" like mom, Bar thought, with a big breath first, who-wite.

A different orthodox kid with better skin, no glasses, and a Members Only brown leather jacket said, "Excuse me, but Jesse Orosco is from Santa Barbara and is of Mexican descent."

The Latina waved his comment off and turned her head away in dismissal.

"Would you all shut the fuck up? It's bases loaded!" Bar went back to drawing the TV owner. He liked the big, soft hair and made it even bigger than it was, then bigger than that. Too much. His hair made the turn at Horshack, rounded Dr. J., Diana Ross and Angela Davis, and headed home to surreal.

The Eastern European woman (Czechoslovak? He was no longer confident of her being Russian) looked around at everyone talking to one another, concerned, as if wondering if there was some emergency.

"One pitch by Orosco for the big out..." Vin was getting into it.

"You see?" said the Latina woman, vindicated. "Oh! This my stop." She scrambled much more quickly than Bar would have thought possible and left the train at Woodside.

Five girls got on: three blonde, one red-haired, and one brown-haired, occupying a nebulous age that crossed from high-schoolers to a little older. All but one blonde was wearing Mets gear, boyfriend style: a hat with a ponytail through the back, an oversized Mets jacket, or an oversized Mets "official" uniform shirt. The blonde was wearing a black leather miniskirt, fishnet hose, and a black leather jacket with shoulder pads, and her hair had the volume of a Mack truck. She and the Russian woman in the red leather miniskirt looked one another over approvingly and looked away. The girls chewed gum. Blonde rolled her eyes and sat looking out the window at the two-storey houses going by. One of the others said, to someone, "We're not going to the game. We're going to a party near the game." The three orthodox boys stood straighter when these girls pressed close to them to see the screen. "What's the score?" one girl asked one of the boys.

Vin said, "The Mets are desperate to stay in the game and in the Series," and then, "...to right field, and a single for Lee Mazilli. The tying run is aboard!"

"Holy shit, the Mets are going to tie it up!"

The non-participating girl said, "Nah. Mets're going to lose. The Mets always lose." Bar started drawing her on a fresh page.

The zit-faced kid said, "No, smarty-pants. The Red Sox always lose. The Mets won in 1969. Last time the Sox won was 1918."

"The past is not proof of the present," one of the ortho boys said. The good-looking one. The other two looked at him. One of the girls asked him, "You like baseball? I kinda think it's boring. Lotta standing around."

They listened to Vin. "Dyskstra's looking to bunt. Schiraldi's going to go to seconnnnd- IN THE DIRT! EVERYBODY'S SAFE!"

The handsome boy explained, "This is when I like it. This is exciting. The Mets are only down by one. Look, Bachman's going to bunt too. It's like chess." The girl seemed unimpressed.

Vin called: "The bunt is down, and Schiraldi...HAS TO GO TO FIRST."

"See? Now the Mets have runners on second and third. With one out. Lots of possibilities open up," said the orthodox boy confidently. He had an Israeli multi-colored kippah. The other two just had black ones.

"You know a lot about it," the girl said to the smooth boy.

"Yeah, I guess," he laughed a little, nervously. She smiled at him. One of the Black men had a good seat next to the TV owner and was glued to the screen, but the other, further off, was listening to the boy and girl talk. He looked up, caught Bar's eye, and winked.

"This train's takin' forevah!" said fishnets. Bar drew her face in that state of outrage on the same page, one face next to another, as he had seen in Rembrandt's sketchbooks.

Vin: "One out, second and third, and for the third time tonight, the Mets have a gooooo-lden opportunity."

The orthodox boy gently explained the tactic of walking Herandez to the girl who, Bar suspected, knew all about it. Probably her dad explained it to her a hundred times. The nerdier orthodox boy said, "Hernandez's Mexican too."

"No, he's not," said the third one. "He's Spanish and Irish."

One of the girls said, "Hernandez? Irish?"

The third Orthodox boy said, "His father's Spanish. Mom's Irish."

Bar heard Vin's voice, "And the chant, 'Gah-ree, Gah-ree,' and THE PEOPLE ARE UP. AND SHEA STADIUM IS A MADHOUSE!"

"Why're they chanting?"

"They're gonna lose," said fishnets. Bar hated her. He stopped drawing her and started drawing the ortho boys.

"Mamabicho," the TV owner said to her.

Bar was becoming sorry he was going to get off.

The TV owner and the Black man with the coat started arguing over Gary Carter.

Vin announced, "And a turn of the screw, as far as the tension is concerned. BALL THREE! OH, THIS'LL KILL YA!"

"Sho, nuff." "That's right." "Wow!" "Esta brutal!"

"CARTER'S LINED TO RIGHT! TAGGING UP IS MAZILLI AT THIRD, AND DOWN TO THIRD GOES DYKSTRA! IT'S A BRAND NEW BALLGAME!"

Everyone burst into cheers and a corner of fishnets' mouth curled up in a proto-smile. The TV owner dumped his appliance on the lap of the man sitting next to him and imitated Lee Mazilli running down the third base line toward home, his arms straight up in the air as he tied the game up. Just then the train lurched and the man's high center of gravity forced him to grab a pole right in front of 'nets. He gave her a long stare before she popped a bubble with her gum at him. He went back to his seat and took the television back. Bar felt an exhilarating rush of hope. He looked at the group, the boys and girls, and zoned in, drawing well now.

"What happened, anyway?" asked fishnets.

No one answered her. "Lookit. Strawberry's my man. He's gonna homer. You watch."

The train pulled into the 74th Street Station, a stop before Bar's. He decided he couldn't get off the train now. The train doors remained open for a good long time, the wind rushing through in gusts. Bar looked at the girls in front of him. Two of them had drifted closer to their friend fishnets and were looking at the three Jewish boys and whispering to one another, covering their mouths with their hands. The less attractive two boys were employing different strategies for looking at the girls while appearing not to.

Two slim and clean-shaven white men, maybe in their twenties, stepped onto the train, having run upstairs from the other lines that connected at this station underground. They looked at the unclosing doors and then at one another, acknowledging the effort they wasted. They were both in white business shirts, clean dark slacks, and expensive shoes. One had a tie folded up in his shirt pocket. One was slightly taller and had a pointy, hooked nose, and the other was a little fuller in the arms. Fishnets followed them with her eyes.

The thicker one said, "Sucks that we had to stay so late. Arty's an ass. He's an ass, right?"

"He's an ass. He tries to get everyone else to do his job, is what bothers me."

"What an ass! But then takes credit, like in that Citibank thing."

"Dude, that's never going to happen. A skyscraper in Queens. Yeah, right."

"You don't think? It'd be a smart move."

"Come on."

"Dude, you are in Queens."

Fishnets was staring at the two finance guys like a laser. Her hair was the thing, he decided: its artificiality was wild, odd, and powerful. Deciding not to hate her, he started a new drawing of her in a pose of intent stare.

"Rick Aguilera's Puerto Rican. I'm pretty sure," nerdy boy said.

"Excuse me. He's an American," said the winker, frowning. "He was born in California."

"Oh, yes, yes, I know he's American. I know that. I'm not saying he's not American."

"Then why'd you say he was Puerto Rican?"

"Mano. Puerto Rico, in America," said the TV owner.

The two financials shared suppressed condescending looks.

Fishnets smiled as if in cahoots with them. But they didn't notice her.

Nerdy boy dug in, "I'm just saying, Aguilera's a common name in Puerto Rico."

"Now how you know that?" asked winker.

"My family goes on vacation there, like every year."

"On vacation?"

The Puerto Rican guy said, "Aguilera's Boricua, man. He right."

"See?"

"Do you even speak Spanish?" Winker demanded of Nerdy.

"Si," said Nerdy, pushing his thick glasses back up his nose. His friend

Smoothie missed a question from his car-ride girlfriend out of concern for the trajectory of this conflict.

"¿Dónde se va de vacaciones en Puerto Rico?"

"A veces vamos a San Juan, a veces a Rincón, a veces a El Yunque," he replied.

The financial guy with the tie looked over, "Hey, is that the game?"

"Yes," "yes," "sí!"

"Come on, man, fill us in!" They did.

Bar decided the tie guy was Syrian-Jewish, based on no real information other than a nose. Fishnets was still staring at them, sadly unrequited.

"Henderson up. Look, we all got to shut the fuck up again. It's on loudest."

Vin Scully chatted about possible pinch hitters for the Red Sox. The train doors closed. The train pulled out slowly, lurching East. There was a crack and Vin started yelling, "AND A DRIVE TO LEFT, GOING BACK ON IT IS MOOKIE WILSON, AND THIS ONE IS...GONE! HENDERSON HAS DONE IT AGAIN!"

The train crowd booed and said, "Aw man!" and "Come on!"

"Puto culo de Puerto Rico," Juan said.

"You can say that again," said nerdy.

"I toldja they was going to lose," fishnets piped in, now for once getting the Syrian Jew to look at her.

"Oh, why don't you just be quiet," Winky said to her.

The train pulled into 82nd Street, Bar's stop. Bar sat, unable to think about moving. The doors closed and the train pulled away with Bar still on it.

Two tall Black men had entered train. They had extremely high cheekbones and round faces, were tall and thin, and wore clothes that struck Bar as vaguely Euro. They started speaking French, but not a French Bar's high-school lessons could decipher. They saw the crowd and one of them asked what was going on.

"The World Fuckin' Series, man."

"Oh, thank you," he said, telling his friend, "La Baseball."

"Oh, alors. Trè raz." They went left to the empty double seat at that end of the car.

The crowd inside the TV started chanting, "Let's go Mets! Let's go Mets!" The crowd on the train mimicked them, "Let's go Mets! Let's go Mets!" Everyone on the train chanted, including Bar, except the Haitians (unless they were French), fishnets, and Winkie, whose mood matched the probabilities with finer sensitivity. The finance guys chanted while looking at one another to confirm their ironic stance with respect to chanting with strangers on the Queens subway.

"They're putting up Schiraldi."

The redhead asked, "Don't pitchers not have to hit?"

Smoothie opened his mouth to answer, but was scooped by Bar, who surprised himself by saying, "That's the American League. In the Series, they use National League rules."

Three people looked at him. He regretted having spoken. Now they might see what he was doing and want to see the pictures and ask for one and …

"Come on, everybody knows that," nerdy said. No one was looking at Bar any more.

Redhead glared at him. She said to Smoothie, "I'm Eilish."

"Zeke."

"Hey Zeke," she smiled.

"Boggs just hit a double. Fuckin' maricon."

"You got a mouth on you, huh, Juan," Winkie said.

"Hey, you want me to fuckin' switch this shit off? What's you name, anyways?"

"What's the difference?"

"You know me. You know my name. What's you name? Let's get everybody's name. We watchin' this shit together."

"William."

His friend with the patchwork jacket said, "Jimmy."

"Bar," "Zeke," "Eilish,"

Jeremy, Bruce, Maeve, Anne, and Jennifer. Fishnets' said her name, Saoirse, to the finance guys, Timothy and Abraham (the Syrian – the name not dispositive, Bar decided; could be "Ibrahim" originally).

Juan said, "Alright, we all family now. So family? Shut the fuck up."

Bar added some marks to Saoirse's portrait.

"And it's hit into center, base hit. Here comes Boggs. He. Will. Score!"

"Maricon, man! It's fuckin' five-three!"

"We can all hear it, Juan," William said. He was in a very bad mood now. The girls were jubilant, the finance guys concerned but having a good time, not committing, Saoirse trying to read and copy their complex reaction, and Bar saying to himself, he wished his friend Jon were there.

Vin on Davey Johnson: "As so often happens when you make one decision, something else happens to make you rue that decision."

"What's on the screen?" from Saoirse.

"I thought you didn't care none about the game," William said.

"Keep your willy on, William," she retorted.

He stared at her. "You just a two-bit whore. If you were a man, I'd smack you. I sure hope your daddy does."

She gave him the finger in a tired, over-it gesture, looking away. He nodded and said, "Mmm-hm."

Juan said, "Mets are going to fuck them up."

The train pulled into 103rd Street, two stations from Willets Point. An elderly Chinese couple got on and sat near the French-Haitians. The couple spoke to one another in

Cantonese.

Sculley: "Base hit for Carter, and the Mets are still alive."

"That what I'm fucking talking about!"

"Still alive, honey," William said to Saoirse.

"I ain't your honey," she spit back. She stuck her gum under the bench she was sitting on, and William shook his head in disbelief at this incivility.

"Hey, mister, William," said Timothy the finance guy. "She's just a kid."

"Mind your own business," William said.

Vin: "And the Mets refuse to go quietly."

The train pulled into Willets Point and opened the doors. The enormous sound of the crowd washed over them, but they could still hear Vin Scully cut through with, "It's UP TO Mookie Wilson. And the crowd is alive again!"

Juan stood and led them, holding his little television aloft onto the platform. Bar, exiting by another door, was struck at the resemblance to the Delacroix painting. Juan Leading the People. He quickly roughed in a sketch of the scene, including "7" trains at each station off into the distance, like an awaiting army. The extra-wide station was full of people, some trying to watch the game from the station itself, and some kids jumping onto a lower platform where you could see it better. Bar saw a blue cop snag one of those people and haul him off.

They could hear the sound of the canned trumpet calling for attack from the stadium and from the TV at once as Vin Scully gave some stats about Mookie.

Bar thought, what kind of name is that? Or Saoirse? How do you even spell that?

Saoirse opened her mouth to speak, but looked at the stadium with its awesome lights and its massive curve and lost heart.

Bar looked at the stadium, realizing he had never gone to a game, and was reminded of pictures of the Roman Coliseum.

The Wall Street guys strained to see over the girls' shoulders. Saoirse walked around behind Timothy and stood looking at his back. Zeke was holding Eilish's hand now. Maeve saw and whispered to Anne. Jeremy saw and nodded to Bruce, who shrugged.

Mookie fouled one off. "Fifty-five thousand and seventy-eight and they've reaaally been put through the ringer," Vin said.

"Hey, mano, me too," Juan said.

Bar looked around at the clear night. No possibility of seeing stars, not with that mighty machine of light and sound roaring next to them. He thought about being at the center of the universe this once in his life. The World Series. The importance of it. Just a game. But by agreement, much more. An aesthetic experience if you were open to it, a national drama in which everyone achieved perfect authenticity for a brief moment if they let themselves. As Jon said, it was like Greek drama in the age in which it had been written.

The live crowd's sound was like being in the middle of a riot, yet it was curiously calm. No one touched him. Together and apart, like playing baseball. Bar could still observe.

Another train pulled in.

"The picture shows the Mets' dugout and the stadium crowd," Juan said mildly, but loud enough to be heard. "They all jumping up and down." He struck Bar as calm: called upon to do his duty, he did it. But then he Bar saw tears on his face. The tears made him seem gentle and gangly, whereas before he was towering. Bar could see some acne scars on that face now, glistening wet. "Now they showing the Red Sox. Kinda down."

"No shit," Jimmy said. William was smiling at someone. It was Saoirse. Saoirse was smiling back at him, not sarcastically.

Bar found a spot net to the railing where there was a newly installed faux-old lamppost. He hooked his arm around it to steady himself as he drew with the other hand. They were all in the corner of the train platform, and Bar was observing from this edge.

"There's more fuckin' toilet paper behind home plate. Fuckin' fans, man."

Vin said, "Can you believe this ball game at Shea?"

"Oh, brother!" Joe Garagiola answered him on the TV.

"Mookie swings. It's a little roller up along first, BEHIND THE BAG!!! IT GETS THROUGH BUCHNER!!! HERE COMES KNIGHT AND THE METS WIN IT!!!"

After a beat, the crowd at Shea burst into a higher pitch of screaming and mayhem whose volume and intensity no one hearing even the previous volume plateau could have thought possible. The "family" circle screamed along with them. William, Jimmy, and Juan formed a tighter circle of three around the TV, now on the platform cement, and were locking arms and shoulders and jumping around clockwise. The girls were screaming, including Saoirse, and the orthodox boys along with them. Eilish and Zeke were hugging each other.

Bar felt his heart beating madly, his body itself hearing the roars of the mass of humanity in common ecstasy. Bar felt an odd calm, an eye-of-the-storm feeling of happiness and contentment as opposed to the tumultuous excitement around him and the stirring yet threatening crowd sound coming from just over the coliseum bleachers. He was inside the moment, yet also strangely detached, watching and listening. He said to no one, and no one heard, "It's my birthday." He wondered if he would ever be in a situation, in a place like this again in his life, with the wills and hearts of so many people throbbing and vibrating together, including his, even if he watched all of it, even himself, as if … what?

Whaa..t? All of a sudden, he had a weird double vision, as if he were looking at what he was looking at, and also looking at Saorise's ass. But Saorise is facing me. *What the hell's that about? She's looking at me, smiling, knowing her effect. Caught looking. From two angles? What the hell was this? In addition to the two angles, which wasn't quite like vertigo or dizziness but akin to both, he was receiving feeling that he couldn't recognize, that wasn't his, but then it was, and he had no words to explain it. It was inside of him and outside of him, willing and forced. He was receiving militant indifference to what he saw going on even as he, the real he, felt exuberance and couldn't fathom anyone who did not. Indifference, but other feelings as well. Shame at looking at Saorise because she's so young. But I am the same age, he thought. It made no sense, especially when the feelings from the other self kept coming but the vision suddenly stopped, or clicked off as if he had closed his eyes, though his eyes were wide open.*

But the dizzy/not dizziness made him grab the lamppost again. In a moment he was fine, except for the vivid memory of just having seen the Willets Point station from two points of view at once. Then it was done. It had taken all of ten seconds. Slowly, he let go of the pole and found that he didn't need it to be steady any longer. What had happened?

Music started playing from the Stadium; the change in sound and the continued merriment of all about him made Bar let the strange phenomenon go. Bar saw the first people leaving the stadium and heading toward the parking lots and the 7 train, trying to beat the crowd. He thought about beating all of them as he watched a Manhattan-bound train coming on the other side, but he felt attached to the group even after game was done.

The "family" was giving each other hugs. Bar and William shook hands the cool way. Saorise hugged Bar and whispered in his ear, "I saw you drawing me." She moved off backward, smiled at him wryly, and went to grab Abraham/Ibrahim before he could get away.

Is that the Chanel lady on the other platform? Her presence snapped him away from the "family" and he ran to catch her. Oddly, she stayed and waited for him this time.

"Hey!" He yelled over the sound of the crowd and the trains. "Did you do that to me? That thing that just happened! I was seeing double and I …"

"It is a fold," she said, explaining nothing. "It may happen again. A re-writing. You will understand. This was the nodal point." She turned and went down the stairs and Bar was held back from following her by a group that suddenly raced into place ahead of him and though he yelled for her to stop, she disappeared, again.

The Seven train took its time getting him back to 82nd Street.

In the hall outside the apartment, Bar, exhausted, dropped his heavy set of keychain holding keys to this apartment, his mother's apartment, the studio at Cooper, and his own place. He thought he heard yelling through the door. Was that a woman's shriek? "Ai, Papi, THAT HURT TOO MUCH! YOU BASTARD!" Bar thought they were playing. He was amused at how she said the word, "Bas-tard," really emphasizing the "tard."

As Bar opened the apartment door, Claudia burst out of the bedroom. Claudia in a bra, no bottom, her hair loose and streaming behind her, one hand holding her eye, ran to the bathroom, seeing him with the other as she fled. Bar heard his father's laughter from the bedroom. Running water from the bathroom. It seemed less like play and more like something serious. That door open, he saw Claudia's ass, which he helplessly catalogued: rounder than Stacey's, similar to… Claudia turned suddenly and slammed the bathroom door. Bar remained frozen with his hand still on the key in the front door. He realized with shame that the front door had been open while Claudia was running through the apartment. He closed it. Claudia came out of the bathroom with a towel around her waist; dropping it once she got to the bedroom door, she wielded a wooden shower brush and attacked the figure behind the wall.

She screamed, "me pegas, te mato, maldito!" and he bellowed, "zonna!" The pair of them appeared in a violent embrace at the doorway, Saul laughing, naked, his full belly and his black and white hairs covering his body, Claudia as before. They fell, he on top of her, and lay still next to the bed.

She spat out a bitter laugh, "Ha! You son, he is right there!" Saul said nothing. "Get off me, old goat," she said, not at all amused, and shoved him off. She retreated into the bedroom, an instant later appearing in a nightgown. She went slowly back to the bathroom and ran the sink, yelling back, "The fuck you can do that shit to me and get away with it. I call my brother and half dozen bad boys come here and break you nose, just to start, eh, papi?" Saul snorted.

The snort did not sound like amusement. Saul made another. Bar did not recognize that sound as something usual from his dad. Bar went to the bedroom door and saw his father naked on his back, clutching his chest. "Dad?" Bar went over to him and shook him. "Dad?" Saul started shaking on his own.

Bar ran to the kitchen phone and dialed 911, or rather he tried to dial the phone but was hit with a double vision: he felt his father slap him, which made no sense, since he could see his father lying in front of him. But the slap came somewhere else, or they were both in that other place. Bar tried to scream for Claudia to call. The other place disappeared. He picked up the phone and called the ambulance.

The next events happened quickly: Claudia's expert CPR had no effect, the Elmhurst Hospital's EMT guys lifting his father onto a stretcher, Bar and Claudia in ambulance to the hospital, the words "coma," and "myocardial infarction," seeing his mother, Judit, seeing Judit, Claudia, and Schlomo talking together. "You can't go in the I.C.U.," "wait and see," "usually these things…" Going back to the apartment in a taxi with Claudia in silence, except for when she said, "he fucked me." It seemed to Bar that she was talking to herself; he didn't reply, thought he saw her looking at him just after saying it.

Bar slept a few hours in his childhood bed. He came back the next day. Saul had emergency triple bypass surgery in the night.

The doctor was a forty-five-ish nebbishy man with a curly red blond beard. "Next of kin?" he said. "I'm so sorry. We tried what we could. He was strong but his heart couldn't take it."

There were the calls, mostly to Israel. Bar's uncle Moshe came on a redeye, not from Israel but from Chile. Moshe had been a commando in the IDF and now did security work; he and Judit paid for the burial. Moshe and Bar shoveled the dirt onto Saul's grave. It was like zoning in, but in a universe in which only bad things happened. He was unable to think, yet also unable to escape his consciousness. His father was in that unadorned pine box. Or was he? Was that his father, or was his father gone, disappeared, never to return?

Shiva in the apartment. Some of the men from the Jackson Heights Jewish Center, where Bar had his Bar Mitzvah, came over and said Kaddish. Saul hated the synagogue for being Ashkenazi yet the only one convenient to their home. Some darker men came from the inconveniently far shul in Brooklyn. That rabbi said the Kaddish too quickly.

Abigail came and looked out of place among all the Jews with her blond hair, blue eyes, black lace dress and turquoise jewelry. But after kissing Bar, she went bravely into the kitchen and asked to help. Sleeping with her in his childhood bedroom made no sense to him, but nothing made any sense. His father had died at the age of sixty-two.

Lots of people came and went. Bar's mother told him to call his school, which he did. He had trouble not glaring at her whenever she spoke to him.

Bar spent a day of shiva eating whatever food people brought, then going back into his room to study art history for his midterm when Abi went to work. Once, a relative he did not remember tried to talk with him, to observe the custom of talking about the deceased, and Bar never turned to face him, spending the whole five-minute period of this person speaking about his father facing into his room, angling away, until he finally walked into the room and shut the door.

Whereas before, reading about Rembrandt was like reading a map for making art, now it was a set of facts to be remembered, no different than chemical equations or French verbs. Let all the world's art burn, he thought. The midterm might be shorter that way. Yet it was easier to focus on the book than the alternative. The art books let him escape the default mode: most of the time he was a prisoner of consciousness. His father was dead, he thought, brushing his teeth. His father was dead, he thought, drinking tea, eating a bagel and sable with raw onion. Bar's father was dead as Bar sat on the toilet, as he washed his hands, and as he went back to Rembrandt. He tried to ignore the prison cell; the cell returned: his father's goneness became present.

He spoke with in single word replies. Do you want some more sable? My father is dead. "No." Do you want some herring? My father is dead. "No." He's dead. I don't eat herring, you fucking Europeans. Moshe had stayed two nights and taken the plane back to Chile leaving Bar with Judit's relatives and friends. And Schlomo.

When his mother tried to sit with him her presence caused him nausea and he left the room, angry with her even for his understanding that she was trying to comfort him.

On Friday the doorbell rang; Bar answered it. A little boy waited in the hallway. He was wearing a Superman costume. He held up a small bucket with a few pieces of candy in it. Bar stared at him, not understanding for some seconds until it clicked. He felt shock at first. People are doing Halloween? Don't they know my father died? But he said, "Wait a minute," and came back with a piece of chocolate rugelach.

"I'm not a-posed to take something not wrapped," the boy said.

"Oh, sorry. That's what I've got. Look, it's good," Bar said, and took a bite. The boy dropped his head, not prepared to "trick," and walked away.

Bar went back to school and made up missed exams. He spoke to no other students. There was a study group meeting for one of the exams. He walked past it. He came home for the last night of official mourning. Claudia spooned "manteca de cerdo" from a can into a pot of beans. She had put Saul's things in boxes and asked Bar if he "wants nothing before I go to Salvation Army?" Still in Bar's room were clothes that no longer fit, notebooks from high school, his sci-fi and fantasy figurine collections, sailboat bedsheets, and half a dozen drawings he had made, including one of Saul, tacked into the plaster. He ran his finger on some of the joints of the bed, chair, and desk his father had made by hand. He took an old suitcase with the zipper stuck midway, packed what he wanted to save, and told Claudia where he stowed it in the closet.

Her eye was healing but still showed a faint black circular bruise ten days later. They did not discuss the circumstances of Saul's death; it did not occur to Bar to bring it up. As he was getting ready to leave, he puttered around the kitchen, now full of unfamiliar smells, not wanting to sit. Claudia turned from the stove where she was stirring a pot.

"You stay and eat, no?"

"No, thanks. Gotta go."

She stepped over and hugged him close, her head turned to one side. He put his hands on her waist rather than hug her back. Her female body felt delicate and small, and he let himself experience that horror of knowing why his father desired her as her body pressed against his. She let him go and went back to the stove. He realized she was merely trying to comfort him. He left, confused, not understanding whose apartment this now was, not saying the word "goodbye" to this person who was not his dead father, not his mother, not nearly old enough to be either. Just as he closed the door, he saw Saul's living room chair empty, an image that stayed with him when he lay down to sleep and when he woke suddenly in the night.

Crossing the Queensborough Bridge, he wondered if he should have left the keys on the table for Claudia, which would have meant he would have to call the apartment where he was living, not "college-home," but home.

Saturday, October 25, 1986, around midnight. Life Two.

They asked me to keep a journal. Day by day, moment by moment. They said to do some moments. Which? You'll know.

The actual duration of the travel from their office to Willets Point station was a moment, a flash of existence, like the Star Trek transporter device but faster. In that time, I saw in my mind a huge drawing, life size on eight-foot-high paper of me flailing as I fell, like one of Robert Longo's big paintings of men in suits dangling, or falling, in mid-air, except naked, not in a suit, and not standing on anything. I imagined a drawing that moved in which the flailing would take place in front of the viewer, like a ten-second film but all images done in ink, a black and white cartoon of precise detail, the flailing showing pitch and yaw and twist and then snap back to the original position for as disturbing and sea-sickening an effect as I could imagine.

It felt like vertigo. More like being thrown than falling. Like sleeping and waking up somewhere else and dreaming the whole time of being thrown off a building. This is...Willet's Point. I can't believe it worked. I believe it because the alternative would be that I'm inside an utterly real-seeming delusion.

I'm landing onto the elevated 7 train station, dropping onto it from a meter up, and simultaneously being jolted by the sound of the wildly loud baseball stadium and the crowd's wall of roars, as if yelling at me to WAKE UP! At least there's a big metal pole I can hold.

My legs feel like jelly. I can feel strength rushing into them. I can't take a step. Right, now I can. It's like ... no words. I need to keep grabbing that blue railing. It's so blue. So 1980s, so real? What is real? Is two and two really seven and no one told me?

Youth is: the body unspoiled, the mind, unformed. What am I, then? A perfect human being, my mind experienced, my body fresh? I can see my hand from twelve inches without reading glasses. I think I could get hard from seeing a woman at a hundred yards in a stiff wind. As I gaze upon these young women who aren't even all that attractive (to me; they are hot to those boys looking at them), I think I'd agree to sex if asked. No spiritual connection would be required. I feel poisoned by testosterone. Perhaps I have always been so poisoned.

I miss Eva. Don't want sex with these girls. It's as if my body were being emptied out into a hollow shell. Eva-nostalgia feels like a devil on my shoulder. It's 1986; Eva is fourteen. I left her alone in 2006. No: she's still "there," whatever that means. Only she hasn't met me yet, in 2004. It will happen. It might happen. What if it doesn't? My head is spinning. I need to work all of that time stuff out, but not now.

Perhaps the testosterone "poisoning" has been the defining feature of my life, art, and relationships. I am my own devil on my shoulder. No! I've come back! I can save dad!

Shit, now's a palimpsest...but it's from the other perspective! There's Saorise's ass, cute, too small, so young. What am I doing looking at a child? She's my age. But now I also see her face from the other point of view. I remember this. This is what these are! I feel the confusion from my younger self at feeling shame for looking at the young girl. It's as if I'm talking with myself. I see what I saw in 1986 (fool: it *is* 1986) plus what I see now... until I close my eyes. Keep them closed. Even then, the feeling bleeds in from the other perspective. Of course. This is what they always were.

The feeling I am receiving from the "other" point of view is elation, excitement, surprise, thrill, and a warm togetherness with everyone around. These feelings jar against my current antipathy. I spent the last hour in the Chanel Lady's office, which turned out to have lots of big machines with beeps and flashing lights, not on the train with these folks, and not listening to the game. What difference did a game from decades ago make?

There is the Chanel Lady across the platform. She's nodding, so I'll nod back. She's going down the stairs. Gone. Like the last time, except she doesn't need to explain what's going on. She called it a "fold" last time, what I called a palimpsest. She might consider buying a few other outfits.

"Hey man, you alright?"

"Yeah, sure, don't worry about it." That is be one of those Jewish kids I saw. See. See-aw? Amazing how I remember that from ... ? No, now. Amazing Mets. This is craziness. Use Logic. Use Reason. Open your eyes.

The palimpsest is gone thankfully. That's good; that and how I don't need to cling to a post for dear life any more. There's an old Seven train lumbering past, screeching a little, it's lights flickering, signaling its need for maintenance and more generally the same need on the part of The City of New York. The cost of faking that one thing? Think it through. Prohibitive, mind boggling. Graffiti everywhere. It would be like a billion-dollar movie set to construct all of this. There's a monstrous crowd here. A million extras? In 1980s fashion and hair ugliness? Impossible. This can't be faked, and who would bother?

I feel unnaturally strong. Dizzy, but hungry. Horny. I remembered Saorise for years. She is so much less attractive than in my memory. I painted her in my mind with my balls....she's a kid. She's a kid? *I'm* a kid. No, I'm not a kid. No? She has Dallas hair and an ugly 80s outfit. At least I never wore embarrassing shit. If I touched her I'd feel like a child molester, though we are the same physical age. My age, all of it, it will all have to be negotiated, calibrated, somehow.

Wake up. Be aware. There is a roar of people. There's a breeze. People all around. Going home. Game over. I have been sent back in time and even though I am forty years old, I am now in my twenty-year old body, twenty years ago, in 1986. I need to repeat that, hold onto it like this pole. Actually, I can let go of the pole. Look at the street.

It's not faked. Those old buses, down on Roosevelt Avenue must have the old pull cords. The tech difference: it's not what matters. Yes, material conditions determine mental ones. That graffiti is scary. It doesn't strike me as art so much as evidence of social decrepitude. Or both. I didn't used to think of it that way. It looks like a decrepit artistic representation of decrepitude. Yet, just yesterday, I might have thought of it as preserved, archaeological hip hop culture. Now, it's everywhere, and mostly not even attempted art. I'm old, crotchety, and I've had to clean up graffiti from the bike shop gate.

What is art? Re-calibrate. Don't ask stupid questions now.

If a delusion, I will have to go with it. The surface of reality is utterly convincing.

Un-virginity: I was excited, once, to find out that the Mets won Game 6, but not anymore. I had a family feeling with these people. We lived through something together.

I'm supposed to go back to Dad's. I do not care about anyone here. I will never see them again.

"Hey, Bar!" What was this guy's name? Is.

Dad is alive. Is. He is still alive! A couple of miles from here!

"Take it easy."

I feel the tears on my face.

"Bar, ain't you celebrating?"

Yes, but not what you're celebrating, not this twenty-year-old ballgame. It's going to be difficult not to think fools of people who don't know what I know. Don't plan that now. Don't plan anything. Just go.

Celebrate being twenty!

Save dad..

"Let him alone, man. Can't you see he's ballin'?"

"Yeah, I gotta go. Thanks. It was, uh. Great." I've no idea what I'm saying.

My hand doesn't have the scar I got from burning myself in '96. Was it 1997?

"Bar!"

These people don't matter. Go moment-to-moment. Go.

Take the train back to 82nd Street and Jackson Heights. Remember: I am Bar Mizrachi, Artist. (No matter what the galleries say). I Observe. I see, record, and reflect. I am of this world and not of it at the same time. That was always true. Ever since…I drew Stacey back in high school. (Don't get distracted. Her body distracts me even now, twenty years…no, this year? She would be twenty also, young and sexy and possibly willing to see me. Where did she go to school again? Stop.) Artists know adversity, rejection, trouble. They are the gadflies, the permanent outsiders; they learn things, understand things others cannot; they see. As an artist, I will be able to adjust.

Here is the apartment. I grew up here. I haven't been here in decades. Claudia lives here now. Wait – yes, she should be here. Do I have the key? Yes, it's in my pocket. I put it there, twenty years ago, meaning today.

"Ai! PAPI YOU HURT ME!" Claudia, from the mom and dad bedroom, once my mom's and dad's, now and for many years, dad's.

"SHUT UP, YOU FACKING WHORE!"

Hurry.

"Ai, it's the son." Claudia is so young. I don't want to look at her, but have to: no black eye. Yet. She's wearing a white bra. Nothing lingerie-like but also she's not wearing anything else and the triangle of her pubic hair is irresistibly present.

Focus. Claudia's smirking at me on her way to the bathroom. She saw me see. Caught looking.

The kitchen has a telephone attached to the wall. A rotary dial, incredibly slow. "Hi, yes, there's a man having a heart attack. Queens, Jackson Heights."

"What man!" Dad yelled. He always yelled. This is the first time I've has seen him in twenty years. I should be elated but he is also annoying. I'm crying at seeing him, of course.

"Dad. Eighty-six-ten, Thirty-fourth Avenue, apartment six-thirteen. Elevator, yes. Six-thirteen, sixth floor. Come quickly."

"What the fack are you calling…uh. I feel…it's the facking whore. Wore me in."

"Out, dad."

"Why you think he has a heart attack?"

"Come on, Claudia. You're a nurse. Look at him. He's not breathing right. Take his pulse or something."

"That's how papi gets when he's excited…when we…"

"He can't breathe. Come on. Let's get him downstairs. Every minute counts."

"El idiota me golpeó y me dijo que lo estaba engañando! No estaba! Juro que no estaba en Santa María!"

There's a chance… I have to calm her down. "Claudia." (She's wearing jeans and a t-shirt now but…Don't look at her body. Do. Not. Why am I so horny?)

"I no whore!" She's yelling into Dad's ear. "You sonoffabitch." Wow, she spat at him. At least I never made a woman spit at me.

"I like it? You like it, estúpida vieja cabra! You know? I go along with you but no mas. I am leaving. You son is better than you. Look, he is gentle. You are dirty."

"How come you have that mark? On your neck?"

"I tole you, cabra! I get that in the hospital. Working, that is something you…"

"You're a facking whore."

"Help me get him downstairs. We shouldn't wait for the ambulance. Or, get his things. Pack a bag for the hospital."

"What for? He's not…"

"LISTEN TO ME. HE'LL DIE…"

"He should die, the goat motherfucker, calling ME a whore!"

"No, NO! I came all this way!"

"Don't you facking order me, boy…"

He's falling. We're almost out of time.

"Dios mio, you were right."

"Dad"? This is harder. Watching him fall is harder.

I remember the cardio doc's beard.

"It was touch and go," he says. "An hour later, or if he had tried to exert himself…"

"When can I get out of here?" Saul is disoriented, as if drunk.

"It's a miracle you figured it out, with even a trained nurse not seeing it."

"Yes, my son, he knows, Doctor. Bar, I need my cologne."

"It's not in the bag, dad." He's winking at the doc. He has no idea what I know and don't know. "I'll bring it tomorrow."

"You go back to the apartment?"

"Yeah."

"You want to fack my woman, ha, Bar?" Saul wheezes a laugh.

"That's disgusting, dad."

"Ha, ha, I am making joke. Only, I was going to fack her, and here you come, you say 'No, No, you have to go to the hospital.' I have heart attacks for twenty year. So now I need to go see a doctor? When you see my woman's ass?"

"What do you mean you've been having a heart attack for twenty years?"

"Nah, nothing, nothing."

"Should I have let you drop dead, dad?" He's starting to consider the answer to that question unclear. Dad isn't the human being that I remembered. Yet preventing his death, it felt triumphant, as if this impossible, insane idea,…and now I have to wait…what will dad end up doing?

"Ach!"

"You can't even lift your left arm."

"Ach, get out of here." He's trying to punch me with his right. This is dad, alive.

"You're welcome."

Claudia's making rice and beans with chicken. Her food was always good. She looks cute in her scrubs. That's because she's a pretty woman whom I will leave be.

I did it. I saved dad. That makes everything else that follows worth it, come what may.

(Claudia the sexy nurse; a stereotype. Watch the testosterone poisoning your brain, Bar. It's endemic among twenty-year-olds. Every girl turns your head.)

Stay on target, I'm here for Eva. And dad. However, I can't possibly last through decades of abstinence until I can meet Eva again, for the first time. Might as well have a good time.

Not with Claudia.

"I saved him."

"Que? Yes, well, the doctor. You, too. Good son. Here. Salsa picante?"

And not with Abigail? I don't live in Jackson Heights any more. That part doesn't promise to be a smooth transition. Technically, I'm living with Abigail. Meaning I am having sex with her about six times per week, as if it were the usual thing, but it is not the usual thing. This is not something the body can simply hand me, like horniness and a bigger VO_2 max. I haven't seen her since '94. If then.

I remember 3rd Street between B and C well enough. What branches grow out of this stony rubbish? Did I know that poem, then? Doubtful. "My" apartment where "my" girlfriend is waiting for me. I feel dread and anticipation, feelings I did not have and I do not have the feeling for her that I once did. I am angry with her, yes, after this long space, for what she did, and yet didn't do yet. Maybe she would never do those things. What's the difference, though? Isn't she responsible either way? The simplest thing would be to play it cool, pretend I'm still excited with relatively new love. She's about twenty-one, right? She was a couple of years older. Is. I'm forty; it's wrong-ish. Try not to tip her off that I've become someone else in one day, that I've aged twenty years since I walked out that door two nights before.

It was a mundane moment, like nothing, coming in the door to the apartment I shared with Abigail, a domestic scene.

"Baby, baby, baby," she said. "You took care of your poppa?"

"Yeah," he said and let her kiss him.

"How's he doing, baby?"

"He'll be okay. The cardiologist …"

"Oh, Art's here." Of course he is. "I made a pesto. What's wrong? The cardiologist? What did he say?"

"Nothing. Dad's going to be alright. I was there in time." I can't hide from

Abi, but I can't level with her, either. "I...Art, don't get up for me." He's getting up. He's giving me the flourish. Why does he raise hairs on my neck? In less than two weeks he's going to kill himself, is one good reason. Or at least, that's what happened last time. It smells like garlic and Italian cheese and there's that good cheap wine we used to drink, Italian table wine. This was my home. That woman and me, for a few magical months, had played house very well, until she spun it out of control, and are now in the middle of playing house, as far as she knows.

"Are you going to give me a kiss?"

Yes, he decided quickly, seeing her face, I can kiss her. She is beautiful. The white hippy, the American girl, descended from communists and capitalists, Blue and Grey soldiers, maybe even Puritan witches. Army brat, rebel against her daddy but so much like him. Fiercely herself. I do feel strong respect and love, or memory of love once lost for Abigail Greenfield, returning like a rising of my heart. I can kiss her with the memory.

"Your Black stud seems mopey this evening, his dear."

"I'll have to revive his spirits."

"I could fluff him up for you. If you like. La Negre. Je le veux." He gives a flourish and an arch smile.

"Bar, you look stunned."

"Wow! I'm not a Black stud. What the fuck …"

Art is surprised, as if he had made a very light joke. Things have – will change.

"Honey, you're a stud, and you're …" Art begins.

"Not Black. I'm half middle-eastern. Get it right."

"Whew. Brown stud, then."

I'm glaring at him and should stop. But I do hate him. I can't remember if I had enough reason yet, aside from his racist stupidity.

"Baby? Is your dad going to be okay? You said, on the phone..."

"My dad's okay. Art's the sick one. Abi, this, …" This is hard. Why not wait? Just one night. It wouldn't kill anyone.

"What do you mean that he's sick? Art, are you...you're sick? What's the matter with you?"

"I am in the pink, my dear. A mere manner of speaking. I meant no harm, of course. It was a compliment." Flourish.

Alright, recover. "Never mind that. You're a great artist, Art. Have I ever said that to you?"

He's laughing. "Usually such a statement precedes something less pleasant."

"No, I mean it. That painting of yours hanging in the E.V. Gallery, it's important." And it'll be worth about two hundred thousand in fifteen years. They're both staring at me. What am I doing? Did I not used to talk like this? "So, like, there's a lot to live for. Just saying." Art's amazed. It's gratifying to mystify him for once. He used to do that to me all the time.

"What the fuck are you talking about, Bar?" she asks, smiling.

"I don't know. I guess I'm talking about hope. There's always hope."

"Hope for what?" Art asks him, with no spin on his voice. No flourish now.

"Hope for one's art. So to speak. Hope for a cure...hope against hope. And other things."

He's staring at me, unsure. They're all staring at one another.

"I'm hungry, guys." Abi's voice is lower than I remember.

"I think, sadly, my dear, your Art must take his leave." This flourish had a little hesitation that I'm savoring. With a few more flourishes, he's gone.

"What was that about, Bar?"

"I don't know. I was, I'm sorry. I didn't mean to kill a mood. Pasta smells good."

The window outside showed stars, and if I sit up and strain my head, the whole Lower East Side north of 3rd Street.

If I lay back down on my side I can look at the landscape of her back. The semi-circular dimple-creases. The many freckles. I wouldn't say she "has freckles." Tens, not hundreds. Asleep, her body's wound-upness is unstrung. I let my eye follow the line of her leg leading up to the hip, down the waist, up sharply at the elbow that rests on her side, down at the shoulder into her neck and head. If I put my hand close to her back I can register the shades of lightness and darkness between us. I like this moment; I can observe her without interruption, without interaction. Let her sink into me.

I remember staring at her just this way in my first life when I first woke up once at dawn after a falling asleep together naked, staring at her freckles and the marks of the sheets on her skin and the blond down on the small of her back. I see this same view again after two decades of not seeing her, pretending that it had only been a short while. The memory twinged of having been so afraid lest she discover that I had been almost a virgin and the silliness of that term and the way as a young man I had thought of it as a clear threshold, a physical ritual like a bar mitzvah, once done, something that would utterly change me but didn't. Yet there were events that utterly changed me, but sex had taken longer.

Even my bar mitzvah wasn't transformational. Its immediate effect was that I would not have to memorize the parsha in Hebrew and Aramaic like the Yemenites still did, ever again. What a bummer, in high school, to discover from Jon that almost no Jews around the world did the Aramaic. They never even heard of memorizing a parsha in fucking Aramaic.

What a rip-off, was my reaction in 9th grade.

Each fact needed to be learned, "the hard way," and usually after it was too late.

My heart is racing. What have I re-begun? I'm on a long, long train ride now and there is no getting off.

What am I doing?

I saved dad. Can't I enjoy a little affection? Abigail is affectionate and sweet. She turns into a tiger later.

This is corrupt. I'm too old.

No, I'm actually a year younger.

But that is a lie.

No, it's unclear. Let the ambiguity be the rationalization.

What if I fall in love with her, the way I felt the first time, when I was an Abi-virgin? Will it all explode the same way?

No, this time I'm not her plaything.

She was on top. Just now.

So? Hadn't I always "let her"?

Eva doesn't like being on top. Won't. The most direction she gave was to pull me on top of her when she was ready.

(Am I not Eva's boyfriend? No. She is a kid. *That* would be wrong and illegal. Also Eva as a kid isn't the person I want.)

The feeling of Abigail on top of me, controlling the rhythm, isn't one of her as the instructor, the revelator, not like it was. This time her direction strikes me as cute, and my attitude is one of magnanimous permission. Cute, or endearing, is her expression of desire for me, or for the "Bar" that exists in her mind. A person that I no longer am.

3. No Listings

August, 1986. Life One before the Return.

As a boy of eight, Bar made a drawing in colored pencils of his "house," meaning his apartment building. This on assignment from his 4th Grade teacher, Mrs. Ross. It showed the six-story building on the avenue and the non-detached two-family buildings on the side street, separated by cement driveways on a tree-lined block. He included the metal plaque in the form of a coat of arms on the front of his building bearing its non-official title, "The Griswold." The picture had pretty good perspective for a kid, the foreshortening a little clunky but passable and consistent; something he learned from the "pull-out" art teacher, Miss Clark, an African-American woman who took a liking to Bar until she asked the kids to draw their "place of worship" and Bar drew the shul with its Star of David front and center.

Before boys of summer went into post-season and the Mets clinched the pennant, and before Bar started at Cooper Union, he went looking for a place near the school. His parents were not involved. What was involved was mostly mental, though Bar was a quick study.

The transition from the leafy blocks of Jackson Heights to the bleak checkerboard of tenements and abandoned bombscapes of the Lower East Side was not smooth or simple, given Bar's financial limitations, among other things. Yes, Bar had grown up in this metropolis, but it was a galaxy with many solar systems, some of which seemed forever far, far away. In Jackson Heights, there were bullies, at first, but not much real danger. The wholesale drug dealers that Bar heard about later on only started doing business after Bar reached his late teens, and in any case they mostly shot at one another. The retail market, and its junkies, were elsewhere. Bar attended a neighborhood public school that led to high school in "The City," meaning Manhattan, and took the subway to school after that. He heard of a lot more crime than he ever saw.

His experience as a crime victim of being mugged consisted of giving a tall man a dollar once after being challenged on his way home one night at midnight. He might not have been perceived a target, even then, but he was walking home in a daze after making out with Stacey Abramovitz until both of their lips were numb and his gait appeared possibly alcoholic. His friends got mugged in richer neighborhoods. Jon, his high school buddy from the Upper West Side, had taken to walking from his apartment on 86th Street and West End Avenue, away from the 86th street crosstown bus to the 79th Street crosstown to avoid a group of teenagers who had shaken him down six or seven times right on Broadway and 86th, as if he were an ATM. But Jon did not have dark skin.

 In high school, Bar continued his lack of criminal experience by not becoming a perp. Bar knew of the kids who went into Central Park at lunch to smoke joints, and he heard of the private-school kids who had money for coke, but he didn't get invited to those parties, and didn't see much of any of that. He played Dungeons and Dragons in late-night (not all-night) sessions in which the boys (no girls) made batches of chocolate-chip cookies. He got drunk at a few high school parties, which was illegal, but behind closed doors, and was not the one to do the purchase.

 In high school, Bar had one girlfriend. No one he knew got pregnant, or arrested, or badly injured; they all went to one college or another. Bar had never been in Harlem or Bed Stuy and the closest he ever got to the Lower East Side before going to Cooper was CBGBs and his main impression of the punk center of the universe was that the speakers were too loud.

 Of the ten Black kids in his high school class, two went back to their neighborhood schools before the end of tenth grade, and none happened to be Bar's close friend.

 Now, though, he would have to live near the school and Cooper Union did not have dorms and the richer area to the West, where NYU and Dojos and the Violet Café and that movie theater where they played *Rocky Horror* at midnight and the rich gays and the twee three-story brick carriage houses – all that was far too pricey for him. Between the amount he was able to wring out of his mother and a small scholarship, Bar's budget did not cover costs for a decent room west of First Avenue. East of there was a place he was told – by his mother, his father, and Cooper Union's orientation – not to set foot. This gap surprised him considering, one he did start looking there, how many vacant buildings there were all over the area. How could rent be high at the same time? There were no vacant buildings in Jackson Heights, not through the downturn and loss of population New York City suffered from suburbanization in the 1950s until re-urbanization in the 1990s, and certainly not after Bar left the Heights in the mid-1980s, missing out on the radical diversification of the neighborhood; it became the nation's most diverse place around 1995.

 (Dad was not involved in Bar's financial discussions; his contribution to Bar's education was made up of advice about how to get girls who did not at first understand their need for his male potency. He never even asked Bar where he was going in the morning and seemed not to know about Bar's gallery-sitting job or that it was a key piece of Bar's cash flow. He did not always seem to comprehend that Bar was transitioning to higher education; sometimes he brought up going "away" to school and sometimes, when Bar talked about Cooper, his father stared blankly, thought that may have been the effect of the sixth beer.)

Bar awoke on a Saturday in his room in Jackson Heights, went into the kitchen and made himself coffee and shakshuka. He stocked the fridge himself with more than just the beer that occupied one whole shelf. In the year since his mother had left, Bar had taken to paying the bills. This was best done on Friday afternoons, paydays, before that money could be misspent. Dishes and garbage and other chores were never done unless Bar did them, including changing his bed sheets, but excluding cleaning the toilet, the only task dad took upon himself to do regardless of his alcoholic intake, and that represented a floor to dad's active self-care.

Dad had been doing a little better recently, getting steady work throughout the summer. He seemed lighter, easier. Bar noted that he had been coming home after work, not going to a bar, and only drinking a couple of beers before bed.

This Saturday morning, Bar was startled to find a woman a little older than himself in the kitchen wearing what looked like a large t-shirt of his father's, and underwear. She was staring at the now-uncovered plate of poached eggs with tomato sauce, onion, peppers, and an inviting cumin scent. Was she a cousin? Did he forget about an announced visit?

"Oh! You are the son? You look like Saul," she said, smiling and holding out her thin, brown, bird-like arm and delicate hand.

He took it. "Sorry, um. Hi?" She had very long black hair, down almost to the end of the shirt. She looked and sounded Spanish, not Yemenite.

"I am Claudia," she said. She had a Spanish accent. Bar noted her dimples and long black hair. She seemed smart, sharp. Pretty.

"Bar."

"Yes, of course. Your father, he spoke of you, of course." Pointing to the eggs, "You made this?"

"Yes. Is dad, uh, Saul up?"

"No, he is a-sleeping." Still smiling. She quickly went into his father's room and emerged wearing a pair of gym shorts.

"You call him Saul?"

"Yeah, sometimes. Not a lot."

She laughed.

Was it possible for dad to have a girl? Bar sat and ate his breakfast and drank his coffee. He looked at her as she went about making her own breakfast of eggs, black beans, and avocado, the first time Bar had seen anyone deploy such a fruit in his house.

"You are finished? With high school?"

"Yeah." He turned to face his interlocutor, but she was reaching for the coffee can on a high shelf. His father couldn't reach that high. He turned back to his food. She's tall, young, with long hair and long legs…stop it.

"You are lucky. I have a test Monday."

"Yeah? In high school?"

She laughed, "No, nursing school."

"Uh-huh."

Why was she here, as a nurse? He finished his food and left to meet Jon in the City. On Northern Boulevard, he considered Claudia. She seemed very comfortable there. when did she start coming to his apartment? Dad's dating? a non-Jewish girl? in nursing school?

He met Jon at their Village spot: The Kiev, in Little Ukraine: 2nd Avenue and 7th Street. Jon was already half way through a plate of pierogis. "I usually get the Matzo Brie," he said, telling Bar about the courses he would be taking at Columbia in their pre-med sequence.

"Ashkenazie food," Bar said wrinkling his nose and requesting a burger with fries and apple pie from a waitress whose blond braids curled around her head.

"Mets are going all the way this year," Jon said, putting the last of the pierogi whole into his mouth.

"Evidence?"

"Doc Gooden. In a good game, the pitching's the thing. The Common People love those games when there's lots of hits and people are running around, chasing the ball. Those are inherently inferior to a real pitching duel. That's your artistic baseball game. Mental. A one-nothing shutout. Ten-six, that's like selling out, like a Madonna song."

"I'd fall asleep. I don't see how you can watch it."

"I listen on the radio, remember? I like to keep the whole thing in my head."

"Uh-huh."

They started walking to the first listing. "How's Columbia?" Bar asked. Columbia had started a week earlier than Cooper.

"Oh, you know. The core classes are not as bad as I feared. Some of the people in the class are pretty smart."

"The Ivy League is sadly fallen off."

"No, the opposite. They're still trying to get rid of the old white families that've been going there for centuries. There's this guy, James Huxley, like, the ninth, in my lit class. He reads, like a page."

"What's stopping them?"

"Folks like that don't ask for financial aid. Columbia's buildings are half rotten."

Jon asked about Bar going to Cooper. Bar said, "I just want to learn to draw better. Draw, paint, use stuff like marble, do photography, shit like that. I already have a 'style'. I don't see why I need another one. *Don't* I have a style? I mean, you can tell a picture I made, right?"

"I don't think you're seeing what people mean by style. It's not just a way your stuff looks."

"It's not?"

"It's who you are. It's the ideas as much as the overtly aesthetic things. Its why you do art. What art is. Like cubism. Suddenly, a painting isn't a window attempting to be real. The light's all wrong on purpose. So what is a painting, then? Make it new."

Bar felt ashamed of being the one to go to Art School when his friend seemed more qualified. Except for drawing.

After a tour of three places, they returned to the Kiev. Jon ordered the Matzo Brie. "You can't live with those five women from Texas," he said.

"What!? You're breaking my heart."

"They're pigs."

"They liked me!"

"I'd say that two of them might have been up for having sex with you, but they probably won't pick you as a roommate anyway. I would worry about sexually transmitted diseases."

"With them? Or in general?"

"Both."

"It's too expensive anyways."

"I don't see any of the other ones we saw working out, but if you live with those girls you'll probably get crabs, maybe syphilis, also botulism, asthma, lice, at the very least, maybe AIDS, certainly one STD or another. Possibly a roach will crawl into your mouth while you're asleep."

"I'm in love with two of them. The red-haired one, what was her name? I thought AIDS..."

Jon cut him off. "That's not love. Learn the difference. Also, she's not one of the two who thought you were cute."

"How could you tell?"

Jon gave him a withering look. "Freud was wrong," he said. "Not everything is motivated by sexual desire."

"But a lot is."

"You can be in control of it."

"Yeah. They'd let Gary Mitchell move in for free, I'd bet." A group of two men and two women occupied a booth across the room. Green, bright pink, and orange hair (one was natural black, long and covering one eye). One fifties checker shirt, one repurposed gas station uniform shirt, one green army tank top, and one white button shirt with a bow tie. Three pairs of Doc Martens. Bar looked around the room, anticipation rising at the idea that he would soon live among these coolest of the cool. If he could find a place he could afford.

"I wonder if he'll ever come back from The Coast." Jon seemed very serious for a moment.

"Yeah. How about the place on 3rd street? Unclean."

"They have mice. It's only a matter of time before the vermin conquer New York. We're all doomed," he said, shoveling the last of the food into his mouth. "Nuclear war would be a relief, in a sense."

"Plus, no chicks," Bar said, not even mentioning that he could not afford that one, either.

"You look at these buildings from the street and never imagine the way people live inside."

"There are a million lives in this Naked City."

"Which leaves the nice Ukrainian lady across the street."

"Maybe she's watching us."

"We are eating in a Ukrainian establishment. Kiev being the capital of The Ukraine."

"What was that? Let me look." Bar looked over scrawled notes on the back of a flyer announcing a student art show from the previous July. "She wants three hundred for that place."

"Take it."

"I don't want to have sex with her. She's like, *forty*."

"Exactly. Perhaps that is why she has an antiquated price point."

"I *do* want to have sex with three of the five Texans."

"Invite them over to the Ukrainian place. There's a high probability of an intersection of sets between the ones you like and the ones who like you."

"You think that place is like the nunnery in Monty Python."

"Yes, that is apt."

"So, Jon, you asking girls back to your dorm? How does one do that?"

"Huh?" Jon looked out the window, smile suddenly vanishing.

Twenty minutes later.
"I can't believe it," Bar said.
"I'm sorry. It's my fault."
"No, no."
"If I hadn't had that coffee,..."
"No, she said twenty minutes. She rented it twenty minutes ago. It was the Matzo Brie."
"I'm so sorry. I'm a fool."
"No, no. I would've had to take it when we saw it. She said the girl who took it, she got there and wrote a check."

"It's a tough market. Anything slightly below it gets filled immediately. Brooklyn?"

"Why would I do that instead of just living at home?"

"I don't know. I don't really get the emergency here anyway. You could, in truth, live at home."

"I can't live there. I'm afraid I would have sex with my father's girlfriend. I have to finagle something."

"That's unlikely. Mom's?"

"It's a big glass and steel one-bedroom. I don't like the aesthetics and I don't like my mom. No, no."

"I just think, how're you going to be the one person to find the one place that no one else has found? This is a transparent marketplace..."

"Yeah. But I don't think like everyone else. I'm going to finagle something. You'll see."

They were near the northeast corner of Second Avenue and Seventh Street coming out of the vestibule of the apartment Bar narrowly missed renting. As they continued to confer, Jon was nearly knocked down buy the shoulder of one of three men in their early twenties. The leader who shoved him wore a black leather motorcycle jacket with a hooded sweatshirt underneath. The other two wore varsity leather jackets with hooded sweatshirts underneath.

"What the FUCK do we have here, boys? Is this what we came here for, or WHAT?" He was smiling broadly. His two buddies smiled with only a little less cockiness.

Bar noticed that they all had Yankees hats, one backwards.

Backwards Hat said, "Fucking FAGS, man. This one's definitely a fag. Other one's his black bitch."

Jon said, "Leave us alone" evenly, looking them in the eye, one by one. "We don't take that kind of shit any more."

As he said that, the evident leader tried to swipe Bar's cycling hat off his head but Bar saw him coming and pulled his head back suddenly.

Jon said, "Ha ha! You missed! That's so embarrassing!"

Shit, Jon, don't say that! What was he doing? Jon suddenly seemed to grow an edge to himself.

One of them said, "We should fuck this smart ass up!" Then, turning to his compatriots, he repeated it: "He's fucking *smart* ass!"

Jon said, dryly and with just a hint of sarcasm, "I know a cop in your town."

Follower number two shoved Jon's left shoulder and said, "What the fuck? What town is that, asshole?"

Jon said, "Your high school jacket says Weehauken, genius. Nice place, very safe. Kind of tough after the factories started closing, but still, if you can get work, good place to raise kids, huh? You guys live around The Shades or what? You went to Union Hill, and Weehauken High? Shouldn't be hard to find, if it came to that. You know Officer Donal? He's my cousin's friend."

Bar was at once annoyed yet impressed by Jon. They should just yell for the cops but no one was around and yelling for police would underline his and Jon's present military inferiority.

"You ain't never been to Weehauken," one said, but his bravado had weakened.

"My uncle lives there. He probably knows you shitheads on sight."

Black Leather said, "Hey Benny, either let's dance or let's hit it. What are we fuckin' standin' around fa?"

Backward said to him, "Well, douche-brain, if you're going to tell them my fucking *name*."

The three jackets, dropping "fag" and "fucking faggot," left.

Bar and Jon watched them. Bar said, "I don't even get what that was about."

"Neither do they."

Bar saw Jon's left hand twitching. Jon noticed that he noticed and shoved his hand into his pocket. Bar was excited, in a mood almost opposite anger.

"What do I look like? I'm wearing jeans and..."

"And an Italian biking jersey."

"That's faggy?"

"To these guys? You don't have a leather jacket, so you're gay."

"Ha. You scared the shit out of them."

"Hmm," Jon said. "What're you going to do about getting a place?"

"I don't know. Ride around, maybe."

"Okay, just not east of 1st."

Jon left to walk across 8th Street to Christopher to the 1 Train. Bar rode his bike down 2nd Avenue to 6th Street. He went east, past the Indian restaurants on 6th Street and 1st Avenue. Despite Jon's warning, he kept going, past Avenue A where the buildings started to become sparser and the empty lots more frequent, the rubble with chain-link fences, and then no fences. Despite everyone's warning never to cross A into B, C, and certainly not D, he went all the way to where the federal housing projects near the East River were. These streets had people walking on them in the early evening light. The landscape, apart from the "projects," looked more like the Blitz after the detritus had been cleaned out, not right after the bombing, the lots nearly flat fields of broken bricks or just packed dirt, sometimes with a stray giant black 1970s El Dorado-ish car on wheels or cinder blocks. An ancient, leathery Puerto Rican man wearing a feathered fedora gave him an evil squint eye as he rode to the river. There was no access to the waterfront. Past the chain-link fence topped with barbed wire, it was all tires, dog shit, garbage, and endless broken glass that made him nervous about his tires. A couple of unhealthy-looking men looked up from something they had been bending over. They seemed surprised to see him, or anyone at all. Bar thought he saw dominoes on their card table. A family of four walked by, the older sister, maybe eight, pushing the stroller.

He rode D to 3rd Street, back west to Avenue C. There was a lone deli on the corner like a general store in the middle of a Western movie town set. Locking his bike to a parking sign that ruled over no cars for the short time he would go into the store, he bought an ice cream sandwich and a seltzer, his personal "mobile egg cream." He balanced eating the ice cream and walking his bike west again on 3rd. A man sitting on the stoop of a lonely building, playing an electric guitar with no amp followed Bar creepily with his eyes. The building was remarkable in that there were no others on either side or in back of it.

Bar circled back. He rode past 3rd Street and the lonely building between B and C. In the lurid light of the streetlamp, the building's white terra cotta ornaments and red brick façade looked like a dirty conch Bar remembered from when he was on the beach in Springs. Though at first, Bar had felt the tense fear of the warnings, he was quickly liking the feeling of emptiness, of a land cut off from the main line in this part of town. He stood in front of this building that had no other touching it and felt that it was perfect in a way that he couldn't articulate. It wasn't just the ornamental façade. How many buildings existed alone like this, alone yet among the thousands of others. As his eyes got used to the light, he saw that man on its stoop staring at him. He rode away, but circled back.

The next time he passed the building, the man yelled from the stoop, "Hey kid. You lost or sumptin'?" Tall guy: leather pants, no shirt, a leather vest, long black hair, bushy eyebrows curling up almost like Salvador Dali's mustache. The guitar, an old Fender. He cultivated his own cool, an aesthetic from some other American city, like maybe New Orleans, some place with music. He held a brown paper bag. He struck Bar as the perfect proprietor of this perfect building, though Bar did not even know if he lived there. Perhaps he was merely passing through. Isn't that what people said in Westerns?

But Bar was wary as well. He stopped, about thirty feet away, in the middle of the street, his left foot on the left pedal. "Yeah?" He looked around trying to look as if he weren't nervous and weren't looking around. The block remained desolate, the sunlight dying over the west, where civilization lay.

The man played the guitar solo at the end of "Stairway to Heaven." Nwwww, duh-nah-nuh-nah-nuh-nah-dw-nw-nw-no, nowwwww. "Hey, Kid, didn't your parents ever tell you never to talk to strangers?" He laughed.

"Yeah," Bar stayed on the street. Ten yards. Maybe enough if this guy rushed him, though that seemed unlikely. He'd have to put down the Fender.

"Look, kid, half the people around here are pushers and the other half buyers. You know what a pusher is?"

"Yeah," Bar said, annoyed.

"You...ever say nothin' else?" He laughed. "Not a pusher or buyer are you? What's with ridin' around here? N.Y.U. kids all get told never come 'round here, ain't so?"

"I don't go to N.Y.U. I'm looking for housing. I go to Cooper Union."

"Cooper! How 'bout that. We a world away from there, kid. You see any decent housing around here? Maybe in that cemented-up heroin den, or the squatter building next to it? You could set up a tent in that empty lot right there." His laugh was half-wheeze.

"No."

"No what? You doin' Engineering? Where you from, kid? California? Ain't you heard of Alphabet City?"

"Art. I'm from Queens."

"Art? Is that your name?"

"Bar."

"Art Bar?"

"I'm in the Art School and my name is Bar Mizrachi."

"No shit? Hmmm, you look too square to be any *art* student. What kinda name's Bar anyway?"

"Yemenite," Bar said. "Israeli." That would be simpler for him. This guy was weird, but his weirdness wasn't what Bar expected. He was too foreign, or not foreign: just out-of-town. American, America being a place outside of New York City.

He said, "Yeah, that's it. Straight edge, kinda. Hey, it's cool. Wait a minute," he said, and popped out the front door onto the stoop. He took a drag from a cigarette, putting it down on the edge of an ashtray he had next to him on the stoop of the surreal building standing amid the ash heaps, with fastidious care. He said, squinting at his own smoke, "What're yah doin'? Knockin' on doors and shit?"

"No, I got listings. People, landlords, list at N.Y.U. and Cooper."

"I see, I see, huh. Fuckin' gentrification. There's that bar on 7th and A with a fuckin' *T.V.*..." He trailed off, smoked. "Listen, seriously kid. I was just shittin' before. Curious. Don't pay me no mind. So full of shit sometimes I might burst one day. Watch out! It'll fly everywhere," he spread his hands wide apart and started a laughing jag that ended in a deep cough that he assuaged with a sip from the brown bag and another go with the cigarette. When he laughed, Bar saw the missing teeth separating the tobacco-stained remaining ones. "Housing! I know a lotta artists. My good artist, sir, I kin show you somethin'. Problem is, you cain't trust me. Hmmm." He smoked the last of the cigarette and put it out in the tray. "Say what. I'll show you a place but not today. The apartment, I'll give it to ya cheap, kid. Support the arts. Do sumptin' for the community," he said, and cough-laughed for a while. He gestured with his thumb behind him as if trying to hitchhike. "Never go in anywhere with a stranger, not round here. I'm saying it to myself; I'm saying it to you. See my address?" he pointed back with his thumb again in the same direction, this time indicating the whole building whose stoop he was on. The building number was painted in careful stencil onto the glass transom. Bar noticed the building's ancient character, its black parapet above a light, almost-white terra cotta curtain wall, the very old stonework Greek columns creating a domestically grand entrance somewhat contradicted by the plain, straight iron gates over the first floor windows.

"Go talk to Professor Cielo. Italian dude. Knows me," Sharpey said.

"Professor Chee-ell-ow?"

"At Cooper. Talk to him. *Then* come back. Bring your troops. Your hombres."

"My hombres? What do you mean?"

He ignored the question. "We kin be formally introduced though," he started another laugh jag, perhaps because Bar was still thirty feet away. "I'm Ely but folks call me Sharpey. This is Picasso on account of his fucked up eyes," Bar noticed for the first time that there was a cat behind Sharpey. Its eyes were disturbingly unaligned. "'Rats on the west side, bedbugs, uptown.' Hey, Bar. See the address?" he repeated.

"Yeah."

"A golden opportunity. One C a month. You could swing that much, huh?"

Right, he means the rent. "Maybe." A hundred for a whole apartment!

"Alright, One, then. Heat's free, such as it is," Sharpey said, "but you'll know if it gets chilly I'm chillin' just as much." He smiled: his missing teeth echoing the missing buildings to his left and right. Bar said nothing for a beat, not sure what to say. Sharpey said, "Close to the vest, good, good. I like it." He went back up the stoop and picked up the cat. The cat seemed displeased but resigned. "After the formal intro by the proper authorities." He was talking to Bar again. "Come back tomorrow."

"Okay. I tell the Professor I met Ely...?"

"Ely Sharpey. Yeah, do that. Then come here mañana."

"What time?"

"Don't much matter. I'm here," he said, and Bar began to wonder how he lived.

"Oh, one thing," he said and squinted at Bar accusingly. "You a Mets fan, or Yankees?"

"Mets."

Sharpey smiled and spat. "That'll do, then. You know they're takin' the Series, right?" Bar nodded and Sharpey went back into the building through the matching old wood and glass doors that closed quietly behind him.

In Jackson Heights, Saul was watching *Dirty Harry,* two empties at his feet, but there was Indian food on the table in the kitchen that smelled good. Bar heard a third person in the bathroom. Claudia would explain the take-out. Bar sat down in the other chair and watched the movie with him for a few minutes.

"Dad, I think I found a place."

"Yah." He sipped his beer.

Bar waited a second. "An apartment," he said.

Saul looked at him with those emptied, after-work eyes that made him feel that his father was put upon by the galaxy. Bar looked away. "In deh Village?"

"Yeah." So dad did know he was going to school. And where.

Saul said, "Good. You mother, she is giving you money for this?"

"Uh, yeah."

Claudia came out of the bathroom in blue scrubs, her hair tied in a ponytail, smiled and said hello to Bar.

Saul sipped his beer again, and got up to change the channel. "You need the car?"

"Uh, maybe yeah, I would. You watch baseball, Dad?"

"This year. Claudia likes it." Bar stood next to his father and watched Lenny Dykstra single to right. "She like Rick Aguilera. Puerto Rican." He sipped his beer.

"Si," she said from the kitchen, making herself a plate.

"Uh huh."

"She say maybe we go dere. Puerto Rico."

"Si. And you, too, Bar?"

Bar nodded but said nothing. He had trouble imagining his father traveling anywhere, though he knew him to be an immigrant who had lived in three countries. In the last ten years, his Saul had not left the five boroughs, not even when his youngest sister overdosed in Jaffa. He seemed rooted to his living room chair more than he seemed like a mobile citizen of the world's airways.

The next day, dad and Claudia were gone by the time Bar woke up at eight with a vague memory of his father kissing him on the cheek before he left, something Bar didn't remember ever happening before. There was also his home-baked Yemenite bread on the table and coffee already made, under a saucer to keep it warm, thermos tech not yet having been introduced into the household. The film of milk fat floating on top told Bar that his father had heated the milk in a pan. And there was a note saying that there were hard-boiled eggs in the fridge, and, something quite new and strange, an admonition from his father to ride the "crazy bisickle carefully."

At ten AM, Bar left Cielo's office as a girl almost crashed into him walking in: punk rock in a plaid skirt over black-dyed ripped jeans, white A-shirt, her mohawk kind of droopy.

No buzzers were on the outside of the place. Bar heard a sharp whistle.

Sharpey was peering down at him from an open window, taking his fingers out of his mouth.

"Hey, Bar. No backup?"

"No."

"Tough kid. Take your bike in. Don't never leave a bike out there. Seen 'em take a two-buh-four, pop open those U-locks."

Each of the four floors was it's own apartment coming off the stairwell. Sharpey lived in the fourth floor, the top. He said he used the second floor for "storage," leaving the third empty as far as Bar knew. He said someone called "Herbert the Troll" lived in the storage apartment, but "you won't see him much. Likes to be private." Sharpey had to wiggle the key on the first floor apartment to open the "police" lock, the kind that inserts a metal rod at a forty-five-degree angle into a seat in the floor. The lock seemed tougher than the simple wood door it held shut.

The place was empty; Bar had not seen one bare floor in the roommate deals he had investigated. Everything was old. A bathroom sink in blue enamel, an ancient white claw foot tub, water stains where the faucet dripped, floors warped near the cast-iron radiators, a kitchen sink made of white porcelain, plaster walls showing in spots through to the brick, and one window in the back missing half its glass, replaced by plywood.

Bar looked at the heavy iron bars on the outside of the windows. "I'll take it," he said.

Sharpey squinted at him. "Kinda scary here, some nights. Even with them bars on the windows."

"I'll be okay."

"You sure 'bout that?" Sharpey took a drag on his home-rolled cigarette.

"I'll be careful. I'll come here by bike and leave by bike."

Sharpey said, "Alright. Nobody ever bothers me. They all know me. You, though."

"I'm...I'll blend in."

This claim caused Sharpey to start cough-laughing and slapping his thigh, the laughter giving way to smiling with his missing teeth. "The hell you will. Hell's bells."

"I brought a check..."

He shrugged, "No checks. I ain't a big banker type. Bring cash. Mañana."

"But, you won't give the to someone else, right?"

"Oh, naw," he said, smiling. "You seen any other callers?"

"No. Who else lives here?"

"Jes me an Picasso. Herbie. An now you, it seems."

"Uh, is there a lease?"

Sharpey stared in response, raising one eyebrow and offering a wry smile. Bar drew this face in his mind.

"We'll just shake, then," Bar said. Sharpey nodded and they shook.

He called Jon. "It sounds like this Sharpey dude read *Walden* and just, like, did it, except there's no pond. There's a big puddle in the back yard. No fish there, I think, though."

"He doesn't sound like Thoreau," Jon said. "He sounds like Thoreau's cousin from Tennessee who moved to New York City."

"And became a gangster."

"He's a criminal?"

"I don't know what he does. He's home all day. He said nobody fucks with him."

"Maybe the natives will think you're a kind of centaur with wheels."

"I didn't see a lot of people."

"They're there. Let them think you're … never mind."

"I'm what?"

"Not a student. Don't let them think you're a student."

"Uh huh. Okay. How'm I supposed to do that? I have art supplies and knapsacks."

"And this Sharpey guy, you don't know what he does for money? If he owns that whole building, he could sell it and get an apartment in a nicer part of town. Why's he out there?"

"I don't know about that. I think there wouldn't be a lot of buyers for this building. I don't know why he's there. All I know is, I have a place I can kind of afford."

Saul fetched his contractor's van. It had not been driven in a month, another unemployment spell, drove Bar and his things to the village and helped him haul them into the first-floor place.

Bar looked from his dad to Sharpey. Saul's black slacks were paint-flecked as were his black sneakers, his chest hair tufting out under the v-neck of a white t-shirt. Sharpey wore his leather vest, no shirt, and stood six inches taller than Bar's father but Saul held his own. Bar, wearing his black-dyed jeans and a black Led Zeppelin t-shirt., introduced them.

Bar took out his wallet. Saul pushed his hand away and reached into his own pocket. He took out a thick fold of bills, surprising Bar, who could not recall having seen his father with so much money. Saul counted out two hundred dollars in twenties as if he were paying ransom or putting a down payment on buying the whole building, then hesitated, looked around the room, said something under his breath, added a third hundred, and gave them to Bar.

"Dad, I can..."

"Please, before I am annoy." He smiled. "Here you can bring some girlfriends, no?"

"Sure, dad."

"I should have played in the field longer," Bar's father told him.

Sharpey smiled at this. Later he would tell Bar that he could tell Saul had been in the army by the way he walked. Bar handed Sharpey two hundred, the deposit and first month.

Saul said, warming to the subject, "More girls is better. Don't let them catch you. You understand? Yes, yes, sex, but no babies, yes? Rubbers, and no love. You are too young for love."

As Bar thanked his father for driving him, if not for the advice, Saul, facing the road, grunted and jerked the vehicle toward Queens. Bar turned to walk up the stone steps so worn in the center that they seemed to sag, and thought about Claudia's sharp, young features and his father's old, goat-like face.

Bar saw Sharpey around from time to time, often during business hours, always wondering what he "did." Sometimes Bar heard the outer door creak open and someone walk up the old wood stairs past his apartment. Once, Bar heard someone come in at one in the morning, lugging something that went clunk, and huffing his way up the staircase. Sometimes, when Bar came home from class, Sharpey greeted him in the same position he had been in that day in August when he called Bar over: sitting on the stoop, cigarette, drink in a bag, cat.

Any hour of any day, Sharpey might let loose on one of his guitars (it turned out that he had a collection). Sometimes this was acoustic, unobtrusive, even possibly classical. Sometimes it was a one-o'clock-in-the-morning wail of slide guitar blues.

Bar heard people going up and down the stairs sometimes but didn't feel that he could ask about it.

In October, on a rainy day, Bar tripped over a body sleeping in the vestibule, inside the outer door but outside the locked inner door. The next day, it wasn't raining, and the same man was sleeping in the same spot, this time blocking the out-swinging inner door. Bar had to knock on his own door and wake the man up just to be able to get out. Once he got to Avenue A and started seeing the girls with day-glo skirts and purple hair and the guys with sombre black wool coats, everyone in black boots, he felt that he had reached civilization again.

For a few weeks, there was no one sleeping in the vestibule, though it did rain overnight twice. Bar wondered what the difference was until one morning he woke in the middle of the night to piss and heard Sharpey yelling at someone outside his door. Outside, it was pouring, the sound of rain gathering through the gutter drains glugging. The other person, a deep male voice with a semi-English accent, said, "How do you do?" Sharpey yelled "Get outta here, fool!" The stranger said, "You wouldn't send a person out in that!? Would you?" Bar opened his apartment door to take a look, and Sharpey turned around suddenly. He was holding what looked to Bar like a giant toy pistol, a white stock and silver barrel like in the Lone Ranger T.V. show. A beat later, Bar saw that it wasn't a toy. The Englishman out of sight was saying, "No, no, that won't be necessary." "Shit, Herbie, you cain't just..." "Yes, yes, my good man, apologies. I won't happen again. If you could assist me this one time, however..." Bar had moved to where he could see them. The man was wearing a tweed brown suit a few shades lighter than his skin. The suit, and the man's unkempt curly hair full of dust, evidently from his having lain in the vestibule. Sharpey held out a hand and lifted the man up to his feet. Herbie managed to put his arm over Sharpey much higher shoulder. Sharpey guided him up to the apartment above Bar's. As he passed, Sharpey said, "Mind your own business next time, huh, Bar?" Over his shoulder, Sharpey said, "This is Herbert. He doesn't live here. He's doin' security. Fer me." Herbie said, "I shall have to introduce myself more formally another time. I understand that you are an artist." "Get going," Sharpey said.

Bar saw Herbert from time to time and wondered how this person could be doing any job whatsoever, least of all "security."

Securing what?

After a week, Bar received a package from a blasé postal employee, the first representative of any level of government Bar had seen in the neighborhood other than one police car on patrol, once. The mail otherwise appearing magically. It was from Mom; an answering machine, which struck Bar as being a present for her as much as for himself. However, since he had yet to set up a phone, the answering machine lay in its packaging in a corner of Bar's spacious pristinely empty living room, devoid of all furniture, unless one counted a sleeping bag.

At the end of the summer there were many days when the apartment looked empty, not spacious. An empty apartment in an empty part of New York City. Sharpey's cat was the only being that greeted him when he walked into the building, and no one said hello once he was in his own space. School was hard right away.

Walden was one of twelve books he had in the apartment. Page 247: "This whole earth which we inhabit is but a point in space. How far apart, think you, dwell the two most distant inhabitants of yonder star, the breadth of whose disk cannot be appreciated by our instruments? Why should I feel lonely? is not our planet in the Milky Way?"

Bar thought, is my loneliness a weakness?

On the days he went to visit his father, just being in the same room with him, watching television, even though there were times when Saul said not a word, was a relief from the apartment. At night in the Village he stared at the ceiling, at the plywood window that he had painted red and white, and dreamed of kissing Stacey, staring at Jessica, drawing their faces, entering the zone.

In a few days, though, he got used to sleeping in an entire apartment alone, knowing that he and Sharpey, if Sharpey were even home, might be the only people on the whole square block. And Herbert, if he made it home from wherever he had gone that night. He stopped hyper-vigilantly checking the block before getting on his bike to go to school. No one would be there; no one ever was. Farther east, there were mostly Puerto Rican families trying to work out why they had been sent from one God-forsaken island to this one, and to the West, the City lived. Right there, the smell of wet bricks after the rain was the only neighbor. It felt as if he were living a mile from the nearest neighbor. Sometimes, in the day, doing his homework, he heard birds and squirrels, and sometimes he heard a far-off tinny recording of old jazz or salsa, and sometimes just the wind whistling through the warped wooden window sashes. He invited a couple of other students to come over and work but when he said where they all declined so he stopped asking, and came to enjoy the undistracted, television-less, solitary existence. His possessions, accumulated on weekends, were a mattress and sheets, kitchen things, a table and a chair, clothing stored in piles on the floor, bathroom things, art supplies, and easel he made, and a few books. On October 15 he found a record player for $10 on the street. He bought a record: Joni Mitchell's *Blue*. Only two serious scratches.

Bar made himself most meals, eating occasionally at the Kiev, and twice succumbing to the temptation to get cannolis at Di Robertis. The most convenient store for staples was a deli on 7th and B,

catty corner from Tompkins Square Park. He rode there, of course, locking his bike for the five-minute shopping experience, hoping a junkie had not stolen it or pissed on it.

A few days later he met Abigail and within a week, in mid-September, she was spending more nights at his place than at her own.

Herbie did come down to Bar one Sunday morning, apologizing for knocking on Bar's door "so early," though it was eleven and Bar had already returned from two laps biking in Central Park and was having a second breakfast, though it was true that Abi was asleep, having worked until three that morning.

Bar offered Herbie some tomato juice and toast, which the latter gratefully accepted. He said he was guarding "Sharpey's art," but when Bar asked if Sharpey had made a lot of valuable art, Herbie looked at him quizzically and proceeded to refuse to talk about it, saying, "it would be best" if Bar went to Sharpey for more information. Herbie asked, "And your work? Is there any of it about that I might see? I was – am something of a connoisseur, you see."

"Oh? You worked in museums or galleries or something?" Bar asked, going to fetch his most recent sketches.

Herbie smiled and said, "Something, yes."

He looked over Bar's sketchpad, turning the pages very slowly. Herbie flipped past a few pictures of Sharpey, saying, "Good, nice, looks like him, yeah," and stopped to study a picture of Kristina Bar had made, a nude, for so long that Bar thought Herbie had fallen asleep, but he had not. "This one is accomplished," he said, and went into detail about the form, composition, the feeling of movement, the light, and the shading, giving Bar some suggestions with great humility but also much sense about how to bring out what was already there implicitly. Bar was impressed and mystified but Herbie deflected questions about himself.

He thanked Bar for the food and the "nourishment for my eyes," and went back upstairs. Just as he was leaving, Herbie said, "Curious, perhaps your lady and I have met?"

Bar shrugged.

"Perhaps not." Herbie smiled and left.

4. Crit

Monday, November 3, 1986.

Life one.
The two drawings were 11x14 pencil and charcoal on paper. One, a full body nude portrait of a a woman with a tennis racquet, Kristina, Bar's devirginizer, the other a drawing of himself (clothed) drawing the woman in the first picture as she posed. Each was realistic, with care to get right all issues of perspective, light, volume, proportion, and anatomy. In the nude, Bar showed her hitting a backhand, the ball a foot from the racquet, a moment from impact. He was pleased that one could not tell if it were just before or just after impact. He showed her athleticism: her gaze, the anatomically correct muscles in her bent thigh, bicep bent back, her neck, all coming to a compositional point off the page where the ball would be. Her body was proportioned so that her body in life, five-foot-four, a hundred and fifteen pounds, muscular, and sinew-y, was easily imaged as real. In the other picture, there was a discarded drawing within this drawing to the pictured artist's right, shown in extreme foreshortening from above and to the side, as well as the same picture as the finished nude, but shown on Bar's easel at an angle to the viewing plane. The light sources were suggested by bits of window in each, something he picked up from Durer's "preparatory drawings," as if there were a spotlight on the main figures. The cross-hatching was detailed, like Durer's, and when Bar put the pictures up he felt perhaps that the cross-hatching was too busy.

In the apartment, Bar admired his early work. Meaning his current work. Bar remembered the crit in Life One. He had been exhausted, having stayed up most of the weekend to turn in four midterm projects in Painting, Drawing, Sculpture, and 2-d.
Just as he had twenty years earlier, meaning today, he worked seventy-five of the last ninety-six hours, then threw himself into bed the night before and slept in his day clothes.

This is what happened in Life One:

The next day, on October 21ˢᵗ, he went to Mac's class in high anxiety. Professor MacIntyre's critiques class made him feel sure that he was a fraud, a fool, or both. He hated being judged, a common hatred, but for Bar it was tantamount to ruining the purpose of making the art at all. Having it discussed in front of him was an invasion of his deeply private world, turning him inside-out, making social that which was a refuge from social things.

The professor had a uniform of a long black wool skirt and black turtleneck sweater, short sleeve in warmer weather, hair pulled back as if by a winch. She was happy to go on about a bad mark or idea as about a good one, and then there was her Modernist agenda, which Bar only understood enough to make him more nervous. Something about abstraction as the apotheosis. He looked that word up after the first class.

Could he really draw as well as everyone always said to him? Here in Cooper, almost everyone could draw well. Only Chauncey was merely adequate, but then he had the conceptual edge, which was part of Bar's feeling like a fool: everyone else's work seemed to have a book of philosophy behind it, at least a small manifesto, or an idea. Something. He just drew. In high school that had been enough. In high school, girls talked to him when he drew. That phenom was almost the entirety of why he had applied to art schools. The goal going into the crit was not adulation but merely to escape without too much shame.

The other students, Sun, Calliope, Gatik, the Girl in Lace (what was her name?), Chauncey, were arguing about an artist. Prof. Mac wasn't in yet.

"I heard he grew up across town in a carriage house converted into a fabulous live and work space by his father."

"Whose his father? Anyone we know?" Lace asked, gossipy.

Sun replied with the name of a student not present, and an eye roll. His father was a successful mono-named painter whose last solo show was a fabulous post-sixties happening sixteen years earlier, who made twenty-by-thirty foot abstract expressionist canvases using only two colors, though the colors varied. "Green/Orange" had sold for forty-five thousand dollars four years ago.

Chauncey changed the subject to talk about Art, meaning Abigail's friend of that name. "The question is," Chauncey said, lisping ("the queth-thion ith") "whether Arthur is always posing, or if the pose is him. If he is pure pose per se."

"Huh?" Sun asked.

"It's like," Lace offered, "is his surfacy fakeness real?"

"Exactly," Chauncey agreed.

"He's just fake," Calliope said. "Don't think too hard about it. Same with Warhol and his bullshit 'Business Art.' It's just games."

"Art is not a game? Art is a game because everything is a game."

"I'm not here to be playing a game." Calliope said. Bar drew her face in his head: huge Mediterranean eyes, dark wavy hair, olive skin, large, impressive nose, and an expression of imposing assuredness, looking as if she were descended from Athena. She intimidated him differently from the way Chauncey did. She was a brass section; he played a piano. Bar wished he could sit in on this class and never have to show his own work. It was fun listening to the rest of them but not while sitting in the hot seat.

"Then you merely play the game of not playing games." Chauncey said. His pale face struck Bar as childlike, the hairs on his chin, under his nose, and sideburns seemingly not yet shaven, but his small blue eyes seemed to look through people, his blond, flat hair flipped off to one side of his head, but covering one eye unless he continually pushed it away.

Bar tried to shift away from their power to intimidate by ignoring their gossip and thinking about each of them on his own ground: Chauncey couldn't draw, Calliope could but not dazzlingly, Sun could draw as well or better than Bar himself, and Gatik could too, but was unoriginal.

Professor Mac walked into the room and went directly over to a student's chair/desk combo among the kids: she put her notebook on the desk part and the ominous red pencil on her ear like a red gash among her black clothing and pale white skin.

She signaled to Sun: you're up. Sun's short black hair gelled into spikes, blue jeans and a white t-shirt with the sleeves rolled up, controlled fear in her eyes. She struck Bar as half-Asian, half something else.

She put up her stuff. Four sixteen-by-twenty landscape drawings on paper, in each an amoeba-like shape, a big paisley, or half a yin/yang. One of the drawings was a thousand white marks on black paper, the second white paper with black ink wash and charcoal, the third the same shape in primary colors, and the fourth the same in florescent day-glo.

The class stared at the work.

Calliope fidgeted.

The blonde girl in the lace shirt doodled in purple on her notebook.

Bar tried to decide which of the pictures was most spermatozoic.

Chauncey played continuously with his pretentious hair. He slouched his long, string bean body that, suggesting a disease of the spine. He would suddenly lean forward on his desk and start tapping his nose between his thumb and forefinger, incredibly quickly. He buttoned his cowboy shirts to the top. He wore thick glasses that distended his eyes.

Chauncey said, "This piece, qua abstraction, hath a certain balance because of this line here and the weight of that piece."

"What do you mean, 'qua abstraction'?" Mac asked.

Bar hated the mysterious word "qua."

Bar contemplated the cool the way the amoebas were tapered and seemed to wiggle until they ended. He wondered if she used a French curve or was able to draw that freehand.

"Given the constraints of...uh...uh...m-m-modern art 'conventions'," Chauncey replied, using air quotes. Mac seemed to glare at him, but perhaps she was merely thinking.

Gatik raised his hand. "They are formally interesting," he began. He once told the class that he was from Uttar Pradesh, which to Bar meant very far away. He seemed to be the kind of person entirely without the guile or the need to use sarcasm, yet more than once, in exasperation at a question about where he was from, Bar heard him say he lived in the Taj Mahal. Gatik tossed his head subtly when he spoke, always came to class in slacks, dress shoes, and a clean tennis shirt with a collar. "The bottom of this one seems to be similar in form to a Kandinsky that I remember, is this not true?"

Bar picked up on Gatik's subtle accusation, and then accused himself: is my work original?

McIntyre said, "Yes, very good. I remember the work also. 'Curved Line Undulating Freely,' from 1925. Sun, did you have that work in mind?"

Bar wondered, what does originality even mean, but he didn't ask that aloud.

The class discussed Sun's work in relation to Kandinsky.

McIntyre said, "Abstraction is the most politically revolutionary of all modes of art."

Calliope said, "Yeah, sure, but, I mean, Sun's Asian."

Sun's face froze into an unreadable smile, until she said, "I'm from Queens."

"What does her nationality have to do..." Mac began.

"My nationality is American," Sun said.

"I mean, she has this huge culture she can draw on. That's like, not respected enough. In the West," Calliope said. *"Ignored..."*

"Anyone may use any art," the Professor said. "All is available. Modernity is global."

Sun said to Calli, "I, like, was using Asian culture. Totally."

She and Mac were talking over one another, "The project of the artist is international because ultimate."

Calliope said to Sun, "You don't have to get snippy."

Sun crossed her eyes at Calliope. Calliope shrugged.

Sun fished in her bag again and brought out a set of Chinese characters. "The mark here was supposed to look like part of this character. It means, 'woman.'"

Calliope said, "See?" looking around at everyone and no one.

Mac stood, mysteriously, and looked at Sun's work, saying nothing. She sat. There had to be some meaning to these kinds of moves she made, but Bar could not tell what. They made him nervous, again. Mac wrote some things in a notebook, using a fountain pen (of course). Bar watched her. She would be worth drawing, he thought. They all would, but Mac particularly. Even if she's old.

Looking over half-glasses, McIntyre indicated that the girl in lace would be next. She stood and showed a single, large drawing she had done of a figure somewhat obscured by tall grass, and rays of light coming from above and behind...her. As they looked, the figure cohered into a girl with long, bright hair and a thin naked body, her legs spread wide right at the viewer, her pubic hair difficult to separate from the reeds.

As the teacher looked at the work, Bar tried to decide whether it was softcore porn. Mac said, "This is good work, Gail. Did you use a mirror?" Oh, right, Bar thought. "Gail." Bar felt relief that a girl drew a girl naked. He had not realized it was of herself. Her drawing wasn't as precise as Sun's. Or his own.

"No, see? It's on the beach. It's from a photograph."

Questions in Bar's mind regarding the circumstances of the picture's creation momentarily crowded out his ability to look at it. He looked at Gail. Her lacy, hippy attire matched the aesthetics of the drawing, somehow.

Mac stood and pointed out a few more formal effects of the shading and lines. No one else said a word. Mac asked Gail what she thought of the picture.

Gail had a breathy, high voice of few decibels. In context it was jarring: "Well? When I made it, my boyfriend Miles and I had just made love and I was feeling so free and happy and I don't know, joyful and it was late afternoon, you know? And there's this something about the light on the beach in the late afternoon; it's so spiritual. I felt so open, you know? So at peace with the world and everything in it. Miles was taking pictures of the landscape, and me, and I asked him to print this one for me. I have it here in my bag somewhere. Sorry, it's such a mess..." She started ruffling through a large tote bag with a Merce Cunningham logo.

Mac said, "That won't be necessary, Gail. Let's just look at your composition. Can anyone comment on the relationship between figure and ground?"

No one could, so Mac answered her own question.

Mac signaled to Calliope that it was her turn.

She went to the front with a green army duffle bag out of which she pulled a canvas onto which was sewn shreds and rags of vintage clothing, some painted, some not. She smiled at the class and the teacher, confidently, Bar thought, in her paint-splattered jeans, black engineer boots and black leather motorcycle jacket. She turned toward her piece. "Oh," she said, and shook it out. After that, it became clear that the rags depicted a body with oversized breasts from which were flowing a stream of white cotton. "So, like, I'm into re-imagining female myth? Like Medusa, Venus -- of Botticelli and Titian -- Cassandra, Cleopatra, Briseus, Calliope, and Eratos, Calliope said. "I'm making illegitimate children. Men artists get to be fathers, so we have to be mothers. I'm destroying these clothes and re-

assembling them together on the canvas to show how even the idea of clothes oppresses women."

Bar thought it looked like rags shaped into a caricature of a woman. He repeated some of Mac's words from September about retaining an open, available mindset, one that allowed for the possibility of future understanding, though Mac herself did not seem terribly open all the time.

"It's very punk rock," Calliope said. *"I think."*

"It's beyond punk," Gail said.

"Way," Calliope agreed. *"It's totally post-punk."*

"You must work on the craft," Mac said. *"Your statement, it is not yet as strong from the..."*

"But..."

"Simplify the forms and the..."

"Messy is part of the point."

Bar watched as Calliope argued with Mac, something he did not think he could do. After a discussion in which Chauncey defended the work, Calli stuffed the canvas back into the army bag. She sat down with a dramatic thump.

Mac, writing in her notebook, said, "Bar? What do you have today?"

Bar stood awkwardly, almost tripping on himself. He put up his two pictures of Kristina and of himself drawing her. His hands shook; he put them behind his back.

It started happening again – the feeling he had on Willet's Point station. He was doing the same thing this time, though, and his visual perspective was almost the same, just a few inches off, and it went in an out, as if the "other" point of view were trying to match this one. The feeling he received from the "other" was pity and as if in explanation, confidence, the thing he lacked. Then it popped off.

Sun got up to help him. She held his wrist tentatively to steady him."Thank you," he said to her. "I'm okay." She smiled and sat down. He thought, she's nice. I'm about to be skewered, and maybe I'm going nuts, but Sun's a nice person.

No one spoke right away. Bar clutched his hands behind his back. It was one of those infinite moments, stretched by anxiety the way modern physics predicts time to stretch near the edge of a black hole. He looked at the picture of Kristina, thought about the night with her after the party Jon took him to, her body, then the morning, and then not getting his phone calls returned by her, and then he thought of her body again. He squashed those thoughts. This is art class. Be in fucking art class.

Don't think of the word "fucking" while in art class because then you'll inevitably remember fucking Kristina, losing your virginity to her, though the loss (perhaps removal was the right word) was not reciprocal, and she was highly disappointed at the alacrity of his completion, practically accusing him, yelling, "don't tell me you're a fucking virgin, are you? You could have said something!" And her hyper-organized apartment with the closet labels for umbrellas, sneakers, heels, winter coats, fall jackets, etcetera, and the forty tennis racquets, the bedroom closet with innumerable little white skirts (turning him on). The way he had seduced her without meaning to, misrepresenting himself without meaning to by wearing a tux to a black-tie event that he did not even understand to be an AIDS fundraiser because Jon had invited him without explaining, and then Jon's odd behavior the whole time, chatting with a bunch of other penguin-attired guys, though that left him, Bar, the sole hetero male for Kristina's field of vision. Her hottt little black dress, kissing in the taxi, and STOP IT and how could you stop thinking about dad for a moment? Dad would've wanted him to push, with Kristina but he didn't push, no, not at all; it was she who …

"Wow," Chauncey said, bringing Bar's head back from Kristina's apartment.

"Can you be more specific," Mac asked him.

"Dude can draw," Chauncey replied.

Mac asked Bar to talk about the pictures. He felt most awkward explaining a drawing, as if he were automatically lying. Yes, he used Durer, he had a book open to a page from Durer the whole time he had drawn Kristina, and yet while Bar nervously explained the Durer reference and the idea of capturing movement, the tautness of her physique, and her energy in person, commanding yet agitated, always in movement, the energy contained in her small, sprung body, he thought, I just drew.

"Yes, yes, but what drove the making?" Mac asked.

Bar thought for a while, looking at them. He said, "I …uh…"

"More specif…"

"Yeah, so, the bodies blow me away. People. How they look." Stupid, he thought. "And what they're like. People do that. I draw the Human Form Divine," he said.

Mac snorted at the clunky Blake reference but made no other reaction to Bar's artistic theory. He could see on her face, though, that it was as if a fifth-grader had said it. She said, "I think this piece is very strong, as drawing." She went to the lone nude and using thumbs and forefingers as "L's" made a frame around her hair, then half of her tennis arm, and then parts of the wall. One almost never knew what she would seize on as either good or bad. She took the "L's" away. "I'm not as keen on the whole thing. What's wrong with it?" she asked the class.

Gatik said, "It's too simple. Also the cross-hatching, it is too much."

Gail fidgeted nervously and started doodling; she glanced at Bar's face, then away.

Mac asked, "Is the common portrait enough?"

The class discussed the common portrait. Humanism, the "human form divine," the geometry of the face.

Mac asked about the two pictures, "Do they have a distracting narrative or performative element? Does this distract from the composition, the lines and volumes? Of the pieces as art?"

Chauncey sat up, or slouched less. "May I...I would like to interject? That it is a rather arbitrary, if not wholly precarious valuation? This valorization of the non-performative? The pure essence of art qua Art? Bar drew a g-g, a p-p-p-person, doing a th-thing. And himself, doing his thing. It's quite moving."

"How hetero of you, Chaunce," Calliope said, smirking.

Bar looked at Chauncey, wanting to feel grateful, but unsure of what he meant. Chauncey's gaze was on Calliope. Sun looked at Bar and smiled. She's nice, he thought. He should ask her out. Or something.

It was impossible to avoid awkwardness with so many people present.

McIntyre gave Chauncey the look of disappointment she reserved for really bad drawings. "It's not 'rather arbitrary,' Mr. Egan. It is the basis of Art. If Bar wants to be a cartoonist, let him, but here, we aspire to more; here, we long to understand the way each medium leads us to contemplate it as such."

Chauncey started tapping his nose. Thumb-forefinger-thumb-forefinger, like a hummingbird. "Raphael made cartoons," he said. "And no one is talking about the quality of the drawing. Do first-years normally draw this well?"

So it was war. Bar felt brief respite while they fought this out.

"Mister Egan. Drawing quality is for the 2-d class, as you know. I admit, Bar's quality is high, almost too high. We do not aspire to the condition of Norman Rockwell. As for Raphael, his cartoons were made under commission from a Pope, in pre-modern times. He arranged Jesus and the disciples with utmost care about composition, light, and color. We may say, therefore, that despite the degrading presence of narration, the Raphael Cartoons are examples of Art ..." She went on about Raphael and Bar thought, yes, yes, go on about Raphael. Did Raphael have to go through the crit? "Bar," she said, and he flinched and he saw that Sun saw this because she smiled and looked at her feet, "unless I am mistaken, has no Papal commission, and may therefore use his drawing skill to approach the question of what drawing is, rather than make...illustrations." She went on again, ending by turning to him and saying, "you should draw a series of wall pieces. The walls are the best parts here."

"Just walls?" Chauncey stopped his tapping. "If he w-w-wants to pursue an agenda of abstraction maybe. He seems to be involved with the g-g-girl." Calliope grunted. Bar panicked, then realized "involved" meant artistically.

McIntrye laughed. "Well, Bar? Were you involved with the girl?"

The class tittered. Sun studied her tall black army boots.

Bar said, "I...I drew what I felt and saw. I wasn't thinking. I ... uh, was artistically involved. With her body. I drew her life, I felt that her strength ..."

Calliope jumped in, exasperated, "It doesn't matter. It's just porn! It's conservative art so it isn't art at all! Does she actually play tennis in the fucking nude?"

Fucking again. Kristina's self-administered orgasm after his disappointingly brief performance. Jon calling the next day, mad that Bar had left the party Jon had taken him to without saying goodbye. "But Jon, I scored with a girl." That only seemed to make Jon madder.

Sun opened her mouth as if to say something.

Mac was faster: "Only if it is sentimental," she said. "All pornography is sentimental, a descent into what we share with...cuttlefish, with bears, ocelots, squirrels, among other creatures." Gail looked distinctly uncomfortable. "Art should lift us above the beasts." She contemplated Kristina's taut body again. "That is the question for you to answer, Bar. Is it sentimental, or not?"

Bar tried again, "But she…this is how I felt. About her. It's really … it's how she looks. The … she's strong and intense." I don't have the words. "I drew how I felt about myself, too. I didn't...isn't it porn if I … Professor Hildreth said porn is when you idealize. I was trying to be real."

"So you're 'real' is that you're a horny straight guy. So what? It's demeaning," Calliope said.

"I do not think it is necessarily demeaning. Not a priori. The nude qua nude." Gatik said. Bar hated that. Latin shit he had no idea about.

Calliope cut him off. "Because you're a guy. What if Bar saw the 'strength' of another guy and we're all sitting here looking at some dude's big dick? Would you find that demeaning? I mean a priori."

McIntyre said something about "…the problem of the male gaze…"

Gail said, "The female body is the goddess body."

Gatik offered, "The female nude has a vaunted and storied place in the history of art of the West...and of the East."

"That's the problem!" Calliope said smacking her desk.

The class debated whether the identity of the artist mattered. Calliope said, "For example, I shouldn't make that drawing of the stuffy guy. But Bar can."

"Why?" Chauncey asked.

"Duh," Calliope said, "because they're both Black. He should've drawn a Black girl. I've seen white girls before."

Bar opened his mouth to say he was not, in fact, "Black" in the way Calli meant it, but Gail cut him off, her high voice, quavering now, "I was hoping people would see something spiritual in what I made."

Calliope rolled her eyes. Chauncey raised his index finger to reply. Bar opened his mouth again.

But Mac took the floor, "Bar, if you create art depicting women's bodies, you will be judged according to what new formal insights you reveal," Mac said, "not about the bodies. About the forms."

Bar, from his standing position, could see that Gail was sketching a picture of Chauncey in the act of tapping his nose, sneaking glances at him.

The doodle reminded Bar: he pointed to the Kristina's non-racquet hand in the picture and said, "That's her, that thing she does with her hand. I was looking at her doing it and seeing how she did it with her whole body. I didn't make her."

Calliope said. "You want credit for not raping your 'friend'?" The class shifted in their seats uncomfortably, avoiding Bar's eyes.

"No, I mean, I didn't make her, uh, do that gesture; it's her gesture. I tried to show her, what I saw."

"It's porn," Calliope said.

"It is neither porn nor true, advanced art, because the artist was too involved in the subject as a word or set of words, as opposed to image as image. That is the universal truth of all art," Mac said.

"Nothing's universal!" Calliope cried.

"Actually," Gatik continued, "that's what I was saying. The nude, the human in action, and the artist in his studio, are all traditional. The first is like the 'Discobolus,' a sculpture of a man ... " he hesitated, remembering. The class waited.

"I'm not Black," Bar said in what he thought was a clear voice.

"What? Please repeat," Mac said.

Bar realized he had said it to the floor, to himself. "I'm not Black. I'm Jewish. My dad's from Yemen,..."

"This is a distraction," Mac said, "The art, in and of itself,..."

"No, it isn't," Calli jumped in. "Then show us some naked Yemenite guys."

Mac frowned at Calliope and the class fell into small group arguments, Chauncey and Calli, Sun, Gatik, and Gail, while Mac did her standing up thing and silently looked at Bar's work.

Finally, she spoke, "You have astonishing skill, Mr. Mizrachi," she said. She turned away from the art and spoke directly to him: "But you have not conceived of it. You merely do it. Unless you think your art, it will never become. You must think it."

Bar felt he had escaped, but was scathed by Mac's gnomic statement. He did not understand how to do what MacIntyre was demanding. He had no idea how to draw for the form of the thing and not the thing itself, or what she meant by "think." All he knew was the zoning in, the melting of himself into what he saw, not the art qua art stuff, not the modernist ideology, not flatness, or how to conceive of what he felt came naturally or not at all.

November 3, 1986

I recalled all of these things that happened in Life One from Life Two, in the minutes before the class just as I had been remembering it for the last twenty years. It was the last crit for me before I was expelled. Now I won't be expelled. Now I can remain, or leave, as I wish.

The room before Mac enters is a map of desires. Calli and Chauncey will date for years while attending Cooper, move in together, break up when Calli decides she is gay, get back together, and then finally split when she moves to Chile in the late 1990s. Gail is going to become wildly successful with her book cover illustrations. Sun will follow Mac as professor, teaching this very class in twenty years, after an academic career in the hinterlands. Chauncey will never have an art career. He's going to write books of great importance to a few thousand people, and teach. His class will be among the most popular humanities courses in his university.

They are beautiful young artists now, some of whom I've gotten to know well in the years to come. I hope to again, especially Calli and Chauncey. They are revitalized, restored to their youth. I love them for being the child-parents of who they would each become. I am overwrought with love for them. I don't know if I will be able to answer the simplest questions.

Sun is distracting me out of this maudlin pit; she's staring in a way I did not remember from One. No, she did used to stare, but was there this subtext, or am I imagining it now? Ah, now she's looking away. I do not remember everything, it seems.

That's Mac. She's hott with two "t"s. I do not remember being attracted to her. She was old! But now, look at her in her black wool pencil skirt and dancer's hair. Severe, smart, sexy.

Stop it.

Try to say something nice about Sun's stuff even though it's boring art. Don't comment on Gail's narcissistic porn. Don't say anything about Calli's work, either. She has a way of taking a compliment as an insult, like she did (will do) at her first major opening, in ten years. Try to remember not to say anything when that happens, either. Like anything about "an advance for women in art." Don't say that.

Mac, writing in her notebook, said, "Bar? What do you have today?"

I'm putting up the same two drawings of Kristina and me drawing Kristina, as I did before, plus a new picture of Summer in the Schiele style I've been working on, and also in that style a drawing I made of one of the women who earned spare cash posing for the art students, four pictures in all. They're all in debt to Schiele, even the pictures I made in One. Or is my "hindsight" determining my seeing? (Please ignore the way Mac's long skirt has that long slit, showing her left leg when she sits down, all the way up to the thigh.)

They're talking about the work. Uhg, it's hitting me – the palimpsest I remembered. The fear from Life One floods in, a strong feeling that could overwhelm me. Fight it. Hey original self: calm the fuck down. Who cares about this crit anyway? I – we – know what we're doing and always did. Always, ugh. There: I shut he palimpsest off, or it ended, or something.

"Bar, are you well?" Mac asks me, standing and coming to me.

"Yes, yes. I ... forgot to have lunch. I'm fine."

"I have a muffin. If you want," Gail offers me.

"No, uh, okay. Thanks, that's nice. It's good." She smiles.

"Bar, why don't you explain the work?" Mac tells me.

"I drew elongated arms and legs in the Summer drawing – her name is Summer – her stomach extra-concave and her waist intentionally too narrow, her face suggesting ecstasy or a trance, with parted lips, like Klimt's painting *Judith and the head of Holofernes*." Gatik is impressed. What ever happened to him. Did he go back to India? I'm an ass for not knowing. "She's not attractive in any human standard of beauty, particularly compared with Kristina – that's this person – in the two older pictures. I hope Summer's disturbing, mutant-ish. The point was to go with the lines suggested by her body in nature but past nature. I preserved that piece of her face's beauty: its perfect symmetry, but the oddness of her body fights with the naturalness of the face. Anyway, that was the idea."

I remember having sex with Kristina. A comedy of the errors of youth. She had been mad that did not tell her of my inexperience but I was so inexperienced that it had not occurred to me to tell her. The other model – what was her name again? Wow, just last week and I can't remember. She was beautiful, and drawing her I zoned in quickly, something I had not allowed myself recently with Eva. ("Recently.")

"I uh, worked for a long time with the model" Jessie? Janie? Lara. Not Lara. " ... on doing a twist pose, trying to get her to do something almost unreal, until she finally began a yoga routine. I was surprised that she knows yoga now, before it – I mean, not a lot of people know the poses." Not yet. "Her twist was perfect for my exaggeration idea. The twist I drew is just beyond the geometry of what she actually did, and just beyond belief. I also kept her beautiful face, her deep, dark eyes and brows, and her strong facial bones, and suggested a curvature of her strong sinewy arms that would have broken them."

"Emancipation from the arbitrariness of realism," Chauncey says. In apprehension, how like a god. "These two, and those two, it's like two different artists. The figures in those," he says, pointing to Summer and the model, "are inhuman, their faces pulled, as if drawn by a monster."

"Yes, but it is loving as well?" Sun says, "A monster who loved these people?" Sun's energy toward me is odd. If only I caught the clues in One ...? But she deserves better than me in my current form. I am the monster now. I will have to figure out how not to be one, for Eva.

Chauncey is nodding at Sun's remark.

"It's like Holbein," Gatik says.

"It's like *Playboy*." Calli says. "No, that's too good for this. This is more like *Penthouse*. The tennis player is *Playboy* and the other women are some kind of sick fetish magazine I don't even know." Calli is fabulously militant. Honest, bright, and tough. A tough broad. She's worth all these kids put together. No, they're all worth a lot. A great deal. I could teach them so much. But I am not the teacher.

"It seems almost impossible that you're really the one who made all four of these," Chauncey says. "I mean, given your last – the last stuff you brought in. Which is like those," he says, pointing at the Kristinas.

I'm nodding. I agree with the observation. Two Bars. Two Me's.

McIntyre says, "In our last critique, we were discussing the problem of the male gaze with respect to your work. You seem to have decided, not exactly to throw this problem back at us, but perhaps to stay your course regardless of our comments."

"I am not trying to respond to that. I'm trying to show what I felt about each person. Visually. What I saw. I use different styles to express different feelings."

"Oh, come on," Chauncey says.

"No, really, I..."

"'Come on' is right," Calli says. "Don't give us boilerplate shit."

Being tough on me helped me so much, later, when I did get stuck sometimes. They're the ones that helped me evolve to this style. Why did I let the three of us fall out of touch? It was the shame. Chauncey, now, (not "now" – later) at Binghamton. He was up there a lot, anyway. Calli – but I did stay in touch with her for a while. Then an unanswered phone call gets harder to answer and finally fades into we're-not-in-touch.

"What happened to her," Calli asks, pointing at Summer. "She dumped you?"

I have to laugh. Me and Summer? "Not yet." I've met Summer by now but certainly never dated her. I don't think she'd recognize me on the sidewalk. This is all from memory.

"She should," Calli adds. "And her, too," she points at the model. "Though at least you drew a Black woman."

I'll let that go. Just smile at Calli. Ah, but she's taking it as a smirk, parodying a smirk back. "I think it's *Playboy* if it's idealized a certain way. The drawing equal of air-brushing. It's *Penthouse* if there's sex. I don't think I share either of those aesthetics. I didn't try to fit them into a pre-existing fantasy. I tried to listen to their bodies."

Mac says, "Your conversation is interesting but not about the formal problems of art and therefore somewhat beside the point. An artist is not a man or a woman, a Black or white person, tall or short, European, American, Asian, what have you. An artist is a prophet of the new society in which art replaces theology and the artist is the medium through which the society learns to see again. You all did the homework on Agnes Martin?"

We all nod. Professor, I did that homework many decades ago, so I'm sorry but I don't remember what I wrote.

Mac lets that sit while Calli purses her lips. McIntyre says, "Can you show us a little of your process?"

Calli interrupts, "It's porn if he's taking sexual pleasure in the female body and treating her as an object. Listen to their bodies my fine ass. I don't care if he's a prophet if he's a misogynist."

"What if a woman draws a man," I ask her.

"Not the same history of oppression and objectification," she says.

"But this one," I say, pointing to the elongated Summer portrait, "isn't realistic enough to say with certainty that I derived or suggest sexual pleasure from seeing the form."

Calli frowns and won't answer, but I see the wheels turning and know I'm not off the hook with her yet – I've merely poked a bear.

Mac repeats her request.

"You mean, draw something?" Oh, Mac is testing me, not that she definitely thinks I'm showing someone else's work, does she? Perhaps to put that idea to rest? It has been a big jump. Decades-worth. "Sure." Whom should I draw? Also, did I bring the right things? Yes: a 16x20 sketchbook, a few pencils. Enough. Each person's beauty is radiant. Sun's face, though, has classic symmetry. Her flawless skin's subtle way of reflecting light. "Sun?"

"Sure."

Mac directs. "Sun can face the class and Bar's large sketchpad on the easel face her. Yes. The class behind you. Yes, at a bit of an angle so that they can see you work." I'm beginning by drawing a vertical line down the center of the page. In about five minutes, I've drawn half of Sun's face in my older way, though I'm not in practice of being absolutely faithful any more. I'm glad I can still pull it out. The other half should be in my Schiele-inflected style, almost a caricature of Sun, not insulting or unflattering, but exaggerated, here, and here, taking an idea of what he see and pushing it. High cheekbones higher, her small mouth smaller, her cool triangular haircut hipper and more severe than it is. Pretty raw, done quickly.

"Is it clear that this is the same artist who has drawn both sets of pictures?" Mac asks and everyone nods yes.

Mac walks right up to the drawing, bending over to examine it closely. Now she's looking at Summer and the model – Lisa! Right, her name's Lisa, and she's a French major at N.Y.U. – then the Kristina pictures, examining them all, and grunting something, unconsciously?

She stands suddenly whirls, facing me. I'm waiting for her to speak, but she does not. She's so oddly herself. The class waits. "What Bar shows us...no." She pauses. "That he is like Holbein and Cranach, and so on, yes. Durer, perhaps, in these," she says, pointing to the "old" pictures. "Insofar," she begins, "as Bar uses simple lines and forms, as if he were Calder, or Diebenkorn, or Dubuffet, or Okeke, the artist I showed you last time, he is modern. Here," she points in the new one, "and here," pointing at the Summer's foot, which I barely sketched in so that it's possible to disintegrate it into lines in one's mind, "he is modern. Insofar as he is trying to represent, he is not modern." She stops but still does not turn to face the class, or me, and we all wait for her to elaborate. Chauncey clears his throat to speak but Mac holds up her left index finger, stopping him. We all think she's going to say something about the art but she suddenly turns and ended the crit, reminding us of when we would next meet and what's coming due.

Calli says, "I still think it's porn. Even if it's very good pornography."

"Thank you," I say, and bow. That gets a smile.

Taking down my work requires an extra minute during which the rest of the kids leave. I was much more nervous when I was a kid. I am still a kid, and being alone with Mac still makes me nervous, but not as a kid would be nervous. No one may avoid being judged. But I want her to appreciate me as a peer, not as a kid, a request to myself that embodies my the predicament of my opportunity.

Mac, sitting in the chair Calli had used, asked, "How did this happen, Mr. Mizrachi? It is like a miracle, except there are no miracles," she says, "except aesthetic ones."

"I am more than flattered by your approbation. I ..."

"Yes, yes," she says, batting away my remark with a toss of her head, "but explain this."

"I cannot. I...worked hard. I've been...thinking."

She considers my non-explanation. She looks at me blankly. "I have never had such a student, not like this, not ... " She turns to me again and says, "You will be a great star. Do you know this?"

I'm facing away from her. I feel my face heat up. If I had been pale, it would have shown. "You don't know that."

"I do."

"It's not like there is a one-to-one relationship between one's skills and the recognition one receives."

"No, that is true. But you are unique. A surprise. You are not what you seem." I'm starting at that. She seems not to notice. "You are right; it is not one-to-one, but it does not matter. The skills, your skills, because they are yours...You will need to prepare for this, Bar. A star in this world is not necessarily happy. People will say ugly things along with the good. They will say you have not thought through what you are doing. That you have not shown us what you are and where you are from."

"What do you mean?"

"Do not pretend to be naive."

"I'm not Black. I'm not an African-American. My father is from Yemen. I..."

"Does this matter? How will you be perceived?"

"I can't control that."

"Good. So you understand. You must play the chess game."

"Five moves ahead," I say. "But ..."

"Yes. You are not a child."

"No." Not any more.

As I am leaving it occurs to me that I can't do the sitting in class with older children any more. It is not beneath me, but it is not useful. The time, the need for this is past. I could talk with Mac as a friend, almost like we did, but not as a child. I can't go back. I won't be expelled but I won't finish, either.

5. Out to Lunch

Mid-October, 1986, Life Two

The one item in my mother's (really Schlomo's) apartment that strikes me as old world is a painting she brought to America of her grandfather, a real oil painting that confused me because first, how did she get it from Hungary if they lost everything fleeing, and second, why did this guy seem so goyische? I finally asked her fifteen years from now (meaning about five years ago, in my life span) and she told me that it wasn't really him; it was someone she claimed looked like him. "So it's fake." "It is *not* fake. It is better this way. He was not such a handsome man as this, your great-grandfather." I looked at it fairly closely. There's good paint-pushing, decent light on the face, the eyes, the visible hand looks like a hand, which is hard: a competent job. The portraiture seemed specific enough to be of someone; it isn't just a random Scot. His features, a slight smile and a jolly glint in his blue eyes, indeed strikes my eye as Scottish, his hair slightly red where it isn't blond-turned-gray. The relation of this person to my own black-haired ancestors is most likely as distant as someone from China or a Cherokee tribe. (What makes a person "handsome" in this global context?) This man, unlike my real great-grandfather, had probably not been force-marched in 1944 into the woods outside of Budapest to dig his own grave before being shot and pushed into it. Mom picked a picture of an old white dude who looked "European," as if Europe had not done that and other similar things to her and hers, teaching her come to this land of milk and honey to struggle with the white settlers who got here first.

I'm thinking about this painting as I rise in the elevator in Schlomo and Judit's glass and steel apartment building. The rest of the apartment has no old world charm whatsoever. It's as different from my pre-war childhood home as could be and still be in the same city within Western civilization. While the Jackson Heights sixth floor apartment has dark oak floors, a hundred little Arabic rugs, fabric-covered furniture, built-in shelving dad made himself, double-hung windows, and ten-foot ceilings, this twentieth-floor place had unopenable floor-to-ceiling windows that give me vertigo when I look out on the little ant people. The windows distract from the low ceilings. Then there is the wall-to-wall white shag carpeting, and shiny chromed furniture everywhere. Every tabletop was glass, and every seat is black or white leather.

I arrive and they're ready to go. "I'm sorry that I'm late," he say, "I was..."
"Ha! Schloimy, a miracle! He is apologizing for being late! For anything! What happened; something hit you in the head, so you've been civilized?"
Time to smile and keep smiling. In the twenty years since this date in Life One, I've learned to let her comments, however annoying, bead up on my surface and roll away. We walk over to the Russian bistro nearby, on the corner of 64th and Lex. Schlomo won't be able to go this fast later. When's his hip operation? 2000? The tablecloths are white, the waiters in uniforms, mom in a stiff black skirt suit with 1940/80s shoulders, Schlomo his usual schlumpy self in a striped buttoned shirt open at the collar through which show his chest hair. I remember this lunch; in Life One I wore paint-splattered jeans and my Rolling Stones t-shirt, the one with the big tongue, stained with bicycle grease. This time I have clean jeans and a blue buttoned shirt. I remember mom's grimace at my t-shirt; today, she smiles at me.

I'm not wearing these clothes because I want to please my mother. I'm wearing them because I think of myself as wearing them.

I am nearly Judit's age
Schlomo tried talking for once, wheezing a little; he seems fatter than before. Schlomo describes a couple of development/rehab projects on the Lower East Side. His main problem is attracting quality labor. "For reliable people, I would pay," he says, leaning toward me. He wears an incomprehensible and unpleasant cologne.
"Uh-huh."
"You did good work, was it last summer?"
"Yeah. My dad taught me," I say, unable to help myself. I remember that I said exactly that the first time. Judit looks up from her menu; she looks back down.
"You should go work for Schlomo," she says to the menu.
Last time I whined about wanting to be an artist and then got into a pointless argument, again, about the wisdom of studying art. I don't need to do that today. I didn't need to then, either.

In the short time since I "arrived" at Willet's Point, my stocks went from the four hundred dollars I saved from my bar mitzvah to several thousand. A trade I'm about to make should triple that in another week, and another trade will make it all go up ten times on top of that. Far from needing to do manual labor for Schlomo, I'll be going into art from the capitalist's end. No need to say any of that, either.

"Bah. Look, he is thinking it over. Boy, boy, studying art will lead to nothing," Judit said anyway. "It is unfortunate, but you will end with a degree, it doesn't matter in what. That is what I tell myself when I am in a panic that my only son will be destitute. After the degree, we can see."

"'We' can see what?" he asked.

"There is law school," she said with a smile.

She ordered a martini with lunch. We eat: three kinds of smoked fish, boiled potatoes with dill, "real European" bread, and lemon cakes, tea in a Russian samovar.

Judit fishes an envelope out of a new leather purse and holds it in her hand halfway between us. Oh yes. She used to give me money to live on. Almost enough money. Never enough.

"I don't …" he begins.

Clutching the envelope, she interrupts, "You say you learned from your father. Well. Maybe he wasn't such a total loss as I think. Schlomo says you did fine work for him. So, you learned something good. You can learn the business part. You were good at math, always. Bar,"

"I don't need the money. I have enough." I wanted that money badly in Life One and was equally ashamed of wanting it and taking it and wishing that I did not have to. I reconciled myself, swallowing the bitter pill, saying that I was finagling with her, getting her to do what I wanted but it wasn't entirely true. Among other things, she did manage to plant her way of thinking about money in a desperate way into my brain. "I don't need it. Thank you."

"Ach, what is this? What does this mean, 'enough'?"

"Don't do this, Bar," Schlomo says. "Don't push away your mother. She is your mother."

"That's not what I mean," I say, noting Schlomo's signature way of pronouncing moral certitudes. "I only mean I don't need it. I'm fine." Remember to smile. Not sarcastically.

Judit sits back against the high leather banquette, a skeptical look on her face, the envelope still in her hand.

"Such a macher? How? And by the way, what is her name, she who is living with you? Do you think I cannot tell if she is on this answering machine? And you don't say anything to me? You don't bring her to me and yet she lives there? Why? You are ashamed of her for some reason? She is not Jewish. You don't need to tell me. Abigail? Well? Is she Jewish?"

I have to laugh. I got indignant when we talked about Abi in Life One. Time to say nothing.

"A not-Jewish girl is okay for the time being," Judit says magnanimously. "But you are still living there, in that dump. Where I cannot visit, it is so frightening a place. So Abigail is not an heiress. And you don't need the money? Bah. Listen to me. When we were hiding in the barn a penny would have mattered to us."

"But you're not hiding in the barn any more. I'm not hiding in a barn."

"Living on Avenue B is like hiding in the barn."

"No, it isn't. I'm not being chased by Nazis."

"Nazis, junkies, what's the difference? You think I don't know what is there? Schlomo and I drove by."

"I thought you couldn't visit."

"I told him to go faster," she says, laughing. "I wanted to push his foot down on the pedal."

"I'm not pursued by soldiers of the state. The Lower East Side is full of artistic energy."

"That's what they need down there, some soldiers. Listen, I didn't struggle in the barn and then on that boat where everyone threw up except your uncle and we almost starved and then working here like a dog, always finagling something to make the little pay go farther so my son could make himself into a poor person living with the Blecks and the Puerto Ricans."

"It's not your choice."

"A starving artist."

"I'm not starving. You encouraged me to do art. When I was little. You took me to the Met. And MOMA." I'm slipping into pit. It's as if I can see it a hundred yards off and am saying to myself, don't walk into that pit, and yet, I am doing so.

"To do it, yes, as a hobby, as a child, yes. I encouraged you to become who you are, my boy. But you can paint after you finish the workday as stock broker, or a doctor, no? Almost every artist fails. Why should you suffer?"

"Why shouldn't I try?"

"The life is horrible."

"Perhaps the life will be horrible if I don't try."

"Ach but you never finish knowing. You are always thinking, maybe another year and I won't fail. I know this from my uncle."

"The artist from Berlin."

"Yes. He wasn't an artist. He was a shoemaker." I have heard this enough times to finish her sentences. But I won't interrupt. She thought of her uncle as a tragedy of social class. "An educated man, making shoes because he thought he must be an artist."

"I am able to live with the uncertainty." Am I? Then what's this?

"Ach," mom says and turns her head. "I have had enough uncertainty. Perhaps you should be a refugee for a year, to taste it, and see whether you want such a thing again," she spits out with bitterness suffusing her voice and twisting her face.

"Kinehora," Schlomo says.

I am tempted to genuflect, just to bother him, but I don't. I used to rage at her attitude toward art but now I feel sorry for her, having to watch her son make a terrible choice, as she sees it. She's merely telling me her own most pressing truth, and I threw it back at her to gain my independence. It's hard not to throw it back again, today. I pity her for being unable to let go from trying to control something that, the more she tries, the less she succeeds. What would I have been like if she had never said a word about me becoming an artist? I wonder. Why do we allow another person perturb the orbit we choose for ourselves? Even one's mother? And if I am like a comet, returned to this system after a long elliptical journey, why must I allow the same gravitational mass to bother me again? You'd think I could see it coming. I realize that in my life I fulfilled, will fulfill everything she predicted, bicycle mechanic being the same as shoemaker, regardless of some Thoreauvian philosophical stance justifying voluntary poverty as an artist's sacrifice, and regardless of my idea of keeping faith with my art. Perhaps I need not fulfill it again.

But still, in clutching, she is annoying. "You don't mind if I order the steak frites, do you? I mean to go. So I have something for dinner. As I travel like a refugee to my hovel in the lower east side." On the one hand, I am trying to be sarcastic. On the other, I do think it a hovel. Also, her point of view isn't stupid, either. That isn't its problem. She doesn't see the freedom in living cheaply, or more generally, the freedom of being an artist. She only sees the prison of penury.

"Wait, let me see," Judit says, looking over the menu again. "The steak is the most expensive thing here."

"Why don't you give me the envelope. I can pay for it from that. Maybe there's enough there so I can get a few steaks, bring 'em home, put 'em in the fridge. You don't mind if I share a little with the shiksa?"

"That is wasteful. You said you don't need the money. Yes, you should take it, but not to spend here. An artist's life is never sure. Take it, in case."

"Judit," Schlomo says. "He's thin. He should eat a steak."

"Tell me something," Judit says, "is your father eating? I don't want you to take after him. Are you making yourself poor because he is poor? He is poor because of his drinking. I don't believe you that you have some money. From what? Not from Saul. He's not working and getting depressed when everyone else is working. Are you drinking? I heard there are a lot of drugs down there …"

"Thus the junkies. Let's not talk about my father, shall we? I'm not starving. I said that about the steak to make a point." Yes, it was a good idea to come back and save dad if only for him to show mom that he's better than she thought, that her act of abandoning him was ill-considered after all.

She stops. "No. Alright," she says, putting the envelope back into her pocketbook. "Waiter!" She closes it with a click. "You can come and stay with us, of course, boy-boy. In case things turn. If you want to get away from the drug addicts and the shiksa."

"That won't be necessary. I like the shiksa. And the drug addicts." Actually, I don't like the addicts and I'm not so sure about Abi, either.

"You don't know for sure. Waiter! We want a steak to go. Tell him what kind, boy-boy."

"The filet mignon, medium, and the steak fries." I should've had the cabernet, too. Next time.

"Such a macher, doesn't need mamma's money. Another miracle," she says, smiling. "I will make you french toast in the morning, like you like it."

Meaning the way you like it, with too much milk.

"I know your father never makes you anything."

Just because something's true doesn't mean it's a good idea to say it.

He had said, in Life One, "You made him unhappy. That's why he drank. I understand that your buddy Schlomo here fired him. Isn't that right, Schlomo?"

And Schlomo had replied,

"I was forced. He was using electrical tools, after lunch it was dangerous. He would hurt himself. I am sorry, I..."

"Forget it."

"How dare you!" Bar's mother said, said raising her voice. "You blame me for him? What's for his death? Outrageous!"

She had said,"I. Don't. Want. You. To. Become. A. Drunk. Like. Him. Boy-boy," catching her breath and slowing herself down visibly. "I want what's the best for you. Is that clear? I don't want this… for you to be a druggie. A bum."

They got into it, arguing over whether she should give him the money she had clutched in her hand, and she saying she would not because he, Bar, had accused her of murder and she had left in a huff and Bar said to Schlomo that he had to pay because Bar was broke and Schlomo had shrugged, saying, "Then come to work." He paid the check and Bar felt the shame of having nothing, of being reliant on those who would presume to tell him who he could be and what he could do.

A memory from when Bar was ten. In Jackson Heights, mom is making breakfast. He is sitting at the kitchen table as she cooks. She started explaining about how to finagle while Saul occupied his usual chair in front the of television, his fingers curled around a beer. She gave Bar examples: the aforementioned Great Uncle, Jozsef, who built a wine-trading business, and his wife, Bar's Great Aunt Rosa. "She was a professor of German Literature at Berlin University when there were maybe two other women of her professional level in the whole city. The Nazis put her and her family on a train but they didn't know what hit them in Aunt Rosa's case. She was strong, a personality. She finagled her way off that train where all the regular Jews were herded together and onto a much less crowded train that she was certain had to be better. The SS were no match for her," Judit said proudly.

"How come I didn't meet her, mom?" Bar asked, assuming that this was a story of escape, like the one Judit liked to repeat of her family hiding in a barn.

"Ach, but, it's tragic. The train she got off was going to a work camp and the one she finagled herself and her family onto, that one just hadn't been loaded up yet. That one went straight to Auschwitz."

"What's Ow-shwitz?"

"Never mind that. Can you get the maple syrup, boy-boy? If you grandfather wasn't so clever, we would have gone there. A bad place. You have to be a macher to make yourself something. And now I am here with that lump," she said, waving the fork she was using to scramble eggs in the general direction of the living room and shaking her head in disbelief at her misfortune. She pours milk into the eggs and Bar thinks, not too much.

She can't stop herself. She has to reiterate how she is the better parent. When they were having their affair, Schlomo would leave messages on the family answering machine that Saul could hear. No cell phones then. (Or now.) She should've gotten a beeper to be more discreet. She should simply have gotten a divorce without having an affair at all. Schlomo had a lot of guts, calling the house like that.

But that was the whole point, wasn't it? Schlomo had the guts to run a contracting business, and dad didn't. The people skills, the management skills. Though, maybe, and this is today's experiment, it was partly about access to capital, a family like Schlomo's with money for each son to start something. I will see whether Saul might do better with some seed money.

"Before I go, I have a question for you, mom, since you insist on bringing him up. Why did you ever marry him?"

"Who. Saul?" She had also married Schlomo. But that was not a mystery.

"Yes. Saul. My father."

She looks uncomfortable for a moment, then with a sidelong glance at Schlomo, says, "Because he was sexy." The colloquial word seemed out of place in her mouth. "And I was a fool," she adds. "I took a chance. We were young. Everyone was poor. Some would do well in the world. He seemed like one of those. A strong man. Of course, I regretted it, maybe even since the day of the marriage."

You mean the day of the wedding. "Amid a general lack of information about the future, you chose on beauty, an arbitrary and capricious criterion. And you would pretend to be qualified to give me advice."

"I have learned," she says haughtily, but she looks dejected and ashamed and hurriedly rises and goes to the bathroom, uncharacteristically fleeing the field of battle.

"You have shamed her," Schlomo says to me.

"She's a woman less sinned against than sinning."

"You need to do this? For what? To teach a new lesson to an old person? All she wants is to give you some money. To feel she is taking care of you."

"I need freedom from her michigas ..."

"Freedom? All you will get is to be alone."

"Schlomo the wise," I say, too quickly.

Schlomo frowns. Judit returns. I let Schlomo pay as we stand and go out. I walk away from the restaurant and around the corner because I don't want mom to see me have the ability to hail and pay for a cab. Yes, the money is that fraught. There lies the whole tragedy of Judit's post-war life. She had the misfortune of not being able to get, in one Jewish male, both kinds of sexy at the same time: a sexy body with a sexy bank statement.

6. A Party

November 7, 1986

Later, I drew a scene of the party in Soho from memory in charcoal and ink for the most part. I used red color pencil to draw Abigail's hair tie and her lips, less than 1% of the surface area of the picture. The guy with the torch was there, as were the two in plastic dresses and the all different outfits, but all of them were smaller figures in the background. The critics were in the center, bickering. I tried to catch the energetic gesticulation of one of them, the reserved, arch sarcasm of another, and the flat, affectless pose of the third. I drew myself underneath them, listening, not saying anything, brows knit. Abigail and Art were standing in a corner near a bathroom, pitching their heads toward one another, licking one another's tongues, oddly, but there were many odd behaviors in the picture. In another corner, the top left, a group of four people faced a framed image hanging on the wall, a bit of wish-fulfillment, since it was a picture of mine they attended to.

I wake thinking it's the mid-2000s, that I'm in my bedroom on Riverside Drive and 135th, that Eva's probably angry with me, and that if I told her my dream of having had sex with Abigail, it would throw lighter fluid on that fire.

The window is in the wrong place, at the foot of the bed, not the side. There's an empty lot outside, not the Hudson. Urban rubble.

The blond hair of the woman sleeping next to me is strewn across her naked back. Eva's not blond. Who's this? Where's Eva? Where am I?

Abigail moans in her sleep but doesn't not wake. "It's alright," I say aloud, mostly to myself. The lines of bed marks on her skin remind me of the lines on Eva's face and I am homesick, right here at home. Abi's smooth, young white skin is human and beautiful. Very young. What am I doing? The youthfulness of her body is not a turn-on. It ought to be, but it isn't. She is beautiful, but not because of that. Her youth creeps me out. Her movements, gestures, expressions, and most of all her life agenda are all strange to me, things I left behind, kid stuff, all that punk rock at the E.V. Club, except the stuff she does that shows her desire for me, a formidable force. She says "like" too much, like a teenager, and chews gum. I wasn't sure I'd stay. I was sure I wouldn't. Not that I could realistically go back to Jackson Heights. Sleeping with Abi sure beats staying at mom's. I supposed I could've gotten a hotel room. But she wanted me last night. I missed that. The way the timeline is going it will turn out exactly the same as before: Abi will have been my ex.

Don't make your mistakes Eva's fault. They are your own fault, fucker.

What does "fault" mean in this instance?

Ow, fuck. Banging one's foot trying to get out of the mattress on the floor shows the value of a proper bed; when will I get re-used used to this mattress on the ground. Also, sleeping naked. Time to carry the boner to the bathroom to pee.

I am tempted to gently remove the sheet from her body and draw. I would if I knew she'd not wake. Go. Just go.

In the bathroom mirror I see a young fool who, faced with the possibility of eighteen years of celibacy, until he starts seeing Eva again, took the nearest way. That defense is only partly successful, even with me. There's the rule against seeing exes. Technically, Abi isn't an ex. Yes she is. No she's not. There should be a simple way to figure this out.

I could simply make some money in stocks and go live in Japan for a decade and a half.

I don't want that; I want the same thing that I had before, but corrected. I want to see why I ended up where I did. I can't do that if I change absolutely everything.

I don't have that scar on my knee from the accident in the bike shop in, I think, 1996. I don't have joint pain. I wonder whether I can still do an eighteen-minute lap in the park. "Still." I have no ear hair.

What's the ethical status of physically expressing love for someone you know with certainty you will not remain with at some not-too-distant future?

What's the ethical status of … wait: in theory, Abi and I could stay together for the rest of our lives. But we won't, and I have prior knowledge about that. Is my prior knowledge a self-fulfilling prophecy?

No, no stick to the main problem: she's too young.

My body in this shower is quite young. Abi can feel that for herself.

Won't everyone be too young, when it comes to that? Eva will be in her thirties and I'll be – in my fifties, except physically.

Don't solve all of these problems now. Abi seemed determined to have a good time last night. In the last twenty years, I haven't thought about how she has sex like a guy, always on top, always making sure she gets off first, not so interested in things after that. I'm going to let that procedure justify me being older. She's still the more powerful personality of the two of us. Who's taking advantage of whom?

Actually, it was nice.

At least my past self always understood the importance of decent coffee, middle-eastern bread, good tomatoes, stuff to make a decent omelet. The cereal in the cabinet and the mayo in the fridge must be hers.

What strikes me is the difficulty of things. For instance, having to call information to get a phone number simply to make an appointment with a real estate broker. I leave Abi a note on paper. No individual phones, no texting, none of that.

No, don't focus on the tech side. It's not what matters. You were able to deal with this state of things once.

Yet, that's emblematic, isn't it? Of the return, of it being impossible to forget the future.

I hope she'll be at work when I'm back.

My clothes are all kid clothes. Which concert t should I wear, The Who or Frank Zappa? Should I wear dyed-black paint-splattered jeans or dyed-black ones that are merely dirty? How could I have lived like this? I can't believe I subjected my feet to Keds. At least there are the Doc Martens. Do I need the orthotic inserts yet? Do they exist yet?

Walking outside, the neighborhood is a shock because, among other things, I saw it transform.

There is malevolence in the emptiness, the broken down building, the one with empty windows as if it had missing eyes, the rubble lots that look like missing teeth, as if the frequently used "bombed-out" metaphor were real, and the natural response of the remaining survivors is understandably to attack anyone who might have been in on the blitz. Isolated men walk quickly through from the projects on Avenue D to work or a grocery store further west. They look like Bedouins crossing the waste. This cool autumn Friday morning the streets might as well be in the Gobi desert. One sad car on three wheels is parked across the street from Sharpey's. The other parking spots remain available for whomsoever does not value their vehicle, or is a gangster whose ride no one would touch. (Don't say "ride" for car.) No one looks me in the eye. To say "hello" seems impossible. The edge of this area was once not merely tolerable but appealing; the feeling of the edge, edginess. Instead, it's making me feel on edge.

What do I need now? I need to stop living with Abigail Greenfield, pretty, adventurous, up-for-anything white girl, charismatic artist, seducer of my body, once upon a time older than me, a person who led me into error. No longer.

The brokers don't want to deal with buildings east of First Avenue, until I said to one of them, "What about something like the Christadora?"

"I thought you were asking about whole buildings."

"That's later. I need an apartment sooner."

"Oh, my, yes, I can get you an apartment in there. Sure. The Christadora's a lot more expensive than the rest of the neighborhood. I didn't know you're in that range. Maybe four vacancies right now. Frankly, I don't know what they are thinking. They spent a lot renovating so they think they're entitled. People are so optimistic about the future when it comes to grabbing a piece of it now. You're like an entrepreneur. The nabe could go gentrified, or it could stay like it is." She laughed. "Though I do think it will..."

"Yeah, I'd like to see what's there. There and near Washington Square also."

I stop by Cooper to talk to former/present classmates to see what assignments I have that need immediate attention, and what could wait. I'm on the fence about finishing the semester. I need to plan an orderly withdrawal, do things like an adult. Burn no bridges. Not like the last time. Blame yourself for that, not her.

I return to the apartment at six with groceries for dinner, and find Abigail and Art on the kitchen stools touching foreheads intimately, not like friends discovering something funny, but more like a lovers' conference. Something about this vision of their rapport makes me nauseous, Art pulling at her arm, Abigail's thigh next to his thigh. It's not even that I don't want them to have sex. It's my memory of how they acted later (long ago).

Abi's smile as she runs to me is genuine. She sees no contradiction between living with me, having sex with me, or maybe it was making love, that hackneyed phrase, and her thing with Art. She throws her arms around my neck and kisses me and it feels good but strange. She is a stranger I know intimately.

"I gotta change," she says, running into "our" room. Yes, it is ours, our clothes stored on wood planks separated by cinder blocks, her hippy thrift store dress collection on a repaired clothing rack salvaged off the street. I found that. My late-teen/early twenties t-shirt collection, jeans, and antique bike clothes (chamois!), and one "nice" outfit are all on pine 1x10s.

Abi seems in a hurry to go change. Her hair is tousled. Had they been making out?

Art says, to her, "And I, too, must assume the proper attire."

Art changes in the bathroom, coming out in a white t-shirt, white jeans, and antique, long white tuxedo jacket. Abi returns wearing tight black leather pants that fit closely to her ankles, a tight, midriff-bearing little black t-shirt, sneakers traded for silver heels that made her an inch taller than me, and hair pulled to the side by a red scrunchie matching red lipstick. She looks like Olivia Newton John in *Grease*. Oh, yes, we're going to that party in Soho that we went to. Maybe I can talk to Cielo there.

Abi twirls and says to me, "You could say I look nice."

I'm considering it. She's sexy but it's inorganic. She only wore this outfit once, in my memory, so while it might be clothes to someone else, it's a costume on her. Art, in the breach, says, "You're so sexy I want to come in my pants."

"Messy," she says, wrinkling her nose.

She is profoundly sexy in that getup. It bothers me. Why?

I need to maintain the idea that I don't know what I shouldn't know. "What's going on?"

"That party? That I told you about? Delilah invited us."

"Why do you all need to dress up?"

They both reply at once. Abigail says, "Come on, let's have fun," and Art says, "Because everyone's dying." He gives an elaborate flourish, rises. "I am untested. I cannot be tested. Society is testy. Are you testy, too, Bar? My friend James Galligan, a nice Irish boy from Troy, New York, gave a great blow-job in his day, he died last week. That is why I must dress for the party."

I don't answer. Abi gives me a look as if to say, nice work blowing the mood, and I think, I can't win here.

We leave. Abigail takes Art's arm walking west to the party. I walk behind them, and it's obvious to me that I'm a third their couplehood. Even though Art was always gay (that is, I always knew, even clueless me, even then) it was never clear that they couldn't be screwing. She'd do anything for the "experience" and he for the nihilistic, apocalyptic hedonism.

I used to pretend to want the same things that she wanted and that I can't imagine wanting at all. Mostly I wanted her approval.

Her sexiness is affecting me more. She knows. She's turning every now and then to see if I'm paying sufficient attention, catching me checking out her body, and turns back to Art and laughs.

Passing First Avenue, we enter civilization and Abigail starts getting a lot of attention from men on the street. She's enjoying it, oblivious to any danger. The costume is working. But it'll be me who's forced to fight if it comes to that. Thoughtless of her.

She stops. I'm a few feet behind and she comes to whisper now into my ear, "I'm going to open you up, baby. Let me open you up."

"What does that mean?"

"You'll see," she says, and kisses me. She goes back to walking arm in arm with Art.

At a red light, we wait to cross. Art says something I can't hear that's apparently quite amusing, giving a feminine flourish that would signal him as a gay man from a hundred yards. Abi runs her fingers through his hair. His reaction is not that of a boyfriend, but of a friend tolerating a friendly touch. He puts his hair back where he wants it. He's her Exotic Friend, the embodiment of an experience she can't have and that tantalizes her. Also, it works to tease me.

Passing Washington Square Park. I hope to get that apartment to the north, there, on the tenth floor with big windows overlooking the park. When to tell her? She'll be okay, at least financially. I don't actually know how she'll take it emotionally. I can't tell, for all her desire, whether she cares about me as a person or as a pet.

The N.Y.U. undergrad males give Abigail second looks that she would not have received in her usual peasant skirt, paisley or white t-shirt, sandals, and straight long hair. I wasn't aware, back then, of what guys like this were capable of in the basements of their frats.

Greene Street. We've been hearing music from different parties compete with one another for many blocks: frat parties, dorm parties, parties for grownups. Art stops at a building with an industrial elevator opening onto the street, once intended for easy loading of mechanical equipment by men with blue-collar jobs, now convenient for loading lots of people, or big paintings and sculptures, or collectors with bleached white collars. Art rings an almost invisible bell painted black set in a black metal column. The elevator's interior is covered in pages from one of the ubiquitous xeroxed 'zines featuring dense, unreadable text and solarized photographs. We get in.

The elevator opens into an enormous loft space, thick with people, the music deafening. Eighteen-foot-high stamped tin ceilings reflect back the sound waves of the DJ's choices. It's an eighty-foot distance to the far wall, white columns, dancing crowd, and lots of big paintings on the walls. The music is loud enough to hear in one's bones. A hundred attempts to have conversations are visible but inaudible. A man with mostly gray hair, mid-fifties? ogles Abi, who is still arm-in-arm with Art.

I scan the room. A serving girl offers her tray to an older woman with a Susan Sontag shock of white amid a black coif, wearing a long black dress. The young woman is one of many with trays that hung from straps around their necks, all in the same style of dress: voluminous tulle skirts, tight bodysuits, and fishnet stockings. They're handing out cigarette packs, fancy chocolates, and little open smoked-salmon sandwiches on tiny pieces of brown bread. This one has a Mr. Clean t-shirt, modified with slices taken out of various places at various angles. The older woman says, "You know you hurt women when you agree to wear clothes like that to work." The younger woman rolls her eyes and says, "Yeah but it's ironic," with an air of ennui.

There are a dozen sexy girls whose revealing clothing registered on various levels of self-conscious irony. And, if I focus, men as well. The males, females, and those sporting an ambiguous stance compete on several planes, intellectual and physical being only the most obvious. The party as occasion for denial of a conflict between smart and hot.

A long, old wooden bar that seems purchased from a closed pub is half covered in pre-poured glasses of wine. Some people sway-dance while cradling a glass.

Someone suddenly turns the music down to half its former volume. The dancing corner groans and boos.

Art points out to us various art stars, including my Professor Cielo, who nods to me and gives Abigail a hard up-and-down. I know where many of these people will end up. Some will retain their stardust and some will not, of course. Knowing which is which gives me a feeling of power that I must check. Don't get arrogant, or you'll assume something will happen that maybe you're misremembering or that you're changing by being different. Beware becoming a butterfly with an effect. Beware becoming like Gary Mitchell.

I remember the last time he spoke with Ceilo, in Life One, when I was still in school.

Cielo's office at Cooper Union. Quietly, as if conspiratorially, Cielo said, "Of course you draw the girls." He shrugged dramatically, standing up as if to get more leverage. He sat down again. A piece of paper from his desk was dislodged by the air flow and settled eventually in a small pile of papers on the floor next to it. The desk itself was covered in books, papers, pens, paper clips, several student works including drawings and a small oil on canvas, a cardboard box in which Bar saw copies of Cielo's book, spines up: Art and Desire: The Shock of the Modern in Futurism's Aesthetics of the Sublime. Cielo sat and wheeled the office chair close to Bar, Cielo's nose almost touching Bar's. "You draw the girls because that is what you draw well, eh? You draw like you..." he entered the last word with a gesture or pushing his fist straight forward, a motion Bar understood. "That's good. I try forever to get kids to draw like a-this." He suddenly wheeled around and whisked Bar's sketchpad from his desk, sending two more papers onto the floor. They all seemed to land in the same place. "Here, this one is perfect, no?" It was a nude of Abigail in pencil and ink wash. "Her form is perfect. Not only as a woman. As a form. Look upside down at it." He flipped the page over and showed it to both of them. "As a picture, as a form. It's a-perfect. The diagonal of the body, no? Like Rembrandt. Also the face, like Rembrandt. You don't throw this away, eh?" He flipped it back over. "And she is, well." He smiled. "In Italian we say you talk with no hair on your tongue, eh?" Bar's feeling was mixed as Cielo turned the picture over slowly, making a complete circle, staring at the work. "You can draw this, so you can draw a Black girl. I only say what is leads to success in America. The artist does what is upside-down. America, Europe, say no to Blacks. The artist must say yes."

"But..."

"Yes, yes, you already say. Good for today, eh? This is why the art world is ready for you," he near-shouted from his desk to Bar's chair, a distance of five feet. *"Another Basquiat. The danger of the jungle. The fear of the Black man."* He rested his voice on *"fear,"* drawing it out, and using his hands in that quintessence of Italian hand gestures, the fingers pointed up and together, as if feeling an invisible piece of cloth.

"But, uh, I'm not Black."

"Bah. You must study this movement, Black Arts! From the 60s, when all was possibility! The poet says, Bliss it was in that dawn, eh? This fear, this...this danger, it is a primal thing, eh? The Europeans always will fear the African, always. But this is not so simple, like racism. The Europeans, they like this fear. They like to get close," he said, making a fist and bringing his face close to Bar's. "Close to danger!"

"I'm ...not Black," Bar said quietly, turning his face slightly away from Cielo's nose hairs and old-man spots.

Cielo drew back. "You say this. What does it mean?"

Bar explained being Jewish and Yemenite.

"So? Eh? You are whatever you want, no? You are not white, would you say?"

"I'm Jewish."

"There is no point in that. Jews, not Jews. So? It's like Italians. Too many Italians in art. There is no sympathy for us, eh? But the Blacks, no? Do you not see?"

"My mother hid from the Nazis in a barn. My dad fled from Yemen in 1948...," Bar said with more edge to his voice than he meant.

Cielo bent over Bar, putting his hand on Bar's shoulder. "It does not matter. The Jews own ninety percent of the galleries in New York." Bar tried to control his face. He thought he might be revealing hatred to Cielo by squinting; he relaxed his eyes. Cielo seemed not to notice. He said, "Beside, you don't draw this. Why not? You could draw your mother in the barn. Why do you not?"

Bar looked down. "I don't know," he said, his desire to refute Cielo deflated.

Bar left feeling that if he had to be thinking about the things Cielo wanted him to think about, he wouldn't be able to draw a thing.

A tall woman in a complicated boxy suit outfit with ridiculously high shoulders comes to Art and air-kisses with him before declaring in a theater-ready voice, "Art, I'm sorry but you are too evil for me to talk to you. I love you. But I must walk away."

"You bitch! I love you! You're high society! You are couture! You are … "

"I walk away!" she says. "High society? I am not such a thing, my goodness..." she yells over the music as she strolls toward another area, turning her hands up in a corkscrew twist like Gloria Swanson with the elephants. After I stop watching her, I see that Abi and Art are nowhere in sight. Yes, they are planning a trap for me.

I was in a conversation with some writers, wasn't I. Where are they? Oh, yes, over there. I get myself a cube of cheese and a glass of white wine. They're in the middle of it.

Bar looked around, wondering where Art and Abi went. A corner of the giant room was cordoned off with wooden police sawhorses and filled with sculptures, minimalist, futurist, and other. Bar thought a very tall thin metal sculpture was a Giacometti; he could not tell whether a carefully laid thick rope was a sculpture or just a rope. Not to mention the sawhorses. At least one of the paintings was a Motherwell, as if there to represent former revolutionaries. A Cindy Sherman poster turned out to be one of her original prints, according to some admirers near it.

A group of three women in hot pants and bikini tops danced in a circle, fending off all males who came to shave one of them off for himself. One of the girls was a boy of fifteen.

A man in an orange suit walked around holding a lit torch. No one seemed to think him worth interrupting, until a very large man, one of the only ones wearing a simple business suit, came over to talk him into dousing the torch in the sink behind the bar.

A tall woman with West African features, Bar thought, in a dress made of small white stones sewn together, clinked by, while an extremely pale woman dressed in a plastic translucent dress, her underwear, and lack of a bra, asked a friend to get her a drink. A moment later a muscular man in the same plastic dress, his Hanes showing through, walked by as if in search of his mate.

Bar found himself in a conversation with one of the serving girls and a couple, maybe in their fifties. The woman had another long black dress and a streak of white in her hair almost identical to the earlier one. The serving girl was excited about her own upcoming show of photographs of the things of her life, coming up at a gallery on Sixth Street, above an Indian restaurant. "It's my first show in New York!"

"We should go. We'll go," said the man of the couple as he stared at her retro plunging neckline a bit too obviously and got a kick in the calf from his wife. He ignored the kick and kept talking to her. "What do you mean, the things of your life?"

"Condoms, maxipads, undies, ciggie butts, beer bottles, stuff like that." The husband seemed intrigued; he pulled out a business card that he neatly placed between her breasts. His wife smacked him in the side of his head harder than a joke would merit. The man merely smoothed his hair and said he worked at a gallery nearby. Bar assumed he meant that he owned it. The woman giggled like Maralyn Monroe, bringing her shoulder to her chin, knocking her knees together.

His wife said "I write about art, my dear. For ArtForum. And what do you do, young man.

"I'm at Cooper Union?"

"You are asking me?"

"Yes. No. I mean, yes, Cooper. I'm a student."

"Very impressive. I know some of the teachers there. Sheila McIntyre. And Cielo over there...In any case, my dear," she said to the young female artist, "You won't make anything of yourself if you just do conceptual stuff. There also has to be craft in it. Is there craft to what you do? Because to be frank, it sounds as if you put a pile of junk on a bed and write a caption."

"That's not true. I don't write the captions. The gallery does."

The art critic smiled.

"Hello Lisa," said a man with a grey punk hairdo (hair gelled straight up) and a black tuxedo jacket over a black shirt.

"Allesandro."

They kissed cheeks, Italian style.

Allesandro, smiling as well, addressed himself to the young woman. "Don't pay the slightest attention to Miz Liebensraum," he said, smirking.

"Leibstein."

"Whatever. Craft is nothing. Craft is a mere ploy. It's merely a popular conceptual tool, a trompe l'oeil, a party trick, like sleight-of-hand. What's your name, anyway?"

"Debbie. Oh, uh, my gallery told me to call myself Elle Vichyssoise. I can't even spell it, half the time." She laughed politely.

"Elle, then? You supply all the beauty your art needs, all by yourself."

Elle laughed politely again. She said, "But isn't it unsatisfying if the art is used up in an idea? Like, if you can get as much from hearing about it as seeing it? Like, my friend? She did this whole performance piece getting naked and covering herself in honey and inviting anyone from the audience who wanted to come up and lick her."

"Uh, that sounds different in person from just hearing about it," Bar said. The old man nodded, slightly stunned by the idea, which it seemed he was imagining with Elle in the lead role.

Someone asked, "What was the point?"

Various people spoke at once:"The artist's relationship with her audience," "The illusory permanence of art," "How quickly social norms can be transgressed or transformed."

"I was gallery sitting once for a Fluxus show." Bar told the story of the rose and the "rose."

"And yet," Allesandro said, "that rose, too, has a presence, no. Both are about presence. Just as Elle here has a presence. The human body has a presence. The presence of the female body …"

"Oh Sandro, would you please shut up? Your smarmy semi-sophisticated slithering will never cease to amaze."

"What do you mean, 'semi'," he said, still smiling.

Bar wondered if he were an art critic also.

"In the piece I wrote for Art in America *last month,"* Allesandro went on, *puffing up his chest only half in self-mockery, "I explained the importance of presence, charisma and fortitude in art."*

A third critic, it soon appeared, arrived in the form of a woman about the same age as the artist the two old guys hovered over. She looked Scandanavian: pale skin and blonde, John Lennon glasses, nearly white hair in a pageboy with bangs, and a blue-and-white striped, bell-shaped dress. She looked intimidating to Bar, not smiling like Allesandro. He called her over from a conversation she was having with the man with the doused torch, "Annette, come, we are having an interesting discussion." He filled Annette in on Elle's practice, Lisa's comment, and his own. Everyone leaned in toward Annette to hear what she would add.

"I'm not sure about the idea of presence, Sandro. I read your piece and found it ... provocative, as usual. I think we're all chasing the next Cubism. Everyone's terrified of being caught with their pants down, unaware, or unready for the new, new thing. The woman who does performance nude with honey is merely being more dramatic about staking a claim to newness."

Bar couldn't tell if she was agreeing with him or not. He sipped his wine. It made him almost bold enough to ask her, but not quite.

Annette looked Bar over. "You're very good-looking," she said. She turned to Lisa and said, "This party's like, wall-to-wall dinky roosters. The guys are strutting. Half these men are wearing eyeliner." She started fishing for something in a large square canvas bag with a print of Picasso's "Woman Ironing" from the blue period. "Who's he?" Annette asked, referring to Bar with her chin while looking at his face.

"He's studying at Cooper Union."

"Oh," Annette said. She took a cigarette out of a silver case. "Got a light?" she asked Bar, who shrugged. Allesandro served her with a zippo. She still stared at Bar, making him squirm. "Name?"

"Bar Mizrachi."

She nodded. "Do you think you were lucky, getting into Cooper?"

"I don't know. I can draw," he said.

She smiled. "I was in the office yesterday..."

"Annette Peterman is the editor in chief for ArtNews,*"* Lisa added.

"Yeah, so I was just listening to these two artists talking," Annette began. *"They weren't talking to me. Just talking. One said, 'You can't be a minimalist now. You had to already be one.' The second one said, 'That's right. It's all over.' The first one said, 'It's all timing and luck. It always was. I keep telling Frank that, but he keeps going out to Jersey to this factory where he drops thousands having them make those big metal spirals.'*

Bar nodded, but did not understand her point.

Allesandro, who thought he did, said, "This wanting what is next, it is itself old. It is superficial, like wanting the next scarf, eh?"

Abi appeared, alone, just outside the circle behind Bar.

"What's wrong?" he asked, turning to her.

"Nothing." But she seemed shaky.

The old man who was possibly Lisa's husband detached himself from Elle and moved toward Abi. "I'd love to take you home and show you my collection of nineteenth-century erotic photographs."

Abi replied dead-toned, "Take your hand off my ass or I'll find out where you live and set the place on fire."

Bar jumped at the sound of a building suddenly falling. Someone laughed, "That's Einstürzende Neubauten."

"It's music?"

"Yes. I guess you only like funk music? Is that what they play 'in the hood' where you're from? Did I say that right?"

"I'm from Queens. Jackson Heights. It's not a 'hood."

Iggy Pop's "The Passenger" abruptly replaced the noise-music, and at club volumes again.

Art danced, or ice-skated, across the floor, back to Abigail.

Allesandro said, "It's a formula I made up. It's based on $E=MC^2$. $E=CrCo^2$," he said, spelling out the letters. "The energy of art depends on its craft multiplied by its conceptions, squared. Just as in Einstein, the constant is enormously high, so is the same thing true of the conception."

Lisa said, "No one is going to understand what you're talking about if you use fake formulas."

Elle said to Sandro, "I think what you're saying is clear." Sandro smiled at her. "You're trying to be obscure. It's like all the guys in my program? The M.F.A. at Hunter? They're always trying to sound smarter than they are." Sandro dropped his smile.

Annette said, "I think I understand it. But yeah, no one else will. You see, Bar, all these people," she said, waving her finger in a semi-circle to indicate the crowd, "think they are in charge of their fates. If only the come up with the right formula, they will succeed. The illusion of control is comforting."

Bar nodded.

"And you are one of the Fates," Sandro said, "cutting their strings in just the right spot. You are the one in control."

"Hardly," she said. I'm only guessing at what's next. I need luck, too. If I am unlucky, people tell me I'm not a Fate but the devil and stupid and say I'm finished. It happens every other week."

Bar said, "I think if you make something beautiful enough you force people to appreciate it."

Annette took a drag and blew the smoke to the side, "I don't even know what beautiful means any more. Beauty itself is often a matter of luck," she said. Bar felt her to be leering at him.

Art gave a flourish, grabbing attention away from Bar, and said, "Artists are the seers. We are the prophets, and our conceptions and abilities are given to us by a god. But not a god in heaven."

"Oh," Lisa said, amused. "Where is he?"

Art gave her an elaborate flourish and pointed to his crotch. Lisa laughed, Elle smiled as if at a misbehaving puppy, and Sandro and Annette remained stoic.

"What do you think, Bar? Bar is the voice of the future. He's at Cooper," Annette asked, ignoring the fact that by this reasoning Debbie/Elle was also the voice of the future. "Is the artist trying to be a God?"

Bar couldn't tell whether she was challenging him or trying to engage him. "I'm not. I just want to draw what I see. I hope other people didn't see the same thing. Isn't that enough?"

Art said, *"No, no, no, no, no. It is not enough! The artist consummates himself in his celebrity. What are your drawings if there is no one to see them? By extrapolation, their importance increases with their audience, as does yours. There is a specialness to seeing a picture of John Lennon or John Cage when they were young, before they were famous. Before they were recognized. The tantalizing cusp of thing. Most of us are never recognized. No one sees us. We are forever on that cusp. Like the lovers on Keats's urn, always about to kiss but never kissing! We make images so that a part of us may be seen. A part of our souls. But usually, it doesn't matter and we may as well have not because most images fail anyway. The failed mark shows the soul, trapped in the body, unable to give a glimpse of itself. We are all trapped in our bodies. Most of us simply live, and die, like the fruit fly. It's special to know the person who does more than live and die before the recognition and then to know about the recognition that comes after. Truly, it is sublime. You know me, for instance,"* Art said, allowing a sly smile to crawl across his face, *"before I am more widely known."*

"You're pretty well known already," Annette said.

"Yes, but only by artists and art people like you. Not regular people."

"That's only for Picasso. Basquiat. Warhol. People on that level of famous," she said.

"Yes," Art said, raising an eyebrow as if in contemplation of his future empire.

"God," Annette said, "isn't Art so sexy that you want to jump on him?" Since no one in particular was addressed, no one replied, though Abigail jumped at what Annette said.

Bar saw Abigail glaring at Annette. Abi grabbed Bar's arm and pulled him toward the door. "We're leaving." Bar began to object, as he was interested in this conversation but had not fully worked out what it was about, but. She yelled over her shoulder at Art, "Let's go!" In Life One, Bar went.

In Life Two, Abi grabs my arm to get us away from Annette. "Just a sec, Abi." I thus perturb Abigail's drugged intensity briefly. She says, "Just one minute. It's important! I'm going to show you something!"

"Okay." I manage to get to Professor Cielo, surprising him, and deliver my message to him, and as I am speaking with him I see Abi getting into the elevator. I go down to the street to find Abigail, who's doing a frenetic dance on the corner of Wooster and Spring. She began performing ballet moves, limited only by the tightness of her pants. She did an arabesque, and tried to make it into a penchée, almost fell, and went into a series of constricted pas de chats. I don't remember talking with her about ballet. She always talked about having absolutely nothing to do back in West Point, as a kid. Apparently there were middle-class things like dance lessons. A couple in black evening clothes on the other side of the street stare at her.

"What're you doing?"

She screams, bending over with the effort to make more sound: "I WANT TO GO!!" Her scream attracts more turned heads.

She smiles; she laughs sweetly as if she were the kind of person incapable of screaming anything, ever. She does another twirl and smiles at him as if expecting him to get it. Her smile strikes me as half possessed. Art emerges from the elevator, dramatically, his arms pushing against the side walls.

Abi takes two steps and hugs me, or grabs me and kisses me, aggressively. Her hand moves down to my pants where she starts rubbing. She pulls her face a few inches away and looks at my face, laughs, releases me, and all at once, takes off. Not running, not in those heels, just walking briskly. She heads east. Art and I follow.

"Where are we going?" I ask, but I remember what was going on.

"I want to show..." breath, "...you something," she says, facing front.

She walks too quickly to stop for cars. I run to her side and make apologetic signs to cars to slow down. We pass through Washington Square Park and the hustlers whisper-hawking their wide-ranging drug choices. One's a sallow kid, maybe sixteen, looking hollow-eyed and despondent who makes me shudder seeing him, remembering him.

We reach Second Avenue. Time to stop this. "No!" I yell, and stop following her. It feels strange, not going with Abigail's lead.

Abi's a couple of car lengths ahead of me. She turns, runs back, grabs my wrist again, and tries to pull me west. "Come ON!!"

"No, Abi. I won't do what you're planning."

"What do you mean? You don't know what I have planned. Or even if I have something planned. What do you mean what do you mean? What do you mean?"

In Life One, Abi rushed Bar home, rushed both him and Art, who objected to the coked-up pace around First Avenue, though he, as well, was coked up, though it seemed to affect him less sharply, perhaps through familiarity and tolerance.

She brought Bar to their bedroom, and Art was still there. Bar submitted to letting her strip him of his clothes, even though Art was standing, smirking, at the opposite corner of the room. Abi, in her leather sat Bar down on one of their cinder-block shelves, knelt in front of him, and got him hard. That done, she put his hand on his own boner and told him to "keep it going. I'll be back." She stripped, unzipping her clothing too quickly to qualify as performing a tease. Bar started to lose his erection the moment she stopped touching him. Even more than Art's presence, Bar felt the effect of Abigail's jittery, frantic energy. It frightened him. He went along with it because it was the easiest thing and because yes, he wanted to let her push him into the experiences she so craved, and so insistently wanted for him as well. But letting her push him didn't turn him on. He felt as if he had been blindfolded, put on a Ferris Wheel, unblinded at the top, and told he must, must! love, love! it. Her body, once naked, did turn him on, but then she unzipped Art and started getting him hard, too, which had a dampening effect on Bar. Abi got on her hands and knees on the bed, facing Bar. Art produced a small glass container of vaseline, got behind Abi, and proceeded to prep her ass. "Look at me, baby," Abi said, but this isn't what he wanted to look at. Art took something out of his jacket pocket – his jacket was still on – that Bar didn't see. But there wasn't the act of ripping a condom wrapper. Whatever it was, Abi's body obscured it. Art put his hands on Abi's hips and looked straight at Bar as he began fucking her. Bar let go of his soft penis. It was the opposite of the pleasure he got from looking and drawing. It was as if someone had found out his refuge, his hiding place (which was the way he drew) and burned it down. He felt a sickening feeling, as if he were in trouble, caught seeing something he ought not. He felt naked in front of this man. He looked away, but Abigail, who was moaning softly, said, "No, baby, look. Look. See it. It's not bad. It's good. Mmm." She reached down to touch herself. Her focus divided, she couldn't always keep her head up to maintain her eye lock on Bar. Looking at Abi, Bar thought, no, you don't see me. That's why you're doing this and thinking I would think it fun. You can't see me.

The double-vision hit again just then. In the other view, he was on the street and Abi was there, and Art, and everyone was yelling. He felt that self-assurance again, like he felt in the crit, knowing what's right, knowing he's right, the very thing he did not know here. The doubling added to his nausea. After maybe fifteen seconds, it popped. She hadn't seen him almost fall off the chair, but Art had. Art was still looking at him as he, Art, finished. On Art's face, Bar let his artist's eye see the range of feeling, physical release, lust for him, Bar, and an arrogant cock-of-the-walk look as well, a look as if to say I, Art, took something from you, as if Bar's momentary trance was because of Art, which it partly was. As if Art were saying to him that he brainwashed Bar's girlfriend, Art's best friend, to do it, "because I wanted to fuck you, Bar, and now I did."

Art went to the bathroom, holding his pants around his thighs to walk. Abi cooed soothing things to Bar as she went to him and licked him to orgasm. In coming, Bar felt his shame deepen. He could not understand or explain it. He could not look her in the eye. Art came to the bedroom door and said goodbye. Bar was grateful that he didn't laugh. Bar and Abi went to bed together, hearing the front door close as Art let himself out. She spooned him, holding him as he lay in a C, stroking his hair, kissing his neck.

Three hours later, Bar woke having to piss. He stretched, breaking Abi's spoon embrace. She groaned and rolled over to the other side. She seemed not to wake. He went to the bathroom, not at first remembering what had happened in his middle-of-the-night haze. When he did remember, he felt again that nauseous fear, as if he had been caught doing something terrible, inexcusable. He threw up in the toilet once, then dry heaved a second time. Calming down over fifteen minutes, he washed his mouth and then brushed his teeth and went back to bed. Abigail, who had woken up, said, "Are you okay, baby?"

"Yeah."

"Spoon me?"

"Okay," he said, and held her as the outer spoon and went to sleep listening to her breathe, and as he drifted off he had the thought that maybe she had seen him after all and didn't like him as he was so she had broken him as if to remold him and that's like not-seeing, like being able to see someone but deciding not to see them.

The next morning Abi was again asleep when Herbie knocked on their door so quietly Bar barely heard though he was in the kitchen right next to it. Herbie had something to show Bar, he said apologetic, not wanting to take up Bar's time, but it might be important. He led Bar up to the second floor apartment and unlocked the door to the hall, saying that he would be right back and that Bar should wait. Bar could see through the half-open door that the apartment also had its kitchen near the entrance, of course, but that the visible part of the apartment was full of paintings and sculptures. He moved to one side to get more of a view; everywhere in that apartment, there were artworks stacked, leaning and hanging. Herbie re-appeared with a page torn out of a 16x20 sketchbook. Bar immediately recognized it as one of his own. It was a portrait he had done of Stacey during the summer. It should have been in a sketchbook full of portraits of her that Bar had in his apartment.

"I am truly sorry," Herbie said, handing it to Bar.

"What's going on? You're going into my place and taking..."

Herbie held up one hand, stopping him. "No, my goodness, no. I see that you do not know."

"No, I don't." In anger, Bar said, "I'm going to tell Sharpey that..."

"Please," Herbie implored. "All of the work in this place," he said, gesturing back behind himself, "has been put here by Eli. Sharpey as you call him."

Bar was confused and alarmed. Sharped was going through his things?

Herbie said, "This piece, which is quite good, I might add, though not as good as the other I have seen, I mean in the light. I would suggest..."

"What the fuck is going on?"

"Yes, yes. Sharpey purchased this drawing for the usual price."

"No, he didn't."

Herbie cleared his throat. "Perhaps not from you."

Bar looked at him, still not catching on.

Herbie said, "Perhaps you would speak with the young lady. Abigail. I must go. I'm sorry. I have violated my trust in telling you this. But I thought, perhaps he..." Herbert shrugged. "Speak to the young lady," he said and retreated in the storage room, slowly closing the door. Bar heard him repeat "I'm very sorry," after the door was closed.

"You're the passive type," she says to me, kissing my neck. "You absorb." I'm half-tempted to go with her, so strong is her hold on me, her personal power, but that hold was broken long ago by my experience of its results, and by my anger. I speak firmly, at a low volume, right in her ear. "While I appreciate your desire to open my sexual horizons, I do not consent to watching you allow yourself to become a pawn in an unspoken power play between Art and me. I don't want to watch. Do you follow? I'm not going..."

"ARRRRRRT!" she screams, hurting her vocal cords. "WHAT HAVE YOU DONE! YOU TOLD HIM! HOW COULD YOU...!"

Art protests, "No, baby, baby, I didn't. I swear on Satan and Lucifer and the Devil. I don't understand..."

"You didn't tell him?"

"No. Why would I? Baby,..." He tries to take her other arm, but Abi wriggles free of us both.

"You want to fuck him yourself! You want too much, Artifice. Arto."

"No, no. My man Bar is straight. Baby, I didn't..."

Abi takes a step back from us, her men, looking from one to the other and back. "I don't get what's going on."

"I know the feeling," I say. I should've extricated myself from their little plan more gently, without revealing that I knew about it. Called in sick, said he has to go to the hospital, or his mommy's house, or whatever. But the memory, called up this way, making me mad, and now I've done it.

"There's something wrong with you," Abi says to me finally. "When I said I wanted to open you up, that's not what I meant. I meant ... I don't think you can understand what I meant." She goes to Art and says, "I want you to take me home."

"You're too fast. I can't go that fast," I say.

"What the fuck does that mean?"

"You're Achilles. You chose the live fast, die young path. After a long time, I might've caught up with you."

"'Enough!'" she screams, "'Or too much!'" Her eyes practically pop out of her head. Yes, I was scared of her. She was way too much for me.

"'Everybody thinks that Hell's the hippest way to go. I don't really think so,'" I sing to her.

"'But I'm gonna take a look around.' Joni Mitchell said she's gonna take a look around, Bar. Can't you take a look?" She suddenly jumps to me and hugs me again but I leave my arms at my sides.

"Hey." I hadn't known in advance when the palimpsest would hit. When it does, the only thing keeping me standing is Abigail's arms hugging me like a boa constrictor. I feel my former self's sickness at what I saw then and in a confusing full-circling I felt jealous of the confidence that I, in my present self, now have, as if from the other point of view. It ends.

Abi says in my ear, "Please. Baby, baby."

"Please right back. Please."

Art says, "Let him go, sweet, sweet girl."

"Okay," she says, releasing me.

###

Bar stood still. "Stop. Art has AIDS, Abi." He saw her whirl again toward him, her eyes flit from side to side in panic. "It's true, Abi."

In a last bit of coke-rage, she turned back toward him and hissed, "Don't you think I know that?"

She stormed off as the men followed. Bar calculated how many times, back in Life One, two decades ago for him, he had sex with her after she had intentionally exposed herself to Art's disease. Which was when? When he saw it, or before that?

In Life Two, the men trailed Abi back to the Sharpey apartment, though every now and then Abi turned and hissed at Bar that he should go somewhere else. "I'm keeping the apartment," she said, having already leaped to the next thing.

"Yeah." Bar said on Avenue A and Third Street. "But I'm buying the building," he said under his breath, though Art heard him and raised his eyebrows.

She turned and ran at Bar, hitting him on the chest with fists that were more effectual than he expected. "Why the fuck are you following us? Who even are you?"

"I'm going to get my things. I won't stay." Staying was the last thing he wanted. He was deciding that he did not like this person, artificially stimulated and in possession of a plan for him without his consent.

She glared at him, then ignored him. All three went into the apartment. Bar packed his panniers in silence, mostly with drawings, leaving the bulk of his clothing behind. He put the panniers on his bike and said goodbye to Abi as she sat in the kitchen with Art. Art nodded to Bar with the slightest smirk. Abi turned away. Bar thought, you can have each other.

He put his hand on the door to leave, the other hand pushing his handlebars. Abi said, to his back, "You're a pussy."

Bar turned. He heard himself say, Don't engage with that; be the adult. But he said, "There's nothing so necessarily horrific about your ... idea. Except for the AIDS part. Yeah, that was horrific. You can have this nihilist fuck you sideways if you want but why not use a condom?"

Abi looked cooly at him and said, "Without danger, without risk, there's no life, no art. You can't know what it's like for someone else unless you take their risk. I was going to show you something but you're going to be a boy forever."

"If you get AIDS, you'll die. You won't have a forever."

"Yeah, sure," she said, "no do-overs. No backsies. Boy."

"You weren't going to give me something. You were going to take. And this guy? Your 'friend'? Art, how can you...?"

"You'll never understand," he said. And to Bar, "that's your blindness."

As Bar was wheeling his bicycle into the hallway, Herbie whispered to him from the floor above, and Bar remembered what was on his mind.

"I have something I feel that I must show you, my good man."

"I know about it, Herbie. Thank you. My picture of Stacey. I know. I know that Abi traded Sharpey for coke or heroin or whatever she got for it. Don't worry about it."

"I am so sorry to have disturbed you. Please do ride carefully in the dark. The drivers are not to be trusted to see folks of our complexion. The world is so very harsh."

"Yeah. But I'm going to take care of you, Herbert."

"Oh, uh, whatever do you mean?" he asked, coming out fully onto the hallway.

"I can't say yet. But I will. I have to go. We'll talk."

He left, and as he biked to First Avenue and passed the nearest functional payphone, not stopping, he remembered leaving her in the first life, calling Jon and asking to stay in his dorm, and Jon's father helping him get the then nearly worthless, ghetto/crack-neighborhood apartment on 135th Street, and not talking with Abigail for a year, blaming her for being expelled from Cooper, yet not applying to any other school, getting the job at the bike shop, burying himself in drawing, drawing, drawing, drawing, and withdrawing. I got really good, doing that, he thought, and thought as well, You're not to mourn for your life, given that you have this chance that no one else returns to have. You're to fix things. You fixed one thing just now.

This time, instead of calling Jon, Bar rode over to the Chelsea Hotel on 23rd, where he put a credit card on the hotel desk and got himself a quiet room.

7. A Time to Break Down and a Time to Build Up

In Life One, the first work that Bar saw of Abigail's, in the E.V. (East Village) Gallery and Club was a series of "Studies," eight-by-ten inch canvasses of one or two figures each in the same style, carefully underdrawn, the paint pushed thick, the swirls of acrylics sculptural. Bar recognized some of the other figures from the club: the waitress whom Abi chose to portray in riotous colors, from behind, showing off her provocative hip-jut in purple stockings, tight orange skirt, tactically ripped red tank, and over-the-shoulder smirk; the bartender, drawn from below, looming over the bar, dour expression with a hint of not taking himself seriously, in a black t-shirt with rolled-up sleeves showing his muscles and a jaunty fedora. One in particular stood out: a portrait of a wide-grinning Mad Hatter sort of person in a white top hat, white tux (with tails), white tie, and white shoes. It was painted with varying shades of white and gray, with the underdrawing visible in places giving an unfinished feeling that, along with the wide-angle lens effect of a big head and small body, looking from above, matched the feeling of the out-of-control borderline-hideous grin.

That one was the most dramatic but not the most important to her. There was a small portrait done in oils in a realistic and therefore, for Abi, juvenile style, her student style, of a sixteen-year-old boy. His insouciant face was off-putting at first and after a good stare gave the viewer the creeps. He was good-looking in a conventional American way, blond with a square jaw that jutted out. Bar did stare at all of the paintings and because he asked about this one, she told him who he was.

"I was just a kid. I hung with James and Errol and Michael and Stephan, not 'stee-ven,' but 'steh-fahn,' who was from Austria. The other three's dads were townies, auto garage and mailman and Mike's dad was a sergeant, and Stephan and I were army brats like Mikey but not like Mikey because our dads were the profs and my dad was, is a colonel. I didn't hang with girls. The five of us were a crew and when we got into a fight, I fought, and when James got a four-by-four he and I took turns cutting up the football field. I played baseball on the boys' team in high school – I was the shortstop – until someone in the league said I couldn't and then my dad made trouble about it but didn't get anywhere. I refused to play girls' softball even though it was fast pitch and in retrospect what was I so angry about, but I didn't think of softball as the real thing.

Stephan did pottery and sculpture in the art class even though the other guys gave him shit for it and I painted on the other side of the studio. He had this stuck up way of looking at you like he's a European and knows shit you'll never know but we had a thing between us – he knew that I knew he wasn't some European sophisticate, that he had lived in D.C. before Upstate New York, not Austria, and that the arrogant thing was a way of having some social power in a strange place. I painted that while he was throwing a pot. I like that picture. It gets some of his twisted conflicts as a person.

Stephan and I were close but not like girls. We didn't gossip or talk about feelings. We had beers that his brother got for him outside, in the woods near school after studio but we never kissed and he never tried anything even when we stripped to swim in the lake together, though I saw he was looking.

I knew Mike wanted to ask me to the prom and I wasn't having it so I asked Stephan and afterwards he took me to the woods we'd been to a hundred times so I didn't see it coming, plus I was drunk, but I had enough sobriety to see him looking at me with that I'm-the-shit look like in the painting and I knew that he was going to try to jump me so I went first. I grabbed his head and kissed him and we had sex and that way I was able to tell myself he never raped me, no one ever did, even though I didn't want to. I got blood all over my white dress so we went to the lake and I went home in a wet dress.

When I left for New York I didn't tell Stephen I was leaving. He figured out where I was in a few months and sent me a postcard that I threw out as soon as I saw who it was from. I heard he was in New York and based on that painting Art thought he saw Stephan in Pyramid seeing drag but who knows if it was him."

Life One:
November 8, 1986, fourteen days after his father's death.

They heard a shout from the street. Abigail, sitting on the folding wooden chair, the one they found on the street that had wobbled because it was a missing crossbar, held Bar's head to her chest as he kneeled in front of her. "Baby, baby, baby," she cooed, stroking his hair with her thin fingers, her rings sometimes catching in his tight curls. "I'm so glad you're home." She hugged his head for a moment. "We need to do something. Your old man really had his hooks into you."

"Yeah."

"We need to get your mind off it."

"Yeah."

They had slept in the same bed almost nightly since the beginning of September, since the night he went to the club where she bartended and took her home and after that she had not spent another night in her own apartment, both preferring the proximity of one another's bodies. Even during the shiva when she spent two nights alone because of her work and his need to observe the strict rule of staying "home" in what was now Claudia's place, she stayed in what was now their shared flat. The sex at first had been what she called "standard operating procedure": him on top, and then she touched herself after while he played with her body, assisting her. Since then, always at her direction, they did other things. She was a year older and had had experiences, other men. The last weeks, before the shiva, she had ended up on top; she was able to finish that way before he did. It struck him that he was merely assisting in that position just as much as in s.o.p., the difference being the order of events. This night, the first after the shiva that he spent back in this apartment, resumed that pattern. He felt limp as she began kissing him, but warmed into it. She undressed them both.

She lay on him, both of them breathing, him feeling her smooth skin and she kissing his neck. Before Abi, Bar had touched Stacey but it wasn't sex-sex. He had sex, once, with Kristina, a total fluke, a lucky break not to be repeated. Stacey was up at Binghamton and Kristina was a twenty-two-year-old tennis pro who didn't return his phone calls when he tried calling her. Bar breathed and held this woman who wanted him as much as he wanted her and considered it a miracle.

They heard the shouts again. Had it been going on the whole time? Bar imagined his desire blocking out any sound.

The apartment had no buzzer. The nearest non-vandalized payphone was not near. They were in the bedroom, which was in the back of the whole-floor, twenty-by-fifty foot apartment. Any shouts from the street had to travel around the building to the brick rubble yard in the back, and up into the window. That is what was happening: "Abigail!" is what they heard.

The bedroom featured the chair, a mattress on a platform Bar constructed from plywood and two-by-fours that stood three inches off the ancient, warped hardwood flooring, a large home-made easel holding a twenty-by-twenty-four inch sketchpad, a stolen rolling clothing rack holding mostly Abigail's things, and an eight foot long by three foot high pine shelf, also made by Bar, holding mostly his clothes, as well as his school books and a few art odds and ends: pencils, ink bottles, compasses, french curves, etcetera. Two big wood-frame windows looked out onto an empty lot behind the building, or rather a lot full of bricks and other rubble, and then a hundred yards away a row of five tenements. In the other direction was the paint-peeling wooden door leading to the hall, bathroom and kitchen in the middle of *the building, and the front room on the other end where the door to the outer hallway was secured with three different kinds of deadbolts and a floor-propped "police" lock. The building stood alone in the middle of a block in the East Village, not on the corner and yet no building on either side, on 3rd Street between Avenues B and C. Alphabet City, a part of the city that emptied out when the real estate powers of the 1960s intentionally replaced the huge manufacturing infrastructure with office space that would remain underused until the 2000s, and because of this catastrophic and selfish choice, reducing the population of New York from eight to seven million, leaving neighborhoods like this one, Red Hook in Brooklyn, the South Bronx, and others, depopulated, dangerous, and worthless to their owners. Only drug dealers, poor people, fools, and artists lived in places like this. Some of the residents qualified in all four categories. Bar moved in to this apartment upon starting The Cooper Union School of Art, half a mile to the west, a world away, in the midst of civilization, not in this burnt-out, bombed-out, rubble-strewn wasteland. He found it by cycling around the neighborhood in search of housing cheaper than the stuff near NYU, and found Sharpey, the building's owner, sitting on the stoop feeding milk to his cat.*

She pushed herself off of him. He took off the condom, then covered himself, curling up. "Come back," he said.

They could hear a mandolin playing above them. It sounded like an aire from the sixteenth century.

"I called Art," she said, pulling on her clothes. "He's going to bring some cans."

"Cans?" Bar flinched at the mention of Art's name. Of her friends, the oddballs, painters, musicians (punk and non-), sculptors, dilettantes, beau brummels, gay men, writers, lesbians, drag queens, and hangers-on, he was not Bar's favorite.

"We're going to go out. I mean, let's go out? Huh? Let's go. It's a nice night. A big world. I'm know you hurt, baby. I know."

"Go out for what? There's a lot of food in the fridge. I don't want to go to E.V. Let's just lie here. Look, we can see stars."

"No, no not that. No people. Except you, me, and Art."

"Art is the devil."

"Don't say that," she scolded, mock-hitting his head. "He's my,... our friend. What's your problem with him, anyway?"

"Mostly the militant archness. The inability to express anything sincerely, ever. The distancing from oneself and everyone around. Not knowing who he is."

"He's only joking."

"That's what I mean." She took his head in her hands and turned it to kiss him. He kissed her back and pulled on her, but she didn't come back into the bed.

Bar dreaded Art's arrival but did not think it meant anything terrible would happen. It only presaged feeling like he was the friend and they were the couple, and feeling as if there were jokes he wasn't in on. If Art weren't gay he would let his jealousy have a voice. Being gay, Art precluded complaints on that score but Bar felt that Art was exploiting a technicality, somehow, and that Abi was closer to him than she could ever be with Bar or with any merely heterosexual boyfriend. It had something to do with the way she seemed to see, or not see him as opposed to how she did the same with Art.

But then he remembered, "Oh yeah, Abi, how come one of my drawings was up in Sharpey's art storage? Herbie told me about it. It's a picture I made of Stacey, you know, my high school girlfriend?"

"I don't know what you're talking about. How come you're asking me?"

"Herbie said, 'ask the young lady.' He meant you."

"He's full of shit. He's not English, you know."

"Yeah, but…"

There was the shout again. The mandolin music stopped while Sharpey banged on the pipe to express his displeasure. "Satan hath arrived," Bar said, disappointed. He got up and went to the bathroom and got dressed.

"I'll let him in," Abi said. Art appeared outside the bathroom as Bar emerged. Art was holding a beat-up guitar case.

"Dude. I am truly sorry." Art's voice was another thing: peculiarly grating, a combination of whiny, nasal, and rich-boy, though that last was wholly put on. Art's artistic output sold enough for him to keep an apartment and not otherwise work, but he came, as he loved to tell anyone who would listen, from "Alabama trash," a blond man drawn to the mecca of culture and away from the locus of homophobia that he had survived, irresistibly at seventeen, the day after high school graduation. Abigail was similar, fleeing her West Point professor-dad's house upstate practically still wearing her mortarboard hat. Both of them were more or less self-taught artists, he successful, she perhaps "up and coming," her work known solely among their wide circle of friends. Only Bar was in the process of being formally trained. It was part of Art's annoying quality that he could effect a bohemian stance while also owning a huge loft on Rivington street, right next to the old Streit's Matzoh factory. Art was the only artist Bar knew whose work sold well but who hung out with artists who weren't invited to the cocktail parties that he was. But then, Bar didn't know that many artists.

Art made an elaborate flourish with his right hand going in circles as he slowly bowed to Bar. Bar had seen him do this many times before. This time it seemed not wholly arch, but Bar was wary. It was theoretically possible that Art could no longer do anything with zero arch.

"Thanks," Bar said, noting that it was a nice night, still. They went up. "I didn't know you played," Bar said by way of asking about the guitar.

"Oh, no, no, no," Art said, without elaborating.

Abigail, who had changed from her white t-shirt into a yellow dress, short-sleeved, with buttons from the scoop neck to the hem at her knees, her leggings underneath, set off Art, who Bar now noticed was in all black. "I thought you liked white?" Bar asked him. Art was wearing black Converse sneakers with the logo painted black, black Indian pants, a black linen shirt, and a black wool hat, despite 60 degree temperature, and wore a black messenger bag across a shoulder. On second look, Bar saw that the hat was a folded ski mask. "Is this," Bar added, "going to be a party or a bank robbery?" Abi was right; Art was a distraction. He was rubbing his hands together, another affected movement he did often. Rubbing his hands obsessively and chuckling to himself disconcertingly.

"What," Art began, "is a party without some crime to add spice, to enliven?"

"We're going bombing." Abi stated, excited. She rubbed her hands together in sympathy, but she more like a child anticipating a treat.

Art opened the messenger bag to reveal a full palette of spray cans. He grinned broadly. "I thought, my lady, that we might leave our marks, not on one of these local hulking buildings that so many have marked before, but on a moving target."

"Do tell," she said.

Art outlined a plan to spray paint some garbage trucks penned nearby behind chain-link fencing in a Sanitation department lot.

"This is stupid," Bar said. "We'll get caught."

"Ah, but I've done it before," Art said blithely. Though he answered Bar, he did not bother looking at him. Art and Abigail shared eyes. The main problem of Art's presence was the close connection, near sexual, though that seemed impossible, given Art's predilections, between the two of them. It was as if they were both the same magnetic pole, yet trying to touch.

"All the more reason we'll be caught," Bar said. "After all those people bombed the trains in the yards," Bar went on, "the City put up two circles of barbed-wire-topped fences with dogs running between."

"They have failed to do so here, however," Art said with determined joyfulness.

"Graffiti is ugly," Bar said. "It's always ugly, done in a hurry."

"Nay, young squire," Art said. He was, like Abi, a year older than Bar. *"Take heart. We artists must remind the people of what is ugly as well as what is beautiful in this fair city. Let the city be our theater of courage. The art I make for sale is but one kind, the collectors fooling themselves of its permanence. But art is ephemeral. All is vanity. We are all ephemera, you see, flotsam, garbage."* As he said this, he looked nervously at Bar and added quickly, *"As I install my gossamer works, an important part of oeuvre, I embrace the warmth of my own eventual demise. Mine is the theater of desperate courage. I quite like the ring of that. We live in times of unquiet desperation."*

Bar, momentarily stunned back into thinking of his father, gave Abigail a look that sunk her heart.

"Come on, I'm totally ready," she said quietly, after a brief moment's pause. She looked at Bar as if to ask if he were up to going.

"Totally," Art said.

"And utterly," she said to Art. "You have any pick-me-up?"

"But of course," Art said, pouring white powder from the box into lines on a hand mirror he produced.

"I'm not doing that," Bar said.

Abigail went to him, kissed him, and said, "You don't have to. You don't mind if I do, do you?"

"Uh,..."

She looked at him imploringly, smiled, and, accepting the coke from Art, tipped her head down to snort. "Whew! Good shit, baby," she said to Art, and kissed him full on his mouth, re-confusing and worrying Bar.

"I adore thee," Art said, giving her a flourish before deftly vacuuming the other line into his nose, pinky in the air.

Art went through the door, then Abigail, and Bar, grabbing his black leather jacket, followed them, locking the door.

They walked east, past the Christadora on B, recently renovated for very intrepid yuppies, and Art made a point of spitting on it, past dead buildings that seemed to peer out through broken windows and that seemed as if no one would ever be so foolish as to renovate and renew, and past the public housing whose residents would have chosen to live almost anywhere else. Underneath the Franklin Delano Roosevelt Drive, a long row of white garbage trucks sat like elephants behind a single chain-link fence. Bar saw that the fence was topped with barbed wire, an image that always made Bar think of 1944.

"You know where the break is?" Abi asked.

"Never in the same place. They fixed that one after last time," he said. They walked, Art looking around every so often.

Under the dark shade of a broken streetlamp, Art opened the guitar case and took out long, commercial-grade bolt cutters. The fence yielded easily to the tool, allowing Art to pull an impromptu triangular piece open with some effort.

"You see," he whispered, though they were completely alone for a hundred yards in every direction, "Their invitation."

"The City just doesn't maintain the fence," Bar said.

"The magic is to understand that there is no City," Art said. "There is no civilization. There's nothing. Look around. Garbage trucks in the garbage town. We're going to decorate the end of time itself."

"This seems like a bad idea." Bar said.

"Come on, Bar, let's stick it to the man," Abi said.

"Man's gonna stick it to us."

"There is no man," Art said, sarcastically emphasizing 'man.'

"Don't wuss out," she said. "I'm, like, vibrating. I want to fuck and fuck and fuck and fuck!"

"Yes, my dear," Art said, "but do fuck at a lower volume." That last calmed Bar slightly; suggesting that Art's concern about being caught wasn't nothing.

"What's this for? I mean, how does this stick it to anyone, exactly?"

"Why can't you be cool?" Abi asked, frowning at him.

Art, then Abi went in. Bar heard a dog barking at some distance and unknown direction. Seeing Art and Abi on the other side of the fence, he imagined them about to be attacked by German shepherds being led by SS officers. He also felt as if he were on someone else's date. Bar forced himself to go through. He remembered the feeling he had when he was ten, watching a friend shop-lift candy from a newspaper and cigarette store. He felt horny for Abi, not having seen her in two days, and when she had come to the shiva, they hadn't done it.

Art bent the 'door' closed to hide it.

One of the big white trucks was parked past the line of others, this elephant a peaceful one. Art pointed to it and handed Abi two cans of spray paint, red and blue. He gave Bar a can of black, and took an array of colors for himself.

As they approached the truck, Bar kept searching for cops. The trucks' smell had been masked in the cool air, but up close it hit them: New York's Most Pungent.

Art sprayed a whole scene on the truck. Bar watched as it gradually took shape: a cartoonish man with eyes literally popping out of his head, connected by tubes to his eye sockets, looking behind his head. He admired Art's technique with the spray can, angling it and controlling its distance from the side of the truck to vary the width of his line. He was forced to admit to himself again that Art could, in fact, draw. What he was making was ugly but despite what he had said in the apartment or maybe because of it, ugly in a highly controlled way. It was fascinating, compelling, perhaps all the more so because Bar was seeing it come into life. The figure was hideous with anxiety, like the sculpture of Ugolino by Carpeaux at the Met, but dressed in an exaggerated business suit. Art drew in carefully readable letters below this figure, "YOU." He then began a new figure that quickly took shape as a black-robed Death, complete with sickle. Below that, Art wrote, "AIDS."

The whole thing, Bar thought, was an elaborate, illegal public service ad.

Abi tugged his sleeve and they went to the other side of the truck. She began spraying a three-foot diameter portrait of Bar. He went back to Art's side and took a can labeled "flesh tone." He went back and painted a portrait of Abigail, hair yellow, eyes bright blue.

Bar yell-whispered, "You done?!" He wanted to leave.

Abi yell-whispered back, "Yeah!"

They went back to where Art was spraying another truck. It was another two-figure: Koch and Reagan, the President sodomizing the Mayor. Art was in more of a hurry with this one, so it was less artistically impressive as art, Bar thought, but the effect would be quite clear.

They tossed their empty cans in the maw of that garbage truck itself. Art took out a small camera with an elaborate flash on top.

"Go to the 'door' and pull it open," he said.

"Don't fire that flash," Bar hissed.

"Go, go. I'm coming."

Bar pulled the fence and he and Abi walked across the street to wait. Art documented their evening's work with the camera, lightning bolt after lightning bolt, the flash filling the whole area. What an asshole, Bar thought, angry at both of them. He could've used a tripod and a long exposure.

When they heard the police siren, Bar's heart sank, but he took off down the street. He turned and saw that Abi had frozen waiting for Art as he came skittering on the gravel to the pulled fence. Bar turned and went back, frustrated, pulling on her arm just as the police car pulled over on the other side of the yard. "Hey, you, stop, POLICE!" One cop chased Art south. Abi and Bar ran north. The one chasing them kept yelling, "Stop! Stop!" as he ran through the sanitation yard right at them. Abi's bright dress caught Bar's eye as she ran and he understood that though she might be fast enough in her sneakers, they wouldn't get all the way to the apartment with that cop not seeing where they went, and she couldn't melt into a crowd. The lights of a deli on the corner at the end of the block appeared as they rounded a corner. On the other side of the street from the deli, a line of people waited to get into a tenement. Getting to the end f the block, Bar made a sudden move to pull Abi inside the deli. He took her to the back between rows of dusty canned food and house cleaner and pulled off his jacket, then his red shirt, giving it to her. "What do you want me to...?" she asked as he tugged off her dress. She stood in the florescent light in her leggings, topless, hugging herself. "Come on! Put on the shirt, c'mon, c'mon, c'mon." She did. He put his jacket back on over his skin and took the dress, which he rolled up and shoved under his left arm inside the jacket.

"You go home," he said. "And walk slow. Like nothing happened. Here's the key." He bought a banana for a quarter, mostly to get the bag. He put the dress in it and briskly walked across the street and joined the queue, his leather jacket rubbing uncomfortably. The cop that had been looking for them walked right by, talking into his walkie, "Naw, they're gone. Yeah, one's a Black fella ... I dunno. No, it's just junkies out there." Bar looked away from him; he felt the fear rise in his throat. They think he was Black. What use would it be to explain his Yemenite background as they took out their sticks? But maybe it was helping. "A car or somethin'? ... Fuck off ... There's gotta be a hundred Blackies ... naw, naw. I'm coming back." Bar kept his face toward the wall, not sure if his shaking from the fear made him more convincing. When the cop was gone, Bar went back into the deli, and bought a six-pack. He kept thinking that they had almost been caught. No, just he had almost been caught. But that was because he saved her. But also because Art took care of himself. But also ... he mind drifted to whether he'd have been thrown out of school and whether his mother would've gotten him a lawyer, and he'd be ignorant of how to deal

with the cops. Would he have gone to Rikers? He heard a lot of bad shit about the jails. At least he saved Abi.

When he got to the vestibule, he heard their laughter and it made him angrier. The beer he bought would not be needed; Abi and Art were sharing the bottle of wine in the kitchen that Bar had been saving. Art nodded and Abi smiled at Bar when he walked in. She was still in his t-shirt, sitting on his high drafting stool with her left leg dangling and her right foot up on the seat. "Come here and kiss me."

"I thought you liked kissing Art."

"Mmmm," she said, kissing him and pulling the lapels of his jacket to her. "I do like kissing him, but let's face it. I need a real man. Hey, what's wrong?"

"I am a real man, my dear," Art said in his nasal voice. He was chuckling to himself in waves of more and less control. "I'd love to show how real. To Bar."

"Fuck you. That was a lot of shit," Bar said, "firing that flash." He took off his jacket and was now shirtless. "And then taking off. First you put us all in fucking danger, and then …

"Mmm, my, my my, ha ha ha," Art said, trying to stifles his laughs, as usual speaking to Abi as he made as if he were checking out Bar's physique. "He does have an athleticism. I'm sure you enjoy that, dear. Hmm ha."

"And you look like shit," Bar said to him.

"I know. Ha, ha. No, no, he's telling the truth. I am so much reduced of late!" He laughed hard until he struggled to breathe.

Abi let a look of concern cross her face. "Hey, baby." She kissed the side of his face and felt his hair. "You had a bad time? We got out alright. I'd've protected you from the big bad cops."

Wordless, he walked to the back room and came back with one of her black t-shirts. "Can I have my shirt back? I'm cold," he said.

Abi laughed and took off the shirt casually and put on her own.

"Art and I had a blast!" she said. "Enough, or too much! Experience! Puissance! Esperance! Let's go out again!" She seemed artificially pumped, inexplicably exuberant. She and Art both.

"You didn't almost get arrested," he said drily.

"Of course we all did," Art said, laughing. "That was an essential element. Were there no danger, it would not have been worth doing."

Bar walked over to the stand by the front window, not drinking the glass of wine in his right hand. Bar felt a wave that combined exhaustion and grief with guiltiness at feeling that he had, in fact, had fun. He broke it down: he wanted to be with Abi then he wanted to see what the bombing was about and then he wanted to see Art paint, then he wanted to protect Abi and himself. Yeah, but it was a ride. Then he felt goosebumps as he thought, I'm having thrills while my father is still dead?

Abi went over to him and stroked his hair. Her hand shook. "You're still coked," he said.

"Yeah. Art's gonna take us to the docks. River to river, baby! The night's young!" She laughed. Her eyes were bloodshot.

"What's at..."

"It's what I've been wanting to show you. Trust me, baby. I love you. Let's go!" she said, and began performing ballet moves around the mostly empty room. She did an arabesque, and tried to make it into a penchée, almost fell, and went into a series of constricted pas de chats. She smiled; she laughed. The laughing temporarily stopped the dance moves: loud, raucous laughter at no specific joke. She did a twirl and showed him a half-possessed smile. She ran into the bedroom and re-appeared almost as quickly in black jeans.

He knew he would have to go. He would have to protect her from whatever she was planning and simply from herself in that state and from the City at night. But that wasn't the only reason; he wanted to go with her. He wanted the next thrill ride, too, just not as much as they did. He let himself get caught in her excitement. He let her push the accelerator.

They all popped out of the apartment as if thrust out. They walked due west, not stopping for cars. Art and Abi speed walked, laughing as they went, competing to be in front. Bar ran to keep up and made apologetic signs to cars to stop instead of running them over. They passed through Washington Square Park and the hustlers whisper-hawking their wide-ranging drug choices. Bar shuddered seeing a sallow kid, maybe sixteen, looking hollow-eyed and despondent. Abi picked up her pace even more.

"Where are we going?" he asked as they sped up to half walking, half running.

"The doh-ocks," Art said, half whining and half speaking as if to an annoying child. Abi started humming, "Mmmmmm-iiiiinnnnng."

When they got near the Hudson River, they had to walk along the highway to get access to a long warehouse on wooden piers that jutted out over the river: The docks. Broken windows, broken glass on the ground, twisted pieces of metal, shards of truck tires, petrified dog shit, garbage, clothing, papers. Large sheets of corrugated metal hung listless off the decrepit structure. "We're going in there?" Bar asked.

"Come on!" She pulled his hand, running now across the highway during a micro-lull in the traffic. She led him onto the rotting pier. Bar imagined the ghosts of dock workers past, hauling barrels and pulling ropes on pulleys leading to huge wood crates.

Abigail pulled his hand, following Art into the dark, cavernous building. Almost immediately they saw movement in the dark corners and heard grunts and whispers. Art walked off and disappeared into a thick gloom.

"Abi, what…"

"Shh. Here." Even in the dark of the building, he saw glints of light reflected in her eyes as she led him to a part of the wall that had a body-sized hole in it, letting in a sliver of moonlight and light reflected from the highway street lamps. Bar's eyes got used to the darkness. He saw a human body bent over another, not fifteen feet away. Skittering sounds that could have been humans or rats. Dirt, and garbage. Smells of piss, tar, rot. Grunts and moans.

Abi pulled him close and kissed him. He responded, confused. Her kissing was insistent and clear.

Why did she want to come here to kiss when they could do that at home? Yet the kissing had its effect, melting his anxious disgust and zoning him into her, only her. She loved him, and he her, and they should go home, but was that apartment their home? They'd only lived there a few months.

Yet, that was where she ... He almost couldn't say what she had done. The kissing spell melted. With Art. She had done that. Here, in this dank, damp place with groaning people doing all sorts of things they, too, should have been doing at home, he let himself think of it again. How could the place where she had done that with him *be their home?*

"You let me take you here," Abi said whispering, smiling, triumphant, significantly. She felt for the front of his pants.

"Yeah. Why...? We came here, great. Let's leave. I'm hungry. Let's go get something at the Kiev..."

"Your beauty lies in passive observation," she said, touching his body. "You see things; you take them in; absorb." She dragged out that word. "Abzzzzooooorb-uh." She kissed him again, as if to stop his reply. She was shivering, though it wasn't cold, even in this dank place. "Your art is about that. The rays of light enter your body and come out your hand. I don't know how you do that. Be so passive, so open. It's cool, Bar."

"Uh-huh."

"I want to show you something," she said, fostering his erection. But it wasn't only his cock that made him stay. He thought about what she was doing now and why and understood before she began and knew he faced a fork right now and had to choose right now to stay and let her take him on this sexual ride or leave and they'd maybe not be together any more and then it wouldn't be home, not to both of them, and just then, holding him, she kissed him again and he stayed with her, chose that side, because otherwise he would have to leave. It was becoming clear he'd have to do this thing, get on the roller-coaster whether he wanted to or not because that was how she lived. After this thing, he though, he could stop, talk with her, but she was pushing now and he let her push. He couldn't observe or draw or be on the side of this. She was kissing him and squeezing his dick and he was in the middle of it.

"It's guys ..." She stopped his mouth with her tongue. She put her finger over his lips.

"I know," she said. She pulled down his pants and took him in her mouth but quickly stood, using one hand to maintain him, the other to find condom in her bag and she put the condom on him and reached into her bag for lotion and she smeared him on his condom and pulled down her pants and bent over. "Push," she hissed. "No, not there. There." She stifled a cry as he did as he was told. She braced herself against the rotting wood in front of her, her breath sharply going in as he moved.

He fucked her hard because if he were gentle he'd stop and think and might not be able to start again so he pushed and she laughed and that made him push harder, with anger.

"You like it?" she hissed loudly.

"Yeah," a guy's baritone voice laughed from somewhere in the dark. "You like it, honey?"

"Shut up, Frank," said another man's voice from the same general direction.

On an out stroke, she reached back and gently pushed him from her. She pulled off his condom and tossed it. He heard it plop in water. She pushed him down in front of her; she tasted wetter than he would have thought. She grabbed his hair hard, pulling him up, holding him away from her, confusing him. "Wait," she said, and took a small metal container out of her bag. She crouched. She made a line on her thigh and handed him a little metal pipe. "Do it," she said.

"Is this what you wanted to show me?"

"Experience. Let me take you there, Bar," she said, smiling luridly in the moon glow coming through the jagged window glass. "Do it," she repeated.

It felt like he was exorcising a demon but didn't understand that her name was Abigail and she was there right next to him. He thought he could punch through to the other side of something but instead he was widening a hole in himself, an emptiness that Abigail had exposed the other night, an inability to receive the inputs, a desire for less experience, not more. He had thought he loved her but there was a difference between loving a person who doesn't exist and loving the actual person and when the delusion is exploded and it turns out that the object of his love didn't exist, he would suffer. She wasn't a nice girl whom he love, who happened to want desperately to learn things; she was closer to a mushroom cloud in a film run backward. She was self-immolating. She needed to implode the person who didn't yet have that experience whether that was her present self, or him. In wanting them both to become someone else, in forcing through that change, she succeeded, but if she had in mind whom they would become, she failed.

He snorted the line. She stood above him and brought him to her again by his hair. "Ow," he said and she let go. He didn't feel much of the drug at first and dared to hope it was a dud. He licked her. She finished quickly, which was unusual. The men around them ignored her sincerely voiced cries. She pulled him back up to standing, kissing and licking his face, pulling up her own pants. "Your turn," she said, grabbing his shoulders and moving him against the wall. She turned him to face the wall, guiding his hands to brace him against it, as she had done a few minutes before.

"I'm feeling it," he said.

"The coke? Good." Standing behind him, she reached around and touched him. He turned his head and looked at her. She guided his head back. His head started to feel as if it were going to explode, his body as if he had ten cups of his father's coffee. He wanted something to happen. Something. She put a condom on her finger, took the jar of goo with the other hand. He twisted around and yanked the scrunchie out of her hair. "Ow!" but she laughed. He just wanted that scrunchie to be gone. He threw it in the crack that led to the river as he felt her finger enter him. He sucked in air at the shock of being entered. "This is what I wanted to show you," she said in his ear, using both hands at once. "Passive-active," she said, moving her hand faster. When the coke hit harder, he thrust against both of her hands and screamed.

"You need me, baby. You feel that? I'm your school. You feel that?"

Bar screamed again, not words.

They race-walked back east, without Art. His ass felt pain with every step, but he didn't imagine it possible to go slowly.

"What's it like?" the demon asked him, straining to keep up with him.

"It's like ten coffees I want to fuck you again I think I can do it maybe in a minute lets go back to the...there, no let's go back to our place ... ," he his racing mind thought, I'mademontooI'mademontooI'mademontoo.

"That's where we're going, baby," she said, laughing.

He started laughing. They almost caused a checker cab to kill them as they ran across 10th Avenue together for no reason, laughing so hard through the angry horn sound that they couldn't see for the tears.

In the apartment he grabbed her but she put him off. "Let's go do a fucking crime," she said. "A CRIME!"

"Yeah, yeah, yeah, yeah, yeah, what?"

"I don't know. Let's go bombing again."

"Yeah, yeah, but not garbage trucks. No cops!"

"What do you want to hit?"

"Let's do real art let's steal some lamb or some side of beef I'm so hungry I know where they keep the meat in the basement at Cooper I'm starving you want to go steal a side of beef!"

"Yeah, that sound very cool."

She put on a black sweatshirt. He grabbed a bicycle tool kit and a canvas army duffle, and she packed a couple of one-inch wide markers in her bag.

They ran to Cooper Union, Bar showing his ID to get into the studio building, mumbling something about drawing her. He was shaking but thinking more clearly, he thought, than he had ever done in his life. It was as if he could play chess and map out ten moves in advance, or calculate the hundredth digit of Pi. He took her in the elevator up one flight to the student studios, letting the guard see that they went that way, then pulled her to the stairs and down to the basement level, where he ran ahead through the underground tunnel to the basement under the cafeteria. Quickly and carefully, with hyper focus, he unscrewed the huge hinges on the walk-in fridge, four screws, placing them carefully and in order on the side. He moved the door out of the way. "I can't fucking see," he said in a loud whisper.

"What're we doing here?" she said.

"Lamb!" In the cold walk-in fridge, he found a plastic-wrapped hunk of meat, putting it in the duffle. He quickly replaced the door and its hinges.

"What the fuck are we going to do with that?" she started one of her laughing jags, ending with a choke. He laughed along with her. "Get your head together," she said, holding his face. Then she slapped him, gently first, then harder until he stopped laughing. She took him by the hand, except she didn't know where things were. "Where's the dean's office?"

He was still chuckling. He indicated with his head. She led him. They went back to the first building and climbed the stairs to the third floor, going down the hall to the door with the plaque, "Office of the Dean of Students." The walls outside of the office had framed pictures of former deans and presidents of the Union, and on the other wall some student paintings, drawings, and photography in frames. Abigail began tagging the wall space between the art, and Bar, getting the idea, put down his burden of meat and tagged the other side. They worked quickly, frenetically, though, Bar noticed, Abigail had slowed down a lot before Bar tired. She'd done the shit earlier, he thought.

They took the elevator down to the ground floor and left. When they got home, Bar put the meat in the fridge and lunged at Abi, but she put him off again. "You'll come down soon, baby. I'm came off it a while ago. I gotta go to bed," she said. She peeled off her clothes, dropping them on the floor in the kitchen, and went to bed naked. Bar tapped nervously, feeling that he was still about the jump out of his skin, but also noticing that the jumpiness was receding.

"I need to," he said, taking out his dick.

"All right," she said, kneeling, naked. He came quickly, feeling again where her finger had lovingly violated him.

She lay down and fell asleep instantly.

By the time he was ready to crash, the dawn light on Abi's nude form had facilitated ten very good – some even great, he thought – drawings.

He woke at noon to the smell of coffee. Abi was sitting in her cutoffs and t-shirt, reading the newspaper with glasses. "Everyone who's in charge of everything's pure evil," she said.

"I didn't know you wore glasses," he said. He found himself having trouble looking her in the eye.

He looked at the first picture he had drawn of her the night before. The technique was his, but the composition sucked. It was stupid, worthless; he had given so much tension to Abigail's body that she seemed monstrous, like someone twisting herself into a corkscrew. He looked at the next one. Worse. He left two thirds of the page empty and crammed her form into the last third, pointlessly seeking big drama at the expense of her humanity. Her face in this one grimaced like the Carpeaux sculpture of Ugolino at the Met, but with no clear cause.

She smiled. "Just to read. You have a headache?"

"Pretty bad."

"Have some coffee. And water. Drink a bunch of water."

Bar took her advice. As he drank his coffee, he looked through the other drawings. Not one decent one. All that work, and he made her into one operatic figure after another.

He looked up at her, wondering if something was going to come of last night. He felt that she'd think differently of him now. How? Looking at her, and thinking about how beautiful she was, and how specific her beauty was. It was something of an escape to let himself sink into her beauty. His father hovered on the edge of his mind.

He felt wonder at the power of the drug to cause ruin.

The answering machine, located on the way back to the bathroom, blinked "4." "You didn't check the messages?" he asked.

"Huh? No."

1) "This is Dean Tavar calling for Bar Mizrachi. Please call me, even on the weekend, at the following number..."

2) Another call from the dean asking Bar to return the call "immediately."

3) A call from Bar's mother saying she received a call from the dean.

4) A call from Art. It was a long vocal missive to Abigail, meandering between self-pity and grandiosity, making obscure references to things only the two of them would remember, thoughts about his most recent art, mentions of hers, a few sentences about mutual friends from E.V., and then forty-two seconds of Art weeping, even sobbing, onto the tape. After a huge snorting sniffle, he summoned his grand voice and said, "I cannot face the ignominy of this illness. I feel my skin falling off! I've seen it and I refuse to let that be my ending! I don't think I ever loved anyone else but you, my dear! This. Is. Goodbye!!"

Abigail, who had been crying herself since the middle of Art's eight-minute oratory, now jumped up, put on sneakers, and fled the apartment. Bar called the police, but it took some time to get through, by which time Abigial had gone and Bar realized two things: he did not know Art's address, and he didn't care.

He called the number the dean had left for him. As the dean explained the certainty of his guilt, the guard having remembered the only entrant the previous night, the consequences of his actions, and her own shock at the childishness of what he had done, Bar felt detached from his body. He looked down at the hand not holding the phone to his ear, coincidentally the hand he used to draw with, and wondered if it were really attached to the rest of himself. He remembered feeling this way when he first tried weed in high school in Stacey's room. Listening to the dean's moralistic denunciations, Bar impatiently wished she would get to the point. So what? What were they going to do, take away his pencils? He was sure that she was going to make him clean and re-paint her hallway. He went over the probably square footage in his head. It'd take about five hours, he thought. Totally worth it. Maybe he'd have to do two coats.

It was only when the dean explained, in a voice that had moved from an edge of rage to calm professional vengeance, that she was "going to recommend expulsion without recourse," that Bar allowed the levee holding back the wave of regret to fail. The feeling washed over him, drowning him in remorse. The wishing for a second chance that he knew would never come painfully caught in his throat. The dean asking him if he were alright sounded like a gloat. Unsure of the proper response to the punishment, Bar considered his mother's likely reactions. Would she tell him to fight, to finagle and push? More likely she'd advise him to leave art school, since it was, after all, an impecunious waste of time.

What would his father think? And then he thought about what happened at the docks...

The dean ended the call asking if Bar wanted to say something. "No. Thank you." Bar placed the phone back in its cradle gently, staring at it as if it were some object of the devil, not merely a plastic-covered set of wires. (Fucked.) He walked around the empty apartment, asking himself that same question again and again: wouldn't this be better? Is this what Jon had told him about the Stoics? He would choose what was happening to him. (No; he was fucked.) This was his choice. It really was. (Fucked. Shamefully, like a woman, that's what dad would say. What was the worth of "experience" if this is what it meant?)

She fucked me, he thought.

No. He said it aloud: "My choice. I fucked myself." He went to the bed and still in his clothes curled himself into a ball and thought how well and truly fucked he now was.

Abigail came home an hour later and told Bar that Art was dead and that Bar "needed to leave. Like, now. You're never going to be an artist. Your idea of art is death. You're more dead than he is. You're dead, dead,..."

"Yeah? You can't draw, Abi. You suck at drawing. How about that? You're not an artist because you can't fucking even draw!"

They went at one another like that for a while as Bar packed some things and left the apartment that was in some semi-legal tenant-status sense, his, and walked over to First, put a quarter in the payphone, and called Jon.

It wasn't long after that Bar was living in the apartment on 135th Street with Hudson

River views, also overlooking a drug mart and ghetto, biking in and out, afraid to take the subway four blocks away, drawing in the evenings, working at the bike shop on Canal Street during the day, trying, and not succeeding, in showing his work to a circle wider than family, friends, dates, and gallery screeners.

All of that happened in Life One.

8. Becoming An Artist

Late 1986

In Life One, Bar had a sketchpad he never showed anyone. It had drawings of the Chanel Lady, including the one he made as a high school senior from when he saw her on the bridge. He drew her from memory, a method that never worked well for him. He didn't know anything about her. The pictures were more like police wanted drawings than portraits.

In Life One, Bar made a series of drawings of Abigail. She wouldn't, or couldn't sit still long enough for a live sitting, and the one time they tried a mutual sitting, he found that her face wasn't still enough for him to draw her that way, either. Bar thought maybe using snapshots would open him up to drawing significant, candid moments. To get her used to being photographed enough to let her guard down, he didn't always put film in the camera, snapping away all the time for days. When he did put film in, he didn't always compose through the viewfinder.

He took a picture of her explaining something to him with her usual passion for a new idea. What, he couldn't remember. The picture showed the intensity of her expression, her face giving away the effort to articulate to herself and to him whatever it was that she was trying to say. Her hands were twisted together in an obscure, difficult to interpret gesture. It was half way to a modern dance pose, but because it was only half way, it was persuasive as her sincere body language. Something's missing from the picture though. Call it her soul. The ornateness of the gesture partly covers this lack but it is nevertheless there for him to see. It was one of the only pictures he made that Art liked.

In Life One, Bar made some photographs of Sharpey, with his permission. One of him stroking his cat, one of him intently playing his guitar. For some reason he never drew those. Sharpey asked after them. Bar gave him the black-and-white prints he had made and the film they came from. Those, too, weren't very good.

The only pictures Bar wanted to show others, that made him proud, were ones he drew with the subject sitting for him. His Stacey pictures, his Summer pictures, a few of his dad, Kristina, and some others were what he liked, in the end.

The Chelsea Hotel isn't clean. There are some pretend or real rockers down the hall. Unsurprisingly, they make noise at all hours. The quarter of a beer I drained from the mini-bar's collection was cold. I never could drink worth a damn, beer or anything else. There is no Lethe for me. I remember wanting some knockout drug when dad died. I tried to get drunk on the Kiddush wine and got sick, and then I couldn't bring myself to drink dad's beer.

It is seven days after my father didn't die. The shiva would've been coming to an end today, but there was no shiva, though I feel like mourning nevertheless, just not his death. At least there is that. Whatever else happens, I did that.

After his mother left the Jackson Heights apartment to live with Schlomo, his father went through a phase of talking to him more than he did before. Bar was in high school, in the throes of sexual slavery to Stacey, hardly around at home, which was maybe why his father felt the need to reach out to his son who would be leaving soon. One afternoon, when Saul woke up in his chair around five-thirty when the beer wore off and Bar was in the kitchen making dinner, his dad came into the kitchen to get another cold beer. Instead of going back to his chair he sat at the small kitchen table and told Bar stories of being a boy in Yemen, some of which Bar had heard and some not. He told Bar about being a teenager in Israel, and then about coming to New York in the early sixties. The last thing he said was, "I live in the middle between Yemen and Israel and here in New York."

"Uh huh."

"In the middle of Atlantic Ocean. You live like thet, you drown. All the time here, I try not to drown."

"Why didn't you tell me this kind of thing before?"

"You were a boy. Look, now you are a man," he said, standing and grabbing his son's strong bicep. "There is always a time for things," he said, and went back to his chair in the living room.

I need to figure out how to make my artistic debut. Presenting myself to Eva as a man of means is not enough. I need to be the same person, but well off and successful. Not for myself. I never needed that for myself. She can't have a reason to think little of me. With a twenty-year head start, that would be intolerable.

(Is it cold of me to think of this immediately after ridding myself of Abigail Greenfield, with whom I shared sweet, delicious body time a mere moment ago? No it is warm: I am in love with Eva.)

I am a humanist. I go into a trance of a kind when I draw. It's as deep a feeling as sexual ones, but it is not sexual, or not only sexual. That hasn't changed. If I don't change my art, will the result change? I will have the marketing, this time. What will I bring to market?

I should've drawn Saul more if only to show that I could make pictures of a man. I could do a series on him now. I should've drawn Stacey a lot more when I was a kid. I wonder where she is. Some state school, not New York. Berkeley?

All the drawings I wanted to make but never did. What have I been doing with my art? Has it been an exponent of loneliness, a sex-substitute, my whole life, and I've been lying to myself, rationalizing a fetish? I've always drawn girls, women, mostly. I said it was not just okay, but traditional. I defied those who accused me of lechery, but there was always some lechery. That, too, is traditional. What kind of argument is it to say, when I draw a portrait of a woman I'm attracted to that it's only thirty percent lust?

The point is, I need to make more art.

Abi thinks that for me to become an artist I need experiences. That's crap. Abigail didn't turn my head; she twisted it right off. After that, she threw it into a sanitation truck. She was cool, up for anything. I wasn't cool. I'm not cool now. I want certain things to happen and not others. Maybe I should go back there and ask to watch Art fuck Abi in her ass, tell her I want the experience, only insist on condoms, and draw that. It'd be like copying Art's art: drama, drama, drama. Let him paint that scene if he feels like it. It'd feel to me like an old man watching live porn, not an "experience." She's not going to do it if I'm not there, is she? It didn't look like it was fun the first time, though I am relying on a memory colored by unpleasant feeling. Anyway, she didn't get AIDS from him. Like I didn't get cool from her. None of that can become the art I produce.

I can't make drawings of horrible, shocking pain that leads to early death.

What would it take for me to have the kind of experience Abigail wanted to give me? Something surprising. This is it, of course. This act of going back is it. Sometimes, it's as mind-blowing a feeling as it was at Willets Point. Yet even that is fading. This, the going back, it's real now, my reality. I suspect that it's only going to be novel at first, like anything else.

I don't want the danger she thinks is the only way to become a person. I want beauty. My experience of seeing an Egon Schiele show once was worth ten "experiences" that Abigail and Art value so much.

I wanted Abi's beauty and didn't tell her and instead she thought I wanted her edge because she never thought of herself as a pretty/pink-and-pigtails/cheerleader. Back in West Point she wore black t-shirts and hung with dudes. I never captured that in any drawing I made of her. I never drew Abigail except from those snapshots. That never works. The quality isn't there because the human being isn't there. I wish I could have drawn Abigail. I'll ask her but I doubt it'll work this time.

Before Abigail there was Summer and before Summer there was Stacey.

Remember Stacey. Remember becoming an artist.

In high school, Stacey was an "it" girl, way out of my league. I was surprised she ever even approached me. She and Gary Mitchell (Uri) had dated, briefly, in junior year, a phenom we called Ken and Barbie or alternatively, Clash of the Gods because they fought in the hallways so much, including that day she screamed at him, "Do you think that tastes good!? You think I'm ever doing that again!?" Gary Mitchell was the one who told me she had heard about my portraits in the studio art elective and that she wanted me to draw her. She came to the art room after classes where I was doing ten times as many drawings as the art teacher had asked for. I asked her to take off her makeup. She came back from the bathroom and said it was the first time she had been in school in four years without it. As I stared at her huge eyes and round, pretty face and tried to keep my eyes away from her v-neck t-shirt, she told me about the guys who stared at her on the subway and the catcalls and how it made her stop wearing mini-skirts. Given the skin-fitted Jordache jeans she daily wore, I wondered at the efficacy of that fashion change.

"My mom goes to parties. She says, I should be thankful I'm still getting attention from men. She puts on these, like, tottering heels and leaves me alone all night."

"She does?" As she spoke, I felt her flowing toward me, and felt myself flowing out through my hand onto the large, thick paper as I marked it with her, with whom I felt she was. Yes, it was like sex, I guessed, but it was not pleasurable in that way, as I discovered when I began having sex. It was me seeing Stacey's self, maybe like sex in the ideal where there is closeness and the feeling of intermingling of the soul, though sometimes, as in this case, it was more of a one-way mingling, her soul, her forcefulness, her will to live, the thing in her that made her move and smile and speak and get dressed and avoid pain, her liveliness, becoming apparent to me.

"I'm like, totally dreading the guy might be in my bathroom in the morning. Like the last guy? I must've screamed to heaven when he was, like, right there when I stepped out of the shower."

"Wow, that's rough," I said, drawing. "I'm sorry."

"Totally not a coincidence."

I was getting her features, her lines, seeing the fear in her face as she spoke about being pretty, transmitting her beauty onto the page, becoming an eye-hand machine. Not the model-beauty. The self-beauty. It felt as if my feeling enveloped her, as if her feelings entered me while hearing about the price of her pretty-beauty. She told me about the time a photographer, a guy in his fifties, once stopped her on Broadway and gave her his card, begging her to let him take her picture and she was creeped out and scared. I said something sympathetic, and then she said something about how I was "totally uncreepy." In retrospect, I'm not sure I agree.

I was working well now. In class, like a hundred other boys, I had I dreamed of what it would be like to kiss her but here I just wanted to listen to her and draw her for as long as possible. I had zoned in.

At the end of the portrait session, she was in tears and full of thanks, for what I hardly knew. Listening seemed like too small of an act, hardly an action at all. She looked at the picture and said I captured her soul. Utterly unexpectedly, she kissed me on the cheek. I felt shock at the softness of her skin as she wiped the tears from her face and smiled and said, "Bar? Aren't you going to ask me out?"

"Yeah."

Dating Stacey meant I became Stacey's shopping companion, forced-marched to stores stocked with feather earrings, lipsticks, and stuffed purple unicorns. I came to know the ground floor of Bloomingdales and its proximity to Serendipity, where she expected to be treated to cherry ice cream, her lips turned a new shade of red.

I complained, not about the shopping, but about, in her room in her mother's apartment in Turtle Bay, how she signaled it was time for kissing by turning out the light, denying me sight of her flesh. At first, with the voices of my father and Gary Mitchell in my head telling me to push, I quickly tried to pull of her shirt. She gently put her fingers around my wrists and whispered, "Not yet." We kissed more. As we did, I tried again, this time to slip my hand under her shirt, but she demurred, saying "don't," so we kissed more and she smiled. I discovered kissing as an activity that consumes the whole of a person, like drawing, only you don't get a picture at the end. I wanted to give her everything when I kissed her, not to feel her breast but to breath in her soul. I forgot about pushing and focused on trying to give her myself. It precluded thinking, and was a refuge from it."Other boys don't kiss the way you do," Stacey said. I worried, after, that I was "too intense," a phrase of Gary Mitchell's (as in, "don't be too intense"). I left her apartment in a thick daze of love.

In April of senior year, I got a phone call at nine AM on a Saturday.
"Stacey?"
"Yeah." (sob, breathing)
"What's wrong? What's going on?"
"It's," (sob, sob, open weeping), I waited, fearful. Was she hurt? Bleeding? His need to pee annoyed him but his fear kept him on the hook. "It's," (sob, sob), "it's my BIRTHDAY BAR IT'S MY BIRTHDAY WHY DIDN'T YOU CALL ME WHY AREN'T YOU SINGING HAPPY BIRTHDAY TO ME WHY AREN'T YOU OUTSIDE MY APARTMENT WITH A PRESENT WHAT'S WRONG WITH YOU I HATE YOU WHY ARE YOU SO MEAN TO ME WHY DO YOU HATE ME?" (more sobbing).

On another weekend, in June, 1986, just before the end of high school, she told me to come over, "by bike," which was odd, because she normally forbade dirty and sweaty arrivals. She ordered me into the shower, followed me in, watched me. She said, "Your thing, it's normal." "Yeah?" "I thought … I like it." She led me naked to her room, where she lay down on a towel. She made clear what she wanted me to do. I knelt as if in prayer (it was Saturday), her soft thighs spread before me. I think she came as much because of the situation as because of what I was doing. Not that I understood then that she was having an orgasm, or even what that meant for a girl. We didn't have sex. I knew and didn't know what was going on. I didn't try to, but if I had, I think she would have let me. We had no condoms. I'm not sure I knew what they were.

I rode home in the dark from her place in Manhattan toward Jackson Heights, the boner making me shift in the seat, distracting me. Maybe that's why I ran straight into the Chanel Lady on the Queensborough Bridge. I fell off the bike and hit my left knee and right hand against the metal grating, but she was unharmed, which made no sense as I was the one with momentum. "You are Bar Mizrachi," she said. There she was in her pink tweedy Chanel skirt suit and heels. How had she even gotten there in that footwear? The wind on the top of the bridge was strong, whistling past us both. The cars and trucks passing a lane away were loud. That was the first time I heard her speak. "Who are you! I've been seeing you my whole life! What are you doing following me!" "I do not follow," she said. "You do not understand," she said. She looked at her watch, a big chunky man watch that seemed out of place on her. "This is incorrect. Not the nodal point," she said. "There has been an error." "What's going on?" I screamed at her over the traffic. "No, I cannot explain before…I will go." With that, she opened a trap door in the metal floor of the bridge and proceeded to climb down, shutting the door behind her. The ladder led to Roosevelt Island and I watched her climb down but after a few seconds she disappeared. I rode on the three more miles to my father's apartment, boner gone.

Then the following Monday Stacey pulled me aside and said it was time to break up. She'd be going to Paris soon and anyway, she said, flipping her hair, they almost had sex and she wasn't ready, except that I was in love with her, but I didn't object because I didn't know I could. As she kissed me on the cheek and left, I regretted not saying anything and also that she hadn't let me do a drawing of her since that first time.

After a couple of weeks, I stopped coming in a cup, imagining Stacey's body on that last day as she led me from the shower. I drew her instead, filling three sketchpads.

I looked at some of that stuff recently. I mean, twenty years from now. Whatever. I think I learned more about how to draw in those weeks after she dumped me than any similar period since.

That was my send-off, my high school graduation present, the burned-in image and memory of the touch of a pretty girl with a round high-school dream body who let me see her, let me touch her, wanted me to touch her, for whom I felt more desire than I thought my body could contain, who demanded my complete adoration that most willingly I gave, and then she left.

In the summer of 1986, between high school and college, I came into close proximity with a real, actual fashion model.

I took a job at Tricheur Gallery West Broadway and Broome, despite the offer by Schlomo to get paid ten an hour to do carpentry, the gallery paying only six. I thought I would learn about a trade I cared about, one that dealt in higher things, not the quotidian business of roofs and kitchen cabinets. I used to be such a virgin.

The first receptionist was a sophomore in a blue Yale t-shirt, hair tied with a rubber band behind her head, sat behind the counter bent over Heidegger, her neck bent and her face so close to the text that I thought she might be asleep.

"Excuse me? I'm supposed to start today?" I gave my name.

She looked up at me with a round face and oddly close-set eyes. She said, "Huh? Oh, yeah. So, Dicky's out. Must've had one too many of the ole Manhattans last night. I'm Wendy. What're you, the new sitter?"

"Sitter?"

"They didn't tell you what you're doing?"

"Uh, not ex…"

"Okay, so I don't know either. Wait here."

'Here' seemed to me to be the undefined location where I was standing. Wendy went back to her book. After ten minutes, she looked up at me again. "I meant here. Come on, I won't bite." I went around the tall white counter to where she was and saw another chair. "Did you bring a book?"

"Uh, yeah."

I remember her asking that, and her not wanting to talk.

When Dicky Tricheur, a tall, older man, portly, with a single curl of white hair emerging from his bald pate, dressed in a blue blazer, chinos, and penny loafers, sailed in an hour later, it became clear that my job, gallery sitting, was to guard the art, not sitting next to Wendy but in the gallery itself. I was also to do some small tasks that for some reason were not in the Wendy's jurisdiction, such as trash emptying and sweeping the floor of crumbs under Dicky's desk after lunch. The last was buying a long-stem red rose each day on the way to work and putting it in a tall, thin vase that was placed next to a photograph of a real rose. I sat next to those.

Wendy smiled at me a lot the second day, seemingly discovering that I existed, when she wasn't reading German philosophy or answering the phone. The gallery was empty most of the time; Tuesday morning through Friday lunchtime there were generally one or no viewers.

The first two days, I sat still, afraid to move lest I be doing something wrong, and I mistook Wendy staring at me when I was supposedly not looking for her checking on his diligence, though it was she who told me it was okay to read.

Dicky's lack of engagement, added to the gallery emptiness, gave me confidence on day three to go around the small gallery to get to know the art. I worried about the idea that someone might ask me about it, something that never happened. I remember the show. It was Fluxus:

-A set of small wooden cubes arranged in a grid, each with a hole covered in black rubber. There were instructions telling the viewer to "TOUCH." There was sand in one cube, and water in another; each was different. "Why's one cube missing."

"It had tacks," she said immediately. "Liability issue."

"Yeah, but it ruins the art," I said. Wendy snorted, amused.

-A group of four metal sculptures in the middle of the room, about half a foot high each, apparently made from cooled molten metal, brown in color. Wendy volunteered, "They look like pieces of shit, right?"

"Is that, uh, intentional?" She snorted again, putting down her book.

-A set of men's neckties cut in half. I've never figured that one out.

-Inside a closed plexiglass box, a box of matches with the logo replaced by "Meta Matches," and a small card that said, "Use these matches to burn some art."

-Inside another plexiglass box was a pad with a quickly-drawn sketch of a man's face and the words, "Take One," signed at the bottom with the name of the movement, not the artist's name.

-A white canvas with words stenciled at the top, "WRITE YOUR MANIFESTO HERE," and a black marker. "You're supposed to allow people to write whatever they want," Wendy said.

"Does anyone?"

"Not since we put it up," she said. "People are afraid of art."

"Who wrote this?" At the top, in black marker, was written, "Art is Money," and "No, it's NOT," in two different kinds of handwriting.

"The artist. Kinda get-the-ball-rolling thing. Gotta love the irony," she said. I had no idea what the irony was in this case and I still don't know.

-A real manifesto, not available for commentary. I remember that it was a framed scrawl that said something like, "Purge the world of bourgeois sickness, 'intellectual,' professional, & commercialized culture, PURGE the world of dead art, imitation, artificial art, abstract art, illusionistic art, mathematical art, -- PURGE THE WORLD OF 'EUROPANISM.'!" Something like that.

"What's mathematical art or "Europanism?"

"Fuck if I know. I assume it's not supposed to make sense," she said.

Wendy was efficient and professional, always on time despite the boss's capricious schedule, answering the phone on one ring, taking accurate, detailed messages, communicating clearly, and handling questions from potential buyers with knowledgeable aplomb. She seemed to understand the art and spoke about the "Fluxus Movement" with callers several times as if it made a lot of sense, despite the dismissal of it she handed me.

She wore jeans and t-shirts: her collection included a Harvard t-shirt, "Rocky" and "Jaws" shirts, and a Dylan concert T.

I remember talking with her about conceptual art, hanging out on the reception desk. "It's like," she said, "once you get the art, each piece is like, not worth looking at any more. That's my whole problem with conceptual."

I would say things like, "Yeah." I hadn't been to school yet. We hadn't discussed conceptual art in high school. We discussed how to throw a pot and how to push paint so it didn't look literally like shit.

"Thought this show's better than the last one," she said. "Pomo Self-Portraiture. Tricky Dicky had me write this pretentiousness about how it's all descended from Durer but self-consciously sending up the tradition. The one piece I'll remember was a drawing of the artist with the face erased. Oh, and a grid of nine paintings, each eight by ten inches, each of the artist but in a different period style, starting in the upper left with an Egyptian profile, passing through a Rembrandt-like painting, a Goya copy, and a Picasso rip-off, and ending with a photo-realistic portrait of the artist painting himself into existence. I kinda liked that one. Like the painting of Pygmalion at the Met?"

"Yeah, yeah, I know that one. That sounds cool."

"It's sooo insincere and empty, don't you think? I mean, the whole pomo pose," she said. I think that was when she got up from her chair and put her face really close to mine.

"Yeah."

"I should go back. To my chair."

At ten minutes to closing, I looked up from my book to see Wendy looking down at me, smiling. "You're cute," she said.

"Uh huh."

"I dated a Black guy, like, freshman year."

"Uh huh."

"Why don't we grab a drink after work?"

"Uh, yeah." Her shirt, up close, revealed food stains. "I mean, yeah. I have a girlfriend." It was a lie, mostly. I still imagined Stacey as my girlfriend but I knew she wasn't.

Wendy stopped smiling, went back to her chair, grabbed her book and her knapsack, and called out, as she left, "This place's a shithole. And Dick's a crook. You'll see." She went to the elevator. "Make sure you get paid," she said without turning around. "'Course," she yelled from inside the elevator, a random man standing next to her, "he probably won't ask you to suck him off."

The next phone call went to a machine inside the office.

It took a day before Richard Tricheur came in looking harried, and noticed Wendy's absence. The gallery was still locked, as I had no key. I was waiting in the entrance hall, holding my rose. Tricheur did not say hello to me or hold the door open or turn on the lights after opening up. He went straight to the phone at the counter and punched in a number in the dim light from the one exterior window.

"Dick. No, I'm Dick. Aubergine, honey, can you send a girl to do reception? No. No, she's not. I don't know. I can't say. Just – you know what I want. Not another nepotism deal, okay? Yes. No, smart ... It's about image. Right." He hung up and saw me standing, waiting for instructions. "You, ah, I'm sorry…?"

"Bar."

"Yes, thank you. If you could sit here, answer the phone, etcetera? Just tell everyone I'll call them. And take everyone's number. And wait a minute, say, 'Hello, Tricheur?'"Say that."

"Hello, Tricheur?"

"Ugh. Could you be nicer? Pretend you're not from New York. You'll have to do for a day. I'll be back in four hours."

"Uh, okay, what if…" I said to Dick's back as he passed through the glass door.

An hour after that, Summer showed up. I remember that moment. "Hi, I'm Summer," she said to a too-obviously, lecherously smiling Dick. "For the reception thing?" She had a slight southern accent, only in the word "Hi" said as "Hai."

She was so beautiful, her luscious long blond hair falling down into a curls as if she had stepped out of a Veronica Lake poster, that I felt as if someone were shining a strong bare bulb into my eyes. She took my typically disappointing uncool puppy-dog male reaction in stride, rolling her eyes. Like, duh? you never saw a pretty girl in your whole life? The kind of stare I gave her had been happening to her since she had turned fourteen somewhere in the recesses of the South.

One of the difficult parts of the job, after that, was to avoid continually staring at her. I tried to focus on my book, but Summer was less efficient than Wendy had been and frequently became overwhelmed at the phone instrument if a second person were calling, for example, let alone three or five, or if someone called while someone else stood before her asking for a price list or the location of the bathroom. Summer would throw up her hands, say, "grrrrr," or "Oh my God!" or "For cryin' out loud!" These exclamations would make me look up and then I would stare at Summer again long after the curtain had come down on the most recent mini-drama.

I stared and drew pictures of her and fantasized with a certain horror of going home with her (since I was still living in Queens with my dad) and her seeing my room and discovering the extent of my ignorance and utter dearth of cool. In my fantasy, I got to stare at her with her knowing I was staring. In my fantasy, she thought me staring at drawing her was nice.

Seeing her face was like looking at an icicle in sunlight, like putting one's head to the speaker, drinking from the bath faucet, eating ice cream for breakfast, swallowing ten sugar packets, or that time I went to CBGBs to hear the Destroyers and the amp volume on a piercing high note broke a wine glass.

Those first pictures were quite poor. I kept them to remind myself of what not really look at what you're looking at means. I might as well have drawn from poses in fashion magazines, or Playboy (same facial expressions). It was what Jon called drawing with my dick, and while he was leveling a general accusation that I did not accept, I took it to heart. It was more a matter of drawing with my heart with words, like "pretty," and not with my eyes. I tried to look at her more carefully, more closely, without being obvious. No words. Lines, tones, shapes, above all shapes.

Richard, as in "call me Richard, Summer, dear," apparently did not have trouble obviously and obtrusively looking at her from very close. He newly found it necessary to spend a lot of time on his cordless phone not in his office, leaning on the white counter, now that Summer sat behind it, something, in the week that Wendy had run the desk, he never once had done. When he did that, I wanted to howitzer his size 42 ass for blocking my view.

Dick Tricheur told me to "clean up a little; wear slacks and a nice white shirt," so I bought one copy of each of those items, wore them daily, and washed them in the bathtub at night. Summer wore whatever she wanted. Often, her work clothes consisted of black-dyed jeans, carefully ripped with punk-like safety pins and a plain black t-shirt with the neck and sleeves cut off. Summer definitely had a hairstyle, not a haircut: a severe bob with a downward slope of forty-five degrees from her ears to her chin, but only on the left side. On the right side she wore an earring miniature of the Eiffel Tower; on her this piece of kitsch trash looked avant-garde. Her black eyebrows seemed like accent marks of some divine language against her white skin. Whenever I looked at her, I half expected her to speak only French.

I spent an entire morning studying her jawline. I made detailed studies of her face, trying to strip off the worshipful feeling that ruined the first ones. Summer's beauty was to Stacey's as the Indy car to the Stock racer, the thoroughbred to the draft animal, the professional is to the amateur. I said all of this to Jon, who groaned and said I might reconsider my metaphors and their implications. "What if someone thought of you as a horse?"

"Will she treat me like one, too? It could work."

"You're like, incorrigible. That's the word. Also, deluded. You're willfully unaware of the degree to which you're inventing the cool knowingness she only seems to exude," he said, accurately. *"Ask her about* Being and Time,*"* he said. *"You should've dated Wendy."*

I wanted to talk with Summer about the gallery's art, maybe to laugh and make fun of it together. I was also scared (on no evidence) that she took it all utterly seriously, understanding it much better than I could ever do. I assumed she must be as incredibly sophisticated about Art as she was about Style. I accepted as axiomatic that I could only ever aspire to be as cool. I tried reading Light in August *but despaired after a few pages.*

Despairing of the shit I was drawing, I tried to stop staring at Summer and read the book my high school teacher recommended for me as a "college book," (Re)Igniting (De)Sires: An Erotics of Artistic Politics. *(I tried reading it later as well, when I was thirty, but by then I knew what it was and tossed it after reading a paragraph.) Junkie-like, I went back to staring at Summer and drawing her.*

Summer generally either studied her magazine or chatted on the company phone and was thus hard to approach. I assumed she was reading Artforum *or* Art in America, *though she seemed too cool for either of those. It was probably one of those cool xeroxed 'zines that used to be in places selling hundreds of publications on lower Broadway, full of crudely cut-and-pasted collages of solarized photographs and ironically collaged political figures. I listened to some of her half of her dialogues, though, and was confused by the counter-evidence of cool.*

"Yah?" "Like, I think so too!" "I'm so fat." "He said 'Blue Velvet' or 'Top Gun,' and I was like, duh, Tom Cruise? Hello?" "I'm a heifer." "No, no, you cut the neckline just under that. I'll show you. It has to be something you don't care about so much. No, not that one. You're so cute in that one!..." The word "I'm" was the only one not accent free, pronounced "Ahm."

Once, a French couple walked into the gallery. The guy took out a cigarette and a silver lighter and lit up for his girlfriend. Summer, seeing this infraction, scowled and got up from her office chair, putting what she was reading on the counter. It was Vogue; *Madonna was on the cover doing an over-the-shoulder in a white maillot and there were headlines about swimsuits and how "Chic hits the streets."*

A week into Summer's tenure there was the guy who came off the elevator, took a look around, and quickly went into the supply closet through a door that was flat and white against a flat white wall. I remember that he was Black because I spent a moment wondering whether I was suspicious of the man because he was Black and I'm a racist, or whether to accord this man full respect, I should be suspicious of him, as I might be of anyone not yet introduced to me as an employee, looking around, then quickly ducking into a closet right off an elevator. Also, there was his long black trench coat with several rips in it, like those worn by the men sleeping in Tompkins Square Park. And the unkempt, matted hair.

I summoned the courage to get up, go to Summer's counter, and say a word: "Uh,"

She looked up. "Yes?"

"Uh, sorry to bother you, but, um, there's a guy in the closet."

"A guy?"

"Yeah, is there someone else working here?"

"What 'guy'?" she said sarcastically, and then in a worried tone, "Is it Richard?"

"Uh, no, not Richard."

"Shit." She went right to the closet and opened it with the inserted sliver handle I hadn't seen before. "Who the FUCK are you?"

From inside the closet, I heard, "This is my saw." The man came out with a small old electric circular saw, probably worth six dollars if he sold it on a blanket in St. Marks Place. He looked at me and tightened his eyes. I remember that look of hate.

Summer said, "I'm calling the police."

"This is my…"

"Hello? We're being robbed. Jesus! Manhattan!"

The elevator opened with a ding and some British tourists emerged. The would-be saw-owner took his chance. "Aw fuck it," he said, throwing the saw back into the closet with a loud clank, shoving the Englishwoman out of the way, and hitting "door close" in the elevator. He disappeared into the New York afternoon, but not before he called out, "Thanks a whole fuckuva LOT, BROTHER!"

I remember thinking, I'm not your brother. But what if I was?

Summer hung up the phone. "Thank you, so much," she said to me, smiling. "Oh my GOD! We could've been killed." She leaped from behind the desk and hugged me with her bony arms. "You're so tough."

"Uh…yeah, uh, thanks." She didn't hear me. From the office Richard guided an older woman in a thick carpet-like skirt suit, huge, outrageous sun hat, and dark glasses, into the gallery.

"Summer, this is Felicity Cooper. Mrs. Cooper, Summer. We hold our staff to the highest standards of beauty, like our art."

Mrs. Cooper looked at me and smiled.

Summer seemed to suppress a gag, and held out her thin hand. She and Felicity Cooper gave one another a mutually limp shake. "Hello."

"Well, you are charming. Are you a fashion model, dear?"

"Trying to be. And an artist."

An artist? I knew it. I was right. Why didn't she ever want to talk with me about art, though?

"Ah, aren't we all trying to be something?"

Richard, chuckling, pretended that this was witty.

"Um, Richard?" Summer began.

"Yes? How has the ship been floating for the past hour? I'm afraid, Felicity, that we have dawdled away for that long."

"Oh, no! I am due uptown an appointment…"

She told Dicky about the attempted burglary.

Richard's face transformed instantly from the self-satisfied grin he was aiming at the Cooper lady to horror. Bar thought Dicky might vomit.

"Don't have a fit. He was just stealing an old saw. Not, like, one of the art…things, or anything."

"Oh, I see." Richard composed himself. "Such a rough town. I can't imagine staying here even one more year. I know that my heart will simply give out. I swear it will. What with the graffiti and the crime and the dirt…"

The rich Cooper lady laughed. "Oh, Richard, this town is tough because of people like you." He chuckled, amused. She asked Summer conspiratorially, "Dear, was he Black?"

"Uh. I guess."

"Oh, then you should have let him have the saw. Don't you think so, Dicky?"

"Uh, of course. I was merely..." He mumbled something liberal about social responsibility of "the better sort" toward downtrodden.

"And I just came from a show where they were selling graffiti, Dicky. Don't," she said, poking his chest, "become a dinosaur." From her raspy voice and Florida-wrinkled skin she seemed to be a hundred and seventy.

Summer waved her bird-like arm leftward. "Bar stopped him."

The three of them now looked at me with different speeds of cognition. The Cooper lady said, "Dicky, maybe you'd better watch this one. It could turn out to be an inside job." Her wink and the grandmotherly smile she gave me did not put me at ease. Richard's face went back to what must have been its normal red cast.

"Well, Bar, you are apparently a regular Sherlock Holmes. Thank you sir."

"Actually," I said, "it's not like I figured it out." The y stared again. "It wasn't a mystery."

They laughed politely and Dicky and Mrs. Cooper turned to talk to one another and it was as if I weren't there. After Mrs. Cooper left for her hairdresser, Dicky went into his office and emerged to solemnly present me with my check for two weeks of work: $350. Apparently I would not be paid for lunch. After fumbling, Dicky fished a ten out of his wallet and added it solemnly to my take.

Biking home, I considered the Problem of Summer. I did not wish to be her boyfriend as much as I wished to worship at her feet. I considered her way too perfect to be a girlfriend. She was the Platonic Form of Beauty. The problem was her awkwardness. Why did she fidget so much as she sat all day? Was it that her bony tush lacked cushioning sufficient to endure the hard surface of her draughtsman's chair? Each day, I continued to draw her, to add to the twenty-three drawings I had already made of her, in quest of her soul.

I could hear everything being said in the office.

"George, you fucking asshole, how's the... no, I wasn't asking about the Motherwell you fucking failed to get, I was...yes. Yes. Well, it was a gamble, no? Non? Mais oui? No, the show isn't doing fucking well at all. How could it? It's not like we've got a Duschamps here. Get me some real art and I'll show you sales...exactly. Exactly! But we've got a buyer for the IM." He laugh-chuckle-snorted. Bar figured out through repetition and context that he meant the Manifesto, which Dicky called the Idiot's Manifesto. "It's fucking formidable. I don't think he knows it's one of a hundred...No...Well, I talked to Simon...Simon's our fucking lawyer for chrissake…twenty years...yeah, baby, so old Simon says fuck disclosure...That's what he said...Well, it's not a

145

fucking fake, George. Really, I don't see why we don't just Xerox the fuck out of half the shit these guys made...No, no, that's a joke, right?" He laughed again.

Dicky's laugh gave me existential dread.

By July, I gathered that French George was Richard's brother and ran a gallery of the same name in Paris. "Fucking wives, George, I love fucking wives...No, that's not what I meant. I don't love fucking the wives; I love wives, and I was using the word 'fucking' as...I could die just like old Cooper. Drop dead, just like that....No, I'm not smoking, you fat French fuck. Listen, Georgie, I have this in hand. There's no need to literally fuck Mrs. Cooper as long as we can make that two hundred percent markup ... No, what do you think? You're so...sordid." *Laughs.* "And that's why I love you. I'm ringing off." *I wasn't sure which was worse, the fake Brit talk, or what he said.*

In the other ear, Summer on the phone with her agent.

"Robby, I can't make my tits grow." "'I'm eating a friggin' banana, like, once an hour." *I could confirm this rate of intake.* "They do so grow your tits...Literally everybody knows that... I need high fashion, not that lingerie crap. Those guys are such assholes. As soon as the last shoot was over...yeah, the one on West 38th...totally skeevy...the photographer's assistant told me he wanted to do a shoot with me for his book. Come on. Duh? Obviously. I mean, he's not even... Yeah, that drooly...Totally. Yeah. Gross. Get me work, 'k?"

Summer's area of concerns forced me, finally, to face the lack of congruence between her exquisite form and shallow content and conclude that She was not Platonic in any way, a realization that required me to advance past my unwillingness to write off the utterly worthless time and thought spent on the Summer I had conjured.

With new sight sharped by disillusioned idealism, I began to note that her agitated face was always moving minutely, and that her eye darted about. I wondered whether she could not become a successful model because of this nervous facial drama. I wondered how she tried to quiet herself for photographs, or if she was even able to. I began to see in her someone who had come to town having added some style and hauteur to an amenable canvas, and who might be afraid lest anyone see through to a frightened, underweight midwestern girl contemplating the price of staying vs. taking the next Chicago-bound Amtrak.

One Friday she arrived late to find me at her reception chair, answering the phones. She didn't put down her bag. She said, "So, like, Bar, hey Bar, how's it going?" Before I answered she continued, "I have this audition? It's kind of a big deal? My agent? Roberto? He says it could be this big break for me. I totally said I can't; I have to work, but he was such a bitch about it on the phone." She laughed nervously. "I swear he screamed at me. So I don't know what to do, you know?" She smiled again.

"I can cover the desk all day."

"You can? Oh my god! I can't believe you even offering that. That is just so friggin' nice. But, like, don't tell Dicky. I totally need the money, okay?"

"Yeah, sure." *I understood I was being used. While sitting in one part of the gallery was the same as sitting in another, I knew how the part of her request involving deceiving our employer would be entail risking my job. I didn't much care, and it wasn't even because I felt any desire for her that could become part of any set of actions in the world; it was more about feeling relief that she wouldn't be there combined with a melancholy feeling for the dying lust I had felt for her a mere four weeks earlier.*

As she left I saw that her walk was as agitated as the rest of herself. She lacked grace, generally. I remember watching her through the gallery's glass door. She looked as if she could actually accomplish the way Scooby Doo hid behind trees. At the desk, I started working on drawings of Summer in a style closer to Egon Schiele, abstract angles and odd perspectives, and adding a suggestion of blur. The stuff I drew when she wasn't there was much better.

In the late afternoon the gallery was empty for a good forty minutes. I read in Clarke: "The nude is not the subject of art, but a form of art." I had only ever seen one person nude, other than myself. I sketched my memory of Stacey Abramovitz's body, worried that I was incorporating porn into the memory, and wondering if it was that she had incorporated porn into her sense of how to move her body around me.

Here's something quite fucked up, I realize as I think through all of this again: I am going to go pick Summer up, and she's going to say yes, and it's a bad idea but now that I've had this bad idea I'm not able to stop it from happening.

I remember seeing Summer years later in a spread in House Beautiful *in a doctor's office. She was on the cover, too, which is why I picked up that particular publication. The profile was headlined "Summer's Summer," and told of how she "always drew, even as a child in Romania," how a designer discovered this and put her large inkwash pieces in the background of her 1992 Paris show, how galleries came flocking, and how Summer — the Summer, his Summer, but not "mine" in any sense — now preferred to live full time in Bridgehampton with her two-year-old son, triple-A-list architect husband, and three thousand square foot, thirteen foot ceiling barn converted into studio. The white crochet dress listed for $6200. She preferred life out there as it was "slower and can be more spiritual, if you pay attention to the light."*

That's afternoon is when Abigail Greenfield of West Point, New York, walked into the gallery, her long blonde hair loose, her dyed-black jeans covered in multi-colored paint, once-white running sneakers graffitied over in marker and covered in paint dots, and a blue and white Indian peasant shirt, cheap Indian jewelry. I didn't know it was Abigail. That is, I didn't know her yet. She was subtly pretty, no make-up, nothing flashy, neither model-y nor feather earrings and feathered hair. Once, when I left after Summer and caught up to her walking uptown on Broadway, I saw her turn men's and women's heads, block after block.

I think it's because I went through whatever it was I went through with Summer that Abi hit me so hard, so quickly. I watched her walking tough in big strides and with some unknown purpose, as if she were hunting. She was beautiful but not obviously so like Summer; I knew she would turn few other heads than mine. She was not soda pop. She was Campari, a more powerful beverage.

She came and looked at me, or rather she looked at the rose/rose, and then at me. She smiled. I remember the intelligence, the generosity, and the charm of that smile. She smiled as if understanding the joke but not thinking it hilarious, which it wasn't. She smiled without having to show off that she got it. I think I forgot completely about Summer then.

She turned and went straight to the "manifesto." She looked back a me and winked, saying, "You look cool. Be cool, okay?" She took up the marker and started drawing on the public manifesto. I couldn't see what; her body blocked my view. She looked behind herself back at me a couple of times. No one said to me to stop anyone from doing what they wanted with that; it was just a giant pad, really. She took her time, then walked to me in a straight line that kept me from seeing what she had made.

She said, "A person could make the mistake of thinking you're part of the exhibit, sitting there next to the picture of Jan Schliermayer."

"Some people have."

"That's a great book."

"Yeah. I like it."

"Those are good," she said, pointing to my open sketchpad showing Summer in a contortion of limbs.

"Thanks."

She took one of the gallery business cards and wrote, "EV Gallery, 295 E. 8th St., opening 6-8pm, Aug. 30, Abigail."

"It's an opening?"

"It's club kinda place. Hope you can come."

I watched her leave with her man-walk and her canvas army surplus knapsack. Later, I found out about her being raised by her single dad, a professor of military history, and about her desperation. That day, I was quietly blown away by a wholly new kind of female person, someone truly cool.

I went to the do-it-yourself Manifesto just as Dickie sailed in with a matron wearing a pink tweedy suit, saying, "Bar, my good man, glad to see you at the helm. Where is the lovely Summer of our youth?"

The words: "Dickhead Tricheur cheated my friend by selling his painting and lying about the price." The picture: my own face, though quickly done with just a marker, was recognizable on a reclining nude. She drew me as an odalisque, nude. I admired the very few lines she needed to capture a recognizable likeness. Plus she credited me an ample member.

"Uh, I don't...Summer! You mean Summer, of course. Yeah, she, uh, is checking on something."

Dickie scowled. Did he sense a coverup? "Ah, shall we take a look at the Basquiat that you came all this way to see? It is right this way," he said, ushering his mark into the office. As he let her in, he gave me a second scowl, and then, sweeping into his view, he saw the additions to the ad-hoc Manifesto. "Patti, would you mind making yourself comfortable just for a moment?"

"Not at all, Richard, I'll just..." Dickie shut the door on what she was saying, walked briskly over to the piece, read it in an instant, and with a practiced motion took down the large paper, rolled it up, and told me to "Trash it." Dicky opened a flat file behind the reception desk, took out another identically sized oaktag, and installed it in the first one's place. The new one had pre-written on it, in two distinct handwritings, "Art is Money," and "No it's NOT."

I went to that show, at the E.V. Gallery and Club. It was a warm night, not too bad for late August, but I was sweating by the time I got there. First I had to walk around Tompkins Square Park from my apartment to the club. I carefully chose the side of the street opposite the park, even though there were some people around. Even amid the urban devastation, the park represented, at night, a special zone of fear and sadness, a nexus of homelessness, narcotics commerce, and psychotic ranting in the day, raw danger at night.

*The club building listed to one side, a leaning tenement of Alphabet City. One had to step down to a mud-floored square across which spanned two pieces of thick lumber. The queue stopped before the square and then re-started after. One was forced to commit traversing this divide into the culture of downtown. Inside the club, the woman taking money and passes was topless, which made odd sense in the late summer heat; her torso was covered in blue body paint and there were gold snakes around her arms and neck. After her, I went down a set of creaky wooden stairs that my carpenter dad would scoff at. Would have scoffed, because he was dead, then, (*and now, he is alive.*) It was five degrees hotter the instant I passed the threshold. Cigarette and pot smoke thickly laced the air, fighting with a dank and mildewy old basement smell. The huge, crowded space had a dirt floor. Most everyone was wearing sneakers or army boots and didn't care. A little stream of black water trickled inaudibly in an irregular diagonal line through the club, marked off by stolen N.Y.C. police traffic cones that the crowd wound around. A "bar" lined one brick wall, slapped together with two-by-fours and plywood. Several plastic inflated Ronald Reagan doll-balloons floated above it, tied to an antique cash register.*

Across from the bar, hanging on masonry nails stuck into the exposed brick, were Abigail's portraits in a line at eye level. Above those floated Art's astonishing depiction of the apocalypse.

The volume from the band's guitar formed a wall of noise that one bumped into as one entered. There were maybe three hundred people in the club by now, with more coming in. I was jostled every few seconds. The energy of the room was dangerously festive, homemade (as in a coven), slapdash, and frantically casual. People were drinking, smoking, sitting, standing, dancing or just swaying, shouting, straining to hear, flirting, kissing with lips or tongues, touching each other, sweating, waiting for the bathroom, for the bartender, and for one another. At least one couple looked like they were having sex, face to face, standing up in a corner, genders unknown.

I drew the scene in my head but it was too mutable. Whenever I stood still to look, I got bumped, so I put my back to a column and hoped it wouldn't move.

I was facing Art's art, though I didn't know who he was. A large painting (lit by a cheap clamp-on spotlight), about ten by ten feet, heightened and chaotic, like a comic book page done by some Pop Hieronymous Bosch, in lurid, alive colors, bright yellows fading into oranges and reds, like a hallucinatory sunset. I stared at it as people passed, some looking at him briefly before moving on. There were at least fifty different figures in the painting, flying off in different directions, fighting, some having sex, at least three defecating or pissing, and one bowling right at the viewer, as if you were a pin. Several of the superheroes were smashing into massive Doric columns along the edges, and a Greek pediment near the top of the painting was cracking. The title was "Civilization Unbound." It was wild. It was a slight exaggeration of the room I was currently in.

Behind me was the band, tuning up, meaning they created feedback on their amps. It was four guys and a woman, each maybe thirty, each in the uniform: dyed black jeans, black sneakers, various t-shirts in various states of torn. Copies of tonight's flyer were everywhere giving the evening's lineup of bands: Sweet Cheeks, Billy The Hero's Dead, Funk You, The Nerda-Voids, Sororicide, Jagger's Tongue, Screw This, and Scent to the Front. The images for Jagger's Tongue and for Sororicde happened to be almost identical (a face with a wide open mouth sticking out its tongue). With a nod, the band started some kind of death-rock that quickly modulated into a schmaltzy Klezmer song with the clarinetist in the lead blowing wha-wha-whyyah style as if from the 1930s. A couple wearing a tux with tails and a fifties tulle prom dress danced swing, which didn't quite fit. The song's end was met by scattered applause.

A tall person appeared next to me and started talking to me. He was glam-rocked out, with a white tuxedo, white sneakers, and a white surgical mask covering his lower face. This person's hair was near-white blonde, and gelled in a wavy line up from his head at least twelve inches, ending at the top in a little wavelet. He said, "Civilization's discontents will inherit the earth," using a high head voice.

"Sorry, what?"

"I know, the band is called Revelations, isn't it?"

"No, the The Nerda-Voids. I'm Bar."

The man in white took down the surgical mask and laughed.

"In that case, I'll have a boilermaker. Get it. Okay. I'm Art. I'm capturing the zeitgeist," he said, stepping into what I considered my space.

"What is the zeitgeist?

"Nothingness."

"Yeah." *Who's this weirdo?* "Are you from the future?" *I asked, trying be clever.*

"Not yet," he said. "Not unless I take more drugs tonight," he said, pointing to the painting. "If you study it carefully, you will learn fruitful despair, Bar."

The 'Voids ended their set, carefully cradling their instruments in their arms as if making a statement opposite to that of Jimmy Hendrix setting his guitar on fire, as if to say that if nothing matters, you might as well guard your shit. The N.A.I.L.S. set up next. Bar moved closer to the poster explicating their acronym: Nihilize, Anarchize, Inhale, Legalize, Sexualize. Next to the acronym was a picture of a woman's hand with red, dripping nails.

Art put the mask back on. "Did you know that the City of New York considers this property to be condemned? The joke's on them: It's the City that's condemned. This place is practically the only part of it that shouldn't be." He did a flourish move, bowing and winding his arm around three times in front of himself.

His eyes were bloodshot and his left hand shook when he didn't keep it hanging from his tux vest pocket.

A female person snuck up behind Art and put her arms over his shoulders. "Hey Art," she said, "What're you on and can I have some?" Her smile emerged from behind her affected friend. "I met this guy at Tricheur the other day."

"Hey Abigail. So Bar, you're straight? Too bad. Abi, my dear, new flaves from the ice-cream man yesterday."

"Fuck off, Art."

"As you wish, my lady," he said, and, "Well, la di da, Bar. See ya later, Abi. I must be off in quest of weak male flesh." *He left, flipping his white tux's tails at them in his wake. He quickly turned back and said,* "You know, we three should do some lines, and then energetically fuck, together."

"Go away," Abi said, not unkindly. "Why weak?" she asked him. She seemed amused by him, as if he were a pet. She pushed an effete lock of his white-dyed hair away from his left eye.

"The flesh is always tragically weak," he said, turned, and moved into the crowd.

Abi said, "Art's the artist I was telling you about."

"This is his?" I asked about the big painting.

"Yeah. My stuff's over there," she said, pointing to her portraits.

"I like yours better," I said.

She smiled. "Yeah, thanks, but Art's the genius."

She was wearing her own uniform, it seemed; this time the Indian peasant shirt was red. She wore a little eyeliner, otherwise no makeup. Her hair was short and spiked with some goo that made it stand straight up in places; it gave the impression that she stopped doing her hair in the middle, bored. Her nose was too big, and her eyebrows too thin. Yet she was beautiful, like a Walker Evans picture. The difference between Summer and Abigail was like the difference between Tim Curry in Rocky Horror and Robert Redford.

Next to her appeared a woman in a short black dress, sleeveless, plunging neckline exposing much roundness, heavy black eye makeup, a beehive, and a cigarette on a long holder. They both had drinks in cartoon-character glasses: Mickey Mouse and Star Wars. She smiled and yelled to her friend over the N.A.I.L.S.'s music.

"Hey," Abi screamed to me, "Thanks for coming! I'm so glad you could! Bar? Is that it?!"

"You're beautiful," I blurted instead of answering her.

She laughed and said, "No I'm not. And so're you." Her laugh was from Marlo Thomas as Atalanta, her smile sunny and open. She drank in gulps.

"You can draw," he shouted.

"Thanks," she shouted back. She smiled, took his hand, and moved close enough to kiss. It was electric, marvelous. As the band ended its set, they kissed in the relative quiet, and they kissed as the D.J. started playing records. She laughed for no apparent reason. She seemed child-like if the child had been raised feral in a community of nomadic hippies. She put her drink down and danced in slow motion to the song, her legs wide and her arms undulating.

Abandoning this, she rushed up to his ear and said, "This is the Lounge Lizards. I saw them here once. You know the saxophone guy's in the movie, Stranger Than Paradise? John Lurie?"

"No, I ..."

"Lotta people think he's like, the essence of cool," *she said.*

"What do you think?"

She shrugged. "Cool's not the coolest thing."

"Yeah," Bar said, considering this proposition.

Art suddenly re-appeared.

"You are an artist, then, Bar? Let us see some of your work." (flourish).

"Okay," he said. Art peered at him with raised white-dyed eyebrows. "Right now?"

"But of course," Art said with his affected flourish.

"I get off now," Abi said.

I was surprised and not entirely thrilled with Art's accompaniment to my place. But he stayed only ten minutes, and was generally complimentary about my work, particularly the newer Summer pictures. He seemed impressed with where I lived, an inversion of my parents' reaction. Abi was thrilled with the place and said, "Anyone who chose to live here is cool. Cooooool," and she kissed me.

After the sex, Abigail skipped back to the front of the apartment in her white underwear, reached into the pocket of her hanging jacket, took out a joint and a pack of matches and lit it, sucking deeply. She came back to the bedroom and fell into a cross-legged sitting position on my mattress on the floor.

I accepted it from her, having never smoked anything. She said it was strange that I lived here but never smoked pot and it reminded me of Kristina falling for me because I borrowed my friend's tux and it worried me but the apartment wasn't the same thing and I smoked the joint with her and it wasn't bad, though I don't think I got high. She was unadorned, unafraid, and so I was unafraid. When I coughed, she smiled, but she didn't laugh. She felt familiar, easy, gentle and strong all at once. Her familiarity extended to the sex, as if we had done this before, despite not moving like either girl I had been naked with, and despite this casualness clashing against the thrill of being naked with her for the first time.

Afterwards, I started humming Madonna's "Like a Virgin." She laughed and hummed along, kazoo-style. Neither of us sang any of the words. At two-fifteen we fell asleep holding one another under my white sheet.

In the morning, I woke first. I made her a cappuccino.

"I basically ran away from home. My dad did his best but what did he know about a misfit kid who wanted to be an artist? His shoes were always shined, and my sneakers were covered in spray paint. Mom's in California somewhere since I was like, seven. When I got off the bus at Port Authority on 8th Avenue I went right to the Village Voice *offices. Art used to work there, some office job. He found me crying outside after they wouldn't let me write art criticism for them on the strength of my high school clippings. I was really young. He let me crash on his couch and showed me the Village scene, introduced me to the E.V. Club folks. I owe him so much."*

"Why'd he leave so fast? Last night?"

"I don't know. He just does things sometimes. Impulse, feeling, whatever. He's a real artist."

Later, she said, "I want to get things done," she said. "I don't ever want to be satisfied. I want to experience everything. You know?" I didn't.

She wanted to hear my life story and to tell me hers. She wanted to talk about art, and go see all of the art in New York. "Experiences" was the refrain. "That's what I'm here for. That's why I took the Greyhound literally every weekend in high school until that last weekend when I bought the one-way ticket."

That was the end of August, 1986. By September first, Abi had moved in, giving up her roommate situation a few blocks away. Sharpey had to approve, so we trudged up to his cave on the top floor.

He was playing one of his guitars, as usual. "What'ya do," he asked her in his taciturn bass voice. I'll have to describe him at some point but for now, he's six-one, a hundred and fifty pounds, long hippy hair turning grey, and at the moment dressed in knee-length cut off fatigues and a wife-beater. No wife. Just the cat, and his many guitars lining the top of the walls.

"I'm an artist," she said.

"She'll do."

"Thanks! That's it? No credit check, no references?"

"Naw," Sharpey said. "There's two of you now. He's been payin' hisself.

With you, it'll be easy."
She smiled.

We talked about modern, contemporary, postmodern, and Village.
"What's 'Village'?
"'Village's like, whatever's in E.V.," she said. *"It's whatever art for rich people isn't."*
"Can't rich people buy art there?"
"Yeah, but they don't."
I thought this over. *"Thoreau said trade curses everything it touches."*
'Fucking-A."
"I once saw a piece," I said leaving out the fact that on that occasion my mother had taken me, "at MOMA, three mirrors installed in a corner, like making the corner on the floor, and sand poured into the corner in a neat pile. Some little kid thought it was like a sandbox and traced his finger through the sand. Me and the guard looked at each other and he shrugged, like, whatever, can't do anything about that now."
"Installations used to be cool. But now I think galleries figure out how to sell them."
"Say it isn't so."
She kissed me.
I told her about zoning in. "It's the opposite of zoning out."
"Tell me," she said.
"It's like flying. I'm here and not here. I'm seeing the person I'm drawing, nothing else, like nothing else exists, the universe is a frame around her face, her body…"
"That's just sex."
"No, no. I don't want it to end in sex. I mean, I do if it's you, but I don't. I want to draw. It's more like being drunk but not groggy."
"It sounds like smack."
"I don't know. I never did that. I wouldn't…"
"You have to draw me. Right fucking now." It was eleven at night and I drew her for two hours and we had sex and fell asleep in each other's arms again.

Another night, she said, "My dad taught me to throw like a boy and be like a boy."
"Your friends were boys?"
"Yeah. The boys did shit. The girls sat around talking about who to invite to a party. And who not to invite: like that was even more important. But you had to get an inner thing. The boys didn't do a lot either because there wasn't a lot to do. It was like, go into yourself or die trying to think of things occupy yourself."
"So you did art."
"Yeah. And other stuff. Some of it hurt."

"Like..."

"I mean, some of the things I did with my so-called friends...It's like we wanted to feel we were alive. Old story. Pain was better than no feeling at all."

"Uh-huh." I had no idea what she meant.

"I want a baby," she said. That froze me and she laughed. "Not now, dummy. Some day. I can't do that now but I want to go through it. I want all things to happen to me. I want to make all things happen. I want to feel it. I want that pain. They say labor pain is like nothing else. I want that."

"That's nuts."

"That makes me want it more," she said, with a look in her eye that frightened and compelled me.

Before the night in September when we went to see Sharpey, I got down on one knee and gave her a copy of my keys. She got down on one knee with me, then changed her mind suddenly, standing and saying, "No, this is better. I dub thee, Knight of Avenue B. You swear fealty to me, like, forever?"

"Sure. What do I have to do?"

"Try things. Be up for Whatever."

"Up for Whatever," I repeated dutifully. Later, she got out of bed naked and shivering, kissed me and grabbed my ass. "The last time I was on a bicycle," she said, "me and my friends did Special-K and rode around the high school parking lot until dawn. It was a Sunday, and Monday morning they found us asleep on the football field."

"Did you get in trouble?" I asked, suspecting Special-K wasn't the cereal.

"In 'trouble'?" She started laughing. She kept laughing. I smiled, less and less comfortably. Her laughing jag went on and on until it scared me.

In Life One, Sharpey had made Bar a deal. On the Sunday after the party in Soho, before the graffiti bombing expedition that led to Bar losing his place at Cooper, on November 2, 1986, a couple of days late, Sharpey threw a Halloween party for a hundred of his closest friends. There had been thirty Harleys parked out front, and another thirty pickup trucks. Men with bandanas on their heads or around their necks, women in bandana dresses, men and women in leather, suede, and denim, some with eye masks, a minority dressed up as something other than themselves, most not, it being not on the date, but rivers of beer, and Sharpey playing lead guitar in a band with friends on bass, drums, and rhythm, the vocals mic changing hands through the night. It was the second time Bar had been in Sharpey's place. Sharpey had taken down all the non-structural walls so that he had a big loft space with the kitchen in the middle, a bed in the back end where the bedroom would be, and the only interior walls around the bathroom. Abi and Bar spent a long time at the party talking with a forty-ish man who looked like all the others, leather jacket over black t-shirt, jeans with steel studs down the side, cowboy boots. He said he was Sharpey's "old friend," and that they "still hung out," but he, this man, "went straight a while ago," so they two of them "kept it casual." The party went until four, or maybe later; four is when Bar and Abi went down and passed out on their bed.

The next afternoon, November 3, is when Bar went up to pay him rent. In Sharpey's top floor loft, the chief difference the night of the party was that one whole wall was covered by a big canvas cloth. Bar looked around; the guitars on all the other walls were still there. "Nice set of axes," he said. Sharpey showed his yellow teeth, flicking an ash.

Sharpey stood and took down a classical acoustic. Still holding the cigarette, the guitar at a forty-five degree angle high on his chest, he played a Bach fugue for a few minutes. He stopped at the end of a section.

"Why'd you stop? That's great."

"Thanks, kid," he said, putting the guitar down against his cupboard. "These guitars, they got some value, don't yah think?"

"Sure. I guess. I wouldn't know."

"Which one's worth the most, do yuh think?"

Bar looked at the instruments. "No idea."

"Venture a guess?"

"That one? It's shiny. But I don't know."

"Good. That one's a cheap Thai copy of a Gibson. But it sounds good."

"Uh huh."

"You didn't say you knew. But you'd know art value, more 'n likely."

"What do you mean?"

"Take a look at this an' tell me how much you think it'd go for? Inna regular ole gallery over in

Soho er Chelsea er way on the Upper East?" Sharpey and Bar gently removed the canvas tarp from what he revealed to be a huge painting leaning against the wall. Bar silently measured it in his head, wondering how it got into the apartment. Maybe it was under 80" and so would fit through the door, but just barely if so. The painted canvas was recognizable: it was clearly byt the artist as Hammet, someone everyone was talking about at school. "Green and Yellow, is what it's called," Sharpey said. It was basically a late Ab-Ex piece, giant swirls of, as he said, green applied with a roller and yellow slapped on the canvas in a second round, after the green had dried, with big house paint brushes. Bar was momentarily stunned. The painting was beautiful, giant in the apartment space, a bold statement, and inexplicably there. "Yeah, yeah, get over yerself, Bar. I own it, legit. I got papers."

"How'd you even get it in here?"

"There's ways. How much? I mean, what's it go fer?"

"I'd have to check. I remember reading, maybe in a magazine, his work goes for mid-fifty thousands. I'm not sure what you'd get..."

"Yeah we gotta discount. Ain't no fancy sell goin' on here."

"That's true. But art people are funny. If they think there's a bargain, for instance..."

"Yeah, yeah. That's it. Get the psychology. I figured you'd be a natural."

"What do you mean, 'we', Sharpey?"

He didn't answer, saying "Come on" instead and leading Bar down to the second floor. Sharpey knocked three times in a specific rhythm, knock, wait, knock-knock. A voice answered, "Yeah?"

"It's me."

After a minute, Herbie opened three locks and let them in. He nodded to Bar. The whole floor, except for a twin bed, a hotplate, the bathroom, a card table, and a couple of folding chairs, was covered in paintings and sculptures haphazardly arranged, some under canvas drop cloths, most leaning on one another and on the walls, confirming Bar's glimpse of it. There were at least a hundred works. It was like that painting of the artist's studio that Bar had to memorize last year: what was it? Something Dutch. "Wow," he said.

"Got a few more upstairs, not countin' the big one I showed you. Special ones."

"Uh huh. Wow."

"Izzat all you got to say?"

"I don't..."

"I want you to sell it. All of it. Unload it."

"I don't..."

"Sure you do. Not all at once, mind."

"I do what?"

"You know how. Or you can figger it out. Ain't nobody gonna buy all this from me, not for close to what it's worth. You, on the other hand. Nice kid, art student at The Cooper Union, fancy school, good boy. You got some shine. You follah?"

Bar walked slowly around the room. What was this painting of sailboats worth? It looked like somebody's grandmother had made it to hang above their Connecticut fireplace. On the other hand, this abstract canvas had bold colors and a strong design that was halfway between a Barnett Newman and a Rothko but when was it made and by whom?

"Galleries take half. That's a big cut, is what I figger. I'll give you half-uh that. Twenty-five percent. Of whatever you kin git."

"I, uh..."

"Alright, alright, you think 'bout it." Bar walked around the floor, stepping over sculptures, wondering how long each one took to make. To end up here? *"I know yuh probably got questions but yuh see, that's the trick. You gotta agree to it without the answers. Except me tellin' you how I got the things and who gave 'em to me. I can tell you all that. Not more."*

"Uh huh."

"You think it over?"

"Yeah, yeah, sure. But, why can't Herbie do it?" Bar was counting the money in his head. Just that one painting upstairs, a quarter of that would be...enough.

Sharpey laughed, and Herbie, obediently, laughed along, though a little less. "Herbie's got some things in his past. Ain't that right?"

"Yes."

"Things that'd make it hard to be taken serious," Sharpey said to Bar, who was looking at a two-by-three foot painting that seemed a lot like Art's style, featuring two magical bug-eyed men with comic-book muscles wrestling. Or something. "An if you ain't taken serious, you don't get top dollar. Right, Bar?" Sharpey said, covering that painting with a cloth. "You ever seen, over on tenth street, that line-a junkies on Sundays? Over on C?"

"Yes, once or twice. I don't go over there."

"Best you don't neither. They's all lined up, like they's buyin' flour an' sugar instead of what they's buyin'. Line snakes inside that shell-uv-a place an' the sales is done right there with the sellers behind a brick wall. You ever wonder why the cops don't just bust it all up? Or them dealers in Tompkins Square Park? Or those guys out at that store front that ain't got no store inside on Avenue B and Fourth street? An' if I know about 'em, and you do know about 'em, how comes the cops don't do nothin'?"

"I don't know."

He leaned back on the back two feet of the metal chair and sipped his beer. "Guess."

"It seems like there's just too much for the police to take care of."

"Naw, that ain't it. They could do it. Bit by bit, sure. And they do. They bust up a lotta places,

mostly to steal the cash and sometimes the produce too. Sell the shit right back to the folks they just

busted."

"How do you...?"

"I talk to cops every day. Every day, Bar. You know what they tell me? City don't much give a shit about those folks. If you try dealin' outside on the street on Park Avenue, see what happens. Now they got dealers in fancy duds goin' inside, past the doorman an' up the elevator to the penthouse makin' drops, but on the street? Naw. City don't care 'bout these Ricans and Black folks and trash like me shootin' up, shootin' each other, snortin', sellin', whorin', what not, Bar. Don't care a bit. Harsh but true, my friend. Sooner you learn something like that..."

Bar gasped. "This one looks like a Basquiat."

"Yup," Sharpey said. "Not that I'm saying it is. Or that I ever met the dude."

"How'd you get it? It must be worth a lot."

"Yup," Sharpey said.

Bar looked at him but Sharpey added nothing. "He O.D.-ed, right?"

"Right around here. Not too long ago, either. He switched to the wrong supplier, somebody cheaper. This nabe is full of cut-rate, discount fuckers, put PCP in the powder, put fuckin' borax in it."

"Uh huh. Maybe he just took too much."

"Could be. Art game's different smell of shit, I figure."

"Uh huh."

"Ain't nothin' to be honest or reliable about. What you see is whatever you fuckin' think you see. They see me, they think bad shit. Bad shit means less money. Like you bein' all surprised I can play Bach. I can play mandolin, too. Spanish songs, real pretty, sixteenth century. People's complicated. Art folks think they know that but they don't, not inside. They see you, they think, honest kid. Reliable. Sin-seer. That's how you get your quarter. That, and the work it'll take."

Bar looked at the expanse of art. He walked slowly through the floor. Sharpey let him walk, taking out his tobacco box and another piece of rolling paper. "I can see you're figurin'," he said, "so let this help you figure." From inside his denim vest, he took out a white envelope and handed it to Bar. It was stuffed with twenties. "You say no, that's all's fine. Just give me back that cash, say you don't want no part of this, and I'll find me someone who do. You want in, that there's money down."

Bar left without committing, saying he'd let Sharpey know. The whole thing made him nervous, the white envelope and what it meant not the least. He thought, I can do it, I can, and then drowned in doubts. How could he? Whom would he call? "Hello, I'm a schmuck selling art that ... what? may have been traded for smack? Yes, I'll hold." He was no art dealer. He'd look like a fool kid, over his head, which was the truth. His main fear was that it was all somehow illegal, Sharpey's "papers" notwithstanding. He'd get caught because he had no idea what laws he was breaking or how to evade scrutiny. That night, he dreamed that after he sold two, three paintings, cops banged on his door in the middle of the night, New York City cops but with Nazi-adjacent arm bands. He hid in a trap door under his floor, and Sharpey walked in and told them no one lived there, but the cops saw his copy of Vogue and started banging on the floor above his head. He woke up sweaty and shaking to the sound of someone banging the grout off a trowel at a new construction site across the empty brick-yard.

Bar began unwinding the collection with one small painting that he took to a certain man of whom he had heart Art talking, Art's sugar daddy was the in-joke, the buyer of half of whatever Art made, and a person who wanted the other half as well. Bar found him in the phone book, made the deal in his Chelsea apartment, in cash, and gave three quarters of it to Sharpey, who was very, very pleased. After that insider deal, Bar had no idea how he would move any of the other pieces.

November 2, 1986.

Things that happened before the Return to Willets Point are unchangeable. There are things that are permanent in me, such as Abigail, whom I met two months before. Had met? Two months of being in love.

Eight days after my return saved dad's life, the afternoon before the party in Soho that ended with me going to the Chelsea Hotel, I am going up to see The Man. From inside Sharpey's place I hear light guitar fiddling. I knock.

"Come!"

"You always leave your door unlocked, Ely?"

Sharpey, shirtless, is sitting next to an open window that lets in the autumn breeze. He is cradling an old Gibson acoustic. An empty plus and half-full second bottle of beer are on the sill. Picasso is asleep on a pillow that says "Dog."

"Nobody needs 'a bust down a lock to see me. Either they come and kill me, lock or no lock, or they won't." The smile takes its time to appear. "What brings you to my doorstep, young blood?"

"Here's the rent."

"Thank-ee."

"Also, I want to buy the art. On two. The stuff that Herbie's looking after, all of it. We can talk price but I wonder if you're even up for something like that." Sharpey sits up. A smile appears on his face, disappears, re-appears, as he goes through stages of surprise. Good, finally that getting caught short thing is happening to someone else. "Herbie didn't intentionally tell me about it, so please don't give him shit about that, and he never let me see any of it."

"Uh-huh."

"Also Art. The artist?"

"Don't recall that name."

"He's one of your customers who paid with his work. The barter system you set up."

"Product A for product B?"

"Yes." I want Sharpey to know that there aren't any more secrets. But I don't want Sharpey to be threatened. Better not to connect the dots too much. Such as the dots between my knowing about those trades and the threatening possibility of Sharpey going to prison. "Am I off base?"

"Naw, naw, you're not off. You got me on my heels, but you're not off."

"For one thing, storing things in there means they're degrading, some fast and some slow. It's not temperature or humidity controlled."

"I got the AC running in there all summer."

"Yeah, that's nice. Better than nothing. But it's like I said. Not archival conditions."

Sharpey looks me over. He sits back in his chair and starts playing the guitar as if I weren't here.

I can wait. I say nothing, not moving, not staring at Sharpey. This goes on for a couple of long minutes. I recognize the music. "One of the cantatas?"

"Twenty-two," Sharpey says, not looking at me. He stops. "Where'd you get the money?"

"That matters?"

"Shit, yeah. You a gangster, Mister Miz?"

"No, no, nothing like that." He would have to be fast, mentally, to have stayed alive. The ability to see angles around corners.

"You got it on you?"

"Come on, Sharp."

Sharpey chuckles. "I do want to know if behind the dollar bills is muscle, and if behind your talk is dollar bills."

"You give me nothing until I pay. And there's no muscle."

"You understand what I mean."

"I'm not capable of enforcing a contract, except by use of the courts." I let myself risk using that word.

"Mm-hm," Sharpey says, and picks up from where he left off in the middle of the Bach piece. "And what'd'you want it fer?"

"I'm setting up a gallery. I need inventory. I don't have a huge list of contacts on the biz side of the art world and I don't want to wait around to buy one painting here, one sculpture there. You have inventory."

"That I do." He stops playing.

"That's really nice, Sharp. One day you'll tell me where you learned…"

"One day maybe I will and one day maybe I won't. You didn't say where you got the cash."

"No, that's right. I didn't. You didn't tell me where you got the art."

Sharpey smiles. "You jess said Art told you."

"Art told me about one painting and one artist, himself." There. In other words, I don't have a big case, so don't worry. "And then there's the drawing Abi sold you. Or traded."

Sharp raises eyebrows "I see," he says, not clarifying what went down with Abigail. He gets up, puts his guitar down carefully on a felt-covered stand, takes up his beer, and walks to the window. "You're jess full of surprises, ain't you, Bar? You know I spend my days in here."

"Yes. You're…keeping track of things."

Sharpey shoots me a look as if to say, that was stupid. "Be nice to get the fuck out. It's like a prison, sometimes."

"Meaning?"

"Meaning you could buy more than the art. Fund my retirement."

"What's more than the art?"

"The building. And I got lots on either side, too."

"Yeah. Wait, you mean *the* lots, not, as in 'many things'?"

"That's what I mean: the land. I expect you already knew that."

Yes, of course I knew.

"So? Your money handle all o' that?"

"Maybe. Depends on…"

"How much. Yeah."

"I have a number here for the art. I'm going to leave it for you to think over." I take an envelope out of my jacket pocket. "I'll come up with a number for the real estate..."

"You can't do that right here? You want me to think you didn't work all this out before you came up them stairs?"

"Nine hundred thousand, art, building, and the two empty lots." I put the envelope back in my pocket.

Sharpey curls his lips and smiles as if pleased that he is able to roll with this new, wheeler-dealer Bar, and knew whom he dealt with. "A million."

"Fine," I say, standing. "You going to give me a beer so we can drink to it, millionaire?"

"Yeah, I am," Sharpey says, this time his smile showing the teeth he had and the ones missing.

A million isn't bad for the art and the three lots, given present markets. I know future markets but no one else would, which matters in me determining the useless and irrelevant calculation of whether I am paying him an ethical amount. No bank would lend on this land for several years, and then the land will be worth more but Sharpey's life will have failed to move on from this prison, as he thinks of it. Yes, it's all fair, even though I will be rich and he will be merely just fine. Isn't that how all capital deals are thought of?

It was that evening that we went to the party in Soho and I told Abi that she was Achilles and I ended sleeping in the Chelsea Hotel.

I go down and knock on the door to which I still have the key. Abi appears in her bed clothes: one of my t-shirts, and underwear. "Okay," she says, letting the door hang open as she goes to the bedroom. She returns in shorts. No more couple-casual. "What's up, Bar. Need your things?"

"Just some of the art supplies." I'm standing in the middle of the apartment near the entry door, near the kitchen. I go to the back and pack a couple of army knapsacks and a canvas portfolio with art-making tools and the art that I made. I come back to the kitchen.

She's leaning a little on the kitchen counter. "I'm going to work in an hour."

"Isn't it in three hours?" I remember her schedule.

"How can I help you, Bar? I hope you're not here to tell me I need to move out. I'm not moving out. I talked to Sharpey..."

"No, you didn't, but I'm not here to say that. You can stay as long as you like as far as I have a say. I never had a written lease so it's not mine to give or not give. Go talk to Sharpey. He doesn't know I'm not here any more. It's still his building. By the way, I paid this month's rent."

Abigail stares at me blankly. She starts making coffee. Enough for two.

"I can't explain everything I know, but I do know some things, and you'd be better off if you ignored the fact that you're pissed at me and take the info for what it's worth."

"What info?"

"Art's going to come over. I can't remember what night but soon. He was going to bring spray cans. The three of us were going to go paint city garbage trucks under the FDR."

Abigail listens, saying nothing.

"Like I said, forget how I know and forget that I'm the one saying this. If you don't, Art will die after that."

"Of what?"

"He's going to kill himself because he doesn't want to go through dying slowly of AIDS. I understand that..."

"You understand nothing. You've done nothing. You've experienced nothing. You're a child spreading lies because you can't have what you want."

"I don't understand what Art is going through from experience, that's true. I understand it intellectually, but not viscerally."

"Who even are you? 'Not viscerally'? You didn't use to talk like that. You talk like you're forty. No fifty. I so want you to leave," she says, but isn't yelling.

Forty's about right. "I'm leaving soon enough. If he doesn't kill himself tonight, or tomorrow night, or any time soon, he might live a long time. There's no cure coming but there is treatment. A drug cocktail, a combo. People will be able to live on it for decades. Not sick all the time. You have to tell him to hold on."

"I have to? Don't order me around, boy. I don't have to do shit."

"No, that's true, too. I don't much care for Art. I consider him a narcissistic, nihilistic potential murderer. He's perfectly happy to go around spreading AIDS like he's Typhoid Mary. How can you accept his willingness to infect you even if you asked him to? Does he care for you or not? I think he's a monster and maybe we'd all be better off with him dead."

Abigail picks up a metal thermos as if to throw it at my head, appears to think about it, puts it down. She calmly pours the coffee in two cups with different amounts of milk, less for her and more for me, as she knows I liked it. "That the first thing you said that I have no problem believing."

"Well, thanks for the coffee," I say without touching it. I leave my key to the apartment itself, though not the main building's door, on the counter next to the cup. He sling my bags on my shoulders and go out to walk over to First Avenue, which is where the taxis might start to appear, never cruising for a fare in the wasteland of Alphabet City. As I stand on First Avenue, wondering why three cabs go by before one stops, I remember, not very long ago, that the idea of taking a taxi would have been unknown to me, and when I sit in the large Crown Vic's black leather seat, he feel the luxury of looking out the window as others walk.

9. Summer of Discontent

Life Two

Fall, 1991. The first leaves are changing out my window on the trees in the park.

I'm asking Summer to pose for a portrait. "Pick a place in the apartment. Make yourself comfortable. You have to be still for a long time."

"What should I wear? What does a muse wear?"

"Whatever you want." She still pronounced "I" as "Ah," reminding me of her request that we go visit her ancestral home in Georgia, a trip in which I felt little interest, especially after she said, by way of removing qualms, that a lot of Black people lived there and she even had a Black boyfriend in high school. We talked through how I, Bar, am not Black and she, Summer, already knew this but she was "from New York now" and others, she said, wouldn't understand it back home.

Summer smirks and quickly strips to nothing, revealing her thin, taut white body.

"Are you sure?"

"I'm a muse," she says, smirking. She goes to the studio, not to pose but to find my copy of Vasari. She comes back to our bed, leading me through the apartment as if I had a leash. The bed isn't made. She props up some pillows, puts on her reading glasses, and reads. "I have homework," for the class she's taking at N.Y.U. "If you're going to take a long time, I might as well get something done."

In half an hour he I'm zoning in, drawing in a trance.

Summer interprets this state as lust, which it partly is. She laughs. "Come to bed."

"No, no," I grunt.

"Don't fight it, baby. Come, I'll make you feel better."

"Be still and stop talking."

She frowns. "Always trouble with this one." But she is silent for a few minutes until she gets up and fetches her own sketchpad and a set of pencils.

"You too," she says.

"What?"

"Clothes." She gestures with her hand as if to remove them using magic.

"Huh? That wasn't my idea."

"If I'm going to pose, then so're you. You know I get a few hundred an hour to do this with anyone else."

"Wait, I don't … No."

"I proposed a better deal but hey, you wanted to work, so work. I have assignments to hand in. Or I'm leaving."

I disrobe. She returns to sitting in bed, smirking again at my tumescence.

After about ninety minutes we both finish a rough sketch of one another. I sit next to her on the bed and we compare. "This is very good," I say.

"Thank you. Yours is okay. I think you were distracted. Better if you finish when I'm not around."

"Later. What do we do now?" I'm leaning over to grab and kiss her but she says she's hungry and scoots to the other side of the bed, fetching her clothes on the way to the bathroom, where she re-robes.

She emerges in jeans and a t-shirt. "C'mon. Let's get Japanese."

"Come back. Please, baby, baby, please. I don't want to wait any longer."

She kisses me, playing with my hair and says in a sexy whisper, "I think I know what you want by now."

She pushes me away. "I'm going to eat." I follow.

September, 1993. At the opening, Summer's wearing a sheer, lacy black dress with embroidered white appliqué flowers from the recent grunge collections that of course had been a gift. The flowers were tactically arranged, and Summer initially wanted to go to the show wearing no underwear, but I put my foot down and made her put on black underwear, though she wore no bra, and even if there weren't a nude of her twenty feet away, she would have drawn attention. It was a group show for the gallery. I watch as men and women look back and forth from the picture to Summer. Some of them don't bother to look at the picture more than once. She's stealing the show, not only from my work but from everyone's, so I'm pissed twice over. I am also unable to stop staring at her myself.

Nick insisted that Summer attend and had spoken with her for an hour in our apartment about what she would wear. After buying Tricheur in '89 and hiring Nick to run it, I've been deferring to his instincts. He has doubled the gallery's revenues over that period, and I don't want to bother running things.

Sometimes I want an explanation, though. "What's the difference?"

"Summer adds special sauce, Bar. Summer, honey, the black. Not the yellow one."

"No? It makes me look fat?"

"Fat chance of that," Nick said. "You don't have the tits for it."

"I know. I've been eating bananas."

"It's not working," Nick said.

"Why's this so important? To the gallery? For the show?"

Nick turned to Bar and stopped smiling and said in a serious tone, "Your work is fabulous and it's going to make a splash and sell fast. But. But, but, but: it's not forward-looking and not conceptual and the collectors need to feel that they're getting in on something sexy and new. Enter Summer, stage left. She's sexy and new."

"So the art doesn't have to be," I said.

"Exactly."

"Excuse me while I go throw up," I said, going to the studio.

"Excuse me, honey. Gotta talk to daddy." He follows me. "What?"

"Nothing. Sometimes it's too much. The pecuniary concern. I would be as happy, no, happier …"

"If it didn't sell. Or if it sold for less than we're going to get. I know all that. I won't be just as happy, though, and neither will the gallery staff if I have to fire one of them. Think of it as arranging a transfer of wealth from those who don't need it."

"To you."

"To us. I pay the workers."

Summer called after me, "You know I don't have to go at all!"

Nick went back and soothed her and guided her toward the transparent black dress and they spent time picking underwear while I sat in the studio that was bereft of art, my pictures already hanging in the gallery in Soho, sulking.

I feel empty and alone amid this crowded Soho loft, ashamed of the success of Nick's marketing, ashamed of my complicity in it, and ashamed of how thrilled I was when at first, it worked. Knowing the future didn't guarantee anything. Now I'm cycling through wanting to crawl under a rock, then feeling re-thrilled at my success, then ashamed at the thrill, and so on. I wanted to hide when photographers ask for a picture of me and Summer together, but I smiled at the camera because to do otherwise would be to act out a petulant claim to purity that I don't deserve.

I detach myself from a group of collectors who've come to see my work. They were talking to me but looking at her. I do not see Summer as they do, the men who stare in lust or admiration, the women who stare in admiration or jealousy or lust or all three. They see a "model," a physically exemplary person, an ideal or aspirational being. In my drawing of her, I set out to reveal all of her mysteries and yet it does nothing of the kind. The drawing is for them a revelation that promises, but does not deliver the secrets of her allure. For me it is the human details of her flesh: the light bruises from exercising, the scar from an appendectomy, the freckles that add to her beauty by being flaws in it, the veins visible under her white skin, the gluteal folds, the folds in her small belly. I see the hair on her head that she spent so much time arranging but that's already showing signs of thinning, the fuzz on the back of her neck and her lower back, her almost invisible arm hair, her pubic hair, supposedly private but that she has shown to photographers on several occasions and the only semi-curly hair she had, and her calf hair, shaved (with a small nick from the razor). All of these details were in the drawing, but I wonder if anyone sees them, if they could see them and not the word in their heads, "model."

"Hey, Bar. You're thoughtful about something."

I am also turned on watching them watch her, and am disgusted by this unavoidable truth.

I am happy to be jarred out of them by Calliope, my colleague and friend. She is holding a plastic cup and popping a cube of cheese in her mouth. "How do you know?"

"I'm an artist. I see people's thoughts. By the way, I've come around," Calli says.

"To?"

"I don't dislike the porn you make any more," she said.

"I truly appreciate the generous, ..."

"Can it. Nice crowd."

"Nicholas."

"Total pro."

"I think, in a few years, or maybe this year, your work will be all anyone remembers. From this show. They'll remember Da Vinci and Rembrandt, too."

She laughs. "I see. Crisis of confidence? Also, there are five artists showing here."

"No comment on the other three. I don't pick everyone. Nick does. He's better at it. The tapestries, your tapestries, are what art should be, at its best. Incredible craft, vision, feeling, devotion."

"Huh."

"What?"

"You're not joking."

"Not even a little."

"Seriously, I do think your work is those things, too."

"Thank you. But still porn."

"I don't know. My friends all tell me they're sex-positive nowadays. The word 'porn' comes from the ancient Israelites. Not exactly a group I would identify myself with. I don't think they'd like me."

"You'd have to convert. And marry a guy."

"That's what I mean."

"Which suggests that political concerns blow with the wind."

"No, it doesn't suggest that. It means people grow and change. Why don't we go play hooky? I would prefer to bash and get bashed by you than stick around this party scene. Who forgot to invite the dykes? Get Summer and let's go to the pub across the street."

"I know for a fact that two of the models Nick invited are gay women. But since they're together, it wouldn't be profitable for me to introduce you. But I can't leave. I don't know if Nick would be more upset if we left or if Summer did."

Calli and I look over to Summer, who is surrounded by people wishing to speak with her. "Hmmm," she says. "I like 'em more zaftig, generally. But Summer's cool. She should show here, too."

"She's not ready."

"According to you?"

"I ... go talk to her about it. Not now. Later."

"Me?"

"Better you than me, the owner, or Nick, the salesman."

A photographer who has been looking at the two of us and back to the brochure Nick made confirms for herself that we're a couple of the artists and asks us for a picture. Calli complies, then goes to get another cup that she takes out onto the street, making her escape.

November, 1995.

Whiz...DOOF! The expensive, very high heeled silver shoe flies past my left ear and thumps against the white wooden column behind me, producing an impressive bass drum sound. I turn and see the mark.

"Violence won't work," I observe without flinching, "unless you kill me. I suggest poison, or perhaps if you slit my carotid artery suddenly, while I'm asleep. Sharp surgical steel is best. You may remember where the carotid artery is from that book of anatomy I gave you. You should study it more. It shows in your drawings of arms and hands. Hands, most of all. But then, even Rodin had trouble with hands. Donatello ..."

"YOU'RE A TOTAL SHIT!"

"Come on, Summer. Not 'total' shit. 'Total' is harsh."

"YOU FUCKED HER! YOU SHIT!"

"Calliope?"

"You know who I mean!" (Who Ah mean.)

Don't say "whom," I say to myself. Don't play. You're playing. Stop. This is a serious thing, even if it's laughably based on nothing. Nothings like this are based on real things. "Calliope's gay." Yes, stick to facts.

"Fuck you!"

"Why don't you call her? Or call Chauncey. She broke his heart in twain. Call them both. Then call Nick and everyone who has ever known her and ask them all."

"You'd love that, wouldn't you? Me and another woman. You fucking perv."

"I'm available to discuss that possibility, but not with Calli. She is one of my oldest friends."

Summer smolders at me, holding the other evening shoe in her hand, thinking about the next pitch. Her arms are at her side, not poised to strike, but the other arm shakes slightly. Her left eye is twitching, as I've noticed it does whenever she's passionate about something: chiefly in anger or in pleasure.

I'm in jeans and a Century Cycling Club of New York t-shirt, barefoot, leaning against the back of a sofa, feeling the specific relaxation of tension after a confrontation, even though it's not over. She's wearing a floor-length sliver sequin dress with a long side slit on the left, also barefoot after weaponizing her footwear, causing the dress to pool on the floor. I didn't want to do this party. If I do them at all, it's out of obligation, and then there are too many of those. She says she likes the socializing but why do we need to dress uncomfortably for that? And usually there isn't even dancing. Calliope and I would've been a more obvious pairing, if I were a woman.

Summer is breathing heavily as if forestalling a good cry. Suddenly, I feel how dear she is to me. "Come and let me hold you."

"No," she says, but relaxes slightly. "Grrrrrrr," she says and stomps off to the bathroom. She has to lift the dress with her hand to walk, and simply drops the other sandal on the floor, where it, too likely made a mark.

Like the mark on my heart. I scold myself for the sickeningly sentimental image. But I feel sentimental. I feel … what I don't think I've felt before for Summer. I feel the way I did, do, toward Eva. Eva, whom I haven't seen in many years. Summer, with whom I am currently sharing my life. How long now? Has it been five years? Five long summers. Almost five since our first date (her idea). Longer than with Eva.

I've grown accustomed to her face. She's not the person whom I met, nor even the one that moved in four years ago. She's my peer. I'd call myself lucky to be her peer. I taught her about art and she taught me about the possibilities of human growth.

She's outstripping her teachers at this point. I don't teach her anymore; we teach each other. I go to her to ask her opinion, and not to be polite. It wasn't too soon to hang her work in public. And there's the cooking, and the reading, and the corresponding lesser emphasis on clothes unless she knows it's going to be a public event … she has surprised me more than I thought could happen.

What have I done?

One of the bitchy fashion people must've told inaccurate gossip about myself and Calli. She came home in a rage. It was like a flash of silver and blondness in the form of a fury, come to destroy art. She stormed into our shared studio, grabbed the picture on my easel, and tore it into shreds before I could react, destroying five hours of not very good work. Not devastating but certainly frustrating enough. At first I was so surprised that I made a joke, something like, so that's what you think of my work, and neither of us laughed, and it sank in that she destroyed something I made. It was confusing because I was thinking of tearing it up myself but then she did it and, stunned for a moment considering this, I said nothing further. I walked away to get a snack, infuriating her more than if I had flown into a rage.

I can hear her in the bedroom. The zipper of her dress, the tumbling about in her drawers, pulling a suitcase down from the top of the closet clumsily such that a bunch of other things fall on top of her, ("Are you alright?") her exclamation, "fuck," and then the rushed packing of her things.

I call to her, "Are you going somewhere?"

She's changed into gym shorts and a Velvet Underground t-shirt. Her face, even with tear-stained black makeup raccooning her eyes and tousled hair, her wild look, is even more beautiful to me than usual. There is never a moment I am with her without desire, but my feeling has a hundred vectors. Often, I feel her youth more than her beauty. I had gotten used to the small crinkles in the corners of Eva's mouth and eyes and found, in the vulnerability of those, much to desire. Because her youth was also and importantly in her appetite for information, for experience, she makes me fear that she would do as Abigail once did, or would somehow spin out of control in some other adolescent flail. Much of my energy was spent restraining myself from trying to restrain her, much as a father might deal with his need to correct an older teen. She never went toward the self-destructive end of cool, though. She grew up with too little to be drawn to that luxury. Summer was already in her mid-twenties and had supported herself from seventeen to twenty-three without me in her life. As she stands there, like a little sun, radiating beauty, I am fearful of her effect.

Why? It's not the intimidation of the way her beauty was perceived by others, her status, not any more, though that lasted for a long time even after she moved in and after many expressions of her desire for me. Eventually, dense though I be, I listened to her tell me how much of a catch she felt I was, though to believe that required me to unravel much I had felt about her for twenty years.

I am afraid of loving her. I simply can't do that. I'm here for Eva, not Summer. I have used Summer, an admirable person, as a way station. I didn't expect to admire her. I thought she'd be a model, not much more. I don't know what I thought. I wanted her.

This whole silliness about me cheating on her isn't baseless. I didn't, but deserve the accusation nevertheless.

"You're a fucking liar," she says, and goes back to packing.

"No."

His father told him you have to push, push, but he was terrified that Stacey wouldn't like him, would humiliate him with rejection and, worse, leave him desiring her regardless of the rejection. But isn't it necessary for a moral person to be afraid of being disliked so that one works hard to be liked? Stacey wasn't afraid. Bar showed her too much of his awe of her body, of kissing. "Not like other boys," she said. How did the other boys kiss? Was it as if to suck life and sex from the girl, or as if attacking them? Bar kissed Stacey as if studying her form, memorizing through touch what his eyes reported, as if to verify the information and memorize it beyond all forgetting. Also as an act of obeisance to acknowledge the immensity of the favor she did him. It did not occur to him that the favor, however large or small, was reciprocal because it did not occur to him that his body might be a thing someone else might want the way he wanted hers.

What I now have to do is not what I want to do. I walk slowly to our threshold of our room. "It's better that you go," I say, thinking the exact opposite. This is a way of pushing, too.

"FUCK YOU!" she screams, pointing at me. She throws a chiffon scarf at me that flutters to the floor between us.

"We should have been franker about what we were doing together," I say, moving closer to her.

"What the fuck does that mean? You know what? I don't even care. Excuse me. I need to get my things."

"I was always drawn to your beauty, and you were always drawn to my cachet."

"Fuck you. I'm not listening. What you're saying is so … ! Oh my god, that is so gross." She is crying again, frantically throwing clothes and a hair dryer and random cosmetics into the suitcase.

"It's true. Let's say hypothetically that I was exactly the same person but without the money and no big art career. No art career at all. Let's say I'm working at a bicycle shop, barely paying the rent. We know each other because, oh, I don't know, I'm doing a second job weekends at Tricheur, which is still owned by Dicky, and I'm the gallery sitter, and you're still modeling but you didn't yet make it the only job so you still have do reception there. Huh? Imagine that situation. Would you give me the time of day, in that scenario? Be honest, if not with me than at least with yourself."

She stands quietly for a moment, looking as if she might be considering it. "No. No time for scrubs."

"Yeah, that's what I thought. So, …"

"That's a totally random supposition," she says. "Why don't we imagine that you're a professional basketball player in China and I'm a librarian in Iowa? We wouldn't even meet, would we?"

"It's not random. It's what happened. It's like, when we were having sex the first few times or let's say the first ten, what was that like? Did you have to grin and bear it? It can't have been all career move and no affection, unless you're an Oscar-worthy actor, but how much of it was because I seemed cool or powerful? Again, tell yourself the truth regardless of what you tell me, or if you even answer me."

"No." She's avoiding my gaze, looking at the north view of the bedroom window, up Fifth.

"No what?"

"No, it wasn't… You're implying … I'm not a whore. You monumental pig."

"I didn't mean that. Everyone has mixed motives. If you were in it for an exchange, well, so was I. I flatter myself that in my case my desire for you led to something more." I look at the window view she's looking at. "I just wonder whether that was ever true for you, in the past."

"Bastard. The past doesn't matter."

"We're all whores, in a sense. But don't let me interrupt your packing." I turn to leave.

"I…" she begins, gesturing at the suitcase vaguely.

I turn back, thinking, you also got an artist's career out of it. How difficult would it have been to get gallery representation, without your boyfriend owning a gallery? It's arguable both ways. I do think she'd have gotten the good notices she got, the paragraph in *Art in America*, the two-sentence listing in *The New Yorker*, not to mention the spread in the October, 1993 issue of *Vogue*. On the other hand, would she even have become an artist if I had not influenced her, given her the leisure to stop all gigs involving travel, given her time and space? Especially time.

Is that Summer? His Summer? Yes, it was, on the cover. (C'mon. She's in no way "his.") He picked up the fashion mag and waded through the immensity of pages preceding the table of contents and then onto a piece called "Summer's perfect Summer." It was about her art. He did not know that she painted. He did not know that she "quit the modeling scene to settle down here, where the light is amazing" and her husband's family has owned an oceanside mansion for generations. He stared at the reproduction of her painting of a sailboat. He did not know that she "always drew, even as a child in Romania," how a designer discovered this and put her large watercolor pieces in the background of her 1992 Paris show, how galleries came flocking, and how Summer — the Summer, his Summer, but not "his" in any real proprietary sense — now preferred to live full time in Watermill with her two-year-old son, husband triple-A-list architect to the stars and three-thousand-square-foot, thirteen-foot-ceiling barn converted into studio. The white crochet dress listed for $6200 at Bloomies. The cost of his apartment for a year, including cable. That she preferred life out there as it was "slower and can be more spiritual, like it was down home in Georgia, if you pay attention to the light."

"It's going to be a few more minutes. I'm sorry. Nick's on with the London office," said the reception dude. He looked like he was Bar's age, but rarefied and ultra-pale in all-black Japanese pajama-like clothing, though not Asian himself.

"It's okay."

Bar had already played the meeting out in his mind and was trying to prep himself for getting nowhere, once again, by saying that this wasn't the last gallery on earth just because the East Village art scene had turned into a burst soap bubble and with it all the smaller galleries that might've taken a risk on him and that just because the only reason this Nick guy was seeing him at all was that he was an acquaintance of a friend of Eva's sister's boyfriend didn't mean that...what? What didn't it mean? What does it mean when Summer's shitty greeting card art with poorly defined light an vague, poorly drawn lines got national press coverage while he...struggled to avoid the consummate bitterness of one who knew that he did not deserve to be bitter, that he had chosen this life, that... god, she was so pretty.

"Bar?"

That must be him. Thin, tanned, and tall, in a tightly fitted light blue suit, no tie, brown shoes and no socks and a gold chain around one ankle. Coiffed, but not as obviously as Geoff.

"Yes?"

"Nick. Come in. Sorry to make you wait. Geoff, could you run this over to Larry? West 23rd."

"Yeah," said Geoff, taking a 30x36" portfolio and stopping to put on a jacket that seemed exactly like another one of his pajama top.

"Come in."

"Thanks."

Nick got to it quickly. "Call it a gimmick if you wish."

"What, like..."

"What art needs right now. An angle. Something to stand out. I like your work. No: I admire your work, Bar. It's not part of the art conversation that happening now. Both are true."

Bar said something vague about humanism and capturing souls.

"Yes, of course, and I do still believe in that," Nick said. "Look, you can't just paint or draw or sculpt anymore. Not since Picasso. Not since Cezanne. Hell, Bar, not since J. M. W. Turner." Nick turned and found a half-full cup of coffee, turned back, and looked down at Bar, studying his face. "Conceptual lifting means you have to have something. Every painter has to reinvent painting. The form. Or the artist himself. Someone we've never heard from before. Frankly, I'm surprised. I mean, given…who you are. I would have thought...I probably should say so, but,"

"Who am I?"

"You're...your own man," Nick said, recovering and smiling and hiding his face with the coffee. Before the smile disappeared, Bar saw perfect teeth to go with the smarmy professionalism, the more pro, the more smarm. "Look, if I put your work on our walls, that's like lying to you. Leading you on."

"I…"

Nick waved off what he assumed to be a coming apology. "It'd be telling you you'll earn money and get recognition, and those things won't happen."

"How do you know?"

"I don't, for sure. There is no knowing the future. We're all guessing out here. I think it won't happen, I should say 'yet.' Thus far, I've been good at predictions and that's why I have this job. Did you see the Biennial?"

"At the Whitney?"

Nick chuckled ever so briefly."Yes. The Holliday video? The Martinez thing?"

"I've heard. It's all…"

Bar said "bad art," as Nick said, "Political."

Nick said, "The critics all hated it." He seemed to be glowing.

"Yeah? So then,…"

"That's why it's the roadmap. They're scared because they can smell that it's the future. It's not going to be all white all the time any more. Or men. Or men looking at women."Nick raised an inscrutable eyebrow saying this. "Why don't you do some self-portraits? Instead of the girls. Women. Whatever. You're a good-looking guy. A subject for art?" he said, standing and moving out from behind his table that acted instead of a desk and sitting next to Bar on the white couch.

Bar stood quickly and thanked him and was walking to the elevator but decided to walk down the six flights on the cement staircase and couldn't stop the sinking, exquisitely sickening feeling akin to being called into the principle's office or told by a cop to pull over or being caught jerking off. This was his best shot and not even because of being treated as a piece of ass but because the gallery represented people so similar, but not as good, no, not with Bar's skills, and he knew that now, he could tell levels of draughtsmanship with the precision of an electron microscope, but he didn't have a gimmick or a political agenda or a sense of what was going to happen in the future and didn't see why he should care. Nick was right, though. He resented the degree to which he knew that Nick was right. He didn't totally believe the line Nick was selling, not after just seeing the parchment white-girl Summer on glossy pages selling art that challenged no one and nothing but he did believe it, too, and understood that it was all happening at once, the old corruption and the new dispensation, and none of it had anything to do with trying to draw as well as Albrecht Durer or Leonardo da Vinci or Käthe Kollwitz or Rembrandt. The trick would be to avoid the self-pity that was threatening to wash over him as if he were sitting under a giant dam with a thousand cracks. The goal, rather. "You've got to have a con in this land of milk and honey." It's not like he's on a train to Dachau. It's not like he's a child hiding in a barn from pitiless men with rifles and utter determination guiding their Jew-hate. But is that the standard? If you're not on your way to Bergen-Belsen then you're happy?

"I taught you to draw."
"I'm eternally grateful. So the fuck what?"
"I saying. We did things for one another. I don't think you are grateful. You were painting vaguely formed sailboats. You couldn't get the light right. You didn't even know what light in paint was."
"I drew better than you thought," she said. "You didn't used to be able to come from a blow-job."
"And I am grateful for your ministrations in that area."
"Why do you talk like you're a professor? Like you're forty. You're twenty-eight."
"Forty-four." I'm counting the total time of consciousness.
"What do you want, Bar? One second it's 'you'd better go.' The next you're arguing that I owe you; you're Pygmalion and I'm your statue. Does that mean you love me and will never, ever consider cheating on me, that you want to marry me and give me children and grow old together, that you'd never think about being with anyone else? What's the deal, Bar, because I'm near done with this bag."
"Where will you go?"
"I don't know. Answer me."
"I will never, ever cheat on you. I did not."
"Not enough. I require an answer in full."
"Why can't we go on as we were? Things were nice. I think… that I do love you."
She sits on the bed and looks up at me. I want to hold her. I want her to leave so I won't have to face Eva with an encumbrance. I want her to stay because she makes me excited to see how she is becoming herself. I want her to leave. She's crying. "That's the worst profession of love I have ever heard, and I've heard a few. If that the best you can, it's not very good."
"Yes, it is."
"Something's wrong with you. You're, I don't know. Deficient. You haven't told me everything. You keep secrets. Why do you think I'm suspicious? What are the secrets about, Bar?"
"I don't." How can I tell her? I turn and walked to the kitchen and sit at the counter. I glance back to see Summer considering her options. She joins me in the kitchen and gets us one beer, sits next to me, and we share it in silence for a long while.

I consider mine. Summer wants kids. We should do that. I could be a good dad. Better than my own.

Peter comes into my head. Peter's dead now. I killed him. I aborted him. What's the word for a person who prevents conception? What kind of father can I be, given that?

Summer comes into the kitchen and takes my free arm and tugs me gently. "Maybe if you fuck me and make me come I'll stay another night," she says. It's the thing to say. I let myself stand and hold her and feel her beauty. Holding her is a drug. An incredibly beautiful woman comes to me and asks for sex, and Peter isn't alive. Those two things are unrelated. Yet, through me, they are parts of a whole. I feel sorry for Summer that she doesn't have what it takes to reject the bad deal I am offering and leave. I hold her closer.

"Tell me the truth," she says.

"Uh-huh."

"Calliope. Why'd you spend all night talking to her. The other night. At the party in that gallery on the Upper East Side."

"Because every single other person at that party, you excepted, was a terrific bore, and you were talking to those gay men forming around you like groupies, talking about the runways of Paris. The people talking to me were in finance, or worse, in real estate. I'd be happy not to have another real estate conversation again for the rest of eternity. Or fashion. Before Calli showed, I was listening to a conversation about handbags. I do not care about handbags."

"No?" Summer cracks a smile. "Not even the ones with gold chains for straps?"

I keep my poker face. "Particularly those. I'm not attracted to Calliope. Nor she to me. However, I do like talking with her. She's trying to push feminism in art into new directions that … "

"Okay."

" … that I don't fully understand and she was explaining this to me … You're not listening."

After, I lie awake, once again amazed at how a thin person can snore so loudly and remember taking Summer to the Met, two years ago, before the college classes and the reading started. We had been together for a couple of years already by then. I asked her to stay on at Tricheur. She asked me to dinner. I should have seen surprises coming when she sprung that one on me. I approached Tricheur because I vaguely knew Dicky's financial shape and resultant desire to get out and because I was hoping to see Summer, of course. What proportion of each motive made up the whole? When I first saw her behind the reception desk, I was excited but I could breathe. She didn't recognize me, maybe because I wasn't wearing a black rock concert t-shirt. (I showed up in a blue buttoned shirt and shoes, not sneakers.) Still, it hurt. I would've recognized her across a veldt full of elephants.

I didn't know what she saw, except my desire. I got caught looking on the second day I went there. I was trying to talk Nick into running the place. Instead of sitting in the office, I stood in the doorway where I could see her.

She knew why even if I did not. I didn't have any sense that I presented an image of a young entrepreneur on the rise but later, on the fifth or sixth date, she told me that's what she saw and it was disappointing both in removing the mystery of her attraction and because it wasn't about anything good in me.

I tried to take her to the Met on one of those dates but at the last minute she said she had been invited to some party at some hot new restaurant opening and would I take her and I said of course but that should have clued me in as well.

She had never been to the Met, not to mention MOMA or the Whitney or the Brooklyn Museum, the Guggenheim, the Frick, or the fucking Morgan Library, though she had been living in New York City for four years, working in an art gallery. There were no museums near her southern town. "What about D.C.? You said you went there sometimes. The National Gallery?"

"Not for that. We went to get me a dress once a year for Christmas, in years when daddy had a job. He took is to the Smithsonian. He liked rockets."

I took her to other art galleries first, and then to the Metropolitan. We were a couple but it still felt new and I didn't understand all of her cues. She arrived at the Met in black culottes, a black turtleneck, black clogs, and a black beret. I didn't get that this was her idea of an artist's outfit until I saw her standing in front of some French paintings.

 She wanted to see the Impressionists. That's what she thought art was. We brought pencils and small sketchpads. I drew her as she copied a Monet picture of a natural rock arch in the ocean. She wouldn't take advice, however gentle, unless she had a problem. When I solved it she told me to be quiet. She learned much more quickly than I thought she could. She worked hard at drawing for weeks and then months and at first I took it as a compliment but it was soon clearly not something she did for me or anyone else.

When we began, she had no language to talk about art but did have an intuition about it from looking at photographs. She understood portraiture, light, space, and what she thought "looked good." Sometimes she let me teach her as long as it didn't feel like teaching. She was every teacher's dream, quick, eager, independent. We became close in ways we wouldn't have for years.

I became more and more aware that Eva and I never did this.

That first day at the Met, I said, "The Impressionists thought that this is how the eye sees."

"It's more realistic, then."

"Yes, in a way. In their minds."

"You don't think it is?" she turned to look at me, her hair falling over one eye. There was not a moment when I did not consider her beautiful, even when I was angry with her or simply bored of her, or when I saw through her model's poses.

"What do you think? What about all these colors?"

Summer considered Degas's "Woman Combing Her Hair," 1890. "They're not wrong. The colors make you see them as right. The artist forces you."

I thought that was interesting and would have replied but a palimpsest hit, one that I thought wouldn't because Peter was dead or wasn't born but it was here in the Met and I was with Peter in Life One. I was teaching him how to draw. I felt my love for Peter mixed with bottomless sorrow, and even as I felt love for Summer I felt guilty for loving her for the betrayal of Eva and then guilty toward Summer for thinking about Eva. As this mix bewildered me, the palimpsest suddenly stopped, as if it were a statement someone or something made to me but that I couldn't understand.

"What's wrong?"

"No. Nothing, it's alright. I'm alright. I'm going to be alright."

"You sure?" She kissed me and told me how handsome I was and how she wanted to make love with me. That made me alright.

Before that day, the sex was too obsequious, too much her being inquisitive after what I might want, too much like she was molding herself to me, with corresponding suggestion that there was nothing pleasurable in it for her, even when she came, yes, even then, as if her orgasms were meant to delay and obscure the idea that they would normally deny. Sex on those terms made me feel the paradoxical limits of power because in giving herself Summer made me feel indebted, less autonomous. That night, after the museum, after my seeing her work on something completely for herself, our bodies moved in ways that felt closer to nature. We felt like lovers.

"Smudge it with your finger. Watch me. Look."

"You're allowed to do that?"

"Allowed? You can do whatever you want. It's just paper."

"Kew-well."

Peter's wide-eyed wonder at learning to draw made Bar smile. Bar drew little sketches of him in a five-by-seven inch pad, and wondered at the insouciance. The child hides nothing. The child is himself, only. He doesn't walk to you; you have to go to him. He have been glad to give Claudia a break on the occasional Saturday and now that it was almost every Saturday, he came to look forward to it, flipping from being the student to being the teacher, glad to show what he knew, to see Peter looking up to him as the big brother not just because that is what he was but because Peter wanted something like this and wasn't getting it at school or from the series of men Claudia had had four-to-eight month relationships with. It was a relief to go to Jackson Heights and see that it was just the two of them living there, Peter in Bar's old room that still had Bar's Star Wars poster up on the wall and Star Trek sheets on the bed.

"You can suggest the illusion of transparency, even in drawing. The painter used a glazing technique but you can do this … and this …"

"That's cool. You stop now."

"Right. Your picture."
"My picture."
"She's cute, that girl."
"She's hot. For a French girl."
"What's that mean?" Bar laughed.
Peter shrugged and continued drawing. "She's just paint."
"But he probably saw a girl like that, long ago."
"So she's really old now."
"No, she'd be dead by now. This is Degas, 1874."
"Creepy."
"No. She's still alive here."
"You be quiet now. I'm working."

Bar nodded and smiled. A palimpsest hit. He had begun calling them that. He was there with a very beautiful woman who was telling him that she wanted to have sex with him and he thought, maybe this is a porn dream but it wasn't because he saw from two different angles: with her he was in front of a Degas on the other end of the room. He felt sorrow from the other self but couldn't understand it, and then it was gone and he was glad Peter hadn't see him go through it.

It was around then, after Summer (temporarily) stopped being suspicious of Calli, and of the girl who replaced Summer at Tricheur, and of the woman in Paris on that long weekend who looked almost exactly like Summer herself, and of others, that we started going to restaurants a lot. It was she who wanted to. I let Summer pick the restaurants because she didn't care about how expensive they were as long as a place was either "hot," meaning it made her feel as if she were seeing the center of things, or someone she knew told her about it and she had to defray her experience-jealousy. I let her order for me; I didn't want to look at the prices because I would calculate how many meals at The Kiev I could have instead, or as opposed to going to the supermarket and buying ingredients to make schwarma and hummus that, in Life One, I had used as a way to remind myself of my father and in any case I could never have afforded to go out, then.

I never imagined what it would be like for money to become no longer an impediment; the thing to consider was simply whether or not I wanted something. I had imagined it being a problem solved, not shifted. I still fought with Summer over her habit of shopping-as-recreation, which it offended me from an aesthetic point of view. I regularly brought up, then, the clothes in her closet with the tags still on a year later that she bought even though she was now being given almost any clothes she wanted directly from designers happy to have her wear them in public. She said I was like someone who lived through the Depression and I thought: Or the Holocaust, of course, like Mom, or someone who lived through being with Mom. I fought with myself to become convinced that even that clothing wastefulness of Summer's should be ignored, indulged as a celebration of living. As long as I continued, I thought, directing large piles of the fruits of capitalism (not my capitalism, not my enterprise or daring, but that of others) to charities that provided what ought to have existed as government programs, but didn't. As long as I gave money to political candidates who advocated for those programs, I should allow myself a less cloudy conscience.

    She soon settled on Odeon as her default bistro. The first time we went there, I came from drawing my father and was wearing sneakers, my black jeans, a black t-shirt, and a blue denim jacket, and the maître d' asked to talk to me as I walked in. At least he pulled me aside before asking, "May I please see your credit card? Or perhaps you could show me cash for tonight's meal?" "Why?" "It is embarrassing but we have had trouble in the past, you understand." "No, I don't. What trouble?" "Please, I am so sorry, however, I must ask this. The last time I paid out of my pocket, you see?" I gave him a long, hard stare and thought about what I should say or do but then took out my credit card and handed it to him as the simplest choice. The maître d' ran it and smiled after a moment and handed it back with more apologies.

    At Odeon, there were artists and fashion people and celebrities and hangers on and sometimes I got to hang out with the artists and sometimes not. A couple of times, seeing no one I wanted to talk with, I turned to leave but Summer took my arm and made me sit at a table of her old or new friends. We tried sitting at different tables but it meant an asexual ending to the evening.

    Half of the purpose of spending money on dinner was to put Summer in the mood. She never said no, but there were times when it felt so wholly my idea, past a ninety-ten split in initiative, that I would rather let it go. A less expensive restaurant was sure to reduce her eagerness later, but a high-end place with no "friends" often failed to do the trick, either.

    As our taxi approached West Broadway on a chilly, wet Tuesday night in November, 1992, the streets empty of people and full of warehouses and old factory buildings with steel gates in front and some with jagged windows above, the cobblestones shiny in the misting rain, I thought about my knowledge of what would be. Only the Odeon's neon red signage provides colors other than brown and black and steel gray, but in years hence there would be stores open and people thronging at dinner time and baby strollers and discussions of the first-grade teachers at P.S. 234. My wool slacks itched my thighs. The sight of Summer's bare feet in strappy, shiny heels and her black Betsy Johnson spaghetti-strap dress made me feel cold.

    We went to a large table where Calliope, Chauncey, and a newly minted art star named Franc of ambiguous gender, and a few others were sitting. (S)he wore a long white suede duster and white wide-brimmed hat that (s)he did not remove and that kept hitting Chaunce's neck, and turquoise-studded rings on each finger and a turquoise hair clip in the back of their neck-length hair. Franc stared continuously at Summer, a phenomenon I had seen so often that I hardly registered it. I knew that Calli had no money and wondered about Chauncey. Franc could probably pay their way. I said, "Night's on me." No one challenged.

Calli did a tally of the room. "There's De Niro. And there's, like, half of Saturday Night Live. And David Johansen. And Keith Haring."

"Haring's dead, dear."

"No, I swear, that's him."

"It's troubling," I said, "when someone as no-sell-out as you points out the celebrated people."

"Should I talk about the death of the East Village art scene instead? Oh, and there's Amber Valetta."

"Who's that?"

"Model." Summer said. "She was nice to me in Milan last year. I lost my underwear and … " We turned to face Summer. "… don't ask. She lent me some. I think I still have it."

"She's beautiful," Calli said, staring.

"You could sell it for a lot of money," Chauncey said. "Don't stare, or people will think you're a lesbian."

"I am a lesbian."

"Not last night," Chauncey said.

"I reserve the right to dump you for Amber Valetta," she said, staring. Amber Valetta smiled at Calli. Calli choked; she looked away.

The waiter came and recited an endless list of specials. People made orders of food and drink, and some, just of drink.

Chauncey pointed out that the art scene was merely moving around, first to from the Village to Soho and now, it seemed, to Chelsea way west.

A person I did not know who turned out to be an art dealer himself confirmed that trend. "Everyone's going to end up there. Or in Brooklyn."

Calli said that Chelsea was "too boring" a place for art. "The whole scene of cheap space and risk-taking it had encouraged seemed to be drying up. Nobody wants to show political art any more. You can't show things like Haacke or even…"

"Of course you can," Chauncey said. "We're going to have to make our own spaces, like Bar is doing."

Chauncey and I spoke over each other about Haacke and capital. Summer interrupted: "Haacke's art is political, but only in a limited, specific sense of 'political.'" Everyone turned to look at her.

"What do you mean?" I asked, wondering if she could keep it up.

"Yes," Franc asked her with a French accent, "what is 'political' if not Haacke?"

"Haacke's work is political because it's, like, about politics and, like, money. He likes to send up the institutions that host his work. Bite the hand that feeds him," Summer said. "But's not, like, *political*-political."

"What's..." I began.

Summer was already continuing and crinkled her nose disapprovingly at my interruption, "I mean, it's like Picasso painting the *Guernica* or David Wojnarowicz. It's all obvious and no one really learns anything, any new way of thinking. It's like Normal Rockwell painting that little Black girl being taken to school, or something. I learn more from something like Jacob Lawrence paintings. Just because of what he paints. Or like Agnes Denes. That wheat field things she made, like seven years ago, in Battery Park before they built it up. It's so, I don't know, things like that..."

"Suggestive," Franc said.

"Make you think much more, and more widely," Chauncey added.

"Beautiful," Summer said. "How they see the world."

"Yeah. I guess I like the obviously political stuff more," Calli said. "Beautiful is passé," she said to Summer. Summer smiled at her as if to disprove the thesis. "I like Barbara Kruger. Hit 'em on the head with a shovel. Don't be subtle."

"But then nothing changes because no one changes how they think," Chauncey said.

The four of them argued this point back and forth while I wondered whom I had been taking Summer for. Now and then she looked at me and seemed to understand that, too.

Someone mentioned Jacob Lawrence again and I said I often liked Lawrence more than Matisse.

"Well, yes, of course" Franc said, "but do not take offense if I say this is because you are a kinsman of his. No?" Franc talked about being French for a while.

Someone asked if the city were going down the drain and whether it was Reagan's fault or Koch's.

Because I had drunk too much, meaning a whole glass of Cabernet, I said, "Yes, but not the way you think. It's going up the drain. Full of rich people. The artists and the whole reason for living here, all the clubs and places to go dancing, the funky people, all that's gone. Soon. But we can't be nostalgic for our lost youth. We have to adapt to the Reaganite dystopia."

"What do you mean, 'lost youth'? We *are* youth," Calliope said, laughing.

Chauncey said, "That's nonsense. Didn't you tell me you paid a hundred a month for that apartment in Alphabet City? It's still a town where you can find a corner and do work. Anyone can. The eighties will be remembered as an explosion of creativity. There's always going to be downtown. It's too scuzzy for the rich. The housing stock in the East Village was originally built for the workers. Reagan's yuppies won't ever pay top dollar …"

"No, you're wrong," I said. "The whole city will be overrun. Those apartments will be renovated. Made into duplexes. Manhattan will be overrun with money. I'm renovating them. I'm rebuilding that place on the Lower East Side. I'm the problem. I'm making the city safe for yuppie-dom. How do you think I'm paying this crazy-ass bill?"

Uncomfortable looks all around.

"Not Harlem," Calliope said. "Yuppies don't go there. Too many racists." "Even Harlem," I insisted. "Those beautiful brownstones and wide avenues near fast subways will get museum restorations and be full of rich whites and Black people and cafés and one-two-five will be a mall with branches of corporate stores."

After there were general expressions of disbelief and dismay, Summer asked, "How can you be so sure?"

I smiled at her but did not answer.

After that the conversation dwelled on whether figuration or conceptual art was more of a sell-out to the market, with Chauncey, whose work was more conceptual, choosing figuration, and me arguing the other way around. "Conceptual art is anti-art. You can't call it commercial. Half of it disintegrates." "Conceptual art that doesn't disintegrate fetches higher prices in the art market. Collectors are snobs who're being told that figurative art is passé and dumb." This comment led to an argument over whether there was a difference between art trends and fashion trends, which led to a discussion of punk rock, and mohawk haircuts, and the Mohawk people, and from there returned to people being pushed out of their neighborhoods.

I spent the whole time looking at Summer, wondering and revising, but not enough.

He remembered, suddenly, a time in One that he had been riding his bike past Odeon, going to meet Abigail at some club on Warren Street. He slowed down and stopped in front of Odeon, wondering why anyone would want to go in there to spend silly amounts of money on drinks and food that they could have at home, this outpost in the middle of nowhere, in the middle of the post-industrial wasteland, an island in the dead land, like Sharpey's building that House he and Abi. Someone came out of the restaurant as he was watching, and Bar followed this person with his eyes because of his (or her?) rushed movements as he turned the corner onto Thomas Street and walked quickly toward Church, looking behind him from time to time as if worried about being followed, which made Bar follow him from thirty yards or so, pretending not to, until he saw this person duck into a doorway where Bar could see through the glass that a transaction was taking place, after which the person emerged and walked just as briskly back to the restaurant, and Bar, from twenty yards, thought he saw Sharpey and a few others come out of that doorway and head toward some motorcycles parked on the street in the other direction. The Odeon patron was wearing a long white coat, quite striking, and Bar remembered marking the event as typical of the people in that time and place.

Abi didn't show at the club, and Bar remembered the music and the night, too, because he turned out to be the only member of the audience and despite this, after a brief conversation, the band decided to play just because they already set up and might as well rehearse and Bar thought throughout the show that he dared not leave early from that this is what it means to be an artist.

Suddenly, Franc looked at his wristwatch, stood, and made for the door, saying, "I'll be back in a minute," and I instinctively got up as well and followed Franc to the door. Franc turned and said, "What are you doing?"
I was ready for them, saying, "I won't bore you with warnings about how you'll die if you don't stop. How about the irony of paying your own murderer?"
"Fuck off. You don't know what you're..."
"Sharpey sells death."
Franc started and looked at me with wide eyes. "You a cop, Mizrachi?"
"No, no. Whatever. I don't know why I cared enough to say anything."

Franc left and Bar answered that question for himself, remembering coming back to the apartment he shared with Abi in Sharpey's building and finding her on the floor next to the bathroom, not O.D.'d but tranquilized, her works sprawled out next to her and thinking, why does she need to go through this? What can she learn this way that can't be learned any other? He picked up the works and put them in the cigar box where she kept them along with a small notebook. He took out the notebook and read in a random page: "Bar scared."

I returned and sat. "You're not Black," Summer said to me quietly, though Calli and Chauncey could hear.
"Yeah. So?"
"Why don't you correct someone when they say you are?"
"You mean Franc? By the way, is Franc male or female?"
Calli said, "Neither. Franc's..."
"Yes, I mean Franc," Summer pressed. "Why not say something? Is it because you want people to think you're Black?"
"No. I don't care what people think I am."
Calli and Chauncey looked at one another. Summer said, "But your show. The pictures of your dad. You're going past suggesting."
"What about them? My dad's not Black, either," I said, seeing Franc coming back into the restaurant.
Summer shook her head. Franc sat back down, avoiding my eyes, sweat coming from their brow.
Just then the maître d' gave them the check and I remind myself that I didn't have to look before putting down a card.
###

"You were talking in your sleep," Summer said as he opened his eyes to a mid-morning sun. Bar had been waking at seven, just after dawn as the days got shorter, and was surprised to see how late it was.

"I drank too much. There was something in my drink."

"You came home and went into a coma. You lay down without taking off your shoes. I took them off for you. I thought about raping you in your sleep, just to see what it was like. But then you had this whole speech. I called your name but you didn't say anything and didn't stop talking."

"I think Frankie roofied me."

"What's that? 'Roofied'?"

"Drugged."

"Maybe. What for?"

"What did I say?"

"You were rattling on. It was kind of boring. I was waiting to hear about your mistresses but I guess you're not lying about not having them."

"How..."

"I was disappointed. Mistresses would be exciting. Dramatic. We could have a threesome. Do you want to have sex with me and someone else, Bar? Would she have to be another model, or do you want a girl with more curves? I hate that I have no ass for you to grab."

"What did I talk about?"

"I guess I'm relieved. I'd be way, way too jealous for that. Someone'd end up dead. Maybe you."

"Tell me."

"Here, I wrote it down. You talked about this guy Peter. Who's Peter, Bar? Okay, never mind. You said Bush versus Gore is the beginning of the end. And why doesn't everyone see that we can't have a dynasty of Bushes. Then you went on about dynasties for a while and how Clinton was bad enough."

"Holy shit." Bar buried his face in his hands.

"Who are all these people? If Clinton is the president then were you talking about the one after him? What's Bush versus Gore? Why would the former president sue the current vice-president? You went on about that for quite a few..."

"It's nonsense. Don't tell anyone what I said, okay? They wouldn't understand."

"*I* don't understand. If it's nonsense then why not..."

"Summer, listen. Do not tell people. Or whatever. You're right. It doesn't matter. I don't know what I was saying. Frankie drugged me."

"Okay, I won't tell anyone," Summer said and he looked at her now and saw clearly on her face that she was calculating something. "How do you know what the stock market is going to do, Bar?"

"I do research."

"No, you don't. I spent a lot of time with you, remember? You just know."

"I need to have coffee. My head is going to split in half."

One morning in late October I wake to find Summer was gone to a seven AM modeling call, the first in a while that she was doing as a favor to a designer friend.

In the studio, my father frowns at me with a sideways glance that follows me around the room, throwing a hostile eye at me as I gather things to work. I attempt to undermine this threat with hyper-realistic renderings of every feature of Saul's skin, his stubble, nose hairs, ear hairs, wayward eyebrows, wrinkles across the forehead, under the nose, near the eyes, everywhere, showing the aging flesh and sorrow in his eyes.

I wasted time reading an article by Roberta Smith about a show of Lichtenstein prints and thinking, this is old art, and thinking, what am I making?

Summer's watercolor portrait of her friend Frankie, a Ukrainian model whom Summer described as "nice." A four-by-five snapshot of Frankie lay on the floor nearby. I pick it up compare. Yes, Summer's painting was a sophisticated balancing act between imposing her own way of viewing and showing and faithfulness. An achievement. Her mastery of bleeding watercolors surpassed anything I ever did with them. Which was part of the point, I guess.

Summer returns mid-afternoon, jeans and white t-shirt. She comes into the studio with a carrot and some of my homemade hummus. Her hair is done in a complicated French twist with a whole bottle of hairspray keeping a fan of hair sticking straight up and enough makeup to get her eyes to pop at two hundred yards, looking like a made-up doll, a girl whose normal beauty was almost unreal and who right now looked like a painted bird.

"How was it?" My father's image silently and pointlessly tells me to "push" and I silently tell him to shut up.

"Okay. I want to talk to you."

I put down my pencil and turn to face her.

"Why do you think I don't keep modeling? Why started taking art classes and why kept at it? Keep at it."

"What does Greg the so-called professor of art think?"

She laughed. "What's so curious about Greg — before I met you I never would've said that, 'curious' or 'interesting.' I never paid attention to what I said. Greg is one of those guys I met by the dozens already who's decades older, in a bad marriage, and imagines me as a ticket out. Even then, he knows things about me more that you do. Did you know that I don't like strawberry ice cream? Or why I paint?"

"I've had endless conversations with you about painting."

"That's true. Did you ever ask me why I'm putting effort into painting, or did you assume it's in tribute to you?"

"I never assumed that."

"You should. It is. It's also that I've been interested in beauty and what's beautiful since I was really little. People always said I was beautiful. To a little kid, what does that mean? Like for instance, why didn't they say it to my sister, too? Unless they actually had manners and did say it to her, but kids know. My face was just my face. I used to look in the mirror and my mom said I was vain but it was me trying to figure it out. It seemed unfair and when my sister bullied me almost all the time, until she left when she was sixteen and I was fourteen, I let it go because I thought it was so completely unfair. She had a boyfriend, this guy Jake, his dad owned Kaminski's Auto Repair, which was like, he probably made twice what my mom the librarian's assistant made, but Jake was kinda rough, you know, not genteel like you — my mom had no city sophistication like your mom had. Like, she hit us. Not much but enough. She came home with cold cuts for dinner and had beer in front of the T.V."

"My dad was a carpenter and had beer in front of the t.v."

"Don't interrupt. So Jake comes over with BethAnn after school and makes out with her in her room and then he says he's going to the john and instead he comes into my room and says he's only making out with my sister so he can be with me and he tells me I'm beautiful and wants to get with me after BethAnn goes to sleep. So of course I'm a stupid kid and I tell my sister, not thinking. First, she beat the crap our of Jake. I think she broke his nose. I'm surprised she didn't end my modeling career before it started. Mom comes home a little later and I have to explain why I have a fat lip and why there's a message from Jake's dad on her machine and so mom beats BethAnn. BethAnn left I think a week after that. BethAnn used to tell me I would never find a normal guy. I would only get boys who liked how I look. That's true, huh?"

"No."

"Do you love me, Bar? Because sometimes I feel not alive, suffocated, bored with myself and bored with you but I think it's not being bored, it's being ignored, like you're making an effort to ignore me. Greg's saying he loves me but he's my professor and he started asking me to dinner after the first class so I think he doesn't have a lot of boundaries, you know? Like the boundary against saying what you might not stick to tomorrow."

"Yes."

"Yes what?"

"I do love you."

"I don't believe you," she said, not smiling, holding his eye. "That's a good piece of work on your dad. It gets your ambivalence about him. Another word you taught me. I want to give credit where it's due. You told me about ambivalence as an abstract idea but it was appropriate, given how you feel about me. You asked me about my dad once and I said there was nothing to tell but there is. No big drama. He lived a town away. He paid child support, not a lot but it kept us from starving. Normally he mailed a check I think because he didn't come around much but once he came to the house to deliver cash and I asked him why he didn't want to live with us any more. He said 'because momma ain't pretty any more, not like you, Summer.'"

"That's horrible."

"Is it? Yes, his saying that to me, sure. He didn't love mom. Should he have lived with us? I'm asking because despite you not being in love with me, I am in love with you. Don't," she said, holding up her hand. "Let me have the last word. Please? I know you could tear whatever I say to bits. Don't? I need to leave because if I don't do it now I'll stay here unhappy forever."

"I don't want you to go."

"You're ambivalent. Otherwise, you'd be on one knee."

She waits for me to do that and I do not. She says, "Uh huh" and asks if it would be alright to stay until the lease started.

"Of course. Do you want me to sleep on the couch?"

She kisses me on the cheek and goes to the bathroom to take off that face.

"Do you need any money?" I call to her.

"No." She laughs but doesn't say why.

"The offer stands. You can change your mind later."

"Yeah? You'd give me a million dollars," she calls from the bathroom.

"Yes." I feel foolish and wrong saying so because though I would give her that, if I did it would mean nothing.

She comes back, her face plain and pretty. She says, "One of the things that bothers me is where your money comes from. It doesn't add up, Bar. Your secrecy makes me think you're crooked. Are you?"

"No."

"There where does it come from?"

"Stocks and real estate."

"Those are a lot easier if you know the future."

I freeze and say nothing. We have another in a series of silent discussions in which she is reading me and I am revealing a great deal without words.

"I know you won't tell me what's going on. I wish you could at least tell me why."

I shake my head no.

"Yeah. I'm going to bed."

She lies down and faces away from me and reads.

I fall asleep thinking how beautiful she looks with the makeup off and in her usual nighttime outfit of a white tank top and reading glasses, reading a book. In the morning, she'll leave and that will be it: six years of her trying to make it work and me trying to delay the end.

Ambivalence: when I went to see her work once, I almost broke it off right then. It was a year into us being us. A tame shoot, as these things go, catalog work, jeans, trousers, t-shirts, button-downs, skirts. No lingerie, no bathing suits. She didn't do anything the other models didn't do. Nevertheless, I was shocked in the most naïve way by the fakeness of her expressions, all the standard moves: bending one's head over and suddenly tossing it back to get some bounce in the hair, or quick scrolling through a series of unmotivated changes in her face. I couldn't reconcile the simple disconnect between inner and outer. That ever-so-easy putting-on of a face, the regular dialing up and down of projection of sexual interest, made me want to vomit. I knew it was a stupid reaction. None of the other models doing the same things bothered me in the least. They seemed merely professional. They seemed merely to be selling clothes. I couldn't help seeing Summer as breaking a sacred trust. It was silly, but I spent months afterwards wondering, when we were having sex, when she laughed at my jokes, or when she cried, whether it was real.

When she left I went through her art at her request to give some items to Nick.

There's a a four-by-six foot canvas, rolled up. I unroll it and clip it to an easel. It's frightful: a picture of a gaunt, near-starving female with grey skin that hangs off her body under her arms and on her thighs. She's biting her the heel of her hand in the pose of the 1930s Dorothea Lang portrait of the woman on the bread line, but not standing. Her other hand's set against her head in a parody of a sexy model pose as she lies on a chaise, wearing a miniskirt and bikini top. The fashion pic from *Harper's Bazaar* that Summer used for the pose was paper-clipped to the canvas, along with a snapshot of one of Summer's model friends wearing only a bikini bottom. The model's body is tall and thin but human, though her ribs show and she has not only no fat but no muscle tone, either. She is mid-laugh and hideously, seems to be having fun at a beach or somewhere with lots of sunlight. In the chiaroscuro-heavy painting, the figure's ribs poke horribly through her grey skin. The exception to the grey of the body is a riot of color on her hyper-made-up face, especially disturbing because one side doesn't match the other: one cheek, lip, and eye is done in day-glo pinks and the other in dark reds and browns. It's a fashion shoot inside a horror film.

It's acrylics, showing lots of control and skill. The composition is clear and strong. The paint is pushed with intentional, strong strokes. I wonder if it is a more powerful picture than any I've ever made.

Instead of feeling jealous, as I was in Life One when I saw her sailboats in the magazine, I feel relief. She doesn't need me any more. It's a clean break.

10. Anger

Fall, 1993

In Life One, Bar had drawn a picture of his father slumped in the Archie chair, his face shadowed and obscured, his right hand gripping a can of beer, his left hanging straight down.

In Life Two, within a year of saving his father's life, Bar drew his father on top of a heap of bicycles, triumphantly holding the Bennotto that he fished out up high over his head. The angle of the viewer was from below, and the light was late afternoon and glorified the figure. Saul smiled benevolently down at a small figure of a boy at the bottom of the pile. It had been hard to get Saul to smile enough for Bar to make a basic sketch that he filled in later.

Bar hated this picture more and more as he went through the 1980s and his father fulfilled Bar's hopes that given access to capital, he could become as successful as Schlomo. In September, 1993, Nick came over and without asking went through Bar's sketchbook and flat file, looking for sellable items. He asked about this picture, remarking that it was one of Bar's best, most fully felt, and a good piece with which to silence his critics who said he was incapable of drawing men. Bar cooly said he would think about it. Soon it was Rosh Hashana, and on the first day, Bar walked over to the Hudson River with the drawing, ripped it into pieces, and threw it in the water.

If I'm at the service door yelling into the intercom explaining to the doorman that I'm not delivering something other than myself, should I be concerned that he assumes that I'm a servant? It's true that I'm not suited up in lycra, but still, I have no packages. Why does he, then?

Inside, the apartment does not cease to surprise me. It has only a single piece fashioned by Saul's own hand: a carved mahogany table lamp. The rest of the stuff's exactly like what mom and Schlomo have chosen: glass, steel, modern, neutral tones, tasteful, boring, characterless. Is that what happens if you're given money? Someone from the government arrives to tell you that you must buy taupe?

A young dyed-blond woman I've never before seen sits on the characterless sofa sectional, her tanned legs up on the chaise portion, along with her white sneakers. "Hi," she says.

"Hello." There must be a school or set of instructional videos that tell young women how to smile, cock their heads to the side obsequiously, and wave from the elbow. It affects me – I'm not immune from a woman successfully being cute -- but also disappoints me. Too obvious.

Here's papa, entering from a side room. He looks fit, strong, and relaxed. A man with low blood pressure. He smiles at me and pulls me to his chest. He says to the girl, "Honey, do me a favor,..."

"And get lost? You're not going to introduce me?" She rises to comply. "You're such a beast."

"Lana, Bar. Bar, Lana. Yes? My son."

"Charmed," she says, offering a limp handshake while smoothing out her short skirt with the other hand. She has a bruise on her left thigh. It isn't too big or nasty but I wonder, nevertheless, if I should call Child Services.

"Hi," I say again. Dad and I watch Lana exit into the hallway from whence Saul had come. I didn't come here to share an ogle with my father.

When she is gone, I ask, "How's Claudia?" partly to be bitchy.

"How should I know? Why you esk me that?"

"How old's Lana?"

"Ach, maybe you better go."

"I'm here to talk to you about your buildings. We need to make something clear."

"Yah, yah, but you have a beer, no?" he says, lightening.

"Okay."

"Beer always good for a serious discussion."

The new fridge is clean and well-organized inside, but there is still a whole shelf dedicated to Israeli beer. Probably the money and the girl are less important for his good mood and relatively less serious alcoholism than his having something to do. Mission accomplished there, as well. No resting on laurels with dad, though. I know he will take what I'm going to say as a contest of wills. Better soften him up. We open the beers and touch cans.

"Dad, tell me the story of leaving Yemen."

"You not so little any more. Thet's for kids, thet one."

"Tell me anyway. The story you used to tell."

"Ach," he turns away, as if not at first willing to travel into that past, but he relents and gives me a wry smile. "You want the story of magic carpet?"

"Yes. Tell it again."

The story that Saul told me in the 1970s, when Saul was a young father full of hopes and I was still a boy. He loved me ferociously, jealously. The story he told was of a carpet so big that the all the Jews of Sana'a could ride on it at once. The carpet rode so smoothly that people could sip their tea just as he, Saul sipped his beer now. Everyone was able to take all of their things. They took their clothing and their furniture and even their goats and my father's father took all of his boats and all of his boat-making tools. People took their houses. The magic carpet stopped by each family's house and people pushed the house onto the carpet using rollers and if they didn't mind not seeing as much they rode to Israel inside their own kitchens. He and his father rode there, but not inside their house, because they wanted to see everything; they left their house in Yemen, never to be seen by the family again. We saw Sana'a as we rode above the minarets, and we saw the sea, and we saw Greece and Italy and Crete and then we saw Israel."

I wait a moment as he seems to be in a semi-trance, perhaps thinking about home and what is now forever lost. I can see where I get this propensity from. "You used to say you brought your house, too," I say. "And the synagogue."

Dad looks at me, his grown son, and says, "We were afraid that the Arabs were angry about the new state and all of them losing to Israel at once. We thought they will kill us. They have pride, the Arabs. We punch them in the nose, make a nosebleed. So, we have to get out of there. We get on the plane the next day, sold all the boats, tools, everything, and we get nothing for them because everyone knows, the Arabs know they can give us joke money for the house, furniture boats. Nothing left. Nothing."

"I'm sorry. When you said, 'we,' as in 'we punched them in the nose,' you mean the Israelis?"

"Of course. The Jews."

"I thought you said the Israelis could go to hell. You said Israelis treated you like shit, like Black people…"

"What do you mean? We are Jews," Saul says, but he's looking through me. "Ach, no such thing as a magic carpet. A plane. My first plane ride. My second was to Tel Aviv to New York and my third, thet one didn't happen yet. Lana wants to go see her mama and her auntie in Kiev. Mebbe I take her there."

"Do you ever think you want to go back to Yemen, to see…"

"Nothing! Don't I tell you this? There is nothing there. Thet is not a place," he says, sawing the air. "Yemen means: you, get out of here! Yemen is the bigger people tell the smaller people what to do. Yemen is shit. Yemen is dead. Death, and nothing."

We sit with our beers for a while and I wait while his blood pressure floats back to where Lana is maintaining it. It occurs to me that I spent a lot of time waiting for my dad, often waiting for him to wake up from a stupor.

"I liked the kid story."

We sip our beers.

"Tell me about your work, when you got to New York," I ask.

"Ach, what is this with stories? Are you such a boy again, sudden?"

"Tell me."

Again, Saul waves the request away, but after a moment, starts talking. "First, I work at the yards. The big boats. They taught me carpenter. Car-pen-tree. The Navy. They need worker here, worker there, everything. I didn't know how to do it. T-square from my asshole." He laughs.

"That was what, until the sixties?"

"I don't know. Yeah, sixties. You were baby."

"Late sixties. Then they let you go?"

"Let go? No. They fire everybody."

"That's what 'let go' means."

"Ach. Some guys go to Philly, some go to the bar."

"That's when you started drinking a lot?"

"I never started drinking a lot. What you talking?"

"Dad,"

"That's when I start my business. I make carpentry for people. Tables, chairs, cabinets, everything."

"Uh-huh. That was in the seventies?"

"Yeah. I don't know. Time for everything. I make some money. But you mother," he says, poking me with his index finger as if I were to blame, "she is always unhappy. Always."

"Because. Why is she, why was she unhappy, dad?"

"Not enough money, of course. So I go work for Schlomo. That's when I make some money. Good money."

"As a carpenter."

"No, no. Burning. We do the burning. I make money, I take momma to the movies, I take the family to the country. To the beach, you remember? You remember the bicycle I get for you?

"The Bennotto."

"Yes, a real Italian racing bicycle."

"Yes, I remember. What burning? What's 'the burning'?" I had never heard this part of my father's work story before. Dad had always told it as being a carpenter for the Navy and then for Schlomo. What's...?

"Burning." Saul says, blinking. "We do it for the money."

"Burning what? Burning junk instead of taking it to the dump to...?"

"No, no, no. Bigger. For the money."

"Dad, what are you...?"

"We burn the buildings." Saul shrugs as if in apology or as if the whole set of actions of which he had been a part were mystifying to him. "He get the insurance money, Schlomo. That's how it worked. Sometimes for Schlomo, sometimes for his friend."

Now I'm getting angry. "You? You made the wastelands?"

"Not just me. I'm a small fish. Small fry."

"What, you mean in the Bronx? You burned … the Bronx? People were living there."

"Bronx, sure. Manhattan. Brooklyn."

"Manhattan? Where in Manhattan?"

"Down by you. Lower East Side. We did that, maybe two years. Maybe forty, fifty buildings. Nice work..."

"It was you. I can't believe it. You destroyed..."

"Nah. It was destroy before me. Empty building. Nobody there."

"Fifty? You made sure they were empty? What the fuck, dad? How often did you do this?"

"Maybe every two weeks. I do furniture in mean time but you mother, she's right. No money in that. She blame me for not making money making furniture. I say, what does she know? Does she go try selling furniture? I ask her, help me sell, and what does she say? No, she's get a job. A lawyer. Not real lawyer,"

"Paralegal. Who the fuck cares? You're one of the people who ruined New York!"

Saul looks at me with sad condescension and keeps going. "Para-legal, for Schlomo lawyer, guy named Yaffo. That's how I meet Schlomo, from mom. You know what's wrong with furniture? Americans want cheapo, fast, cheap, cheap junk. I make dovetails, I do the planing, careful, I take time, beautiful stuffs, but nobody want this."

"So you started drinking when the furniture business didn't work?"

"What is 'start drinking'? I'm always drinking. I drink. People drink. This is nothing, drinking. I eat, I drink, I shit, breathe, what is this? What, you are angry? Angry for what? I burn buildings falling down anyways?"

"So wait, you were burning buildings for Schlomo, and then it stopped? That stopped?"

"Insurance stop to pay. I told Schlomo, at the time, I told him, they gonna stop, not a bunch of stupids, and you get a burnt building instead of a fixed one. And no money. They gonna stop. Did they stop? Yes, insurance stop. I can fix them up. I can do, just let me…"

"Did he…?"

"Yes, yes, after insurance people figure, stop stupid paying, Schlomo got buildings and I fix them. After that, just fix-ups, but fast, fast, not quality. Just like with furniture business. No one want quality. No miters, shiplap, nothing. Slap it up. Glue and nails. Not even wood. Particle wood. You know what is particle wood? Shit. It last two year, three, maybe." Saul's ready to produce tears but pulls himself away from that cliff, pointing his finger at his son closer and closer until he pokes me again, saying, "Now, now I know what to do. Do and never get done. Do, do, do," (poke, poke, poke: I almost grab and break his finger). "I do the fixing up and selling."

I take a breath. I can't do anything about what he did in the past. But: "Yeah, but dad, you have to stop evicting people."

"What you say, I have to stop? I don't stop anything. I don't stop, so?"

"I'm going to take my money out, then."

"Ach, fack you. You don't take nothing."

"Yes, I will. Otherwise, I'm helping you put people on the street."

"Nah, nah. I got tenant, five tenant on Avenue C. Shit building in bad shapes and I fix nothing. Do they leave? No. No heat, do they leave? No, again no. Do they pay? Again no! Fack them, I evict them. This woman, Eva Perez, fack her. She made the strike."

"A rent strike?"

"What you think I am talking? Of course, rent strike."

"What did she say?"

"She say I don't fix, don't do services? Then they don't pay."

"But that's true."

"Ach, simple boy. I offer them to pay them to leave."

"That's not ... this is the ten-story we're discussing?"

"Yes, yes, ten stories, storefront, whole thing. There's banks wants to know what's happened. Schlomo wants to know. Do you know, smart boy? You want to lose all them monies? Banks to lose, and they never pick up phone calls anymore? Almost out of time for this shit."

"Alright, go ahead."

"You see?"

"Evict these people. And then that's it. Then you stop."

"It's only Eva Perez left, bitch cunt woman. Also," Saul says conspiratorially, whispering as if in secret though his girlfriend isn't in earshot, "she is drunk. I sent her a case of Nesher beers."

"I doubt she like Israeli beer, dad."

"No, not because she likes. Because maybe she dies."

"Charming. After this building, though, you can't buy buildings unless they're delivered empty. Nothing with tenants. Or I will pull my end."

"You don't like evicting? You want burning instead, hah? You know what happen, when we burnt buildings?"

"What happened, dad?" What's he talking about now?

"Somebody die. A boy, ten, eleven. Stupid boy, playing in empty building. Nighttime, even. Signs up all over the place, don't come in here, private. Where is his parents? Letting him out like that. He got burnt."

I'm staying quiet, anger coursing through me. This is the man I saved, the child-killer. Then I think of Peter.

Saul sips his beer. I ask, so quietly he can barely hear me, "So is that when you started drinking?"

"No, no. You think it's so simple. That boy, his time was come. To everything, there is a time."

"That's...you and Schlomo..."

"You know what I see in Yemen, before we left? I saw people die. You, American child, you see nothing. I see *children* die. They are hungry, they get...I see a boy, my friend, Musa, he is a Moslem, doesn't matter, to me, just a boy like me, he gets run over by the big truck. So? That's life. A time for life, and a time to die."

"No. That's murder. You and Schlomo…"

"I have girlfriend before I left for Israel. Moslem girl. We hold hands, kiss once. We kiss, closed lips, little boy and little girl. His father, he beat me for five, ten minutes, then he beat her. Before I leave on the magic carpet. On the plane I was crying for her the whole ride and my mother thinks, he is crying for his home or he is crying for the beat, but no, I cry for her. Halima. I remember Halima forever and forever. Her small lips, small nose, dark eyes. Her hair down to her shoulder. I see her face. I see her purple scarf covering her head. She gets it from her older sister. Yes." He stops and drinks some beer. I wait and listen. I'm thinking that this might be the last time I see this man, that I will let Saul talk to me.

Saul starts again, "You know when I drink more, because I always drink? Drink, eat, shit, piss. I drink more when I work for Schlomo, making shit. I get up, go to job site, make shit, come home, have a beer so I don't have to think about the shit I make. What life is that, making shit from shit board?"

"Oh."

"You my son. You do like I say," he says, poking his own chest.

"You didn't drink because of that boy."

"What boy?"

"The one who died in the fire. That you killed."

"I don't kill nothing. Nah. Time for this, a time for that. It was an accident."

I feel the shame of seeing things I should already have seen and let the anger turn toward myself. "I'm stopping the evictions. You can't keep – you can't do that anymore. I won't let you."

"You say I can, so. I do what I do. You are the son. I am the father," Saul says, putting his hand vertically, pinky down on the table, as if cutting it to showing the separation. "My son. You go now. Get out." Saul gets off Bar stool comes behind me and pushes me off mine. "You go. Come back when you my son, not banker." He pushes me toward the apartment door. I do not resist. "Schlomo make more from me, he charge me interest like he is my enemy, but okay, I still make moneys."

Don't talk. I won't let him build on the 3rd Street lots. The deeds are still in my name. He can't start construction without my signature and I won't give it to him. "You're done building with my money. Or my property," I say.

Saul raises his fists. "You don't tell me! Don't you tell me!" Saul slapped me and right there at his front door I lurch into a palimpsest. I'm standing over my father who's shaking on the floor. It takes me a moment to understand that this is Jackson Heights, and my father's already dying and Claudia's trying to give him CPR. As the palimpsest happens I feel that the rules are changing. This isn't the same place or the same date. Something's happening to the way the overlaps are occurring.

The sting on my face from my father slapping me brings me back. Saul comes at me. I stand aside, causing dad to lurch forward and catch himself on a wall. I turn toward the front door just as Lana comes back from the other room. I turn and she smiles prettily at me, "You're not staying for lunch?"

I ride home angry. I almost kill an old lady crossing in front of me and am tempted to tell her to fuck herself, but I do not. When I walk into my place, the answering machine blinks like an angry red eye. There are two messages from Nick asking if I want to come to the gallery, "you know, to get out of the house. Lots for you to do. And I wanted to flag you that we have about half of the Sharpey haul left. It's gotten us this far but…" I delete it. I go into the giant kitchen whose size bothers me now because it's a walk from the fridge to the counter and when I'm making food nothing's in reach. I open the fridge and eye the chilled Sam Adams six-pack and unopened Chablis, and close the fridge.

I get water and go into the spacious, roomy living room. I sit in a chair upholstered so richly that it's hard as marble, swiveling it toward Washington Square, seeing the sun set from the west, and think about what I've done. I sit there for a long time, letting my loneliness wash through, letting the self-pity and shame, and horror at my mistakes bloom in my mind like algae.

I pick up the cordless phone and call my lawyers, though it's late, leaving a message for the one I deal with for real estate to call in the morning.

They do call. They object to pulling the financing from the projects Saul's involved in. There would be contract-breaking fees and legal fees. I tell them to do it anyway. The action merely gives me the belated sense of having washed my hands. It is not satisfying; it corrects no wrongs.

I am restless and want revenge and I want to go back in time again. (To when I was a little kid? With my present consciousness? How horrible!) I want a lot of other things. I want to lose myself in Summer's body but I don't call her because I am too angry with myself to allow myself the pleasure of looking at her. I need to work on something, it doesn't matter what. I go to my large, high-ceilinged, well-lit studio, and pin a four-by-five-foot sheet of paper to a giant easel. I start drawing a building, an ordinary brick six-story, no mansard roof, nothing special, just some cement banding for window cornices and sub-sills, and modest cornices at the roofline. Double-hung windows, six lights on top, one on the bottom. A walkway of about thirty feet to the entrance door, which has some more ornament above the doorway and a cast-iron gate in front of the door. I get involved in the building now. I look at some books I have of New York, flipping through until I see similar ones, though I know this one intimately: it's largely the one I grew up in, the one in Jackson Heights. I put graffiti on it – not artistic, not organized – covering two-thirds of the ground level brick. Garbage in the walkway. Some of the windows are broken, some not there at all. I draw flames. Three open windows on the left show flame and smoke and a small Black child peeping his head out of the fourth, next to the three on fire. His arms are extended toward the viewer, putting that person in the position of impotent savior.

I look at the clock. I've been working for six hours without eating or drinking. I go to the kitchen and desperately swallow some old takeout without heating it up and go to bed, barely taking the time to wash the ink and pencil from my hands and remove my jeans.

I wake at ten and bike to the Bronx with a camera, taking pictures of building after building, noting the addresses. I ride to the New York Public Library and do research on the buildings that I saw. I find the story of the Staten Island fireman who saved four people in a Bronx fire that they know had been set. The fireman died, falling out of the window when a second fire started in the floor below him causing the whole window frame he was leaning on to give way. A librarian tells me to go the City Department of Records; there I look up the collection of 1940s tax photographs of the buildings, sketching some as I go. I draw the building in which Schlomo worked, and the building where the insurance company that paid Schlomo was located.

I go home. I call my lawyers back. They explain that I have no evidence to give a prosecutor a chance in court. I do not know what fire my father had meant, or where, or even if it was true that a child had died. I know nothing and am powerless and a fool.

I draw. I make one large picture after another, going to the library to read the newspaper files, reading about the burnings, calling the insurance companies trying to find someone who could tell me about them (no one would speak), drawing scenes, trying to show what happened. I work from October to December, not seeing anyone who didn't make the trek to his apartment. Nick comes by from time to time with papers for me to sign and with conversations he wants to have that he felt were better in person, and to check on me. I won't let him see the new work. Summer comes by to pick up some things, but we hardly speak. I don't trust myself not to burst with anger that has nothing to do with her, and she, seeming to sense my tinder-box state, stays away.

Her intuitive sense of my mood strikes me now as manipulation and management. I am glad when she leaves. In her wake, I think about making love to her and am glad again that she's not present.

I work on this series throughout the winter until May. Nick come back and tells me I'm looking "strung out," and I discover that I've lost ten pounds. I start feeling that I need to stop, that I'm getting sucked into a vortex, but I wanted to do more than merely to document something. Thus the drama of the moment when the child probably would not be saved. I want to evoke a strong reaction. It isn't enough. The pathos of that moment, when it happened, when I was a kid, doesn't change anything. The insurance companies stopped the fires by changing their financial policies. It's just about the money.

Looking at my big dramatic picture, I feel more anger, not less, anger at the city that allowed this, the society, the nation. The people that let some become garbage or tinder while others can live as I do now. I feel anger, again, at failing as an artist in Life One, and angry that I wasn't able to relinquish that memory, that the successful career that I started in Life Two does not erase the hurt and rejection from the past. I'm angry that I was unsuccessful before, angry that I'm successful now, and angry that I cannot not escape this anger. I'm angry that I'm letting my selfish concerns overshadow the statement I'm trying to make. My giant apartment is too small, and my anger settles on my fancy things: my furniture, my expensive bicycles: all three of them hanging in the small room off the foyer that the architect had designed in the renovation just for that purpose, and into the bedroom, on the designer clothing Summer left there, on my own designer clothes. Seeing myself in Summer's full-length closet mirror, I am sickened.

Summer left her old American Painting homework texts on her small shelf. Flipping through, I see all the familiar icons. Here's Hopper. She and I spent hours looking at a show that put his drawings next to the paintings he made from them, talking about the technique and what it meant. That was some of the best time we spent together. She taught me as much as I her, though I suppose, in the best cases, students do that for teachers.

Here's the *Nighthawks,* a hackneyed victim of its own success. The success it deserved has flattened it into words like "bleakness" or "alienation." It's worth thinking about the paint, color, contrast, shapes, and light and the way the figures are set off against inactive backgrounds, the red dress on the redhead, the white uniform set against the light yellow walls, the angles like de Chirico's but right on the edge of subtle, which de Chirico never was. Flattened, the painting receives no such appraisal. The things I care about are not what others care about.

It would be worth it to fly to Chicago to make a copy and so I will. (I am in the "jet set." I can afford any plane ticket, first class.) In the meantime, I can sketch out what I want to do. What if three of the four figures are Black? Everyone except the worker. That's a nice fuck-you drawing about America. I can make the clothes on Hopper's clean figures ragged and the bar where they sit run-down with peeling paint and the building across the street covered in graffiti, like the neighborhood I lived in, Alphabet City in the 1980s. I'll model the waiter to look like Sharpey.

What else did she study in that class?

Here, this one's perfect. George Bellows boxing painting, *Stag at Sharkey's,* except that I will flip the races of the white boxers and the Black ref, make the patrons all Black instead of a bunch of rabid whites yelling for more Black violence.

I can copy all of the American masterpieces. I can tell Americans what they don't want to hear. I'll call the series, "Fuck you, America" (but Nick probably won't let me).

American Gothic is a bit too kitsch. The *Blackhawks* is on the border of that already. Maybe that's the point, though. Yes, *American Gothic*, but with two Latino farm workers.

Norman Rockwell's *Freedom From Want*, the Thanksgiving picture, I should do it with an all-Black family. No one the least bit undignified, even if they might be in the original. Some of the expressions in Rockwell's original are lovingly hokey on those white faces. I'll have to think about how that transfers.

How about Roy Lichtenstein's *Crying Girl* with a Black girl with dyed blond hair?

Gilbert Stuart's portrait of George Washington, replacing his face with Frederick Douglass's.

John Singer Sargent's *Portrait of Madame X* with a Black woman. Give her bitterness. Give her a withering look.

The photo of Kennedy being shot, but make him and Jackie both Black.

Yes, that would be a good fuck you.

At the end of October of 1995, after I've spent a year obsessively working on this series, Nick calls at ten one morning to tell me that he has papers that needed to be signed. Would I please come to the gallery and grace them with my presence? I tell Nick to come to me.

An hour later, Nick shows up in his crisp blue gallerist suit, tapered pants and no socks in dress shoes, no tie. I greet him at the door wearing a filthy black-and-white Ramones t-shirt, home-cut-off jeans shorts and flip flops. I'm unshaven and my hair is clean but imperfectly self-cut. "You look like absolute shit," Nick says as I open the door.

"Nice to see you, too. Actually, I went for a bike ride yesterday and felt a lot better than I have in I don't know how long. I went up 9W all the way to Nyack."

I rattle on about the bike ride, holding open the door but blocking the doorway until Nick says, "Bar, let me in the apartment."

"Oh, yeah, sorry."

"Were you just released from solitary confinement?"

"Something like that."

Nick asks if there's new work. At first, I don't show him the "Black" pictures, only the ones I did of the Bronx. Nick is enthusiastic about the work, but I can tell the difference between politeness to the boss and genuine enthusiasm. I explain what my father did and discover Nick knows nearly nothing about the fires, not even a footnote in his history. That's exactly what it is, a mere blip, one of a million events in which powerful people do shit to powerless ones. Why focus on that blip among all the others?

We go to the ten-person dining table (where I've never had more than three guests to dine) to sign the papers. I remember to offer him refreshment but Nick wants nothing. The papers are all routine.

"Why'd you come over, Nick? Checking if I'm alive?"

"You're thin," Nick said. "Why don't you come to my place for Thanksgiving? We can fatten you up."

"Who's coming?"

"George, since he lives there, too. My mom and her husband. Her husband's daughter Alice. I think she's an actress or something. She's probably like twenty-six-ish. My dad and his wife, and their twin fourteen-year-olds, Mollie and Janie. A bunch of cousins. Also that intern I mentioned to you, like, thirty times, Camille; she's not local and can't go home this holiday because, well, we pay her shit."

"Give her a raise. Fifty percent."

"Alright."

"I'm serious."

"I know you are. Done. She'll be pleased. She might want to have sex with you."

"No."

"She talks about how great your art is. She wants to learn to draw portraits."

"She's too young."

"For what, portraiture? What the fuck, Bar? She's mid-twenties and you're, what, thirty-one? You're lonely as shit. How long's it been?"

"Summer left more than a year ago."

"Nothing in between? Along the edges? Though, to look at you it seems unlikely."

"What edges? I don't go out. I'm solving an artistic problem."

"Sounds like such fun. But yes, the work's fabulous. Devastating. Heartbreaking. Let's do a show."

"Not yet. Don't pimp the intern. It's gross."

"She wouldn't agree. She's an adult."

"I miss Summer. All the time. I'm confused enough as it is."

Nick nods but doesn't say anything for a while. We go sit on my couches, the headlights of cars creating smears of light on the windows as they pass. Nick agrees to a glass of the white wine that I've kept in the fridge for months for theoretical visitors. I have tea.

"I do love this view," he says.

"Me too."

"You sit here evenings, looking out over the park?"

"Often."

"Sometimes I think that's your default mode," Nick says. "Alone, solving artistic problems, observing things, not giving a shit about anyone else. You're lonely, bossman. You're also a powerful, rich young man. Do you think you'd be the primary beneficiary if you starting going with Camille? Or forget Camille, a young woman who isn't rich and powerful. When's the last time you did something for someone else?" I open my mouth, but I don't have an answer. "You don't have to say anything to me, unless you want to fire me."

"I won't fire you. I want to thank you."

Nick nods. "Are you going to tell me about the other work? I thought I saw some pieces under tarps in there."

I look back at him and say nothing.

"How many?"

"A lot."

"Can I see? Is it a secret?"

"Okay. Go see?"

He gets up immediately. "How many? Done-done, I mean. Ones you don't need to work on any more."

"Twenty-four."

"Wait, I saw maybe nine?"

"I don't want to do a show yet."

"I'm just going to peek."

"You may as well. I'm starting to think the rest are a mistake."

I go with Nick back to the studio and show him the "Black" drawings.

He laughs at first, seeing my *Nighthawks* ripoff/parody, but stifles it, or is overawed into stifling it. As I go through the pieces, he says things like, "Of course," and "unreal." He looks up at me from time to time. He asks to see them all at once, arranged around the studio. This takes time with both of us putting them up. He stands and turns, making a few revolutions. He says, "This work ... this is what you've been preparing for. All the previous work, it all culminates here. This is it. Oh my god, Bar. This is it."

"It's not quite ready."

"Ready? Are you joking? Yes it is. Please? Do you want me to beg?"

"What for, Nick?"

"The work is provocative. It's a thumb in the eye of American politics, of the Art World, of, I don't know, everything!"

I'm pleased that Nick, the one whose discerning eye had not let me through the gates of artistic recognition in Life One, is gushing about my work. But Nick's nothing if not pecuniary in his purview.

"You have to get back into the public eye. Your last show is a distant memory. Don't you want people to see your work?"

"I'm more famous than I ever...than I want to be. Someone bothered me in the supermarket yesterday."

"You mean she adored you."

"That's not what I mean. And I didn't say 'she.' You don't mean 'see' as in letting people see my work. You mean fame. And money. I have money. Fame, it's worse than worthless."

"Uh huh. I'm having trouble feeling sorry …"

"I didn't ask you to!" I thought my anger had receded, that I've been letting go, letting its grip on my heart loosen.

Nick wanders out of the studio to look out at the park.

"I'm sorry," I say, following him before too many moments pass. "Tell me, and try your hardest to be completely honest. If you saw that work and never had heard of me, would you agree to represent me? Imagine it's your gallery …"

"Okay, that part's easy."

I say nothing. He is either thinking or pretending to think about how to con me properly. I should never have asked him this.

He looks at me sidelong and we both smile. "You once said to me that it's better not to own a house. The house comes to own you. I would love to be owned by a house with miraculous sunsets over the ocean located amid the best gay male flesh on the Eastern Seaboard."

That makes me smile. "You already go there. What about George?"

Nick merely smirks at the mention of George. "George and I can barely afford a share. I have to make, like fifty phone calls. And someone always craps out. Someone always finishes the toilet paper and doesn't mention it. It's stressful."

"I'm having trouble…"

"…feeling sorry, okay, touché. Let me sell this work. Yes, I am thinking of the money. So what? Share your gift with the world or stop drawing."

"No," I say to Nick.

"No what?"

"No, I'm going to Thanksgiving at my mom's."

"Bar!"

"I know I have to do a show. I know."

Nick and I talk details and I'm half listening and half plotting out how I could, perhaps, tell Summer what I'm thinking and why including the truth about living this life again. She had figured out a lot of it on her own while I was still vacillating between underestimating her as if she were a dumb model and suspecting her of playing me like a marionette, the strings attached to my prick. She was neither dumb nor so cunning. She could add two and two, and was as observant as me. Maybe that hope, of being able to talk to her, was a large portion of why I knew at that moment that I was in love with her as much as, and yes, more than I loved Eva. I've not seen Eva in thirteen years, and thus, for the last month, after my work was done for the day, poring over the perspective and shading and volumes and faces in the big Bronx drawings, I went to the sketchpad and drew Summer, and then Eva, and then Summer, and so on. I was driving myself mad and I knew it but couldn't stop.

Nick leaves. I wander into the studio and look at my last drawing of a building on fire as if from the perspective of the blimp floating over Yankee Stadium when Howard Cosell, covering a Yankees vs. Dodgers World Series game in 1977 said, "Ladies and Gentlemen, the Bronx is burning." I wonder if it'll sell for a lot and help Nick buy the beach house he's able to go to anyway. I don't believe that it'll do anything else. If it becomes the world's most famous painting it changes not one thing in that world.

I call Nick that afternoon, letting him know that some of the drawings' sales would be donated.

"Why? What's the penance about?"

"I want the money for the one of the kid to go to the family of that kid. For example."

"You told me you paid him already."

"Yeah."

"But anyway."

"Listen, I mean my half, not yours."

"Okay, I accept. It's going to cost you, though."

"What do you mean?"

"That one's going to sell for a hundred grand. You're going to get talked about."

"What if I offend people..."

Nick laughs through the phone and I have a vision of his open mouth, like in a cartoon, widening as he laughs until he swallows me whole. "I'm hoping some people will be offended. No such thing as bad publicity."

I go to look at the pictures and fantasize about tearing them to shreds. When I see the picture of the child in the fire, I think about my own father setting that fire. I make myself walk out of the studio and back to the kitchen and take a cold bottle of Sam Adams from the fridge and press it against my face so that the condensation from the bottle masks my tears, even though there is no one else to see them.

At the opening, I say hello / how are you, kiss a hundred cheeks, and answer questions about the work in neutral, academic tones. After two glasses of the wine I add words about how my anger is behind the work and Nick pulls me aside and tells me to stop that. Annette is there and other writers from the art magazines, and Annette seems displeased. I want to ask her what she thinks, but every time I get near her I'm prevented by some importuning person or other.

All these openings run together. I can't tell which is which. It's supposed to be a gathering of people interested in art but it's like what a well-known actor once said to me about awards shows: it's about the sell.

When I see Summer saying hello to Nick, wearing a simple white cotton dress and no makeup, her hair tied back, her model-in-hiding look, I want to run to her and beg her to leave with me, run away to Thailand or Italy or some other randomly chosen place and use my money to hide from the world. I want to go back with her to my apartment and close the door and hold her and be with her. I recall when I first saw her in Life One, as a kid, the dazzling ray gun of her face, its power increase by some exponent figured for me now by adding up all of my feeling for her soul.

She comes to me and we say hello and she asks how I've been doing. She thinks I look thin. I can't kiss her cheek and it creates an awkward moment but the touch of her face would unman me. I see in her eyes that I'm looking at her too intensely; I force myself to look around the room at all the different people who came because they're interested in art, in ideas, craft, images, and in me, but not the actual me, only the celebrated me, and feel that they're about to discover that I've badly led them astray. I don't say I missed Summer because rationally, according to the plan, I don't want to start up again, though that is what I want more than anything else. When she says she missed me I do say the same, too and when she says she'll call I say, "Thank you," which is wrong but it's what entered my mouth without consulting my brain. She leaves quickly and I suspect I've been too fraught, she and I are too fraught, and when I see that she goes through the door I feel out of breath. I think she looked at the drawings only as she came in.

There are a hundred, maybe a hundred and fifty people milling around now and not all of them know me. For a few minutes, no one speaks to me and I wonder if I'm giving off a bad vibration because Summer left. Perhaps its that the art is so bad, so politically miscued, done with such a tin ear that no one wants to interact with me. They're ashamed for me. It's a disaster. I'll be run out on a rail. The gallery will close. Perhaps I'll be taken to a public stoning or be forced to wear a scarlet letter F for Fool.

Nick appears next to me. "The show's sold. Half was pre-sold, you know, at the collectors' invitational thingy. But now it's all sold."

"That's …"

"I know, I know. I should've asked for more. It sold too fast."

I say nothing and Nick starts complaining about the bartender.

"What's the matter with her?"

"The matter is that she fucking left. She's some kid we got from this agency, underage, somehow that's legal, and she was drinking the wine (which isn't). I was watching – and now she's …"

"I'll do it."

"What? No, you will not …"

"Yes, let me. It'll give me something to do. I'm the host."

I get behind the table with drinks and unbutton my cuffs. "How can I help you?" I ask, and pour.

Annette comes to ask if I know how to make a gin and tonic and I say no and we laugh. I follow her instructions. She says, "At least you can do this."

"Yeah. I can fix bikes, too."

"Good," she says. I don't think she is entirely joking. She drifts away and I see her meander toward the exit.

A group of four visitors come to the bar, three women and a man, all of whom seem just post-college. The man and one woman are redheads of the same height and look like siblings. A shorter woman with black hair and pale skin hooks arms with a taller blond woman. The man looks Irish. Short collarless leather jackets, boiled wool sweaters, university t-shirts, a camo mini-skirt with black ripped hose, a Brooklyn Dodgers cap, and eight black boots. They don't know me. One woman asks me for a refill in her wineglass. Another wants seltzer, and the man wanted a vodka tonic, which I make by adapting the gin-and-tonic recipe and hoping that's what he meant. They stay near the table. Their conversation is initially about mutual friends. I want to draw the twins, as I dub them, but don't say a word. The other two are beautiful, too, merely for being young and energetic and happy to be in one another's company and I gather that they had no deep interest in this particular show and are among those here for the wine and cheese.

"Was that Summer?"

"What?"

"The girl in white. She left. I think that was her."

"Summer who?"

"Duh. The model. Models don't need last names."

"I think I did see her. It's funny how they're so disappointing without the makeup and the art direction."

"I think she's pretty. Gaunt, but pretty."

"I heard she's an artist too."

"Guys, that's why we're here: to see the art. What do you all think?"

"He can draw," says the man.

"I think it's great. People don't know about how the developers are, like, literally killing us. All the real estate people should be shot on sight. Do you know how much my tiny hovel costs?"

"They're not literally killing us."

"Yes they are. It's like …"

"Not literally. And not us."

"I guess. That's not what I meant."

The third woman, the tall blond one says, "I heard he's not really Black." I cringe and want desperately to interject but I dare not give up my momentary anonymity. I can't help but draw them in my mind.

"I heard that too," says the man.

"So, like, it's all fake."

"All? What's fake about it?"

"Jolie just said. He's not Black. He's, like, what's the word for it?"

"Appropriating. Like, stealing things that belong to others."

"But wait, here's a picture of him," one says, holding the program. "He looks Black."

"It's not a good picture. You can hardly tell what he looks like."

"He does look Black."

"Is that enough?"

"Let's ask this dude," says the pale girl.

"No, wait,"

"Hey, Bartender."

I raise my eyebrows in expectation of the question coming from the one who seems youngest. She looks up at me and asks, "What do you think?"

"About what?"

"If the artist isn't really Black, is it even okay for him to make this stuff? I mean, we're asking you …"

"Lilly, stop," her friend says. To me, she says, "I apologize. She didn't mean … I mean, she's not …"

"It's okay," I say. "Truly. But I just work here." I smile less than I want to.

Lilly complains, "Why're you stopping me? He's Black. He should be able to say whether it's acceptable." I keep that neutral smile on my face. "Hi, I'm Lilly," she says, holding out her hand.

"Bar."

"Oh, like the artist!"

"Yes."

"How funny."

Her friend looks at me and then at the photograph in the program and I see realization come to her face like a photograph in developing bath. "I'm so sorry," she says and tugs at Lilly and her friends, pulling them away and I hear Lilly complaining again, "But's he's cute …"

I read the reviews as they came out, not, as in a Broadway show, the next morning, but in dribs and drabs over the next months.

Art Now!!, February, 1996, Don Wachowski, "Around Town: Bar Mizrachi at Tricheur"

Finally, Mizrachi matters. Bar Mizrachi, whose work hitherto consisted of intricate, detailed, exquisitely boring pencil and ink studies of his girlfriends, has made a big splash at Tricheur. By entering the world of acerbic art, he has flipped a switch from "can safely skip" to "must see." The work is funny at times but always dark and pissed off, sort of like the way the rest of us live all the time. Go see this New Yorker's parodies of American canonicals and his devastating reportage drawings about the intentional destruction of the South Bronx, something we should not forget because it's not over. The work is still exquisitely done, but the opposite of the soft core of the past. It's all hard core now. Just don't try to buy any of it because it sold out, day one. Hot show.

ArtNews, March, 1996, Annette Peterman, "Gallery Scene: Mizrachi's Long and Winding Road," Drawings at Tricheur in Soho.

At the opening of Bar Mizrachi's new show at the Tricheur gallery, which he also owns, everyone who's anyone was in attendance, had an opinion, and often, could be heard sharing that opinion at high volumes. The show divides its audience, sharply. We'll get to that effect in a moment. First, we should applaud the gallery director, Nick Gatianne, for achieving in fabulousness what his boss and artist friend could not achieve in the quality of the art. The place was swimming with fashion models of all genders as well as a few stars of stage and screen. There are those of us in the art world who are concerned about this convergence of art, celebrity, and fashion and those of us who call the first group names like conservative and worse, no fun. It's not disputable, however, that the point of the glitz is buzz. Buzz supports inflated pricing schemes: Mizrachi's drawings sold out for about fifty percent more, on average, this show than last. Buzz, perhaps for the artist and certainly for the gallerist, is also an end unto itself.

One wonders about the pricing's trajectory and whether it has more to do with financial speculation than with what the artist made.

The art was in two series: a set called "Ladies and Gentlemen, The Bronx is Burning," taken from a line by Howard Cosell, and tells a story in pictures of the human cost of real estate industry's resorting to arson in the 1970s when their housing stock in that borough became worthless. Mizrachi accuses his own father of having partaken in some of these actions. The second set parodies classics of American art such as Hopper's *Nighthawks* and the Stuart portrait of George Washington to make blunt statements about a history of disenfranchisement and impoverishment among white and non-white Americans alike, but most non-white. Taken together, the two series are a departure for Mizrachi, who has hitherto made portraiture, mainly of attractive, young women, his oeuvre. Not only are these drawings mostly devoid of women (of any sort, suggesting that when it's time to get serious, women may be ignored), but these are unsubtly political whereas the earlier work was apolitical, except insofar as it may have implied a possibly unconscious politics.

The earlier work is better. Mizrachi may have had his heart in the right place when he decided to complain about inequality, racism, and cruel violence in American culture, but he isn't shedding new light on the history or the issue of American abuse of power. Any artist should consider carefully how they bring political ideas to the fore. Are they merely identifying themselves as belonging to a certain idea group, usually liberal? And providing a happy, unchallenging affirmation of their audience's identities? Are they pushing us or are they merely making a shriller, starker image of the same old ideas than what we've already seen?

Mizrachi used to stand for the quality of the work and made us wonder about how we see. In exploring the nature of beauty, his portraiture challenged the viewer's eye. The older work is, as I have said in this publication, astonishing in more ways than one but mainly astonishing about seeing. The most recent of this older category began to stretch and distort the figures in fascinating ways that maintained powerful appeals to our sense of beauty while also dilating and expanding our view of it. In the pursuit of beauty's ineffable qualities, he was on the cusp of greatness, not just among the most skilled draftspersons of his generation but among the best artists.

Now, he is crying mea culpa around his father's misdeeds of decades ago, which speaks to a complicated family dynamic to be sure, but how useful is that statement for the rest of us? Bar Mizrachi may have been on a road to making great art but now he seems to be on a detour toward making mediocre agit-prop.

This is not to claim that political art is somehow less valuable or even that political art is not becoming ascendant; it certainly is as anyone who attended the Whitney Biennial in 1993 can attest, and the art world's narrowness being forced to open itself to people who are not white men is only for the good of all. Perhaps Mr. Mizrachi was influenced by this show. If he was, and this exhibit is a bid to keep or maintain relevance in a changing field, we advise him to ignore the trends, since they shift in the wind, or at least, to adopt them with more thought. He must think of himself as not white, or else he would never have dared to speak as if from that position. If so, he might have thought it enough to show the world his art, rather than attempt to beat them into submission with his sledgehammer concepts. If he does consider himself white, as we formerly understood, possibly incorrectly, then many would ask what business is it of his to pose as spokesperson for a group of which he is not a member. That's what people were heatedly debating at the show I saw. Mr. Mizrachi is descended from Yemenite and Hungarian Jewish families, not African-Americans. However, we do not take it upon ourselves to decide what someone's race is; merely we ask, once they actively, publicly, and in their art, propose to speak about it, that they clarify this issue.

We should also return, since we are discussing the ethics and politics of art, to the fact that Mizrachi's show is hung in his own gallery. His is not the story of a neglected, downtrodden person, underestimated on account of race. If anything, he is overestimated on account of class, meaning money. It might be worth a conversation about the ethics of purchasing an existing, thriving gallery, inserting oneself into the stable, and showing one's own work there. The conflict of interest is breathtaking. Mizrachi's show complains about the real estate moguls' abuses of power and yes, that's real. But perhaps a look in the mirror, in several senses, is called for first.

11. Department of Returns

In Life One, Bar drew the moment at Willets Point when the Mets won Game Six. He made it a few years after from memory: it was of the people he had met, the guy with the radio, the Irish girl, the Jewish boys, those two men in leather jackets. They were all celebrating together. The picture showed the shared amazement and joy of the moment.

In Life Two, Bar re-drew it. He used the old drawing to show the crowd, whose faces he otherwise didn't remember. In the new one, he included himself in full body, but as small in the composition as Icarus is in Breughel's picture, a figure in the lower right corner: he was falling, almost having landed on the concrete surface, one leg pointed straight down, the other knee bent, as if he were coming off a layup, but his arms were skewed out and up, landing, not jumping, his body lacking grace. His face, only a square inch in the picture, showed shock but not joy. Mostly, it was a picture of a bunch of people on the left celebrating something, and a small man to their right falling onto the platform, apart and unnoticed.

Life One, 1996, Early October.

At Arturo's pizza place on Houston, all dark old wood and the smell of spilled beer, Jon and Bar sat in a booth. Jon had a view of the American League playoffs.

Jon frowned, frustrated. "The Mets went 71-91 this year."

"I'm not following. I don't have a T.V."

"Radio?"

"I never did that. That was you. But yeah, I don't have a radio, either."

"That some Thoreau thing?"

"That's a money thing. My birthday's October 25. I give you permission to buy me a big Sony T.V. and give me the money to pay for the electric bill. Consider it a redistribution of wealth from the health care industry to the arts."

"You think Thoreau's life was simple because he said to simplify? His whole experiment was riddled with contradictions. He ate his Aunt's pie. He had a Harvard education and a dad who owned a pencil factory, which meant he had a safety net, unlike ninety-nine percent of his contemporaries. He wasn't authentic. That's why he liked that authentic people. You can't be authentic either, Bar. Simplicity is not available in the modern world. We live together, not in some fantasy of self-reliance. You've got to stop thinking it's bad to sell out."

"Don't you think I've been trying to sell out? I can't sell shit. No one wants to buy my stuff, Jon. It's not political."

"It's political because you made it."

"What's that supposed to mean? I'm some Jewish kid from Queens."

"No, no, you've got to...you're... I talked about this with Uri. We think..."

But Uri made his entrance, effusive about the East Coast. "Heeeeey, Guys! I love, love, love this place. Real scratch graffiti on real wood. In Cali places like this are all new and the scratches are done by the waiters, pre-opening." Two guy hugs. Uri regaled them with stories of his two business "failures," both of which ended in lucrative buy-outs, and his latest foray. He told them about his sexcapades, including the six-month period during which two women lived with him, but not the same two: women A and B became A and C and then C and D. C hated D and both left at the same time.

"You were alone?" Bar asked with mock incredulity.

"For like, a month. It was heaven. All the ice cream was mine."

"Sounds rough."

"Totally. So Lisa and I are going slow. She's been through the paces too. Very independent. She's in tech, too, so it's like, we're trying to be non-competitive, though I've made a lot more. But how are you guys?" Jon described Bar's refusal of wealth. "I can understand that," Uri said, keeping his eyes wide.

"Yeah? Explain it to me, then," Jon demanded.

"It's like, we're all upper-class, but some of us are upper-class with money, and some of us choose to focus on the education."

"I have neither," Bar said.

"Nah, the degree isn't the shit, man," Uri said. "You know how many times I got asked for my pigskin? That'd be zero. It's all what can you do for me, buddy?"

"I get asked for a resumé every time I show my work to a gallery." Bar said. "I'm thinking I need to go to Hunter to get some kind of M.F.A. They think I'm nothing. They can't judge the work without externals, credentials. They can't tell what I can do for them."

"Maybe I should move out there," Bar said, taking a sip of Uri's beer. "How about you take my apartment in Harlem and I take your place in San Francisco. I'll take A, B, C, and D, in whatever order."

"Nah, nah. Too boring for you out there. Anyway, I dumped my house."

"Sorry to hear that," Bar said.

"Actually, I made a killing on my house," Uri laughed. "Lisa got a job in the City."

"You're turning people into CPU's," Jon said.

"Nah. I'm not. Actually, I'm unemployed. When I was working, I sold shit to the guys turning them into CPU's. I'm up the food chain, baby. Bar, how's the art game? Who's *your representation and what the fuck's the matter with them? What're you doing for Benjamins? What's it like being a contemporary artist at the center of the universe?"*

"I could be bounded in a nutshell, and count myself a king of infinite space, were it not that I have bad dreams," Bar said.

"What's that from?" Uri asked.

"I didn't know you remembered that," Jon said.

"Yeah, so, I'm trying to read books. It's slower than T.V. but watching T.V. used to keep me up at night."

"How's your mom?" Jon asked.

Bar pulled out a small notebook, turned to a page and handed it to Jon, who read it aloud. "Marble ash tray, though no one smokes, Venetian Murano glass vase, cut flowers (fresh), sable (not mere lox) on the glass and steel table, Eames chair, antique chair no one's allowed to sit in,...What's all this?"

"Stuff in her apartment. Hers and Schlomo's."

"What is it, like a list of grievances?"

"That Murano glass thing is grievous." Jon said.

"Ha ha. Who's the snob and where'd he learn to be one?" Uri asked.

"I liked the furnishings my dad made by hand in Jackson Heights. Did I tell you I'm taking Peter to the Met on weekends? When his dad lets me. His step-dad. Who thinks I want to marry Claudia."

Jon raised his eyebrows. Uri asked, "Who's Peter?"

"My half-brother. Also, I did get a raise recently to eighteen an hour."

"Eighteen dollars?" Uri now had his mouth open. "That's, like, illegal, isn't it? I think I paid my cleaning, uh, person, eighteen an hour. You know you're not allowed to call her a 'maid' any more."

"'Maid' is a word for virgin," Jon said drily.

"I can't possibly comment," Uri said.

"The hourly minimum wage is less than eighteen."

Bar got his beer and drank down a fourth of it.

"Fuck the hourly minimum! This man is an artist."

"Not when I'm fixing derailleurs."

"You blame your mom, still?" Jon asked him.

Bar stared in response. He knew Jon was trying to be a friend. "I was going to make some furnishings for my place. You know, instead of boards on cinder blocks? Mom was storing Dad's tools. I asked her about it. She stopped paying the storage bill. His stuff's gone."

"But she..."

"Should've asked me. Lotta money in tools."

Uri looked at him, at Jon, and back to Bar. "Shit, man, I'll get you some fuckin' tools. Why don't you sell drugs? Buy some nice furniture, stop working at a damn bike shop."

Bar laughed. "I am living in the Dominican distribution point, at least according to the New York Times. Cocaine and crack. Also the cops who keep frisking me to see if I'm carrying."

"Because you're so shady looking," Jon said with an attempt at sarcasm.
"Because they think I'm Black," Bar said. "Obviously."
"That's because you are fucking Black! Obviously! Bar! It's not up to you! Draw that! Tell the galleries!"
"They think you're Black? You're a little tan, okay, but still." Uri asked while Jon was still ranting. "So you're telling me you're being shaken down by the fuzz at home, not getting paid or laid, and you're swearing off making art?"
"Not from making. I'm swearing off trying to sell it. For now."
"Shit, man, I think this has to be a case of Uri to the rescue."
"Great!" Jon said.
"You see! The sarcasm! Love, love it! I love New York. It's like, no one is sarcastic out West. At first I thought they were all stupid, and they thought I was rude..."

They exited the dark restaurant and walked downtown on West Broadway. Uri had a list of places he wanted to see that he had gotten from the magazine in the seat pocket on the flight east. The first gallery's minimalist sculptures left them cold. They went to another gallery where the show was of defaced movie posters, contemporary to classic, to fit a theme of political satire; Indecent Proposal was changed so that Demi Moore's and Robert Redford's faces in the act of adulterous sex were replaced by Reagan and Thatcher's. In a third place the show was of a painter Bar had never heard of who used thick layers of paint with bits of glass he stuck in the impasto. The glittering colors were dazzling, even if it was overtly ripping off Schnabel. "People don't remember ten, fifteen years ago," Bar said. Uri and Jon both rocked from side to side to get the glitter effect. Uri asked for a price list. The write-up said the glass was "genuine sidewalk glass from the major cities of the world including New York, Lisbon, and Calcutta." Bar said, "Neo-ex sellout bullshit trash. Don't buy it. This is all decorative. It has no political value."

Jon said, "I thought you despised political art."
"Don't simplify me. I'm just telling him not to buy it. It won't hold its price is all I'm saying."
On Broome, Uri commented on how many of the former gallery storefronts had turned into high-end clothing shops. He nodded to a group of maybe five very tall, skinny young girls in heels tottering away like a herd of giraffes, and said, "Models. The trouble with them is their looks can confuse you into thinking they're human."
"They're as human as we are. They're girls. Children," Bar said.
Jon said, "There were models in San Francisco?"
"Not like here. But yeah. I'm swearing off looking at women, though. It's me and Lisa, steady."
Jon said, "How's that going?"
They stopped in front of a building Bar knew well. "Why do you want to go in there?"
"It's on the Time Out list," Uri said. "Show's on four."
"Four?" Bar asked. He had been in this elevator before, many times. Bar

admired the new white lettering stenciled into the glass door, "Tricheur Gallery."

"I don't want to go here," he said. "This's that place I worked."

"Oh, come on. Who cares? Wait, it's not that one. It's next door. It looks like there's some decent art in there."

They followed Uri in.

The eleven-by-fourteen inch white placard on an easel announced the show: "The Paintings of Abigail Greenfield," and a quote in French. Bar froze.

Near the room where he had gallery-sat, and where he had first seen Abigail, was this gallery, a mirror image of that one on the other side of the building, now filled with about twenty paintings, all portrait-oriented, ranging from two-by-three feet to four-by-six. Bar walked around the gallery in shock. The paintings were frenetic, energized portraits, not immediately recognizable as portraits because of the swirls of fighting brushstrokes, thick impasto, the paint sculptural, the colors powerful, the palette dominated by a dark purples, haunted by strokes of lamp black, but with small, delicate yet bold curves of thin yellow, sometimes in a corner. She had done brushwork with big brushes first: three-inch wide down to one and a half, creating an almost-flat surface as the ground, punctuated with thicker paint and some hints of space, carefully controlled. Bar slowly understood that the yellows, done after the larger brushes and on top of those strokes, but in very small brushes, were Abigail's hair. There was also small-brush work in dark brown, also in curves suggesting a head. There -- there was an eye and teeth: a face. The work had complexity and rewarded attention, like early high cubist stuff. Faces were disembodied and broken up, and you could re-assemble them but the painting's driving energy resisted total comprehension.

Uri looked at them quickly, and then went to chat with the girl at the reception desk: thin, striking, kohl-eyed, with dark skin and long, frizzy hair tied with a yellow and white scarf over her head. Sitting in what could have been Summer's throne, an equally radiant replacement, suggesting the similarly cheesy management style.

Bar went from painting to painting. In one, Abigail appeared to be curled in a ball in the corner of a large room. A wave of paint attacked her, threatened to drown her. In another, she was pretty clearly shooting up, her head so far back that it looked about to fall off her neck in a hideous, monstrous parody of the ecstasy of opium. In another, there was a screaming figure, all darkness except for his big teeth and flashing eyes. He had curly black hair done in small brushes, like in the other pictures. The shooting gallery picture had a red dot next to it on the wall.

"That's you," Jon said behind him. "Isn't it?" He forgotten that Jon, or anyone else, was there.

He said, "Yeah, she..." There were no words.

The work was vulnerable, yet was full of boldness, fearless self-revelation, like Nan

Goldin but with bold, creative painting. The Abigail figure held some stereotyped poses, like the classic prostitute pose of Picasso's Demoiselles D'Avignon, one arm held back of the head showing the elbow, the hip pushed out to the side. In Abigail's painting, though, the yellow-haired figure doing this looked like she was under attack by thick lines of paint emanating from the male figure dressed in white and four times larger. Yet she held her own; she was formidable. The complex political message, whatever it ultimately was, in no way stopped the painting from being carefully composed, gorgeously painted, full of electric charge and human emotion.

The work changed styles as they toured the show. Abigail had gone through a neo-cubist phase, a photo-realist phase that blew Bar away with her mastery of craft, and had a sprinkling of abstract pieces throughout the years. She had figured it out. She had done what she wanted to do. Her work was its own thing. Despite the stylistic range, there were signatures like color choices, bold navy blues and strong siennas. Her abstractions used shapes like spirals and ear-like forms that rhymed with the representational pieces.

Jon said, "Her work's like in the Picabia quote over there."

"What's it say?" Bar asked.

"Notre tête est ronde pour permettre à la pensée de changer de direction. It's a famous quote from him."

"Translation, please?" Uri said.

"Something like, our heads are round to permit the thoughts to be able to change direction."

"Yeah," Bar said.

Bar laughed seeing Art depicted with devil's horns in an early painting, a needle sticking up from his white suit jacket's pocket.

In the largest painting, five by seven feet, placed at the end of the series, was much more explicitly about volume, showing a gigantic, awesome space, in fact, like in a John Martin painting, and with some of Martin's hellish red fire-light. But not hell: a warehouse. There was that strong blue and set against white on one side: the water? A dock? Just left of center were two figures. One must be Abigail, with the telltale thin yellow hair. The other was -- a dark figure with dark curly hair. The female figure seemed vampirish, preying on the male. Bar noticed the little red sticker-dot next to that one, too. He quickly scanned the room: half of the paintings were sold.

As well they should be, he thought.

Bar walked over to the receptionist and said, "That large one, what's the price on that?"

She looked at him without expression, it being obvious that he couldn't possibly buy anything in the gallery, and said, "It's eight thousand."

"Okay, thanks."

Bar understood the math. Abigail's going to be able to live on this. Abigail has grown up and is now an artist.

He felt the palimpsest come on, helpless to stop it, as usual. He felt his present body crumple to the floor, but as if cushioned, as if it weren't the body he was really in. Suddenly he was in shoes that hurt his feet, white slacks and a white buttoned shirt, and he was screaming at someone. The person came in and out of focus. He couldn't quite figure out who. Then it ended.

Bar was looking at the floor. Jon was feeling his pulse. Bar said, "It's alright."

Jon asked him a series of questions about his blood pressure, whether he ever fainted like that before, and others, but Bar brushed him off. "I'm fine."

"You dropped like a sack of potatoes."

"Yeah, but I'm okay now. Look at me."

"I think you need to get yourself checked out. Do you even have health insurance? Come by the hospital and I'll do a work-up. Off the books. I've got nurses owing me a lot of favors."

"No, no, it's alright. I just, hey, I can stand on my own now." Jon let his arm go.

They left, Uri complaining that he didn't have time to look at everything after the girl had "bothered" him for so long, insisting on giving him her phone number, and then talking about whether he should get a place right on Washington Square Park or in the Christadora, overlooking Tompkins Square Park, and the light in each place, and the food shopping, the restaurants, the night life, and whether it would be easy to find an ATM nearby.

Same Day, Life Two.

A week earlier, Uri called me from California. I felt angry at him for what he tried to do with Eva in Life One but reminded myself that this didn't happen yet and would not, not anymore. I allowed my feeling for an old friend to come forward.

His bravado shot through the transcontinental wires, "What're you doing day after tomorrow, hot shot? Publicity for your gallery or your show? Getting yourself photographed in Odeon for *Vanity Fair*? Dating four models whose ages add to yours? What. Tell me. Talk to me, baby. Got time for an old friend?"

"The math doesn't work."

"What math?"

"The four models. We're thirty."

"Two models?"

"Creepy, as always."

"So? Busy?"

"Not too busy for you. What's your deal?"

"I'm flying back east tomorrow. I've got three brokers' appointments lined up. I'm thinking Village, maybe West Village. Or Brooklyn. Where you at these days?"

"Near Washington Square."

"You got a view of the park?"

"Yes. You should stay here while you're looking."

"Hey, maybe I will. If you're lucky. It'd mean a ton of hot women traipsing through, mostly interested in me but hey, there's always spillover."

"Your generosity is astounding."

Two days later, Uri, on west coast time, woke at ten in my spare bedroom, complained that his room had no view and that he had to walk all the way to the common room to see the park. I had already done laps in Central Park and work in the studio. "You're going to tell me why you're moving back?"

"I totally will but I have a thing with a broker in half an hour. How long does it take to get to Canal and East Broadway?"

"Half an hour. Don't live there."

"Don't worry. We're only meeting there, making our way up."

"Lunch?"

"Tell me the name of the place again?"

I get to Arturo's at quarter past one and regret being there fifteen minutes early. I rushed out of the house wearing white pants that don't quite fit and tight shoes. I'm getting fat because I'm not riding enough. It was better living on 135th for riding. Fifteen minutes over the bridge to Jersey from up there. Plus I'm working too hard and for what?

(Why should I make art at all? Why bother to keep the gallery? I could give it to Nick.)

In Life One I was a late person until about this year and then I wasn't. In Life Two I've been an on-time person since I arrived. I act old.

I sat there thinking about my friends, Uri and Jon. Jon isn't currently my friend. How can he know that I'm changed? Changed from what? But he does know, or maybe he's attached to a me that's gone.

I can't shake my objection to Uri, despite its tortured logic. What are the ethics of holding someone accountable for what I know them capable of doing, know beyond any doubt, but which they haven't done?

If you could kill Hitler when he's a teenager, would you do so? It's a bad question, because too pure. Obviously, you'd kill Hitler. What about someone who murdered one person, not millions? Kill that person beforehand?

The four young white women in short dresses, heels, and lots of makeup, talking to one another excitedly two tables over, giggle too loudly. Out-of-towner. New Yorkers are too dour for that. The other two people here are more like it: a salt-and-pepper Black dude in a black leather jacket and black, paint-splattered jeans (is he an artist or a house painter?), reading a book at the bar while he eats his burger, and an olive-skinned woman in an ugly business skirt suit having a salad and white wine.

If you were sitting at a table for two with Adolf Hitler in 1914, he's fifteen years old, it's before the war and before he started turning into an anti-Semitic monster, before he killed anyone even as a soldier, you'd feel angry for what you know him to be headed toward. You wouldn't merely want to deflect his trajectory, say, by kidnapping him and dumping him (alive, maybe with a deforming injury) in Australia, get him a place in one of their art schools, maybe, so he'd stick around and where he'd sit out the Great War and never develop his hatreds. No. You'd want to kill him, and not just to stop him. Kill for revenge.

The man with paint splatter also has dots of blue. Still, people paint their walls blue sometimes. Maybe he's an artist, maybe a house painter, maybe both, like me in One. The waitress seems middle-eastern, hairstyle spiky in random places, otherwise chin-length, as if a flapper from the twenties had been attacked by a violent hairdresser. Her short black cotton dress on top of a black long-sleeve t-shirt, black hose, black boots, and black lipstick make the place feel like a café in a hip section of Fez. Not that I'd ever been. An imagined Fez. I should try to visit Yemen, though dad would never take me and I speak no Arabic.

Summer might go. She liked to travel, though mostly to boutique hotels. Not only: be fair. She went with me to that rustic place in Mexico. Though it was on the beach. The surfing school. It maks me smile to think of her and not just because that memory has her in a swimsuit. Was that the last time we were together for longer than twelve hours? My smile fades.

What if, instead of going back in time and killing Hitler to prevent mass murder, you went back in time and prevented the birth of someone? Was that similar to murder, or was it illogical to hold oneself to account for a mere potentiality?

I think it's the sixth year of having sex with Summer, two years longer than my relationship with Eva, which hasn't begun. Though "relationship" was a broad term, it had implications that might not include what I and Summer are doing with one another. Mutual use? Division of labor? At first, Summer agreeing to speak with me at all, when I became her boss, gave me a flush feeling. It took months for that feeling to wear off, and in truth it never entirely did. What wore off was how juiced she was by the thrill she caused in me.

I don't blame her for tiring of me and moving out or even for dating several other men, given the number of them who knock on her door. She said she'd keep in touch. She did. Sometimes this meant staying with her for a week. Sometimes it meant a one-night stand. It was a fantasy version of a "relationship" and I agreed to it as if looking at it objectively, as if I were describing this arrangement to someone and saying of course I would have no-strings sex with the hottest girl in New York, but the dynamic always also included my hesitation lest Summer eclipse Eva, and Summer always sensing this as any even moderately emotionally attuned person would, and always resenting the emotional pull-back, and sending me back home again when she did. She'd refer to me as her frigid housewife. She said I was her existential philosopher.

This is because we had an argument, early on, in the first two years, in which I accused her of not reading books, she asked me what to read, what was really hard, and I told her to read *The Stranger* by Camus. Her takeaway was that Meursault wouldn't allow himself to love.

"That's not what it means," I said. "It's about the loss of any fellow feeling that results from no longer being able to believe in one's religion, or in any system of belief whatsoever. That's existentialism."

"Well," she said, "that's not how I thought about it. You think I'm stupid, don't you? A dumb blond."

"No."

"That's why you don't love me."

"No."

"Then why don't you?"

I couldn't answer because even then I was coming to love her and because … how could I? I refused simply to lie. I couldn't answer that I had spent a decade away from my true love and would spend another many years the same way to re-meet her as a worthier mate and give her everything she ever wanted because that's not just unbelievable. It's unbelievably stupid. Am I a prisoner to a plan made by a past self? I remember I went to the bathroom to throw up. Summer didn't take that as a sign that she should keep trying.

At 1:40, Uri arrives. "Why's Jon being such a bitch?" he asks me. Uri invited him. I warned that he wouldn't come.

"He says I've sold out."

"So the fuck what? Everyone's sold out. It's either that or starve. We're supposed to be old friends."

"There are levels. That's not all he said."

"Yeah, fine. I love this place," he says, looking around, losing interest in Jon's non-appearance. "Character. Nothing in Cali has character like this. Not even Northern Cali. It's so cool you're showing me the New York art scene. I was getting into it on the coast but I have no idea what's going on here."

"There's a million things going on. The stuff that people write about as 'going on' is mostly political."

"Yeah, yeah, like race-political or some other political?"

"Everything. FYI we're seeing maybe five galleries. It's hardly the 'scene'," I warn.

"I get it. It's like, everyone always talks about the scene around the Mission district but there's other stuff. It's kind of sad, I think."

"Sad?"

"Oh, you know, the artists have been there, like ten, fifteen years and the rents are already pricing them out."

"Like the East Village."

"I suppose. I don't think I ever saw that stuff."

"It was … one of the things we're going to see is Abi Greenfield's work. She's an artist, I uh, used to know pretty well."

"Oh? Do tell." Uri's eyebrows raise.

I deflect with, "How's this Lisa person you're with? She's got work in New York? You're giving up on multiple partners?"

"Wow, you're a step ahead. What multiple partners? Is that a joke? I don't get New York humor any more. I'm out of practice."

"You don't have sex regularly with several women or persons at the same time?"

"Ha, ha, ha, wow. Is that what you think California is like? Sure, Bar, like ten. Maybe you mean you're having sex with ten women at the same time. Huh? You're, like the king of the New York art world."

"I'm a little prince. Tiny."

"Oh? I heard different. I read that article in Art-something by Annette Vichy. Does she want to have sex with you, by the way, because the article was half foreplay, half art criticism."

"I don't talk with critics. If I can avoid it."

"Is she attractive?"

"All God's creatures … blah, blah. So you never had sex with more than one person, any gender, at the same time. Never happened. That was all lies?"

"What lies? When did I ever claim this?"

I think I made an error. It's hard to keep up a clear border between Lives of information. "How old is Lisa? May I ask?"

"Uh, okay? Lisa's, like, a month younger than me. What did Jon say?"

"I … sorry."

"Did Jon say that I go around fucking crowds? It's a fantasy of his, right? 'Persons' – don't think I didn't hear that. Not that I am homophobic in the least. But you know Jon is gay, right?"

"Of course, I …"

"You two have got to stop calling me Gary Mitchell. I have no super powers. I no longer attract that kind of …"

"Yes, you do," I laugh. "Check out the four mid-afternoon party chicks at your five o'clock. The other five o'clock. Yeah, don't be too obvious. The question is, are they going to a party later, or are they still partying?"

"They might've been looking at you, dude."

"They did not look over here the entire time I was alone."

"Sorry I was a little late. I forgot how long things take here. Walking. What a concept."

"Don't you walk in San Fran?"

"Yes, but I was in Menlo Park for years."

Uri thinks the food, when it comes, is "amazing" and "authentic." He never used to gush, to overpraise that which needs no praise at all.

Suddenly, Uri drops his smile and starts talking in so serious a tone that I think he must be joking. "There's this thing that happened," he starts. "You can't tell anyone."

I put a finger to my lips.

"There's this girl, back in Frisco," he says, checking around the restaurant for possible spies. "I didn't know she was that young. I made her show me I.D. but she had a fake one so she could drink. They all have fake I.D.s now. Did you know that?"

I shake my head.

"I should've known. It's not an excuse. If I'm having sex with girls who look like they might possibly in some other multiverse be under twenty, shit, under twenty-five, I should make it my business to know about the I.D.s, right?"

I nod yes. Maybe I can get through this conversation with head shakes only. Whatever Uri has done, he wouldn't tell me about it last time, in One. Was it that Jon was there, or that it was the three of us, a crowd, too much shame? Or does he consider me an actual person now, not an object of pity?

"She got pregnant."

"Shit."

"Shit is right. I got her pregnant, okay? Me. She was a month short of her eighteenth birthday. I paid for the procedure. Of course."

"I'm …" I felt like saying I'm sorry but it makes no sense. "I don't know what to say. Was this…? Does Lisa know about it?"

Uri shakes his head. "The girl, … she's just a kid. She's emotionally, like, I don't know. She calls me, leaves ten-minute messages. Says she's in love with me. She says all kinds of shit. I've offered her money. She screamed and cried and hung up on me. I pray that she meets a cute boy her age. It's not, like blackmail, but it might as well be. I can't cut her off. There's a paper trail because I paid for the … thing. Still, it's not proof I had sex with her. I won't go to jail. It is enough for Lisa to legitimately ask me what the fuck. And why the fuck do I have so many phone calls from a recent high school grad, real pretty, lives a block away from where we just moved?"

Uri's choking up, getting tomato sauce on his face as he tries to hide his sobbing with his napkin. I sit, thinking mean thoughts. I feel like standing and walking through the door and not looking back, but I sit. I have no words for him but I'll stay still.

"What gets me is that she hit on me, not the other way around," he goes on. "I was working from home. I know the girl's dad's cousin, a business connection. She comes by with two friends, another girl and a guy, and asks to use my pool. I'm on the phone, doing my thing. I wave at the pool and say sure. Next thing I know, the other two are making out in the pool or some shit, and this girl's all over me in the house. Beautiful, Bar, I mean movie-star looks, in a bikini, and even then I kick her out without touching her, but I'm thinking about it and she knows she planted a seed in my cock-brain, so she's there the next day, like half an hour after Lisa's in her car and off to work and now there's no one else around and she's in cutoffs and there's her body and, … there's no excuse. It's my fault. I don't know what's wrong with me. I failed a moral test. She showed me her I.D. I should've known because she whipped it out without my asking, you know? Like she was practically telling me she was lying and underage, like there was a problem."

"Yeah."

"What do you mean, 'yeah'? You got any words of comfort other than that?"

I consider this for a good long minute during which he is visibly getting angry; he thinks he deserves solace and its clear that despite his good words about taking responsibility he has done no such thing. "It's not so bad not getting everything one wants," I say finally.

"Thanks a lot. That's the lamest …"

"I know. I think you'll get lucky. I think we've gotten luckier than we deserve, generally. I don't have words of comfort. I've done bad things, too."

"Like what?"

I merely shake my head.

While he goes to the bathroom to wash his face, I think about how attractive he is, even more now than when he was a fresh young man in high school and college. The girls in the booth behind us watched him get up and go to the bathroom. It's not a test I ever faced. Still feeling sorry for him is too much.

Uri insisted on paying and I let him.

We walk up West Broadway. He's flipped back into a good mood, surprisingly, disturbingly.

"I'm so impressed at how you're positioning yourself as a Black man," he says, utterly unaware of how this makes me feel. "I mean, artistically, right? It's brilliant, considering how you're ahem, not Black, right? Sure, not exactly white, either. This is it. It's right next to your gallery. You're going to give me a tour, right?"

"We can go in Tricheur after we see this one, but they'll try to get me to do work."

"Work? What's that? Is that something people do? What's so hard about deciding what art to buy?"

"Nick tries to get me to make decisions like what kind of toilet paper to buy. He likes to duck responsibility."

"Employees, dude. I used to have those. Pain in the ass. That's why half the people in tech are inventing robots."

"This is it. Wait, maybe it's the wrong place. Those aren't the paintings.

They look like her work, but..."

I've not kept in touch with Abigail much in the time between when I left for the Chelsea hotel and now, ten years later. I tried to give Abi an apartment, a super-soft eviction from Sharpey's building when we were ready to do the demolition, but she wasn't there and Sharpey didn't know where she went, and neither did anyone in E.V.

The poster for the show, mounted on a board that sat on an easel as they walked in, confused him at first. It said, "Paintings for Abigail Greenfield." *For.*

Then Bar spotted the *by.*

"Arturo," he said. "This is my friend since high school, Uri Jorgensen."

Uri made a joke about the pizza place that Art didn't get. Awkward silence followed. I see the differences: Art no longer affects the annoying theatrical flourishes of his past, wears black jeans and a black t-shirt, not a tux, and no longer colors his blond hair. He has almost no affect. Is this hostility? Actually, the most important change is, Art isn't dead. "Why's this your show," I ask him.

"As opposed to what?"

"Hers. Abi's. Where is she?"

Art is hostile now, showing affect in his brows knitting slowly from confusion to anger as he seems to be making an effort to control himself. "Why don't you see the show and then ask me."

"Alright."

First are portraits of Abi: there's Abigail laughing at the E.V. club, Abigail painting a portrait of Art, Abi biking in some countryside spot, Abi looking at a piece of paper with consternation, a painting that recalls the Dorothea Lange photograph of a woman during the Depression. I don't know what that last one's about but the others make me miss her. I almost called her a few times when I remembered from One that she must be in this show or that show but I didn't. I never stopped blaming her for what happened in One, illogical though that may be. The work is reminiscent of Art's early style, the colors too bright, almost Day-Glo, or simply wrong, like Van Gogh's, but the painting is restrained and balanced between real and stylized, like Cezanne or certain Picassos. There is consistency and there is mastery.

Another series starts in a second room. Abi is sitting in a hospital chair reading while getting an I.V. drip. Abi is clutching Art's hands in a doctor's office, the point of view from behind the doctor's head, as if she is receiving news and he is there with her. Abi in a hospital bed with the monitors and rolling tray holder. A fantasy picture of Abi floating on a stream, fully clothed, like the Ophelia by Millais. By now I read through tears that the series is called "AIDS Sequence."

As I become enraged, I see Art smiling at one of the office workers about some random thing. I lose control of my mind and body. I scream at him,

"Murderer!! You murderer! You killed her! You did it! I'm going to kill you!" I jump around the reception desk, where the young woman is yelling back at me. "Get out! Who the fuck are you!" Out of the gallery office rush two other women, one older and one younger, and they start yelling at me, too.

I find what I'm looking for, push the three of them away and pick up a pair of scissors. I come back around the reception desk, heading for Art. I don't know what I'm doing. I have no plan to kill him; I feel rage and want badly to hurt him.

Uri catches me before I get two steps closer to Art. "What the fuck, dude?"

"Let me go! He killed Abi and now he's laughing he's got the guts to use her make these fucking pictures you're a murderer!"

Art stands still. "Let him go," he says to the room. "I don't much care. I didn't kill her. Your sudden concern for Miss Greenfield is odd. Where were you when she was dying, old friend of ours? Old boyfriend? Didn't much give a shit then, huh? The truth is you were never one of us. You always did your cramped, constipated, effete little drawing thing. She tried to get to you to see that the universe extended past your dick but you did your level best to be a bad student. And then you turned tail and ran."

I feel limp and strengthless, as if I'm fainting but not losing consciousness. Uri isn't holding me up; he's stopping my forward motion. I fall onto the hardwood as if shot. I know it's a palimpsest and know which one, too, when I feel my One self's reaction to Abigail's artistic achievement, here in this same gallery. I feel the awe, pride, and jealousy that I felt for Abigail's work then, in Life One. I'm overwrought in Two, lying on the floor; I am weeping for the loss of Abigail and all she had once done, even as I know she is gone. Who killed her suddenly becomes unimportant.

The palimpsest ends after a minute. I get up, shaking off the Uri's queries and offers of help. "If you didn't kill her," I say to Art, calmly now, "then how come that didn't happen before?"

"I don't know," Art said "What do you mean, before? Susie, please don't call the police. That's the last thing we need."

Susie says into the phone, "It's a mistake. Nothing's going on."

I realize my error. "Explain how she got AIDS if not from you."

Art says nothing at first. I see that I'm still holding the scissors. I place them gently on the reception desk and the young woman takes them quickly.

Art says, "I am a gay man. Are you saying I had sex with Abigail?"

"So what? You were going..."

"We were going to do some silly stunt to disrupt your determined stance against living life, but we never did it, and in any case, she wouldn't have been infected."

"How do you know?"

"I don't have AIDS."

"Liar. Yes you do. You did – you were about to kill yourself."

Art is startled by that, but recovers quickly. "I don't know how you heard about that but I never had AIDS. There are always reasons to end one's life."

I don't know what to say to that. He has no reason to lie. He doesn't even owe me as much explanation as he is giving.

Art went on, "No, poor little Abi gave herself AIDS the straight-girl way, by sharing needles with some feckless heroin salespeople. As for my using Abi, on the contrary, these pictures are a tribute. Anyone else would think so. I painted them in her own style, as best I could train myself to copy it. She taught me so much. For instance, Abigail taught me to love her. What did she teach you? I get the sense that you go through women like paintbrushes. Do give Summer – that model who got your picture into *Vanity Fair* – my love, and while you do that, please do stick your righteous indignation up your ass. You might find, while doing so, that your own artistic ethics are to be found right there, my belle 'negre'. You've made yourself quite the talk of the town with your reverse passing."

"Bar, I think we should go," Uri says.

The three women working in the gallery agree in a chorus-like assent. Susie adds, "I think the cops are on their way anyway."

"By the way," Art says, "that Black American Gothic is so clichéd. I wanted to wretch."

I want to say I'm sorry. I'm so sorry, but I can't. Not to Art. I hate him but my energy is spent. At the door, I turn back. "Was all that experience you two were chasing worth it?"

"We were being alive. You call that chasing experience? Everything we did seemed necessary, at the time. Stupid question."

As we go out into the hallway, Nick runs out through Tricheur's glass door, buttonholes me into signing some papers before Uri tells him no, no more; we have to go.

12. The Child is the Father of the Man

He made an endless series of drawings of Stacey in high school. One stood out for him, partially replacing his memory of her face. It wasn't very different from the others in composition; all were head-and-shoulders portraits, some bare shoulders, but nothing past the collar bone. In each of the one he made prior to this he began sketching in Stacey's presence, sometimes reaching half an hour before she wanted started getting bored at which point she called her friend on the phone line in her room (she was the only teen he knew to have her own line) or wanted to make out. Later, he spent an hour, maybe one and a half, on each of the others in Kincaid's classroom before giving up on getting what he wanted. They looked enough like her, but didn't express the inner feeling he was after. He began to despair of ever achieving this elusive idea, one he could not even put words to. At Kincaid's suggestion, he laid out the six least mediocre portraits that he had done in front of him, and worked from those on the one that became the successful portrait. He held, for him, inner as well as outer beauty, though how that worked, he did not know. Kincaid saw it, too, and said so.

That was the picture Abigail ripped out of his sketchbook and sold to Sharpey for heroin. He remembered thinking, Abi knows; she can see. He remembered his pride. It had been his first sale.

An unremembered dream – fear, then,
... The green L.E.D. said 3:30. The window showed dark buildings across the park and twinkling lights up Fifth Avenue. Next to him, summer's small shoulder and thin white arm. Her snoring. Had it woken him, or was it the dream? He had been waking regularly around this time. Sometimes he got up and drew her. No, no, that was when she lived with him. He wouldn't do that any more. Three nights ago she woke when he did and coaxed him back to bed for sex and he had half wished she had not woken. He could have drawn her again.

He went to take a piss, then lay down and tried to remember the dream.

He dreamed he was opening the door with his own key in Jackson Heights, home from school, fifth grade, his dad Saul half asleep sitting in his chair, the T.V. on, the beer already fallen. Saul hadn't worked that day.

That night, an argument, one of a series.

"Stop to being a drunk!"

"Schlomo is a crooked, he..."

The feeling of fear that they would hit each other. The hope that dad would leave, and the fear that mom would instead.

With mamma in supermarket. "Everything here is cheap and fake. Americans and their Wonder bread and mayonnaise and they conquered the world! Ha! Bologna, not real Austrian sausage or Polish Kielbasa. In Budapest, we bought food from all over Europe: French cheese and wine, Swiss chocolate." She picked up a jar of jelly, read the ingredients, put it back on the shelf. "Why conquer the world if we have to live like this?"

Something else is happening. He sees a girl from his class down an aisle. His mother is talking. What was mom saying? "We were hiding in the barn in hungry!"

No, Hungary. You're not a child any more.

(A car horn. This is from his present. It interrupts the dream but he floats back down into it.)

Mom stood. "At home my mother was going to give me the cookware that her mother gave her."

"Why didn't she?"

"I told you. We had to run. In the barn in Hungary there was no room for pots. No kitchen."

"Did you have kielbasa?"

Lisa Lussuria. (Must be fourth grade?) With her own mother, at the end of the aisle. Lisa gave me "the eye," pointing her head down and to the side and looking at me with one eye, the other covered by her long black hair. I walked toward her. She's dark, like me and dad.

"Bar, don't go that way. Our family sold wine to the emperor in Vienna, and the Czar. On my mother's side. I should have been a lawyer, like Father. I was going to study in Vienna," she said. I saw the tears forming and mamma's stifling a sob. She said, "I should not have married … at all."

A woman about mom's age and her son, about my age, pass behind Judit. It says "sliced ham" on the cold cuts paper. Bread in plastic in their cart. Mom said never buy that, the bread in plastic. The ham sandwich family goes around a corner. Mamma is kneeling down to be eye to eye with me and lowering her voice to an anxious whisper, "Don't ever let anyone tell you are a Bleck. Promise me."

Momma is talking about Zabar's and then Murano glassware. The grand piano back in the house in Hungary that she hid under when company came and the vase on top with fresh flowers every day.

You had to flee. You had an hour. You left your cat, whom you loved. Your nanny cried when you left. After the war you found out that the nanny collaborated.

"What's kollabrated?"

"Bad. She said bad things about Jews."

Sometimes I would look around my room at night thinking about what I'd take if I had only an hour.

Lisa's mother is ahead of momma at the checkout. Lisa gives me "the eye" again. It feels queer. Lisa laughs, and becomes Stacey, in high school. She has blonde hair and you can see her breasts under the bodysuit with a chevron pattern in front, a round ass and full lips, and she comes close to kiss me and smells of fruity shampoo. What would happen if she discovered that I was "a Black"? No, not Stacey, Lisa. Stacey. Looking at Stacey until she smiles and says, "What? I like how you look at me."

At the country house in Springs. (No, go back to Stacey. Please.) The man, mom and dad. The man is Ido, a friend from Israel, another Yemenite Jew. He is an architect, very successful, mom says to dad. She already said that. Dad makes a bad face. Why does mom have to try to make dad mad? There's no beer in the fridge. I can see when I open it. Dad will have to go get some.

We can stay there weekdays when the owners are working and the boy's in camp. The boy's name is Itamar. He has a wood coat peg rack with his name in Hebrew. Itamar has a summer house and goes to sleep-away, too. He has a bike but it's too big.

Me and dad going to the dump in the old white pickup truck. On Three Mile Harbor Road, the smell of tar at the docks, the smell of the open pits at the dump, the pits full of garbage bags, the seagulls there, a whole mountain of dead bikes, a graveyard of broken spokes, rusted chains and metal tubes, cracking tires, and bursting seats. Dad, climbing the mountain, tossing aside one bike after another, staring at the pile of bikes now and again as if it were a giant hieroglyphic. Dad saying, "fack, fack, fack," then in Hebrew. Fifteen minutes, half an hour. The dump guy calls out from a little shack, closing soon. Dad sweating.

Dad finds it, a small Bennotto ten speed. "Ha!"

Dad in the garage, replacing the chain, the pedals, the seat, fixing the derailleurs. Dad pushing Bar on the bike, yelling, "Go! Pedal, turn the wheel! The hendleburs! Yes!" Wind and speed and joy and dad smiling.

Riding in the car on Montauk highway. Listening to 8-track tapes of Broadway musicals. That is what Americans listen to. My Fair Lady West Side

Story All I want is a room somewhere there's a place for us.

In the room in Springs that belonged to the other boy are a lot of matchbox cars and I want one but I don't steal. I make a drawing of one.

In the apartment in the City, Dad is angry. Dad comes into my room and yells. Dad throws the radio on the floor.

The radio guts. I tinker with it. Look, the wires and pulleys turn when the knobs turn. I fix it. It plays music.

Dad sitting on his bed, another day. They are listening to the broken radio. Dad's tears. I draw that. Drawing is good because I can be silent. Talking with dad is sometimes good, sometimes bad.

Dad at the supermarket. Dad in his painter's overalls, his clothes all splattered with white paint. "I hate that job," he says in the apartment. Mom yelling at him for saying that.

The flecks of white paint on his dad's hairy hands, and a spot of white on dad's chin.

Mom's list on roll paper.

"Cereal." I silently spell dad's pronunciations. "Thet" for "that."

"No, not that one, this one," I tell him. "Mom says buy the big one."

"Ya, ya, okay, next." Not "next," but "necks."

"Coffee."

"Yes, coffee, not the shit. Do they have the not-shit coffee? Yes, ah. Next."

I read the list.

"Amerrrrican apples," Saul rolled his r's.

"Milk, mom says we should get low fat."

"Shit-milk, tastes like water. In Yemen I remember milking the goat. Lots of work and the goat, she smells and maybe she doesn't feel like it now and maybe she's gonna kick, hah? Goat's milk much better, Bar. With the cream, too. Okay, okay, don't look like that, we get momma her milk, okay? *and* not-shit milk, yes?"

"Pap-rik-a."

"Yes, yes, where is that? She wants...the Hungarian c... Is that it? Now, is your mother going to get madder if I don't buy any paprika. The wrong kind of paprika." Saul is muttering.

"Um..." Not "madder," but "medder" or "meddair." Between those.

Dad is muttering, loading six-pack after six-pack of cheap beer until the tower of sixes reached the edge of the cart.

In the apartment, yelling about paprika. "You are my great disappointment!" mom yells at dad. "My regret!"

"You got lots of regret. Doesn't matter who you get married." Dad snapping on the television, throwing himself into his chair and sitting aggressively still. There is anger radiating from that corner. I'm tiptoeing into my room.

Mom's paprika chicken and paprika and garlic potatoes.
Dad's shakshuka.
Mom's goulash.
Dad's spicy peppers. Dad's hummus and falafel. Dad's shwarma. Dad's *lamb* shwarma. Dad's coffee, starting when I'm thirteen.

I'm reciting my Bar Mitzvah portion at the Jackson Heights Jewish Center, the terror of reciting not only in Hebrew but, in accordance with Yemenite tradition, in Aramaic, all the Ashkenazi Jews from Europe not understanding the Aramaic, my father smiling up at me, my mother...where was she? Is she in the bathroom? She didn't care about it. "I'm not Jewish that way." The synagogue's carpet smell.

The synagogue reception hall. I remove the itchy clip-on tie. Dad smells of beer. He tells me (again) about flirting with the nurse while mom was giving birth. He says, "you hev to push," and makes a motion with his fist punching the air and almost falls.

By tenth grade, mom walks more often. Dad talked about it. "You mother is downstairs," he said. I can see through my window walk briskly down the block and around a corner. She has her new sneakers, Tretorns, like the girls in school, except not decorated with magic marker hearts. Sometimes mom didn't leave cash to pay the delivery person.

Mom doesn't live here.
We order Chinese food.
At first, it was just the dishes that I had to do.

Senior year of high school. I'm doing the shopping and the dishes and the *Yemenite Cooking For Lovers* book that Saul gave Judit long ago. It was new, never used. Mom was having "a thing" with Schlomo, dad's old boss, who called in the evenings enough that dad stopped answering the phone. Mom bought a tape answering machine and Schlomo left terse messages like, "It's me," with his baritone Yiddish accent.

I have not yet had a girlfriend. "I think Stacey likes you," Jon says in the art room. (Jon is in the art room not because he can do any art well, not drawing, not painting, not ceramics, but because it is a refuge from boys following him down the hall and asking him out sarcastically, or shoving him, or asking him to throw a ball to them and laughing because he threw "like a girl." We became friends in the art room in 9th grade without me understanding why Jon was there or why Jon didn't even do art there; he read books not necessarily assigned for homework of any class or talked to Kincaid. She did seem to think Jon should be there.) Jon's senior year news seems monumentally significant. Kincaid at her desk, grading 10th grade watercolors, suppressed a smile.

(Bar turns to his side and spoons Summer and then remembers they are not a couple.)

Stacey at his locker, Jordache jeans, white sneakers, a tight cotton purple v-neck. "Bar? I heard you're like, really good at drawing faces?"
Wanting, and fear.

Telling mom, "I want to go to art school."
"You will be poor. A nothing, like you father."

Stacey said, "Do you want to, like, draw me?" That smile, head turned thirty degrees to the side, disarmed me. "I heard you're, like really good."
In the art room, I'm scowling at my pad, flipping to a new page.
"You're starting already?"
"Yes."
"I don't normally not wear make-up," she says.
"I know." I focus on the light on her face.
"I mean, I know how my face is. It's too round. My mom says I have a fat face. Do …?"
"Can you look at me?"
"Okay. I mean, it's tiring to be looked at; it's like, a job." Silence. She can't take silence. "A guy asked me for a kiss on the subway last week. Like a forty-year-old creep. Like, can't I go to a fucking party in a nice dress on public transportation?"
"Could you, uh, look at me?"
I feel ashamed that she said that word. No, it's cool. No, it's … "Okay."
"My mom goes to parties. She says I should be thankful I'm still getting catcalls." Silence. She is going to talk. I can feel it. "She puts on these, like, tottering heels and leaves me alone all night."
She is flowing toward me and I'm flowing out through my hand onto paper, marking it with her beauty. I become lost in the faces, hers and the one I'm making. I'm afraid of being caught feeling so close to her, as if I had touched her without permission.
She is talking.
I am getting her features, her lines, seeing the anxious feeling in her face as she spoke, becoming an eye-hand machine. She's saying things about her beauty's price. I'm working well. I feel close to her, but I'm not listening to her. I want to draw her and pretend to listen to her forever.

(Summer groans. He had been squeezing her.)

"Maybe I could, like, put together the portfolio for F.I.T. and become a designer. Not a model. Tasha says if you're a model, you're like, a piece of meat." Silence: I call it "quiet." "This guy once gave me his card on the street and told me he was a photographer and begged me to call him."

"Uh huh."

"Isn't that creepy?"

"Yeah." I'm drawing. This is the first time, the first zoning in. It's trans-, more than-.

"Bar, are you okay?"

"Yeah." Silence. She seems … "Can you look this way?"

"Are you done? Can I see?"

She comes to me. I'm not done. I don't want to be … She takes my face in her hands and kisses me.

I am lost in kissing. I wonder if I'm kissing her correctly, as she wishes to be kissed?

Her hair smells of fruity shampoo, like a girl. Abigail's hair smelled of soap.

(Summer's hair smells like an expensive color treatment. A slightly different blond.)

"Uh, yeah, Stacey, would you, uh, go out with me?"

She laughs. She kisses me again. "You don't kiss like other boys."

"No?"

"You're so, I don't know. Intense."

"I am?"

A store selling feather earrings, lipsticks, and stuffed purple unicorns. I am bored. I want to leave but don't want to let go of her hand.

(Summer is saying something.)

Jon is listening. My friend, Jon. It is after school; we are in the schoolyard. "The zoning in was transcendent. More than kissing. Different. Trans-sexual."

"That's not what you mean," Jon is saying. Jon is blushing. It's a block away. We are walking to the train. Why am I not on my bike? It's raining; the smell of new rain. "Transcendent. That – other – means something else."

(Go back to Stacey. Please.)

I'm with Stacey, inside. A big place, noisy. The smell is changed. The ground floor of Bloomingdales, the horrible smells of perfume.

(Summer is grinding her small ass against him.)

We're in Serendipity and I'm staring at Stacey's plump ass as she orders strawberry and I'm paying for the ice cream. Her lips become a new shade of red.

We are kissing in her room. It is an activity that consumes the whole of a person, I think. It is like drawing.

"Other boys don't kiss the way you do," Stacey says, not remembering she told me that before. What boys?

Kincaid is looking at a couple of my drawings of Stacey. Kincaid's my art teacher. She snickers, "They are sentimental. Try drawing with your eyes, Bar."

There is a fascinating freckle on Stacey's bare shoulder. I'm behind her, holding her breast. It is round and there is a freckle on it, too, that I've never seen. The freckle shows the volume and the shape. I want to hold her breast draw but I don't want to let go.

(He reaches over her body and holds Summer's breast. It is small. I'm too old for her, too, not just Stacey. I'm too old. It's too late.)

Gary Mitchell says, "It's not too late to get it right, Bar. Listen, I've done this before." We're in the same schoolyard. Public school, cracked concrete. A handball wall with graffiti. Toy writers. "You can get whatever you want. I'm telling you. How'd you think I got Jasmine?" Jasmine is a pretty ninth grader. I had to explain a couple of jokes to her. GM could have any girl; we're seniors. We rule the school. "Tell her she's hot all the time, even if she said you only like her for her looks, that puts the looks thing to rest. Then you replace it with 'love.'" GM says, using air quotes.

I do love Stacey.

(He doesn't love Summer. No, that's not whom he means. Can he love Summer? Isn't what they are doing love? "How are the body and soul connected?"

Summer laughs. "I don't know, Bar. Are you awake?")

"Also, write down her birthday in your calendar," GM says. "Ask her what she wants a month or two in advance. Make sure to give it to her on the day itself. Get her a gold chain." GM uses air quotes when saying "gold," too. "You'll get to third base, fast. Trust me."

"Trust him. He's a slut, so he knows," Jon says.

"I'm a slut and you're a fag," GM says.

Stacey asks, "Why do you guys call him Gary Mitchell? His name is Uri."We're in her room. Her hair smells fruity.

"It's a *Star Trek* thing. It's from the original pilot. Gary Mitchell's power doubles every few hours. He becomes invincible. But he's eventually defeated."

"How?"

"His girlfriend makes him weak."

Her room, the purple shag rug and girl's underwear on the floor and those shirts that aren't shirts that just have little straps (camisoles? body suits?). Each of her girl's things is fascinating and frightening. I want to hold and kiss her. "Is Gary Mitchell going to ask out Jessica?"

"I don't know."

("You don't know what?" Summer asks. "You don't know if you're awake?")

Ring, ring. It's Saturday just after the end of senior year. I lets the phone ring six times before thinking of getting out of bed. Where is everyone? Ring, ring. Oh yeah, Mom and Dad are trying a new Sephardic shul in Brooklyn. Ring, ring. I'm whipping the covers off and racing to the phone in the kitchen. I didn't pee yet.

"Stacey?" She's sobbing. "Hello?" Fear.

"It's," sob, sob, labored breathing, "it's," sob.

"Stacey?"

"Yeah." sob, breathing

"What's wrong? What's going on?"

"It's," sob, sob, open weeping. I'm waiting in fear. Is she hurt? Bleeding? My need to pee. "It's," sob, sob, "it's my BIRTHDAY Bar IT'S MY BIRTHDAY WHY DIDN'T YOU CALL ME WHY AREN'T YOU SINGING HAPPY BIRTHDAY TO ME WHY AREN'T YOU OUTSIDE MY APARTMENT WITH A PRESENT WHAT'S WRONG WITH YOU I HATE YOU WHY ARE YOU SO MEAN TO ME WHY DO YOU HATE ME?" more sobbing.

I need to piss. I put the phone down on a dish towel so there won't be sound and fetch a glass. I'm filling the glass. "Hey Stacey, I'm so sorry, I just woke up."

("Sorry."

"What's going on? You're talking in your sleep."

"I just need to pee."

He goes to pee, trying to remember what he dreamt.

"Come back to bed, baby. Let me hold you.")

"It's okay," sniffle, "it's just, I didn't want my *father* to say happy birthday to me before my *boyfriend*. You know?"
"Yeah,"
"It's okay, Bar, so, like, are you coming over?" She has a small voice. Feminine. (Eva never did that kind of shit. The little voice manipulation shit.)
"Yeah, just a sec."
"Bar!" His mother walks through the apartment door.
"WHAT!!?"
I drop the glass on my foot while yanking my underwear up. I yell "OW!" into the phone and apartment. There is piss all over the kitchen.
"Stacey? Call you back."
"No, don't go. I have something to tell you. I figured out …"
I hung up.
"What's this, Bar?" Mom is at the edge of the kitchen.

("Bar? What is it," Summer asks. "Are you hurt? Wake up! You're scaring me."
"I'm sorry. Sorry. Go back to sleep.")

Another night, After being with Stacey, I'm riding over the Queensborough bridge at five in the morning, feeling the bliss in that early morning light to be alive, to be strong, to feel the juice in my balls and the blood in my legs.

(Summer moans. She is naked. He is naked. How did that happen?)

That night, before riding home, in her room, lying on the rug. Her touch is magical, yet melancholy. "I'm seventeen now, Bar," she says, with some significance I do not know. (I know now. She wanted to have sex. But she didn't want to. She was afraid.) We are naked, not even in our underwear. She is on her back on the three towels. She is pulling me down, not on top of her. Down.

"Draw with your eyes, Bar," Kincaid said.

I'm contemplating the female anatomy, exposed. (I can't see this close any more. Yes, I can, I came back. My body is young. I'm young!) Her approbations cease. What's wrong? I'm thinking of *that word*. She is pulling my hair, …
"What's wr…"
"Don't stop."
"Okay."

"DON'T STOP!" Stacey's hand's stroking my hair and then pulling my hair but now her hand is hovering over my head. After thirty seconds, she begins to shake, her hand yanking my hair again, and then this stops. She is cooing.

I don't know what to do.

(How could I not have known?)

("Do you want to do it, Bar?"
"Yes.")

Stacey is quiet. I roll over and get a condom.
(I knew something; I knew enough.)

(Bar reaches over to the side table under the digital clock and gets a condom.)

Stacey's phone is ringing. It's a plastic phone in the shape of Mick Jagger's lips. "Hello?"
"Who is it?"
"I don't know. They hung up," she says. We are naked, a few feet away from one another. She is flushed, her hair messy. She stays seated, not moving toward me. "We better stop," she says.
"Stop?"
She smiles. "I'm not ready. I guess."
We talk about it.
She puts on her underwear and pajamas and gets into her bed and clutches a three-foot teddy bear. She says, "I think you draw me to stop time."
"What?"
"That's what I wanted to tell you on my birthday. Forget it. I'm sorry. Maybe I'll be ready soon."
I say I understand thought I do not but I do sense that it's not helpful to push.
On the ride home, I wonder if we could have had sex. (Of course. I just had to push.) I ride faster in the wind at dawn, the roads empty, the bridge empty, the city asleep and astoundingly unaware of what just went down in Stacey Abramovitz's bedroom.

(Summer says, "Yeah.")

Jon is saying, "I think Stacey likes you. I mean, you could get a bunch of different girls. You have that exotic thing. Not *Black* black, but dark and cool. I hope that's not, like offensive or anything."

I'm sitting in Professor Cielo's office that first month of college. Not college, art school. "But I'm not Black."

Cielo laughs.

Jon and Gary Mitchell. My friend, Jon. (Jon is a doctor now but now he isn't yet.) We're in the cathedral-like darkness of the Medieval Room of the Metropolitan Museum. (We are just kids. We are beautiful.) Long tapestries and huge gnomish art. Gary Mitchell says, "I think I'll ask Jessica out. Or maybe Neena. Jon, why don't you ask Jessica out? You've got that non-threatening, sports-are-alien, nerdezoid-dweebezoid, one-of-the-girls, I-understand-you thing. Take advantage…" Jon tells Gary Mitchell that he is crude, crass, wrong, and bad.

"Fuck off, Jon. You're gay."

Jon is a gay man. Are any of us men? In his dorm at Columbia I'm getting ready for a party, borrowing Jon's tux and Jon is telling me that he is gay. I'm going to a party without him. It's a party for AIDS, a fundraiser, and I don't know that but Jon does. He doesn't tell me because he thinks it's obvious, but I was invited without an invitation card. When I get there it's all gay men, thought I don't know that, and a guy a Cooper who invited me who is in my Art History. I'm thinking about how Jon told me he is gay and asked me, does the guy who invited me think I'm gay, and because I do not know the party is for AIDS I don't understand why Jon asks this. Jon wants to tell me something. What?

"You're the thoughtful type, huh?"

Kristina is at the party and picks me up because I'm in a tux and not gay. She is sexy in a short black dress, her body taut, her arm muscles capable of sudden strength. I sing to her at the party. Singing along to Whitney Houston with four men who chime in with perfect four-part harmony making me sound decent. She laughs and is charmed. She thinks it's cool that I'm an art student. She and I talk on the huge penthouse terrace. She elicits from me that I am, as she suspects, not gay. I can tell when we are together on the roof deck looking out onto the lights across the Hudson and she's looking at me but I can't be sure. I don't know how to push. I wasn't sure and let the fear push me to act cool.

She pays for the taxi, which is good because I have five dollars including the quarters. In her apartment nearby, she thinks I'm older because of the tuxedo. I might have been the only straight guy at the party under sixty. It's my first time and I don't know how to use a condom but she does and she puts it on me. I draw this after but I was embarrassed and destroyed the page.

Her closets are organized with labels for things like umbrellas.

(Summer is putting the condom on him.)

Kristina's disappointed but she tells me what to do and makes herself come and she lets me draw her naked for five minutes. She's a tennis player. She might get into The Open this year. Her closet: "short umbrellas," "long umbrellas," "sneakers." It has twenty-seven tennis racquets. Her arms and legs are as muscular as mine, woman-muscles, and my drawing is good though I'm tired after sex.

Jon points to a map behind glass. It's the Met. (No: Kristina. Go back to her. Please.) It's a circle, the world. "See the hands, the feet, the head? The world is the Body of Christ."

"Wacky," I say for lack of any other response. The world is a body. The Jesus on the map turns to me and says, "Eva loves you." This is a dream.

Jon is calling Gary Mitchell a slut. Gary Mitchell is saying only girls can be sluts. "Guys get what they can get." Jon denies this. I look at the Jesus again to see if he will do anything else but he's just a picture.

(Summer is pushing him, turning him over onto his back and getting on top of him. She says, "You're such a slut. All I have to do is shake my ass.")

I say to both of them, "But then, we're all sluts, in a sense."
Gary Mitchell says, "That's the most brilliant fucking thing I've ever heard."
"It's pretty brilliant." Jon is looking at me with wonder.

Mom is showing me a painting in the Met. I'm little. She took me there almost every weekend for a while. Was it to get away from Dad? Dad never entered a museum or gallery in his life. Dad said that only "fegs" become artists. Dad was dying for years before he died. Before I saved him. We are sitting on a bench and I'm drawing a copy of a Rembrandt while mom reads her book. "It's almost a European museum," she says. "Prague." "What?" Something about Paris. "Look at the illusion of the thin dress," she says, "her tulle is transparent, delicate, elegant; see the thinned white paint..."

Mom killed dad but I saved him.

It's not Picasso or Rembrandt; it's Degas, the ballerinas. I think the one whose face is visible is pretty. "Aren't they beautiful?" Mom says. "What's tranzpahrunt?" "See-through. Look, boy-boy." "I can't make it see-through." "No, that's with paint. Glazing. You can learn, if you want." "Okay." "You are making good drawings, boy-boy. You like that girl? For a girlfriend?" "No, mom. Come on." "Nothing wrong with that. You have the elegant gesture of her arms. That's ballet. Would you like to see a ballet?" "No." "There are girls there like this one." "Hmm." "Maybe, then." "Maybe."

Dad's carpenter shop, a messy place full of sawdust with a prior year's *Playboy* calendar on the wall and a mini-fridge. I draw dad eyeing a line on the table saw. This must be before he stopped being a carpenter.

Peter is copying the picture with the giant in another room in the Met. The Poussin. "Blind Orion Searching for the Rising Sun," 1658, four by six feet, oil on canvas. Orion, the giant, was wooing a girl but the father got him drunk. He fell asleep and the father put out his eyes. The picture shows Orion striding toward the sun to be healed. We are all drunks in a sense. We are all slutty, drunken, blind, lumbering giants, in a sense. Peter has copied this one a few times. He's getting better. It's slow. Have patience.

(Summer kisses his neck.)

"Hev patience," dad is saying, "listen to the grain. Paint beck and forth, like this."

(Summer is using him. He is using Summer. For now it's pleasant. But what will happen later? He felt blind, lumbering, next to Summer's delicate body. Summer was also wiry, strong, insistent. She was finagling his cock. Cock-brain. Cock-a-doodle-doo. Time to get it up.)

Ms. Kincaid, the art teacher says, "I like this one. In this one, you were less literal. It's not just about her. You were thinking about composition, light. The arrangement of the whole scene, here," she points, "and here." Kincaid is staring at last portrait of Stacey I did before she broke up with me in that summer after high school, a picture made from six other pictures, not from life. "Something's different. You weren't, I don't know, distracted." Stacey hadn't been there, only the pictures of her. I had tried to make this one perfect.

I'm rocking back and forth on my sneaker heels. Kincaid is wearing a smock printed with, "Women belong in the house…And in the Senate." Her art room is full of sayings done in student calligraphy. "Art is a record of the process of making art." "Drawing is the Center of Art."

She is telling me I, "could go to art school. You should talk to your parents."

She talks with me for a while about being an artist.

"Are you an artist, too?"

"Of course."

"I thought you were a teacher. I mean …"

"I'm both. I like both. Each one gives me joys and sorrows."

"Cooper Union is free. It's *free!*" I'm yelling at mom.

Schlomo says, "Judit, a Jew doesn't speak in rashness."

But she does speak rashly in her panic, calling me "*A nothing!* You are blind but I can see it."

(Summer is coming. Her ecstasy is impossible to resist. Soon, Bar is coming. He is not completely sorry he no longer dreaming. It's five-eleven and Summer wants to cuddle after and he is tired enough and falls asleep again with her head on his shoulder, wondering whether he loves Summer. He misses Stacey. He misses Eva and even Kristina, whom he had seen long ago for less than twenty-four hours and every tenth of a ray of light from every moment of love both physical and spiritual that he has ever had including Abigail and he even misses Summer though she is right there. Stacey.

Not Stacey, but that feeling. Instead, there's the melancholy of post-sex, sleep-needing, nighttime hunger, inextricable from the sadness. He sits up, seeing Summer already asleep and snoring every sixth breath and he is feeling that he would be happier if she weren't there. Just as happy. He goes to the kitchen and eats some fruit at the large marble counter, standing. He is hungry because he went on a long ride that day, feeling his body's power and now again with Summer, feeling it. How much time does he spend eating, exercising, sleeping, excreting, and fucking? How much of him is merely body, and how much comes through his hand and becomes soul? Does he not love Summer because he finished having sex, and will he love her when he wants her again in let's say ten, twelve hours? Is he such an animal?

He heads back to bed. As he falls asleep he remembers the view from the East Village apartment, of rubble and junkies and dead cats, and felt the warmth of the duvet, as if the lights out the window were giving off heat.

When he falls asleep, he dreams of meeting the Chanel Lady in Springs. In the dream, he doesn't call her that yet; he doesn't know what "Chanel" is and understands her attire as meaning that she is a grown-up, dressed for going to "the office," a place where moms work. His father can't see her because he is casting the fishing rod out over the water, on the dock. He has caught three fish but wants another for Ido. Ido talks a lot with dad in Hebrew and Arabic and Bar can't understand. Bar "helped" catch the fish and got bored and went to the beach part. He found flat rocks for skipping. He saw little fish but they swam away, so he went back up onto the dock and looked out over the water where it was deeper. He leaned out over the water, holding the tar-stained pier with one hand. He leaned more and slipped and whoosh! she grabbed his other arm and pulled him back. In a strange accent, not like dad's, not like mom's, she said, "Don't fall in the water." "I wouldna fell!" he yells but feels ashamed because she's not his mom or dad. She must've been hot in those clothes. She said she would see him later. "Are you my dad's friend?" She didn't answer. She said, "It is not yet the time. I will return. You will see me at the nodal point." "What's that?" "I am here for you to remember." "Remember what?" She walked away on her black clicky shoes. Bar ran over to his father. "Hah!" dad yelled, pulling in the fourth fish. Saul gave

Bar the rod and reel and held Bar as Bar reeled in the fish and it was fun and Bar forgot to ask about the office lady.

13. A Friend

Saturday, July 9, 2002.

"You think she saved your life? You would have drowned?"
"I don't know. Would I have? I think I learned to swim before that."
"The inlet, though, right? Currents?"
"It's hard to say."
"And you're sure it happened. It's not actually your mom who pulled you back from the edge of the dock," Jon asked. "Or someone, whoever."
"Not mom. We came home – I mean to the house we borrowed – and she made the fish my dad caught. I remember it as well as I remember anything. I remember her on the Queensborough Bridge. The Chanel Lady."
"And if what you're saying is true and you're not pulling my leg or lying for some reason or delusional, you don't need to have those memories to know she's real."
"Because I'm here."
"You'd be here anyway."
"I'm, like, fifty-six years old."
"You look well," Jon says, laughing.

"My body-age is thirty-five."

"What a coincidence. I'm thirty-five too."

I shrug.

"You look normal. For a thirty-five-year-old."

"Come on. I'm in good shape."

"Whatever. Or you wouldn't be here."

We're at Jon's country house, overlooking a small lake in Berkshire County, Mass. Jon's partner, Ekon, is making dinner. I rode up from the City, a hundred miles. I woke up at five and left at five-thirty, just before dawn. I came from a long outdoor shower on Jon and Ekon's deck, near their pool.

That the relationship with Jon had thawed, I attributed to Ekon's influence. Thawed but not fully unfrozen. Jon met Ekon on a residency in Lagos and when it was done Jon moved heaven and earth to get Ekon a visa so that Ekon would not be killed by his relatives. Once he landed on American soil Ekon felt free to share all sorts of wisdom from the old country with Jon such as that one ought not to lose touch with old friends. It was against human nature. Jon pointed out that in Ekon's culture, their living together was against human nature.

Ekon made some traditional Nigerian dishes. As we sit, he explains each one, how to eat it, and in what order. He says that his mother and sister taught him to cook reluctantly because in his family, men do not cook, though that is not the case in all Nigerian families that he knows. As we eat, I say, "This is lovely, sitting here out on your deck, under the stars, in the woods, listening to the insects, eating this food with an old friend and a new friend. I wish we had done this before."

Jon grunted. "That would be about me."

"It is quite about you," Ekon says.

"I should have confronted you," Jon says to me. "Instead, I abandoned you. I'm sorry."

"Confronted me about what?"

Jon takes a breath and says, as if he had prepared a speech, "I was disgusted. It was too much. The magazine interviews, the photographs of you at parties full of rich people, the gallery openings. Dating Summer. I underestimated her. I'm sorry about that. Ironically, I bought the hype that you were fabulous or trying to be because of pictures of you and her together. Then you suddenly becoming art's homeboy. I'm still having a hard time with that, to be honest. I don't get it. Do you even have a Black friend? Yo, Bar, my homie, where you head be at?"

"I don't think that's how you say it."

"How can you let people write about you as a Black person without correcting them? Doesn't your gallery, that guy Nick, who by the way, is one of the sleazier people I've ever seen across a room, doesn't he put out press releases saying you're Black, or implying it? That's appropriation, at best and at worst, fraud."

"Nicholas is an energetic finagler. He's for what works."

"You're the owner, right? He does what you tell him? Or what you let him?"

"Yes, that's right. I'll answer you if you let me."

"Go ahead."

Ekon starts laughing.

"What?" Jon asks him. "What's with you?"

"You two," Ekon says, "a couple of white men discussing this. It's funny. I'm sorry. I apologize, how rude of me, Bar. Please." He gestures to me to speak.

"I spent a long time not making it as an artist. A long, long time, Jon. Longer than you can know. No one looked at my work. For decades."

"That remains to be proven."

"Not to me. Then, they did look at it. Who did I harm? I've done shows with maybe fifteen or sixteen unknown Black artists, all of whom are now doing well enough that they don't need day jobs. Would it be better for them if I never said I was Black? They were in shows people went to because my work was the draw. I'm like Paul Simon,..."

Ekon laughs, "But Paul Simon never said he was a Black South African man."

"That's true. But in the sense that I introduced artists to the public that the public would otherwise never have seen."

"Come on, Bar," Jon says. "You did it for yourself."

"That's true, too."

"I am in agreement with your friend, Jon," Ekon says. "Why should he defend himself? You both come from a rich nation where you have the luxury of your ethical finery. I come from a place where everyone does what they can. It is eat or be eaten."

"It's eat or be eaten in New York City, too."

"You have no idea what it is like in Lagos, despite being there for a short while, my beautiful friend," Ekon says to Jon.

"No, probably not," Jon admits.

"Besides, it is time for the Black man in America to get off his behind and work harder for success. I know many Africans coming here, doing very well. My friend Elsie, Jon? She …"

"With due respect, my beautiful African friend," Jon says, "You have no idea what it is like to be an African-American. You are not descended from slavery."

"But I am African-American. I am African and American. Thanks to you."

"It's not the same. Bar …"

"Did what he had to do. As he said, he was unsuccessful for too long."

"How long was that, Bar?" Jon asks.

"Decades. But that is a different conversation."

"Indeed."

"I am confused. Unless Mr. Bar is much older than you, Jon. But you said you were schoolboys together."

"I'll tell you later," Jon says. "It's crazy."

I say nothing. We all drink Nigerian wine. I stop finishing my glass because when anyone drops below half, Ekon refills it. Thought it's only nine, I am exhausted and want to go to bed. But I have to answer Jon. This might be the last time he lets me in for another decade. "I don't agree with what you said about Black people, Black Americans," I say to Ekon. "You sound like my parents. Scrappy immigrants. It's a different thing. Listen, Jon, I'm tired of the attention at this point. I haven't gone to one of those parties in years. I used to go because I thought I had to. Nick told me to. I should've listened to myself and said no but I thought, that's what artists did. It was a new kind of ignorance for me. I can't undo it now. I can't un-publish the pieces that were printed about me or my gallery. People have stopped writing about me as Black. Did you see Annette's article on my work last year?"

"No."

"It was about how I'm fundamentally not a Black artist. She went into the whole thing. She made the case that I was celebrated by people who were looking for the next Basquiat, for their own purposes. That I was being used as much as I used others. I'm a man more sinned against than sinning."

"I'll read it," Jon says. "But tell me, did Nick suggest it to Annette? Did he call her or otherwise plant the idea."

"I don't ... I didn't tell him to do that."

"But it's possible."

"Nick does things on his own, yeah, sometimes."

I go to bed with twitching muscles and a twitching brain. I wake three hours later, around 12:30, and can't sleep for an hour while the wine metabolizes.

I know that I've failed. So far.

After Jon serves cappuccinos and smoked fish, I ask if he's be up for talking about the jump. Jon's provisional. He says he yes, intellectually. Hypothetically. Not seriously.

"It's literally unbelievable."

"I know."

"Yet you believe it. You don't think you're delusional."

"No. You're a doctor ..."

"Pediatricians do a three-month rotation in the psych unit. That's it. Despite the fact that you do seem stable, I'm not an expert. You're not on any meds?"

"Nothing. Ibuprofen."

"Let me say it and you correct me. You lived until 2006. You had a relationship with this woman whom you're about to meet, right?"

"Yes. Soon. Maybe next week."

"You were poor. In the sense of being able to pay bills but check-to-check poor."

"Yes. A fair account."

"But she's a lawyer..."

"She's in legal aid. So she's not – she makes a bit. More than me."

"And she wants a kid and you think you can't afford it and you would need to stop being an artist so you go back in time, with all of your memories, back to when you were nineteen, first semester at Cooper Union,"

"On my birthday. The day of the Mets Game Six."

"You save your dad's life. He's dead otherwise."

"Yeah."

"You know the future enough to get some money in the stock market."

"Some. I didn't memorize enough."

"Something of an oversight?"

"I didn't have months to study."

"And real estate. And art, of course."

"Sharpey's collection."

"Which is this whole other can of ethical worms. Art for smack."

"Yeah."

"You buy Tricheur; more ethical shit."

"No. I didn't do what Dicky did."

"You inherit their legacy. Whatever. You hire Nick, whom you're saying rejected you in...wait, how do I talk about the past? I mean, the past that now didn't happen?"

"I say Life One and Life Two."

"That works. In Life One, Nick's having nothing to do with you."

"Like everyone else."

"Like Summer, too?"

"Summer, ha!"

"I get it. She wouldn't have given you the time of day in Life One. Not a starving artist."

"No, no, no."

"It's Nick's idea that you're Black?"

"No, Cielo's. My art history teacher at Cooper."

"But that was true in Life One as well, no?"

"Yes, but I didn't listen to him, then."

"This time you did."

"Yeah."

"And you shack up with Summer. In fact, you hit on Summer."

"No, not true. She hit on me."

"I see. And how much of buying this specific gallery has to do with Summer being an employee?"

"Greater than zero percent."

"So here you are.

"There's other stuff."

Jon gestures as if to say, go on.

"In Life One I came later to my dad's apartment. It was too late to save him, and I didn't know he was having a heart attack, but not too late for him to impregnate his girlfriend, Claudia. This time, I interrupted that … process. There was no way to save him without getting there before, uh."

"Before they 'uh'."

"Yes. There was a child."

"No. In Life One."

"Yes. Peter. I helped raise him. Not so hands-on but a lot of weekends and taking him to the Met and such. He's hasn't been born. Hasn't been conceived, this time."

Jon doesn't react except to look off into the woods behind the house. I follow his eyes. A hawk settles onto a high branch. A squirrel fusses over something below, not showing awareness of the danger. He points and I nod. We watch as the hawk leaves the branch silently, circles for a while, then swoops. But the squirrel calmly squeezes into a hidey hole inside the tree that had not been visible from where we are sitting.

"Did you see that?"

"Yeah. There's nature here."

"We're lucky to be able to come here. Get out of the city. When we were kids, you talked about being like Thoreau. I thought you'd become this artist upstate somewhere, living in a big house that used to be an old Jewish Catskills hotel that you would've renovated by hand. Listen to the ghosts of dead comedians and tummlers. Living on art sales, not that much, maybe teaching kids in the local schools."

"You never told me that particular fantasy."

"It didn't need to be that. Something like that. Maybe you living in Marrakesh or Chile. I never imagined I would see you in a fashion magazine standing arm in arm with fabulousness and European runways, very rich, the very glass of fashion."

"I..."

"It's still very odd. Maybe it's the oddness of that world in general."

"Yeah."

"And then the Black thing. You deliberately misled people. You're like Elvis, but worse. Are you a taker, Bar? You spoke for people you had no right speaking for. Have you even lived in that kind of ghetto, a place like the one you drew, where there's graffiti on all the buildings and everyone's Black or Spanish?"

"I did. For twenty years. I was angry. I expressed …"

"In Life One?"

"In Life One. Also, I made almost nothing on that work."

"You were angry but your anger wasn't the same as the anger of people who have the history that actual Black people have."

"You don't know."

After a while, Jon faces me, "I honestly don't believe in Life One. But it does suggest things."

"Like?"

"Like according to the Life One Life Two idea, you spent these years correcting old mistakes. What about doing something to save people not necessarily related to you? Like preventing the 9/11? Or bigger, like climate change. Conceivably you could have spent some time memorizing enough facts to tell a scientist how to make 2002 solar panels in 1986 or you could've made sure somehow that Al Gore became president."

"I couldn't …"

"It would've mattered. You could've blown Exxon's cover and revealed their reports saying burning fossil fuels causes global warming and then 'invented' the better solar panel. You had a chance to save the world, and instead …"

"Jon. I didn't have that chance. They, the people who sent me back. They said I couldn't make historical changes."

"And you listened to them and didn't even try."

I say nothing.

After a minute, Jon asks, "Is it worth it? I want to reiterate that I am speaking provisionally. I don't, I guess I can't believe what you're saying. About the jump. Even a minimal knowledge of the science says you can't go back, only jump forward by traveling at the speed of light for a period. So my accusation just now is moot, at least to me, because I don't believe you could have saved the world. I believe the believable things. In a way it doesn't matter, even though you're hinging your authenticity as someone who gets to express anger on having lived where you clearly never have, except for a few months in 1986. But let's say it's all true, the magic is real, you're not deluded, you did live in penury, and you jumped back in time, even though that is impossible, and also you couldn't do more for more people. Has it been worth coming back? That's the question."

"I agree. That's it."

"You don't know."

"No."

"Then it doesn't matter whether you came back because what you're figuring out is whether your life as currently constituted is the way it should be."

"I am." We sit for a while longer, maybe another half an hour, saying nothing until I say, "One of the things I lost is you."

"I ..."

"Let me. Please. You have a lot, here, and with Ekon, and being a kid doctor. You have so much."

"I do. I am grateful that ..."

"I am happy for you," I say but I think, then why do you have to be jealous of me?

Ekon appears and we all go into the kitchen to follow his orders in making an elaborate lunch before Jon takes me to the car rental place and I rent the car and drive back to my apartment near Washington Square where I am alone.

14. Hand in Hand with Wandering Steps

Landscapes weren't what Bar had been known for. They weren't appealing for him before he started drawing them. The driving force was a feeling that it didn't matter what he drew, a feeling that began with Eva sitting for him, after his plot with Uri came to fruition and after he regretted that success very much. He asked her to sit and she complied, smiling, looking happy. She was fatter than he remembered from Life One, sexy, round, and content, not living a life of grabbed meals half-eaten before rushing to court, or being so tired at night that sleep was more important than dinner. He didn't cry in front of her, not avoiding it out of pride but out of not wanting to explain.

After that, he asked to go on a bike trip to visit Jon again and he took circuitous routes through the Catskills, through derelict towns never to recover from their heydays decades ago. He was struck by one gas station sign in particular, a metal hoop thirty feet in the air held aloft by its fluted steel column, its circular advertisement long since having fallen out and rolled away. The hoop presented him with a striking eyehole to the sky and he stopped his bike and took pictures of it from several angles before rolling away on his own circles.

He saw empty signs like this everywhere after that. Usually they were rectangles, framing trees, sky, buildings or all of these, and he stopped and took pictures, and when he got home he sketched up several of them, returning often to the circular sign that started it. He made some finished pieces from these and of the ten he liked eight. It was, for him, initially a formal thing, a shape, a frame around the art of heaven that he drew.

Nick came over and had another idea.

Subject Report, Jump Mod. App., October, 2005

These are some of the events that explain the feeling I have now that I've more or less reached the finish line. I've been taking notes. I'm requesting a "modification," in your terminology. Funny word for it. Was what happened in 2006/1986 also a "modification"?

In the months leading up to "meeting" Eva, I had two reasons for fear. Reason one: Summer. I'll deal with that henceforth. Reason two: I did not resemble the person she once met. Who is to say what proportions of body or soul first attracted her? The circumstances had to be similar enough. I had to appear to be who I was, at least. I bought the bike shop, paying about twice its worth. Jerry was overjoyed and fled to Florida on the day of the closing, coming into the lawyers' conference room with a suitcase and a plane ticket. The problem with paying him double wasn't getting ripped off; it's that it doesn't matter to me. How can I be the person she was attracted to if I have successfully removed all money concerns?

Or rather, if I have let (encouraged) Summer to extricate money as a bottleneck from my consciousness. Time, not money, is a problem, and dealing with people who want things from me, and most of all, figuring out what I want. Right before the panic over Eva, Summer was close to talking me into having a full-time servant, whom she called a "personal assistant." It's when I imagined the advantages that I remembered I would have to present myself to Eva after two decades of a life of richness and ease.

When I went to work in the shop, Sally kept asking me why I bothered. She knew who I was – the famous artist who had appeared in magazines once upon a time – and told the other two employees. A week later they came to me and demanded a raise, which I gave them but warned them that the shop was no longer profitable as a result and that they were hastening its demise. I worked there for a good two weeks, in earnest, fixing flats and adjusting derailleurs before Eva showed up a day later than I thought. I had forgotten how hard hard work actually is. Greasy, roughed-up hands that made it hard to draw after work, backache from standing too much. Repressed impatience all day while the people around me said not-unpleasant but simply boring things. Sally and her failed career.

The night after I thought Eva was supposed to show was very bad. I thought I had lost her, that some horrible, untraceable butterfly effect had caused her to get a flat somewhere else, causing her to fall for some other bike mechanic, whose looks and personality I made up to torture myself. He was Argentine (because she had a thing for immigrants or the children thereof), Jewish (not too religious: just right for her), my height, had three-day stubble, a cuter nose than mine, and occupied the right point on some charming/ingenuous axis. I don't know why I went to work the next day, but I did and she appeared. I had almost forgotten my lines. It was probably for the best as I was more spontaneous than I had planned, and closer to my depressed, failed self from Life One. I did remember to repeat my performance of talking too much on the first date and text her an hour after to tell her how much I wanted to see her again.

What's it like to be with someone you were already with for years, many years ago, but it's supposed to be new and everything is supposed to be surprising, wonderful, magical? How can you laugh at jokes if you've already heard them or listen attentively to stories supposedly unfamiliar but whose endings you know? How can sex be the fresh shock of love that it was? How can it become as it was with Kristina, virginal and new, as if "touched for the very first time." I can hear Madonna belt it.

(For the last seventeen years, I have listened to pop songs for the second time.)

My consciousness is fifty-seven years old, my body thirty-six, like an endless jet lag.

My answer was and is: Eva has a charming way of sniffling just before she wakes up. Everything about her is charming. That saves all of it. When she first spent the night, ("first") I wept remembering the other first time. She woke up and wiped tears from my face and made a joke about how the sex must've been lousy for me. I was afraid of going too fast into the emotions we took years to form, in Life One, of which she is unaware. If she became aware she'd think me insane. Her lack of awareness gives me a superiority of intel that I don't want. She was my equal; no, I aspired to equal her, morally and as an adult making one's way. I worshipped her without losing the realism. She saw me; we saw one another. Now it's something else. I got out of bed and made a sketch of her face and gave it to her, in part so that I wouldn't have to talk for a few minutes.

The tears weren't only there from the flush of sentiment making its way through me, and not only from the knowledge that I couldn't tell her of the depth of my feeling; no lovers can ever tell one another how they feel merely using the clunky sledgehammer of words. But my secret is gaping. As I drew I remembered the words I read once, "We are born into the world, and there is something within us which, from the instant that we live, more and more thirsts after its likeness." My Eve, the First Woman. And me, her monster.

One reason for my tears that morning was the tension I felt trying to exclude images of Summer as I made love to this perfect person with me. Yes, so tawdry and degraded have I become. Yet it doesn't feel degraded to admit that I love Summer, too. Why should I not love both? (I am evil.)

Eva's sniffling is not an ordinary thing any longer; "now" it's a trope, something I have come to expect before I had any right to know about it.

Each detail of pleasure I receive via tropes is an abomination.

Each time I think of Summer is an abomination, not least because I do not merely think of Summer. I enjoyed sex with Summer two nights ago and will most likely enjoy it again in a few days, when she gets back from Miami, where she is once again selling underwear, I think, or bathing suits. She's become irrational and inconvenient, insisting on working around the world. I find it highly frustrating when she's not available. I said, "What if I paid you your annual income without you having to work? You could do your art, then."

She said, "Your money is a reason I can't be with you, even if you'd have me. You threaten to swallow me whole. I won't be kept. As long as I think I'm using as much as used, I'm okay. Or not. I don't know. You keep your money. Bye."

"Bye."

The other problem with Summer is the imbalance with Eva. Maybe if Eva were having sex with someone else, too, it would feel balanced.

Uri's Christodora House apartment with a view of Tompkins Square Park is a fabulous irony of which he is entirely unaware. There oughtta be a law against two-story living rooms in a city this crowded. But then he needs the height to display his narcissistic "photography." Uri comforts me regarding my moral decline.

"Uri? I've heard so much about you. I meet so few of Bar's friends from forever." I don't think I've ever seen her kiss cheeks like that before.

"What's up with the drop cloths?"

"Painting. By the way, I need a place for a couple of weeks. Like, pronto. I didn't know. They say if I don't scram they charge double to work around me, so if you know of anything."

"He can stay with us, honey," she says, rather quickly, I think. "Please?"

"Yeah. Sure. Stay with us."

The effect Uri has is surprising even though I've seen it a hundred times. Eva is clearly affected. Every woman I've ever seen in his presence has been taken with him, and not a few men, including at least one previously confirmed, strictly gay woman whose reaction only clarified his charisma. "I never met any of the Legal Aid lawyers," he tells her. "I think you guys should be sainted. I don't think I ever met a saint in person." He can't help but flirt. Crumbs off my table.

"Ha ha. Gary, I'm no saint. I don't even work full time anymore."

"It's Gary Mitchell. You either call him that full nickname, or Uri, his real name."

"Oh, sorry," Eva says, giggling as if she were in tenth grade.

"I'm just a person," Uri says shrugging with faux humility, for he does know his effect. "Look, I'm getting wrinkles and my hair is going gray. You're not doing so bad yourself, Bar."

"Eva said she thinks gray hair on some guys is 'hott' with two 't's'."

"I did," she says her smile lingering too long. "You're not still in Silicon Valley, are you, Uri?"

"I retired."

"At our age? You must have made a killing!"

"I don't see the point," he says, taking in her fawning. "After a while the money's not about money; it's a score people keep. I want to be more like Bar and his Thoreau groove thing."

"I didn't know you were into Thoreau, Bar."

"More when I was younger." More when I was poorer.

She's off to find the bathroom in Uri's cavernous expanse. I remember a stupid high school argument over whether he was really a Jew given that he was blond, a mix of Swedish and Russian parents, both, in fact, Jews. Jon said he was only technically a Jew because of how his looks were too accessible to average Americans to be perceived as a Jew. Uri threatened to take out his circumcised dick and go dig up some piece of paper he got from his synagogue saying he completed his bar mitzvah. His looks are a kind of natural supernaturalism. Time travel is, in comparison, much less impressive than the power of nature.

"What's going on, Bar? You seem lost."

"What? You should stay with us. Definitely."

"Thank you. I thought we agreed on that already."

"Yes, sorry. I'm spacing out."

Still, if you must have a white box apartment with lots of empty space, you could do worse than filling it with cool post-industrial furniture made of rebar and seemingly rusted metal.

Eva comes back, walking ever so slightly more sexily than usual, just a touch more with the hips. It's compelling for me, if not for it's consciously or unconsciously intended target.

"What're you doing now, Eva? You work ... sometimes?" They're chatting. I wonder what she'd think of his penchant for younger babes.

"I take a case or two." "Bar likes to travel,..." "...To get away from oneself..." "Oh, where did you guys go?" "... when we came back, ... " "That sounds ..." "Galapagos was amazing. You should definitely ..." "It's totally different from the massive caseload I used to carry."

"You used to say that it felt like an accomplishment every day you went to work." I can't help myself. I should just can it. I made this happen.

"Do you want me to go back to doing that? We wouldn't have been able to do Galapagos or Italy or even Montreal."

"Uri, you should go to the Galapagos. What? Did she say that? There was a moment, floating, seeing the sea turtles, when I forgot New York existed."

They both laugh. Eva turns away from both of us. Is she interested in that giant picture of a pretty seventeen-year-old wearing a couture dress, or avoiding showing us her face?

She turns back and her smile is gone. "And this way I can concentrate on my cases one at a time. Really help someone."

"That makes sense," Uri says, ingenuously. Eva's tone sounds to me like self-persuasion.

"What're you doing with your time, Uri? You're not really retired."

"Ha! I'm busier than ever! I'm into fashion. As you can see." He waves his hand theatrically at his giant prints. How many times has he done that here, and for what purposes?

"Oooh. These are yours? I'm so dumb. Of course they're yours." She's giggling again? She never played dumb before. She always showed off how smart she was.

"Yes."

"I love this shot of the girl on the beach. It's not just the ordinary swimsuit shot. I guess because of that conch she's holding. It matches the curve of her waist."

"Thank you."

"That was on purpose?"

"I embraced the serendipity, therefore I get to say yes. Actually, it was her idea. She just sort of picked it up," he says. "But I saw the rhyme in the forms."

That's good. He's been reading books. I'm wondering why Jon and I were friends with him. What compelled us?

"Ha ha. But these models are so tall and skinny, like all of them nowadays. It's not like it was in the 90s. It's unreal."

"I assure you this one's very much real. In fact, I think I'm going to represent her."

"You're starting an agency?" I ask. "Isn't that like an alcoholic opening a saloon?"

"Ha, ha, you're so funny," he says and gives me an eye that says shut the fuck up.

"They're so young," Eva says. "How do you talk to teenage girls?"

"I find my ways," he says. He's unable fully to stem the sleaze as he gazes at his own work. Does she see it?

How many of these fields has he plowed? I have a bad thought but answer it: at least Summer's my age. (No, she's not.)

They're talking about his use of light. Take a giraffe-ish girl, one whose entire Midwestern town told her she has to move to New York to be model, a product of capitalist pressures, a person following, being led by, her own body, a body that the designers design for so that the clothes fit her better than they ever would fit ordinary people, who's not old enough to have whips and scorns of time on her skin, cavorting artificially at sunset on a clean, private white-sand beach that is itself so beautiful it's a cliché, let her find a shell, and bam, what an artist you are with the camera.

And yet, I want Eva to flirt with him more.

"It's too bad Jon wouldn't come. I wanted to see you as a trio. Bar told me some of the things you guys did in high school."

"Jon's not talking to me. Again."

"I'm working on it," Uri says to me. He has a look of sincere concern. "He called me. You know he said crazy shit about you, Bar. He said your soul is out of joint, whatever the fuck that was supposed to mean."

"It's Shakespeare."

"So? I know it's fucking Shakespeare."

"I went to see him. He asked me how come I sold out. I told him I'm really an alien from outer space. He didn't seem to like the answer, though."

They laugh politely at my joke. They're tittering politely. I don't like it when Eva does her feminine, polite laugh. This moment is like the palimpsests but entirely normal in its otherness, where I'm present and not present at once because of the history of how I feel about these people. My friend and the love of my life.

"Hey, Uri, what would you do if you had the chance to go back in time into your own body at age nineteen or twenty, but with all of your present memories and knowledge. Do everything again. Would you?"

"Ha ha. Of course. I'd get a chance to score with all the chicks who said no."

"Even though you scored with a thousand women as it is?"

"Hardly. There's always the curiosity." He's looking at Eva as he says this. He's not careful.

"Did I tell you, Bar?" Eva says. "I wasn't supposed to say anything. Jon called me the other day and did say crazy things, sort of like what you just said about going back in time. It made no sense. I couldn't tell if he thought you actually did this or if he thought you thought it. I think he's jealous of you. Of both of you. Two out of three friends become super-successful, and the third…"

"Jon's successful. He heals people and gets paid well for it."

"I know, Bar, but he's just a doctor. Listen to me, 'just' a doctor. What I mean is, that's what he might be thinking. It's possible, because … "

No, that's what you're thinking because Jon, working sixty hours a week, makes low-six-figures and I make high sevens in passive income, mostly rent and interest and stock increases and it's that low because I stopped bothering to make it go up faster.

"I think he's flipping out because of Ekon," Uri says to me. "You know I went there a month ago, Bar? We were all supposed to go skiing? Anyway, Ekon drank himself to incapacity. Jon was furious. It was kind of fucked up."

I don't think he ought to have told me that about Ekon. We chat about

Jon some more. I ignore Eva's comment about what he said to her.

Now they're looking at his other shots. Shouldn't he get some Walker Evans or Berenice Abbot posters instead of gaudily displaying his own work? I'd prefer random needlepoint from a department store. Except as porn: some of the pictures do work that way. Eva glows in the attention he is giving her. GM's nothing if not solicitous. I'd like to leave her alone with him. It'd create…conveniences. Yes, that is a liberating thought. It immediately releases the knot in my stomach. A quadrilateral situation would be much better than the present triangle.

Uri's staying in the studio, which I have not used since I bought that six-thousand-dollar drafting table. Drawing and painting seem dauntingly hard, and the days slip by with long bike rides, reading, watching movies, eating, and sometimes, sex, sometimes with Eva.

The studio has a nice view of our deck from above. This includes a bird's-eye into the outdoor shower, which Eva uses daily after her run in warm weather. I have enjoyed watching this view, and she has enjoyed me watching, waving to me from there, or beckoning.

Will Eva beckon him? Will it be conscious or unconscious? Will Gary Mitchell return to use his powers?

Why exactly do I want this? Is it all about permission to have access to Summer? What have I discovered about myself?

The pictures of the two of them making love are gorgeous, stupendous. The angle from the ceiling light fixture has surprisingly good framing, all unintended, of course. The low-res black and white has the appeal of gritty realism. There's real passion. Eva's face is sincere: he can't see it when he's cheek to cheek with her and she's facing up.

I'm staring at these pictures for too long, scrolling through them to get the time-lapse movement of their bodies. I feel as if I am doing them some deep wrong but isn't it they who did me wrong? I don't know which is which. I don't know what I'm doing. I'm turned on and I don't know why.

It's been making Eva upset. She's going to pop a confession soon, I can tell, and then I'm off the hook with Summer.

Here she is. She's pretending to look out the window. She can't look at me except in little darts of her eye. Now she looks at me. I smile innocently.

"I want to talk, Bar."

"Love of my life. What's up?"

"I called Danny. Daniel Greenberg?"

"Oh. Yeah?"

"What's wrong? You see confused."

"Nothing. I thought … never mind what I thought. Greenberg? I haven't heard his name in twelve – no, thirteen years."

"He told me about the evictions."

"Eva,…"

"He told me you weren't the lead landlord."

"I tried talking them out of it. I pulled my money."

"You mom's … something? Schlomo, and your father?"

"Yes."

"It wasn't all Schlomo."

"Daniel Greenberg doesn't know everything."

"You're trying to change the subject. I'm not angry. I know it was you, too. You filed to evict on fifteen apartments on Avenue C and 3rd Street in 1988. You remember Mickey who works in the Municipal Archives? He pulled it for me."

"Mickey's the woman who stole your boyfriend in law school?"

"Do not change the subject."

"Greenberg's working for some Congressperson. He's not at Legal Aid any more. I forget…"

"He said you did it with class. You gave them nice payouts. Even put some of them in the new building. No harassment."

"Yeah."

"But not all of them."

"I had nothing to do with that."

"One lady died, Bar."

"I didn't …"

"She froze to death in Tompkins Square Park, January 1, 1989."

"I fought with Saul about her. She was drinking. She lost all the money I gave her."

"Her name was Eva, too. That's what got to me. Eva Perez. Maybe if she had been drinking in her apartment on Avenue C she wouldn't have died."

"You can't know that."

"No, I can't."

"Eva,"

"Bar, I'm not, it's not what you think. I didn't try to, I didn't go out of my way. I doesn't even matter. It's a detail. I mean, you're one of the people making the City more expensive. You're a gentrifying force. I knew that way before I found out about this. Isn't that more important? And yet, I've, I'm, I'm coming to understand. I do understand."

"No, you don't. You save people and maybe I don't do that but …"

"I don't save many. I could save more. Before we met …"

"What I've done wasn't such a bad compromise. I built housing for a hundred and thirty-five families where there were decrepit buildings ready to fall down, and empty lots. The government isn't building anything any more. They got out in the 60s. I did the City's set-aside deal. A third of them for low-income tenants. That's ten times the affordables that were there before me. This woman, Eva Perez? I made the mistake of giving her rent money instead of paying her landlord myself. I treated her like she didn't need babysitting."

"And then the rents in the surrounding buildings become unaffordable."

"I can't help that. A neighborhood's either going down or going up. Real estate's not stable. Don't be naïve. Neighborhoods aren't at the end of a rainbow. Isn't it better that there's gentrification if it's done the way I did it?"

"I don't want to argue …"

"People need to understand … "

"I do. Bar, stop. I did a lot of thinking."

" … that when big projects … what?"

"I forgave you already. I didn't like it but I see the big picture."

"Oh."

"It's hard for me because I spend my time one-on-one, trying to stop landlords from evicting people. I don't normally zoom out. Daniel said a lot of what you said. He said you acted better than any developer he had ever heard of."

"That's because of you."

Eva looks confused. I see the problem but it's too late to unsay it. "That can't be. We hadn't met yet."

After a beat I ask her, "When did you find all of this out?"

"Almost two weeks ago. That reminds me of another thing. It was nice to give the store to Sally, Bar, though I don't understand why you bought it at all. It was good to give it to her, and the gallery to Nick. Sometimes, when I'm sitting in the ugly, dirty offices in the Bronx and there's some tough kid I know did exactly what the cops say he did, like stealing an old lady's social security check, just for instance, or beating up his girlfriend, or there's a drunk guy who can't pay his rent and beats his wife and I forget that alcoholism's a disease and I think, you don't deserve what I'm going to do for you, but I'll do my best for the system, or against the system, or something. The police should be held accountable. No planted evidence, and no shaky cases allowed to just get by. No landlord should be able to evict without due process. Do I want to meet this kid in an alley after work? I started taking cabs from the courthouse steps after Jake Finkelstein was killed right outside the Yankee Stadium subway stop, eating a hot dog, after a day defending people like his own killer. The world's complicated, is what I'm saying. We have to have two or three or four ideas in our heads at the same time. I need to hear that you're sorry about Eva Perez."

"I've been sorry for a long time." Because of you, only I can't say it. I'm sorry only because of you. I don't give a shit about Eva Perez; she was in my way when I needed that building vacant so I could raise the capital to get where I fucking-well am today, including this fabulous pad that you like so much, my dear, dear Eva.

"I know you are. I needed to see you say it. I love you, Bar."

"I love you." I'm sorry Eva, my Eva. I'm sorry you had to think about her. Eva's kiss is a drawing, made by God, in which every line, tone, and shade contains brilliance, divine and human, loving, yet fearsome for its power.

"I love you so much."

"Eva,"

"Yes?"

"What else did you find out about me? When you started researching me?"

"I didn't know what to think. One of New York's Most Eligible Bachelors, says Gotham City Magazine, yet sometimes working as a bike mechanic in your own shop. You said you were waiting for me, not just filling in, and I thought you meant you were waiting for someone like me. But you were waiting for me, just me. I don't know how I know that. I know it makes no sense."

"I've been waiting for you almost my whole life." She give me a 'yeah, yeah' smile. "I needed to meet someone who didn't want me for the stuff in the magazine."

"Still, it's so specific."

"I know…I mean, I like bicycles."

"Anyway, I read all the art criticism stuff."

"That says I'm anti-feminist. A misogynist pornographer. A racist appropriator."

"That was among the things I read. There were some defenses of your work, too."

"Yeah. Shelly Moscowitz and John Kline. And Annette."

"And others."

"You didn't care."

"You were so cute, Bar. And so sweet to me. I never had a guy call me ten minutes after our first date and leave a message saying he wants to see me again. I was about to call you, did you know? It feels like you did know. Or that time you got out of bed too fast and got me flowers the next day. You were kind and interested in me and never pushy. You weren't misogynistic to me. That part, I don't see it. I think you're expressing your desires in your art. It kinda turns me on."

"Yeah? You like my art?"

"Yes, I do. I think you're a great artist." She's looking away again. Maybe now's the confession I was waiting for? I see the eyes overflowing with water. Her beautiful water-color eyes.

"Bar, I slept with Uri."

There. The palimpsest hits as soon as she says this.

It's two angles, two apartments. The dingy but spacious place on 135th Street that I lived in for two decades. I am there and I am here. I can see the

Hudson River superimposed over the Washington Square arch, like some tourist film of the city. In One she told me she kissed him – just a kiss – and it floored me and now I hardly feel this revelation of fucking. I feel cheated of the devastation that I felt in Life One and that I can glimpse now, but only telegraphed from there via the palimpsest. I'm dizzy from the two perspectives, but I can see Eva in the other one, much more upset about what she had done.

Like all the others, the palimpsest ends as abruptly as it came.

"I was angry with you," she says, here.

At the same time that I'm elated that it's all working, I am desperately sad. My old self was bewildered by the idea that I could be happy that she kissed Uri. I was the naïve one, then. "I know." She didn't notice. Eva will stay with me forever. I am in my beautiful apartment, and I am rich and successful, and even good sex with a gorgeous man won't take Eva away from me.

Why do I also miss the old life?

"What do you know? Did you know that I know about Summer?" That hurts. That's a surprise. That's not good. "I've known for a while. I didn't know how to bring it up. I guess I wanted you to. I wanted to be even. To feel some dignity. It's humiliating, you know, the idea that I'm not enough. I know that what I'm saying makes no sense and I'm not saying it to be accusing, just to say how I felt. I don't bring us our money, and you're so smart and accomplished, and then that…"

"I'm sorry. I should've ended it with her a long time ago. I don't know why I didn't." Yes, I do know. I liked having sex with someone so absolutely beautiful I could barely look at her, that everyone in the world wants, and I had trouble giving that up, or even understanding why I should. "I should've ended it and come to you and I didn't. You're, I don't want you to be with Uri. I have no right to say that, I know."

"How could you not tell me about her?" Eva asks. "For so long?"

"Uri told you about that? Right? He doesn't know what he's talking about. Whatever he said about how long or how often, …" She doesn't say anything and can't look me in the eye but this time it's not because she's ashamed of herself.

"I don't want to talk about Uri," she says. "But if you do, I will tell you that I know you arranged it. You put Uri and me together."

"How could I have? He needed a place to stay."

"You took us to him. You knew what kind of Don Juan he is. It's not like he couldn't afford a hotel."

"I thought you weren't accusing me."

"Not … I don't know, Bar. I guess I am. There's weirdness. You've arranged a lot of different things. Like the bike shop."

There's danger. "Perhaps it's all fine," I say, sighing. "It's possible to have loving relationships with more than one person."

"I didn't have a loving relationship with Uri." Now it's my turn not to look at her. "Oh, you mean you love Summer." Now she is shedding tears.

"I love you."

"And Summer."

"I don't want this to be a hurting contest. I don't love Summer." Is it a lie if I don't know if it's the truth?

She is crying. "I want to hit you. I love you but you're making me hurt."

"I won't … say things like that any more."

"You don't understand." She is crying harder now. I try to wipe her tear and she doesn't slap my hand but she won't let me touch her face. "I went over to Uri's the other night when I said I was going out shopping with Mickey on West Broadway. I wanted to tell you but I was afraid."

"Why?"

"I was afraid that you actually wanted me to go. I don't want to see Uri any more, Bar. I won't do it again. I'm so, so sorry."

"But did something happen? You just changed your mind?"

"Yes. No. Nothing needed to happen. Tell me you're not seeing Summer any more. Tell me?"

"I'm not." Lie. But I could stop and then it's not a lie. Would stopping be so hard?

"I saw Uri's computer. When he was on the phone talking to someone for a long time, he told me to look around the apartment, at his photography. I wandered into the bedroom. His laptop was just open, and I couldn't help seeing. He's paying a girl, Bar."

"So?"

"For her silence."

"Explain."

"She was fourteen or fifteen, I couldn't tell exactly…"

She comes to me and we hold each other. "I won't see Summer any more," I say,

We go to the bedroom and make love and it's beautiful and we hold each other naked and I'm not floored and not angry, but I can't get out of my head that it's all starting to wobble.

"Bar, wake up. Bar! You're dreaming!"

"What?"

"You kept saying, 'You killed Saul.'"

"So, what's so strange about that? I always blamed her for that."

"Blamed who? Saul … we just saw your dad last week. He's annoying, getting himself a new twenty-old-old girlfriend every few years, but he's not dead."

"Oh, yeah, I meant. I don't know. I'm half asleep."

I asked Eva, what would it be like for her if we gave away most of our money? She said, "You could make more. You have the touch." And what if I didn't? She wrinkled her nose and looked at our view of Washington Square full of young parents with strollers like little mine sweepers, clearing the field before them. I wonder how many of the parents are reminiscent of when they bought a dime bag there in their youths. "It'd be a big change," she said. "What about our children?"

"Isn't this poisoning us? Wouldn't our children be better off if …" I'm thinking, if we have sex at the present rate we won't have any children, but I let that remark go unsaid.

"You get this way sometimes since your mother died. It's like, you don't need to be successful anymore? We should take a trip soon. Let's go back to Ecuador. Like we said we would."

"You can't go back."

"What do you mean? I can book us tickets in a second."

"I mean in general. We'd re-tread paths we were already on. We could change our lives, for the better, I think, if we gave most of it away. I'd run the bike shop, and you could work…"

"Full time, a thousand cases? What do you mean, you'd work at the bike shop? You gave it away, Bar."

"Oh, right."

"I was never a saint. You're in one of your moods."

But I saw you live as a saint, I say to myself.

We have become the "degraded rich." I read that phrase and laughed once. Can I forgive her for what I made her become? I've changed her body-spirit. There can be no forgiveness for what I have done.

Yet, to give it all up? Can I stand to do it?

Doesn't Eva's present opinion matter?

Is this Eva, "Eva"? Which one is properly in quotes?

It's Don't-Ask-don't-Tell, Clinton's re-institutionalization of the closet. Inside the closet is my intuition that Eva is going back to Uri. Whenever I go to the gallery she's meeting Mickey, so she's not really meeting Mickey but I'm sure if I call Mickey she'll cover for Eva and I most definitely don't want to call. I don't want to investigate. Not only that: I'm sure she's having a nice time with Uri. He's a sweet guy, aside from his fetishes. I'm sure he's showering her with the attention of a new thing. It's because of me. My heart has its limits.

The standard operating procedure with Summer is for her to text me a time. I confirm the time, usually. I don't have a busy schedule. I arrive at her apartment. We have sex. I ask about how things are going with her modeling and she tells me how it's so hard to break into acting and sometimes we don't talk at all. Lately less and less. She doesn't ask about me much any more. Eva is not mentioned. I can see that she's been painting but whenever I'm here, the work is covered in cloth. She's taken to picking up her little phone and staring at it and then it's clear she's done with me and I leave.

I ask Eva to sit for a portrait and I very much do not zone in. Her beauty is there and I see it but I can't latch onto it, I can't feel it fully, but I draw it, and she's happy with the work. She's happy in general. We are having sex without condoms and maybe she's going to be pregnant soon. I think Uri is in the past.

But while I'm drawing her, she says, "Uri is using a condom."

"What?"

"We're being safe. I wanted to tell you. Also, I'm obviously not having his child."

I stop and stare.

"You can keep going," she says.

"You enjoyed telling me that?"

"I know you went to see Summer. At least once since you said you wouldn't. So." She is trying to be strong, to tell me to fuck off, which is well deserved, but she's tearing up and looking away again.

I don't understand why the palimpsest with Eva present and we're talking even obliquely about having a child hasn't occurred. I want it to occur. I remember it from One. I felt that in my other life, which should be this one, I felt good about having a child with her. I do not feel that way now. Maybe that's why it's not happening. I've put sand on that fire. I have permanently ruined my alignment with myself. Perhaps I am nobody now, the No Time Man.

Eva seduces me that evening. I don't resist. I lay there, under her, as she attempts to impregnate herself. She has her eyes closed, rising and falling on me. I wonder what she is imagining. I come in her. She doesn't come, but knows I have. She gets off of me and says "thank you" and smiles but doesn't kiss me. She puts on her expensive silk pajamas and lies down, facing away from me.

More recently, I only ever make it to Summer's foyer. I kneel down and service her as she stands. Usually she rests a foot on my shoulder. When she's done, she turns around as I stand up. The first time, I wanted to go before her but she said, "no way," and "you'll just leave." This was not an unreasonable prediction and in any case not a burden as the whole feeling was one of rushing desire and excitement and whatever abuse she wanted to give me would have been fine with me. When I'm standing, I get myself hard and put on my condom and push into her from behind as she holds the wall in front of her. The whole process takes roughly twenty minutes and involves no face-to-face interaction. Twice I saw her crying and wanted to say something but she said, "get out" before I could.

Biking up to see Jon was fun because I was alone. Eva met us there and seemed to be having a good time with him until I showed up.
I came back and made a bunch of big drawings from the photographs of the empty signs and Nick came over to see the new work and that's why we "had" to have a show.
Nick wrote the press release: "Bar Mizrachi is turning his unmatched draughtsmanship and formal skill to the problems of identity and displacement in late capitalism. His new landscapes show the devastating effects of time in communities left behind by our systems of investment, giving new meaning to the cruelty of the phrase 'creative destruction.' The 'Empty Signs' show also serves as metaphor for the confusions circling notions of identity in our time. Mizrachi, whose work has always been about race and identity, suggests in his new work that if identity is cultural, arbitrarily constructed, it's construction is a fragile piece of the infrastructure, yet it remains after the meanings are emptied out by nature's destructive entropies, and that nature will ultimately conquer all framings, all attempts to block it out, even if nature itself is a thing we see depending on where we stand."
I thought it was very good. None of it was remotely on my mind as I drew the landscapes and their shapes. If anything, what I had been thinking about was a far bleaker emptiness.

The thing with Summer in which I never get past her foyer is no longer fun.

Summer sent me a text from Bridgehampton, from the architect guy's place. I admit that even though I introduced them I regret it because now I can't go over to her place any more. The last two times I didn't want to go and then I ended up going.

"Something's wrong, Bar, and I'd like you to tell me what it is. What happened with the bike shop?"
"I gave it to Sally. You know that. I don't know …"
"Fuck you!"
"If you tell me what this is …"
"Tell me about the bike shop, Bar."
"What … ?"
"Fuck you!" Two minutes of sitting and staring. Of course I see Eva's beauty but it's background. I'm losing her and I don't know if I care and if I don't, or not enough, then what do I care about? "You planned this whole

thing without me."

"No, it happened. I didn't plan it. Or if I did, it's centered on you. You're the center."

"The center of what? 'Or if I did'? Not this weird shit with Uri and Summer. I'm not talking about that."

"What, then?"

"Why did you buy a bike shop, Bar? Why did you, an artist and real estate developer, suddenly make yourself into a fixer of flat tires, and then what, a week after you picked me up in that shop, you stopped working there. I talked to Sally. You owned the shop for a couple of months before I wandered in. After we 'met' you owned it for one more month before giving it away." I stare at her. I can't see it the way out. "Aren't you going to answer?"

"I love you, Eva."

"I love you, too, Bar, but I want to know what is going on."

It's bad, but the worst is not being able to confess. "When did you decide to investigate, uh, me? How long I had the shop, my history of evictions, all that. One answer is that I wanted to live simply, like I said to you the other day. I learned I can't escape my life but I met you, the love of my life. You liked me, not the art star and not the guy in magazines."

"Yes, I heard you tell me that story before. Who is is that I met, exactly? Bar Mizrachi. Who's that?"

"How could I have known you would walk into the shop?"

"I don't know. I think you were waiting for a woman, but not necessarily me. Or you were waiting for me. I don't know. Don't ask me questions. Answer mine."

"No, no," I'm shaking my head.

"You *were* waiting for me?"

"No, I can't, Eva, please, let's go away. Let's go on that trip across Canada that your friend took. That you told me about. Or the Ecuador thing."

"'Traveling is a fool's paradise.' Isn't that what you told me? Do you think we can escape from what already happened, what we already did and said?"

"Yes, I believe that."

"Why did you buy the bike shop?"

"Eva," now I'm crying and that can only make it worse, like the man fleeing the scene of a crime he didn't commit, and yet, I did commit the crime. It's like the bare bulb in the police station and the innocent prisoner whose body shakes as if with guilt. I don't have a choice. "I'm going to tell you." The tears are for many things I've done.

"Good."

"You won't believe me."

"Try me."

"I will but I'm asking for patience. We all need patience. Forbearance. The benefit of the doubt."

"I've given the benefit of the doubt to several hundred men, most of whom were almost certainly guilty."

"I came back in time because …"

"Fuck you."

" … we were having trouble and it was about money. I wasn't making enough, so I went back and made a lot and I became successful as an artist to get your respect, and I made sure to meet you again in the same exact way. I was sloppy, though because I should've known that your legal investigative skills would kick in and now we're stuck because you can't believe what I said but I don't have another story."

Eva is looking at me, uncertain, but emotions are flickering over her face, like a sped-up film.

"When Jon called to tell me about that time travel thing, he said he didn't think you were insane."

"Uh-huh."

"That's because he was looking for a delusional insanity, not a sociopathic one."

"I don't know how to prove this."

"Simple. Tell me something that will happen in the future."

"I can't. We are almost at the point when I went back. I don't know anything from here on."

"That's convenient."

I stop talking. I have no arguments. Only regrets.

"Uri asked if I'm unhappy here," she says coldly. "He said he would like me to move in there."

"Please," I say, and now I mean it and I know she can't tell the difference and I've blown everything. "What about Lisa?"

"Lisa lived there for a few weeks, last year. She lives in California. She never actually moved East."

"He'd just do that to you. Uri's …"

"It's not for you to say what Uri is. It's not like you protected me from him," she says, going to the foyer and picking out a short, cute, black leather jacket. "If you want to tell me why you bought the bike shop, really why, then I'll listen. Up to you. I'm going to have dinner."

"With who? Where? Are you coming back?"

"With a girlfriend. Not Mickey. Someone real and female. Yes, I'm coming back."

She comes over to me, kisses me on the cheek, puts on the jacket, and leaves and I'm alone, again.

I have two weeks to decide, and then the "nodal point" returns.

Thoreau said, "A man is rich in proportion to the number of things which he can afford to let alone."

I made a lot of money on the show. Nick did it right, calling Uri's modeling agency and hiring a bunch of girls to get all dolled up and come to the pre-show for the collectors, who bought half of it right there. The show was sold out by fifteen minutes into the opening and Nick's only concern was that he hadn't set the prices high enough. I was glad they were sold: that way, I wouldn't have to look at them again. Annette asked me, with a wry smile, about my turn to 'conceptual' work. She said it that way, with air quotes. I told her to talk to Nick and she said, "So I thought," and said, "By the way, I'm collecting responses from artists for a book I'm writing called 'Art: The Basics.' Why do you make art, Bar?" I try to think of an answer that's pithy and clever and find myself unable to say anything at all and I realize that I haven't made any art in a long time, the works of this show not excepted. I am saved by one of the models Nick hired. She comes over and gushes about my work and as Annette walks away unanswered. She suggests that I come to her place and have a drink. She is beautiful. She looks to be about twenty-four and has the movements and manners of her age. I consider it, I am tempted, I want to look at her for a few minutes longer, but then I decline, not for moral reasons, but merely because I would rather go home and read.

My mom died in the apartment in Jackson Heights that she had so proudly left behind. Saul seduced her, again. Finally, a sexy guy with a bank account. Schlomo found out, kicked her out and Saul wouldn't have her at his place because of his current girl. She called me, begging me to help get her someplace to stay. She asked to stay here, but I didn't want her to be here, so I called Claudia and asked if Judit could move back in there. Into my old room. Peter's room, if Peter had existed. My mother moved into her son's old bedroom and died of self-pity, a disease that only took a couple of months to grip her heart. None of this happened in Life One.

I haven't ridden Manhattan at night since Life One. I remember riding home from work on September 12, 2001, when everything was dark and it was as if the world could be made again.

I used to ride all the time. In the before time, before the dark time. Before the Empire. (I say that aloud trying to get Alec Guinness's enunciation just right.)

I remember the ride around Washington Square. That's what I'm thinking about now. I can see the whole short route from my window as I hold a glass of burgundy.

"I'm going out."

"Where?" Eva's beautiful, of course, but I mean specifically this way, her reading glasses on her nose, her night-time casual outfit of gym shorts and tank top, her hair partially held in a clip, tendrils hanging just so, no makeup. She is getting heavy, earthy in her fourth month. The vomiting has stopped and she's enjoying eating and I'm enjoying cooking for her. She is heavy, tied to the earth. She's reading a novel by a South African writer I admire. She's comfortable. Her belly will start to be obvious in a week or two. Humans ought to be grounded; they ought to know where they are in space and time, and why they are there.

The cloud in this paradise is her crying jags, which come unannounced and last for hours. Hormones, she says. Whenever she is in one of them she repeats that she's lost her way, she's Dorothy and went off the yellow brick road, her life doesn't mean anything, and that she's ashamed. She says she'll go work full-time at Legal Aid, but shudders at the prospect of a million desperate clients.

It's in the depths of these that she proposes that we move into a cheap apartment. That we move from this beautiful, spacious apartment to a place in the East Village, in "some tenement." We went around looking at five or six walkups with leaks and bad renovations, water-stains under the radiators and in the tubs under the faucets, peeling paint, and smelly hallways, and then we'd come back here to the lap of luxury and I'd listen to her talk about not knowing who she is any more and how she knows it's not right to bring the baby into one of those places and how she doesn't know what's going on.

I know, though. I need to do the thinking for both of us, even though that, too, is not even close to fair, but unlike in Life One, she and I are not equal partners. We don't talk about the time travel and she stopped asking about the weird things.

It's my mess, so it's my job, but I can get help.

"I'm going down for a ride."

"Now?"

"Yeah. I'll be back in a couple of hours."

"Okay. Is everything alright?"

"Yes, it is. I'll be back."

It's a continual surprise how quickly one changes neighborhoods in New York. From my Washington Square apartment to Cooper Union is a five-minute leisurely bike ride. From there to Sharpey's is another three. The city at night sparkles like a jewel of great price. Here was an empty lot. Now there's a six-story with a penthouse set back at the top. Schlomo built this one, or maybe the one next door and some alt-Schlomo built this one. Ugliness: modern cheapo, no ornament, quick and dirty housing with fluorescent hallways lighting the way to narrow bedrooms with low ceilings and viewless kitchens. No class, that guy. Avenue A. Here's one dad built, a beautiful piece of work with bay windows, ornamental lintels and interlocking quoins on the corners. He probably wasted money on some of those details. Schlomo made higher margins. Schlomo always chose the sordid boon. On the other hand, for dad it was always about himself.

Has it all been a sordid boon? What, who..? This dude's going to bump me… "Fuck! Watch where …"

"This a hold up, my Black brother." He's laughing? My heart is racing, but I'm curiously unafraid. I'm thinking very quickly. He could kill me, which is scary but not because I'd like not to die. It doesn't bother me. He's very good-looking. Eva would have to agree. The street lamp is a floodlight that flatters his sharp features. He's holding it together on the edge of desperation. I don't care about the bike. What do I care about? I wish Eva were here, but not in danger. To share the moment. Ha ha ha!

"Ain't no laughin' matter, my man."

"Here, take it." I'll have to cab it home. Or I could walk. It's a nice night.

"Wallet too. Don't play."

What do I care about? "You don't… can you just take the cash? The cards …"

"Don't chase me. I'll put you in the hospital."

"I'm not Black."

"What?"

"You said 'Black brother.' I'm dark-skinned but not Black. My dad was, uh, is from Yemen."

"Now that's gross, a man denyin' himself like that. Downright unethical."

"No, really. Don't...don't get on the bike that way. It's delicate carbon steel. You'll throw the frame out of balance."

"Excuse me but please go fuck yourself, Yemenite man."

"You can do better. You're smart. You have guts."

"Listen, mister fuck. You don't know me. You ain't even my brother, like you say. I'm looking at you now. I see you now. You are not a Black man. You not Black at all. You a fake-Black. 'You can do better' my left eyeballs. How do you know how I can do? Lemmie ask you something. You go to college, pretty boy, huh? I bet you went."

"No. I mean, I didn't finish."

"Well I didn't go at all. How about that? Betcha you got a fancy-ass job and pretty-ass woman you fuckin', too. Don't you? Huh? But how's it feel getting all that shit and you ain't even gotta finish college for it? How's that feel? Feel like you can tell me why the fuck is up?"

"I…"

"I ain't hearing what you want to say. I got in. Oh yes, I could go. Place was free, too. All I got to pay is the rent, and I ain't even got that…"

"What, what place is free?"

"What?"

"Where did you get into that was free? You don't mean Cooper Union?"

"I sure as shit do mean Cooper Union."

"In what?"

"Architecture program. I can draw like any motherfucker you know, Mister Do Better."

"But you can't pay the rent. You have to … work. Do this? I'll pay."

"You'll pay what?"

"I'll pay your rent."

"Fuck you. You just trying to get your bike back."

"No. I went…Cooper is where I went for a while. I have the money. If what you're saying is true, I'll…"

"Ha ha! You want to make yourself feel all better. You so not-Black you got white guilt. That, or you just trying to get the bike back. How's it going to work, huh? I tell you who I am and you wait for me with some cops?"

"How much you think you can get for that bike?"

"I don't know. Five hundred? I gotta go, Mister Do Goody."

"You hang on to the bike. You follow me to that bank on the corner, end of the block. You let me buy it back from you. I'll give you five hundred for it. Then all you've got is cash and no one can accuse you of anything."

"Uh huh." He's thinking it over. He's looking around, seeing if I have backup.

"It's a pretty distinctive bike. First thing I'm going to do is report it stolen. You want to try to fence it and maybe end up selling it to a cop?"

He's considering it. "Go, I'll be outside."

I'm walking over there. I shouldn't look back. He can take care of himself. Kind of. Not really. Here's the money. Bike's worth a a few thousand, but he doesn't know that, and then there's the price of convenience for him. Okay, now turn. There he is, ready to ride off. The bike's too big for him. He needs a fifty centimeter frame, like Peter.

"Give me the money first."

"No, it's got to be simultaneous."

"Ha ha! You want to pay for me to go to college, but you ain't going to trust me for shit?"

"You said before you don't play. Get off the bike and I'll give you the cash."

"Give me the cash in my hand and I'll get off. What's it to you anyhow? You got so much money you don't got to care."

That's true. "Just, take it easy. Easy. Your fate and mine are wrapped up tog…" That was a good shove.

"You have yourself a real good night, Mr. Do Better." He's riding away, wobbly on a multi-thousand dollar hand-crafted Italian work of art designed to fit my body like a condom, plus five hundred dollars. The tuition is all mine, however.

"Hey! HEY! DON'T TAKE LESS THAN TWO GRAND FOR THE BIKE!"

Hey Judit, how's that for finagling? (Now? Someone's calling me?) On her deathbed she said to me, "Who would have thought, when I was in the barn hiding from the Nazis, that I would have a son such a big macher?" "You mean as an artist?" "Ach, okay, that too." She died in Elmhurst hospital, where Dad died in Life One. She refused to return her friends' phone calls lest she have to tell them she was back in Jackson Heights, and no one was there in the hospital when she went. Almost no one came to the service. Now that he hasn't died, Dad did come to her funeral, the absolute Gahua. He should have died before and she should have died hereafter.

Here it is. Saul did a good job with this building. Once, there was a frightening, dark opening into a dark, smelly old carpeted brownstone and the front door didn't lock and the buzzer a broken antique. Now, there's a clean, well-lighted vestibule with a video intercom into a ten-story building that's still smells out-of-the-box new. Saul put in moldings and ornamental banding under the windows, and the flooring is nicely patterned old-world one-inch tile and it's roll-in for the wheelchair bound, no steps from the street. Marble walls. The ceiling fixture isn't terrible. There's enough light in here to signal aliens from space.

I'd buzz Herbie, but I don't know what to talk with him about.

Herbie was one of the one-third, the low-income folks whom I installed in here, though on what we are paying him at the gallery, he wouldn't qualify any more. He is living in almost the old coordinates, almost exactly the same spot and elevation, in a new apartment. His living room's about a fourth the size of mine, but it fits a couch, two stuffed chairs, and a small coffee table. Last time I was there, maybe eight years ago, he had all the art zines, as well as *GQ*, and a wine fridge.

I want to buzz and go up and tell Herbie about the jump, about how in Life One, he lived "here" with Abigail Greenfield until she moved out in 1996. How he got a job as an art history teacher at N.Y.U. and received adjunct tenure, but still only earned about twenty thousand a year. None of that happened now, and Abi's dead and Herbie's doing okay, though Nick tells me he goes to a bar and falls off the wagon every six months. It's a pattern: some boy not old enough for him, not looking for a long-term thing, leaves him and after that there's a seven- to fourteen-day incognito recovery. When he returns to work they take it from his vacation time and no one says another word.

I want to ask him about the same things Jon talked with me about, but Jon didn't believe me and of all of the people on the planet, Jon's most qualified to tell if I'm nuts. Herbie knows me as a benefactor, employer, co-worker on some curating projects, and landlord. In other words, he doesn't know me.

"Hey, fella, do you live here?"

"No, sorry, I …"

"This is a private residence, okay? You don't want me to call the cops, do you. Kinda sketchy of you, lurking in here. You at least know someone who lives here?"

"No, no. Sorry." I have an unprovable claim that I actually built this fucking place or at least financed my dad while he did. I used to be its owner.

Who knows me well enough for me to talk?

Here's a list of what I did well, including the bike store and the gallery giveaways. Giving the gallery to Nick was half charity and half a favor I did for myself. I helped Sharpey buy that honky-tonk in Nashville. He seems happy. Summer and the architect: Eva and I were renting a place on Georgica Pond for two weeks. Summer was with ten girlfriends in an illegal rental in Montauk. Eva was going to a bachelorette fest in Montauk so I invited Summer and the architect over for a drink. That's all that was required. His wanting her was a given but I was nervous she wouldn't want him. He seemed too old for her. It looks like she's moving in with him in Bridgehampton, like she did in Life One, only ten years later. There'll be a big wedding I won't attend. So that's, like, a wash.

On the other side of the ledger: my father and my mother, each. My art career, of which I am proud and ashamed. What happened to Eva. Peter, most of all.

I do love Summer. I could see having children with her. Wait, wasn't there a kid in that magazine profile of Summer? Yes, a kid she should already have had. She's thirty-five, now too. I wasted her time. I stole it and gave it to myself. It's that nice? I am now able to say this as I realize what I have done to her.

I am opening the door to my luxurious apartment. Eva may be asleep. In the morning, I will tell the Chanel Lady my answer. It's time for morning work. I wasn't quite awake before; now, no, I'm quite asleep. In my coma-dream I see stretching out before me a life of scurrying and tawdriness, of fool's paradises and pretenses. Of late, I have lain waste my powers, and I am out of tune for everything.

I am dead-and-alive.

15. Life Three

    Each of the transformations or translations or travels or whatever I ought to call them was a jarred my soul. I stand here, in my old studio, with Peter. I am at once overjoyed that he is alive and mournful that for me, his raising happened twenty years ago, in a timeline I have traveled away from and only now have re-entered.

    He is a beautiful young man.

    "This is a painting I'm working on now." I show Peter the five-by-seven foot canvas, landscape orientation, the underdrawing worked out and some of the figures painted but the finished piece not yet clear. "This is the building Sharpey used to own in the East Village as it was. The empty lots on either side. There, and there. It's '86. It's south looking north, across the street."

    "From an elevation. You're on the roof of one of those buildings. Which one is it?"

    "The Sharpey building is in the center, there."

    "I like the slanting afternoon light."

    "That's Sharpey sitting on the stoop next to his cat, playing a lute."

    "I can see it's a lute."

    "That's me."

    "Dawg. You young there."

    "Your age."

"Who's that? In the window next to you? Your girl?"

"Abigail. Her friend Art is walking into the frame."

"Dude in the white tux?"

"With tails."

"Junkies shooting up. Nice background-foreground thing going on. You doing the old masters' groove. But this is acrylics, isn't it?"

"That's what I'm learning at Hunter College. It's a good program."

"It's on my list. Tryin' to get my ass into Cooper."

"You'll get in." I show him how I'm mixing the paint. "The giant here, I want to come out looking between semi-realistic. I see him as striding across 3rd Street, one foot crushing a parked car, the other foot stepping on half a dog; he notices neither. He's wearing what I used to wear, uh, a long time ago."

"You sported all that black shit?"

"It's supposed to be a pretentious artist outfit, all designer things, all imported, Japanese cotton pants that end at my calves, a French linen short-sleeve shirt, and those super-expensive Italian boots, side zip."

"Naw. How'd you ever get the cash-money for that?"

"It's hard to explain. Every crinkle in the clothing needs to be there, and every bit of shine on the boots. I'm going to have to spend a long time on painting the hair, and the brush's hairs. Ideally it'll be possible to tell that the two figures of me are the same. I said semi-realistic because the giant figure is entirely within the laws of perspective, light and shadow, and the whole physics of the painting. I took one thing and changed it to see what the effect would be."

Peter considers it. "I like it so far," he says. "You thinking about an artist? Surrealists? Magritte?"

"Yes. More Picabia. Not Chagall. Not sentimental."

"Poussin. And Bosch?"

"Yes, he gets an emotional effect, even though emotions aren't in the pictures." Trading Saul for Peter is not something I can imagine ever coming to regret. "How's senior year?"

"Hard."

"Stick with it."

He doesn't answer. He returns to the work: "Are you going to make this part green, like that one?"

"I don't know what it's all going to look like. One doesn't always know."

To get Peter back I had to decide. I was in the Chanel Lady's office. The conversation was like trying to turn a drywall screw with a penknife.

"Will I remember Life Two?"

"If by this term you mean the experience past the nodal point, that is not sayable. I cannot, how should I explain, to speak it? I cannot. Some subjects remember. Have remembered. It is possible you will remember some. Perhaps some. Do you wish to proceed? I need the permission."

"Based on not enough knowledge."

"These are the conditions. Were the conditions."

"Fly blind, Bar. Jump off a cliff, Bar. Do you enjoy doing this? Playing with people? Treating them as 'subjects'? Rats circling in the maze you drop us into?"

"I am unable to answer to the word 'enjoy.' Each of us is a subject. We are subject to many things."

"Are you trying to be clever?" She bowed her head, meaning … ? "Do most subjects choose as I am doing?"

"Many do. Some do not. Have not."

"You're a fountain of information, aren't you?"

"The experiment's parameters forbid further release of data. Or of patterns. Forbade."

"To subjects."

"Yes. You have little time."

I don't even bother to point out how she is full of unintended ironies. I don't have much to think over. "Right. Okay, let's go. Experiment on me. Again."

I expected to land at Willet's Point station at the Met game. That would make zero sense. No: I'm in my apartment on 135th Street, and I know. I haven't been here in twenty years, yet I was here a moment ago.

What is happening? Eva's out for a walk. Good that she's not here to see me lying on the floor. I miss her. I saw her yesterday, but it wasn't "her." It was a woman I perverted. I do not know if I will be able to forget that person, or the person who did the perverting.

My body feels sore in every cell, like I ran a marathon and then lifted weights for a few hours and then was bitten by a poisonous snake. I feel asthmatic and nauseous, but it's all fading, and through all, I feel relief.

I'm looking at my blessed old ceiling full of cracks and peeled paint, considering the ramifications. To my left is an easel with art I was making twenty years ago. Yesterday.

Get your ass off the floor, Bar.

Let's see what I used to do. Portrait of my lady, starting to get into the surreal groove but not there yet. Not as advanced as where I went later.

(No: I never went there. All of the art I made in the last twenty years must be gone.)

I am sucker-punched realizing this piece. All my work … ?

Focus: I am released from the fuckups of Life Two. Did it even happen? Is there evidence, a trace? Yes: the trace is in me. However, only I possess it, and I could be insane. But I do not feel insane, and I am not deluded about other things. I don't feel paranoid. I am Bar Mizrachi. I am an artist and I am used to harshness.

I can't know the future any more. I do know things about the past, things I can test. Yes. There are a couple of those. Things I couldn't know had I not returned.

I could make a couple of calls before she gets back. I need to, so I can tell her what's going to happen. I will have to win my love again, this time without tricks.

"Schlomo, I wonder if you have a minute. A bit more than a minute. Yeah, I know it's late. I wanted to talk about the History of the Bronx. No, don't hang up. It won't wait and like a lot of money conversations, it's not a friendly call."

"Hey, Uri. No – don't start talking. Don't explain. If you had a lawyer present, she'd tell you not to talk. So listen, my old friend. You're going to give me a loan. I'll tell you how much in a second, and also at what rate of interest, but first I want to talk about the fifteen-year-old girl you're corresponding with in Oakland."

I hear the tumblers clicking. I have no idea how long she was out. I don't remember that from two decades ago. My mind is sixty-forty years old. The love of my life, walking in that door, is in her mid-thirties. I know things about her that no one should know about someone else, potential things, things she didn't do, but that I saw her do, that I provoked. We shouldn't know what people are capable of doing if they haven't done them. We deserve a presumption of innocence most because of our human frailty. What flocks of cattle would I have to bring to the temple sacrifice to redeem us both? Yes both: I didn't do those things, either. Forgive us our trespasses, and let us forgive the trespasses of others.

Eva enters tentatively. I am so relieved to see her, innocent of it all, washed clean, that I nearly swoon onto the floor again. I am on a ride with many hills: I'm deliriously happy to see her, then down into a trough, knowing nothing is solved from when I "left." She doesn't take the key out of the lock at first. "Hi," she says. She is standing in the doorway as if considering whether to enter, her jacket still on.

"I love you."

"I love you, Bar," she says flatly, pulling the key out of the lock. She takes one step in and closes the door. She leans against it. She moves forward, takes off the jacket and lets it fall to the floor. She has been crying. Was that before she left or after? I don't remember things that happened an hour/twenty years ago. She slides down against the door and sits on the floor in the dark, the vestibule light off.

"There has to be real change," she says. "Time doesn't matter if nothing changes."

"There will be changes. There already are."

My eyes are more used to the dim light now. I see that her eyes are red and her mascara, stained. "I spent the last hour talking with my mom. She says people don't change much. They're set when they're kids and even when there's a big event, it's not like books and movies …"

"Psychologists don't know everything. Those things that are set are general, not specific, like how stubborn a person is, or whether they like cheese. Not professional choices. I can change in specific ways that matter to us."

"It has to be real and it has to be what you want. It can't be me blackmailing you."

"No, no."

"I don't know if this is going to work."

"No one knows."

After a minute, she gets up. I take that as a good sign. She walks slowly to the kitchen and opens the fridge, stares inside, closes it. She turns to me and says, "You sound different."

I manage to say, "I need a week. Only a week," when the palimpsest kicks in but it's fuzzy, as if the reception on a rabbit-ears T.V. needed to be moved. It's us, just before I left. It blinks out before it even gets going, but I did feel the desperation for a moment.

She rushes to me and hugs me, "Are you okay?" and says in my ear, "Please, make it work. Please."

"I will try."

I feel her body shake with sobs against me as I hold her. There is no need to move. Let her cry. I cry too. It's been a long, long time.

"Your mom called," she says, and I am shocked into remembering that my mother, whom I mourned, has not died. As we release our embrace, she senses my surprise and looks quizzical, but lets it go as she smiles and wipes tears. "She said, 'Nu? Tell him, Your birthday is coming. I want to celebrate. I was there, you know. Counts for something.'"

"Mom," I say and we both laugh but the feeling fades quickly into the unknowable horizon.

Five days later, October 26, 2006, I reach Eva in her office. I'm down the street from the bike shop on the corner of Canal and Broadway, at a payphone with no booth and I can hardly hear her as trucks roll by.

"It's tomorrow," I say. "It's set."

"What is? What do you mean? Today's today."

"No, I mean it's happening tomorrow."

"A closing, happening already? That's wonderful, Bar! I don't understand,

though. Where's the money from? I need to be in court in ten minutes."
"That's okay. Go. I need a good lawyer. To read the contract."
"Ha, ha. I work for sex."
"I agree to your terms. But seriously, Schlomo's people wrote it so I assume it has fucked-up clauses."
"I'll comb it. Gotta go. I love you."
I say I love you back but she's hung up, busy helping someone avoid being thrown out onto the street.

We spend a long part of a train ride to the Hamptons discussing how things have changed so quickly for us. Between us. I suppress all knowledge of ironies. I forgive her all. Forgiving myself is slower, since I'm me, and unlike in her case, forgiveness does not become easier every time I look at my face.

Eva, quite round, is in a good mood as we approach the house in Springs that her parents rented for July. She is having early contractions that alarm the shit out of me but are supposedly normal. At least her breathing is easier, though that, too, makes no sense to me.

Getting away from the shop for a three-day weekend took a month of prep. Weekends are the busiest. Here's the bike store situation: it has a ten-year lease in its eighth year desperately needing renegotiation, some bike store stock, and some semi-competent, semi-alienated employees. I also purchased: a fraudulent balance sheet with disbursements disguised (for years) as costs, undisclosed debt I may have to sue over, and unpaid bills that the former owner meant to pay but just forgot. Now Shimano doesn't trust me, and who knows what other key parts or bike makers. I'm taking home what Eva makes, which isn't a lot but is double what I made before. That's after debt service payable to Uri and Schlomo, twice what I earn. So I'm working for them more than for myself; so much for my clever ploy to force open their piggy banks.

My earnings so far satisfy the minimum requirements for qualification as an adult and partner in the reproduction and raising of descendants. That's why I go there six days a week.

I think the shop might last a few years, or not. One big unexpected blow and it's gone. Buying Jerry out I'm able to make more money than before only because I'm doing my old job of repairs instead of paying someone, plus I'm doing his management job.

That painting project I'm doing should take approximately forever, given how tired I am after work.

She thinks it's a girl. I don't understand the idea of predicting based on nothing.

Visiting Summer out here feels like cheating, like I'm cheating on Eva, though neither Eva nor Summer could possibly understand why I would think so. "It's really nice of you to let me come by," I say, rolling in on Eva's dad's bike, a model I could've afforded a hundred of in Life Two but not now, not even wholesale.

"Not at all. No, no, I didn't 'let you come by' – come on, I invited you," Summer says gracefully though inaccurately. Seeing Summer in her Watermill home, I am so fraught with confusing feeling that I wonder if I can do this all the way through. I wish I didn't remember how I loved her, how she unexpectedly affected me. In this life, she has become even more graceful; she was so often frantic before. (Not "before"). When she smiles and I briefly feel the touch of her skin, her hand in mine, and I'm seized with desire and love. I want to hold her almost as much as I want to breathe, and I talk myself down; a man is rich in proportion to the things he can afford to let alone. Possession is unnecessary. Summer and I do not have a history, except in my memory, which may as well be a fantasy. This takes a few moments. She has to ask if I'm okay, do I need water, am I overheated.

She takes me through the light, airy house to the back and I show her my slides.

"I love this one," she says, "with the giant. That's you, right?" She's bent over, peering through my eyepiece.

"Yeah, also me in the window."

"And is that your face on the dog? The one that's under the giant's foot?"

"Most people don't see that even when the painting's in front of them. Bravo."

"It's trippy and cool and my god, you can paint like Caravaggio. You're like, I don't know, an old master."

"Thank you." Older than you think. I am quiet as she goes through the slides. The lawn is landscaped, full of flowers, rhododendrons, and carefully placed trees. The straight hedges form a fortress against the rest of the world. We hear a car on the white gravel.

"Honey!" she calls to her husband, who has just pulled up in some small two-seat sports car I don't recognize through the foliage. "Do you want to see these!"

She looks at the slides again. I wait, looking at the garden and not at her. She is making an effort, studying them. Kindness to a stranger? Genuine interest? I remember not trusting her. What a fool I was, and how smart I thought myself.

"You're here full-time?" I ask her.

"Since last year, yes." She looks up and I look straight at her eyes, but I'm holding steady. "Harry and I looked at each other one night after he got stuck in the subway and we talked and talked forever and asked ourselves what's life for. Harry has enough work out here."

"And modeling?"

"Oh, Bar! I'm old!" There is that smile, like a sharp beam of light.

"You're not old. You look marvelous," but I make it sound like Billy Crystal and she laughs. I want to tell her that her looks are a miracle and that I can't help staring at her with great affection, but it would be nonsense and I am in a state where, if I let myself go I could start to sob. I do not let myself go. If I am suffering, it is only justice, reverberating through universes of time.

"You are sweet!" Summer says, smiling. "No, I'm over the hill. I don't care, though. I think my painting is going okay. My gallery is pounding on the door, you know? But I'm always so full of doubts. I'd love for you to take a look. If you have time. If you don't have to get back."

Here's Harry carrying drinks. He's old, unlike Summer; he must be sixty and for a bad moment I consider rescuing the beautiful princess from the old dragon, but it passes as I remind myself that Harry has already rescued her, and she him, and I'm a visitor. "Bar. Very nice to meet an old flame of Summer's." We shake. "Even if he's a handsome young man dressed in skintight clothing."

"Honey, we're not … Bar and I are old friends."

"Colleagues."

Summer smiles politely. "Yeah, that's right. More like a couple of fuck-up kids. At the world's worst gallery. Though come to think of it I was the fuck-up. You did your job."

I smile back. "They've changed management. I saw a good show there last year. Abigail Greenfield."

"I don't think I could set foot in there ever again. Bad memories of a former self. That guy Dicky was a big sleazebag."

Harry seems to have moved on. "Bar you biked here, obviously. Where from?"

"Springs."

"Nice ride. You must be hot. Dip in the pool? I'm sorry, Summer's looking at me like I'm interrupting."

"We're talking shop," she says. "Look at this one."

He takes the page of slides and looks at the wrong one. "Interesting," he says, unpersuasively.

We do go in the pool, me in one of Harry's bathing suits. I change in their pool house. Summer's wearing a dark t-shirt and shorts, and I'm thinking about how nice it is to live this way and I wonder how Harry has made it to this idyll complete with its nymph and whether he had to struggle or if he had it handed to him, family money, college connections, and in what proportions and whether there was merely the open door of opportunity given him or more than that.

We go inside and I look at Summer's work with both of them and can sincerely give compliments and am reminded of how our best moments were when I was her teacher and remember when I caused her to despise me and fight that off. I was never her teacher, now. I try to stick to technical things, reminding myself that none of that happened. I stick to the work but it's never only about the paint.

Then she shows me a large canvas, four by six feet, that had been covered. It's a multiple self-portrait. She's nude in an infinite mirror setup, looking at the viewer from each of many iterations of herself, each farther one receding in a curved line toward the vanishing point, the largest almost the height of the canvas, the smallest only a few inches. She did not flatter herself. In the smallest iteration, she is a normal human being. In the one closest to us, she is meat. That is, the figures of her gradually change as they are closer and larger, their skin becoming less opaque, until the skin isn't there and we see her muscles, organs, hair, and bared teeth, as if she were simian. The close figure, at almost six feet, dominates the scene horrifically, still recognizable as her, if you know her.

"I used Grey's," she says.

"Quite a fright, isn't it?" Harry says.

"Yes. No. Yes – it's very strong. Almost like a mural, with these stages of revelation of the body."

"Funny you see that right off," she says, "I was thinking about this work in the post office of where I'm from. It's by an Italian guy. I stared at it a lot when I was little, and then I found out there were some by the same person in Queens. Celentano. I went to see them. Anyway, I'm going on. He was a muralist. WPA I think. I don't know if I want to show this one."

"She likes to talk about her work," Harry says. "I've been given an education."

"Yeah," I say. "I hope you show this. Why wouldn't you?"

"It's … I can't look at it. I don't know if I want anyone to see it." Indeed, she had been facing us, not the work.

"It's an achievement. I think."

"Why paint it, if not for other people? Architects don't have the luxury of making buildings for themselves."

"Yeah, but Honey, I need time."

Harry nodded. "At my age," he said, "it's rare to be surprised by a work of art. I mean a movie, a song, a book, visual art, anything. When something's surprising, it's precious."

I hear him say that and think he and I have more in common than I wish to acknowledge.

As Summer covers the painting, I agree with Harry that she must show it.

As I'm leaving, Harry says he wants to ride with me "sometime" and Summer says she wants to show me more work and to meet Eva and come see my work in person. She does promise to call Nick on my behalf.

The entire time I spend with Summer I am expecting a palimpsest but none ever comes and I think with some hope that now, perhaps, they've stopped.

I think that painting of hers is as good as anything I've ever done.

It is certain to me now that I am as in love with Summer as I've ever been in love with anyone. I am sick with love for her as I cycle back to Eva. Yes, of course I love Eva still but I am poisoned, my limbs feeling as if arsenic coursed through them, my heart feeling as if it would drop into my stomach, my stomach as if I ate a cake full of ground glass. I cannot go back, nor can I return.

On the other hand, I learned something from Summer's art.

As I enter Nick's office, I think this is a person on whom I squandered much time. At first, I have to explain that we had met before. He politely denies not remembering me. It's because of Summer coming through that I have a welcome mat at all. (My former employee. Don't think that. You're coming to him hat in hand.) He looks at the work, looks at me, smiles, and goes back to the work. He starts telling me that he is "so excited" about my work, that he has a feeling that I'm going to "become a Black John Currin," and I have to squelch my aggressive response.

"Actually, I'm not Black," I say as mildly as I can.

He talks for a while about how my work reminds him of Gregory Gillespie and and says things like "if Basquiat and Currin had a baby," and half a dozen other things meant to be gushing but offensive to me when he comes back and says, "wait, what did you say?"

"I'm Jewish. Yemenite on my dad's side. Dark-skinned but middle-eastern, not Black. I have no ancestors from Africa or the Middle Passage. My mother was, uh, is Hungarian-Jewish."

"Oh, really?" he says, and goes back to the slides but I can see that much air has escaped the balloon. "Still," he says, brightening a little. He smiles at me more thinly this time and says, "The work's terrific."

"Thank you." Nick doesn't care about the complexities of my case. He doesn't care about my case at all now, I can see.

There's a long moment when I'm sitting there and he's going back to slides he's seen, mumbling "surrealism," "drawing," "more like Picasso?" "photo-real," and "hmm, Rembrandt-ish." "The drawing's certainly there." He looks at me. "Surprising no one's picked you up." He looks at the slides again for another agonizing five minutes, saying nothing and I get the sense that he's not looking at them any more.

My mind drifts into the latest fiasco at the shop in which the new guy who said he could build wheels spent two months building them incorrectly but in such a precise, devilishly almost-okay way that no one could tell and I wonder if anyone's going to die on a wheel I sold them and if my insurance would try to weasel out of covering but so far it's only people coming in with wheels in dire need of truing and we replace them on the spot and do I need to fire this guy if he refuses to give me two months' labor for no extra pay to make me whole, plus my argument in the middle of the night with a guy who spoke maybe fifteen English words from Shimano in Japan, and I haven't had the energy to paint or draw for a week. Indeed, what is life for ...

Nick starts talking before I'm ready and I misunderstand him to be saying "no." He's not saying "no," but he "can't say yes yet," and tells me about a gallery board meeting and promises to "sell the hell" out of my work to the board. There's a bad moment when I ask him about Fire Island and he looks at me suspiciously, wondering how I know his personal business and I say "oh, Summer told me you go there."

"I love Summer," he says. We shake hands. He stands.

Time to leave. "I love her, too."

I remember something. "Nick, there's no board."

"What?"

"If you don't want to 'pick me up,' you can say so. There's no board. This place is you and two other people."

He looks deflated. "How would you know whether we have a board or not? You study the corporate structure of every gallery you approach? Never mind. I don't care. I have to say no all day long and I'm tired of it. Tell me, why do you want me to represent you? Why are you making this work? Why bring it to me or any gallery? Much of your work is personal, like the portraits of people no one else knows, except maybe the ones of Abigail Greenfield. Why do you want recognition from the public? Have you even asked yourself these things?" I've forced the conflict but I am surprised at how vehement it is when it comes.

"What about, if you sell some of my work I get to be an artist? I get to quit my day job."

"So? That answer merely pushes the horizon. Let's say there's a world in which I sell so much of your art for so much money that you can stop working whatever job you have. You'd better live like a pauper for that, but let's just say. Most of my artists work. Did you know that? Most of them are professors. Some swing it part time by living someplace cheap, like Hudson, upstate. One guy's a baker, for real. High end cakes for Odeon and Balthazar. But let's say you can make art all day. What for?"

I did not see this question coming. I answer him by talking about showing the world something beautiful that they had not yet seen as such before but he is non-plussed.

"I think your work is beautiful. Isn't it because I already understand how to see such things? Yes, there's no board as such. It's two other people and it's not really a 'board' but I'll call it whatever I feel like calling it. I'll let you know, Mr. Mizrachi."

I don't know if the bike shop will be able to make rent plus payroll plus utilities starting in three months. Eva's parents offered to buy the loans and extend them but then I'm working for her parents, a poor arrangement with no possibility of default. That is, the shop may be doomed to die right when the baby is due.

Eva's parents want us to move to their suburb. They are arguing that the schools where we live are "unacceptable," but we can't afford a two-bed house there unless we buy one in need of work so badly that it is on the edge of unlivable and then I'm not an artist, I'm my dad, the carpenter who can't make it work. I need a slum to be an artist, but the co-op here on 135th recently voted to increase the maintenance because they're tired of living like we're in a slum.

Eva's request that I act like a grown-up is not pressing at present, but hovers, and I'm not telling her the full extent of what's going on at the shop. She knows about Nick but doesn't seem to get the stakes. She thinks things will work out. They always have, for her.

Summer called her and they made a plan to have dinner, the four of us. Eva thinks she is "charming" and "graceful" and is excited to see someone "so beautiful" and says she has bought at least one pair of pants because Summer modeled them. I'm not looking forward to it. Also, I don't know how we will pay for our half of the bill.

I don't know what stocks will rise or fall tomorrow. I don't know anything. I can hardly say for certain how old I am, what I am doing, or who I am.

October 25, 2006. I told Eva not to make a big deal of my birthday but she ignored me and told Summer and the two of them made me a cake. I see that it has the right number of biological years on it but I consider that number a permanent source of confusion as I do the statement: Summer is not my ex.

The important thing that happened, for me, was when the four of us were in Summer's studio, formerly the car garage but redesigned by Harry with stunning light for his wife. I was talking about her work and she was saying how helpful I was being and Summer turned to me and said, "You should teach," and Eva agreed. I promised to consider it.

I am remaking the Bronx portraits and the parodies of Van Gogh, Picasso, Rembrandt, Da Vinci, Hopper, and Whistler, with "my" people replacing the originals. It's going to take years to do it all in acrylics, but I've finished a pencil and ink sketch of the main Bronx picture, the one of the kid in the burning building, and I made "Nighthawks" with people who aren't white (but aren't Black, either). I made the cook my Yemenite dad, Hopper's blond woman my brunette, Jewish-Ashkenazi-looking mother, and the man who's face is visible one of my Israeli cousins with long curly hair.

I called Nick, who called me once to say he was still thinking about it but not since then, to say I have more work to show him. I said all of that into his voicemail, which he hasn't returned, so I'm going to go over there tomorrow, and if he's not there, I'll go again the next day, and the day after, and then I'll find another Nick until I find someone willing to take a chance.

Eva said she imagined a portrait she would make of me if she could paint or draw.

"I would paint you dark and lovely, with a three-day beard, big, strong nose and powerful chin, curly hair, almost kinky, eyes full of love and pain.

I would make sure people can see how sexy you are from the back. Your ass and your strong, powerful back and strong shoulders. There is that mark you have on the left shoulder that I love to look at when you're on top of me. Your ass when you come out of the shower. Your powerful legs, your thighs like cannons.

I want everyone to see that good porn of your body. I will paint you naked from the front, your face during sex, loving and desiring. My hand running through your chest and all of the curly hairs on it, capturing the exact difference in shade between your black hairs and your cinnamon skin.

I want people to see your face when you're biking, so determined, and when you're painting, so calm and focused. And when you're teaching, so caring, so concerned, so directed at the children.

I want my painting or drawing or whatever I decide to make to show your furrowed brows when you're anxious and afraid. I want them to feel my need to hold you, then, even if I am angry with you, even if we are fighting, and for you to hold me. Also, your face when you're laughing and unguarded and the way your head tosses back when you laugh.

I want them to see how much you love me, though I cannot. I want my picture to differentiate between you looking at me with love and you studying my face when you're drawing. I want to make a picture of when you look at me with desire, and I want the viewer to feel what I feel, then.

In my painting of you I want to show how you talked to me in the bike shop, so calm and gentle but pushy at the same time, gentleness covering the edge of your desire. You were never too insistent; there was only a whisper of a push. I do not know how to paint this. The desire must be like the thin, translucent painting of the ballerina's dress, or the smoke through which the viewer can see the battlefield.

I want to show how much you care about Peter. I would draw him looking up to you and talking about art with you and it's clear, from my painting, that the discussion of art is also about how to see the world so that one might make one's way as an adult and live in the world the way it is.

I want a picture of you that shows your fears and struggles. I want a picture of you dejected, having failed. I won't want to leave that out. The failures are central. I am sure you haven't told me about all of them. Did you think I cannot sense there must be more? I want to show your face when you heard that the shop would have to close, and when you told your workers they were out of work and apologized for failing them, and when you heard from that gallery that they would not take you on, and then, in a later series, the relief you felt in both cases.

One of your great failures is your regret. This propensity comes from your mother's Olympian ability to regret her life, but you've made it your own special, tragic skill that I am teaching you to unlearn. I would paint a portrait of you that radiates this poison feeling so that you can see it and understand how to shun it. It's not true that you "wasted forty years" of your life. You're barely over forty years old.

I want there to be a whole, elaborate portrait of me reflected in your irises that shows how much I love you. The light should be just right, I should be wearing that green dress you like, and I should look pretty (to you) and in my face the is love is visible.

I want to show you taking care of our child, who is not yet born, and loving her. I want a twin portrait of you and her and you're feeding her from a bottle that I made. I will study all of the paintings called Madonna and Child before I begin. I want a family portrait with our six children.

I want to show you drawing, magically creating a person in space using marks on a page, and painting, pushing oil and acrylic colors around until they mean something, but remain colors and brushstrokes and pallet knife marks. I want to show you painting your feeling for me while I paint mine for you.

I want to show you in action in front of your students, making jokes and getting smiles and seeing the one child in the back who is not smiling and thinking about her, and one-on-one with a student, helping them, bringing their best out of them, giving them that gift. The pleasure in your eyes. The frustration that you keep from your face, but that I see, when the students are recalcitrant, unwilling, or slow. The satisfaction when one of those, worst of the worst, turns around.

But I don't want to share the beauty of your body with anyone, and I don't want anyone else to see your face when you're sexual, or when you're privately facing your fears. I have nothing to offer to the world, since everything I see is already known. I don't help people see new things; that's your skill. I see you with cringe-worthy sentimentality. My art looks like the worst greeting cards. I want a portrait of you wearing that one suit of yours, with backlighting around your head, a perfect cliché. But I am erasing that image as well. I want to keep those pictures for myself and in owning them, making them your gift to me alone. I am erasing all of those moments I described. I won't show other people pictures of you and Peter, either, because those moments belong to you, him and me. I won't show you giving milk to our child when she is born, and I won't reveal what your face looks like when you look at me with love. I won't show you teaching, either. I will erase that part. Only your students will see that. I won't show how much I possess you and how much you posses me. My art will show how you give up your life for me and I for you, how you bind to me and take my freedom, and I take yours, how you're like a weighted blanked, restricting my movements, and I am a weighted blanket on you, but to show those things the way I wish, I must show nothing, a white canvas in which you can see only erasure marks and paint covered over and that is all.

    My art is now almost perfectly blank. It's a good thing, too, because I have no skill to draw any of that, and I can't paint. I can see those things, though, and that is enough.

Made in the USA
Middletown, DE
29 April 2024

53622526R00166